RAIN OF FIRE

PRESS®

Gold Imprint
Medallion Press, Inc.
Printed in USA

DEDICATION:

*This book is dedicated to the men and women who have
devoted their lives, and risked them, to study the
deadly potential of modern volcanoes.*

And always, to Richard.

Published 2006 by Medallion Press, Inc.

The MEDALLION PRESS LOGO
is a registered tradmark of Medallion Press, Inc.

Printed in the United States of America

10 9 8 7 6 5 4 3 2 1
First Edition

ACKNOWLEDGEMENTS:

I am particularly indebted to Robert Smith and his Utah Seismic Stations at the University of Utah and must note that none of my characters represent anyone there. I thank Marcos Alvarez of the IRIS/PASSCAL Instrument Lab in Socorro, NM, for information on seismic equipment and the life, Patrick Matheny, Yellowstone National Park Naturalist, for the park tour, and Dr. Lee Whittlesley, of the Yellowstone archives, for showing me around on my several visits there.

As my experience with volcanoes has been on those that are dormant, I untilized the following sources to provide insight into live ones: *Surviving Galeras* by Stanley Williams and Fen Montaigne (Houghton Mifflin, 2001,) *Volcano Cowboys* by Dick Thompson (St. Martin's Press, 2000,) and *Volcanoes: Crucibles of Change* by Richard V. Fisher, Grant Heiken, and Jeffrey B. Hulen (Princeton University Press, 1997.)

Though I have tried to remain true to fact wherever possible, I have created a fictitious mountain named Nez Perce Peak and a world in which my characters alone take on the challenge of an erupting volcano, while park brass and geologists from all over the world sit on the sidelines. In truth, Yellowstone Park Management, USGS, and Utah Seismic Stations are aware of the hazards. In an emergency, teams of scientists would be deployed anywhere in the world.

Thanks to my agent Susan Schulman, my publisher Medallion Press, and to the following for giving critical input on all or part of the manuscript: Stephen Harrigan, Sarah Bird, Robert Vaughan, Michael Garrett, Jim Harris, Evan Fogelman, Marjorie Arsht, Kathryn Brown, Judith Finkel, Bob Hargrove, Elizabeth Hueben, Karen Meinardus, the late Joan Romans, and Jeff Theall.

FOREWORD

We can only guess whether the geologic warnings would be adequate to prompt the evacuation of Yellowstone and surrounding areas and towns to prevent the instantaneous loss of thousands and perhaps tens of thousands of lives.

Devastation would be complete and incomprehensible at the caldera. Imagine Yellowstone Park and everything in it destroyed. Every road, every lodge, every campground, every visitor center, every geyser and scenic feature would either be blown instantly off the face of the Earth or swallowed as the floor of the caldera sank downward during the eruption . . .

We can only speculate on the disaster that society would face during a Yellowstone caldera eruption. As unlikely as such gargantuan explosions seem in our lifetimes, they have happened before and will occur again.

PROLOGUE
AUGUST 17, 1959

Hebgen Lake, Montana

Kyle Stone turned six the night the mountain fell.

In later years, she would treasure the last perfect hours, seeking comfort in the simple details. Sunlight dazzling on water, the way the Madison River shot quicksilver past Rock Creek Campground. Dappled shade and a secret pool where she caught her first trout with only a little help from Dad. Mingled aromas, pine and campfire smoke, while Kyle's fish sautéed in an iron skillet. She even got to help stir German chocolate cake batter.

While the sun sank on her birthday, Kyle watched her mother light the Coleman lantern and suspend it from a branch above the picnic table.

"Mom?" Sitting on a rough bench with her legs

dangling, she tried to imagine being able to reach the lamp. "When I grow up will I be tall like you?"

"We'll find out together." Rachel Stone, with the graceful body of a willow sapling, snugged an arm around Kyle. The sleeves of her flower-sprigged cardigan did not quite cover her fine-boned wrists.

Daniel Stone, a rugged carpenter whose hands could span his daughter's waist, marched into camp and dropped an armload of firewood next to the tent. Max, the family Golden Retriever, followed with his plumed tail high.

After Kyle's ceremonial dinner, buttery trout and potatoes baked in the coals, Dad lit the candles on her cake. He and Mom joined in an off-key rendition of "Happy Birthday" while Max yodeled along. People in a nearby campsite took up the refrain; someone strummed a guitar.

Amid applause, Kyle stared at her flickering symbols. Then she drew a big breath, blew out the flames atop five wax tapers and paused to study the one that was new this year.

She pursed her lips but stopped when Max jumped up and bared his teeth. With his ruff standing on end, he stared out beyond the circle of lantern light.

"What's out there, boy?" Dad set his mug on the ground and pushed up from his camp chair. "Smell a bear?"

Goose bumps raised on Kyle's thin arms. She looked for telltale eyes, a bear or the big bad wolf, though Dad had told her there were no wolves here anymore. Max paced the camp perimeter with a wary eye while her sixth candle guttered out.

Though Dad relit it, and Mom served cake topped by the piercing sweet of coconut caramel, the dog's continued disquiet made Kyle uneasy. After a bit, Dad ordered Max to a place near the fire and gathered her into his lap.

Gradually, the campground quieted. The guitar player put aside his instrument and everyone succumbed to the effect of the diamond-clear evening. The moon sailed from behind a shoulder of mountain. First, a crescent edge, then half a coin; finally a faultless disk emerged to shine upon the forest glen.

Kyle pressed her cheek against the comforting scratchiness of Dad's wool shirt and struggled to stay awake for all of her birthday. Yet, she must have dozed, for when she opened her eyes the fire had reduced to translucent crimson fragments. The moon rode cold and high amidst a sprinkling of heaven's brightest stars.

Her father followed her gaze to the sky. "I make it around eleven-thirty."

"Time for bed." Mom's lips pressed warm on Kyle's cheek, a hint of Breck shampoo wafting from burnished dark hair that matched her daughter's.

"Can't I stay up until midnight?" Kyle entreated.

Mom wagged a slender finger adorned with a turquoise-and-silver ring. "You've already been asleep for over an hour."

"But I just . . ."

Swinging Kyle to his shoulders with a chuckle, Dad carried her toward the Rambler station wagon where she and Max slept. Moonlight cast shadows at odds with the lantern, making her feel like she did when she twirled around too much.

Dad placed her on the blankets, and she smiled up into eyes the same green-blue as hers, turned down a bit at the outer edges. His soft brown beard brushed her cheek and he whispered, "Happy Birthday."

Frozen forever in memory, that was the last perfect moment.

A hard jolt struck. It brought her father to his knees behind the Rambler's tailgate.

Impossibly, the car seemed to drop, while Kyle's stomach swooped like she was on a Ferris wheel. The sensation was of a long fall, but it couldn't have been a second before the wagon bottomed with a jerk. It no sooner landed than it leaped and started jouncing as if a pair of giants jumped on the bumpers.

Max crouched but lost his balance. Dad made it up only to stagger and fall again. The lantern's wild arc threw erratic shifting shadows.

Kyle didn't know how to pray, only the ones that started 'Now I Lay Me . . .' and 'Our Father . . .' She cried into the night, "God, make it stop."

The ground rolled in waves. Braced in the back of the Rambler, she cracked her head on the side window and started to sob.

Dad was back on his feet, arms extended for her. She scrabbled toward the tailgate.

A rough wall of dirt heaved between them, a black ditch opening at the base of the scarp, deeper and wider than she was tall.

"Daddy!" she shouted into the rising thunder coming from earth rather than sky. The bucking ground threatened to throw her off the tailgate into the crevasse.

Pines as thick as Kyle began to whip as though their trunks would snap. The motion added an eerie howl to the din. Down the canyon, a grinding roar increased.

She looked for the place she'd last seen her mother.

"Mommy," she screamed, a raw ripping in her throat.

The lantern went out.

"Please, God." She prayed to wake in warm arms by the fire. They'd eat birthday cake and laugh because she'd dreamed this world turned upside down.

In the next instant, a great banshee howl struck and extinguished the brave blazes in the campground. At the same time, something black, immense and terrible bore down from the mountain. Kyle watched in horror as it blotted out the moon, leaving the most profound darkness she had ever known.

CHAPTER ONE
SEPTEMBER 10

Salt Lake City

In the basement hallway of the Utah Institute, Dr. Kyle Stone opened a door and stared into blackness. It was only ten feet to the seismograph lab's light switch, but darkness took her back.

With clammy palms, she contemplated. Go watch coffee brew and wait for another early riser? Easy enough, but if she tried it too often someone might figure out she was afraid. Poised on the threshold, she heard from within the unmistakable scratch of a match. In the room's depths, a single point of light flared.

"Somebody there?" The raspy voice of Institute Director Stanton Jameson and the rose circlet of his cigarette reassured her.

Nearly thirty years ago, when Kyle arrived at Utah with all her possessions crammed into a rusting Pinto, Professor Stanton had been a lifesaver. His answer to her query about student housing had been to phone his wife to make up their guest room. Four years later, when Kyle completed her Ph.D., she was still boarding in their home.

"Who is that?" This time something querulous in Stanton's tone alarmed her.

With three long strides, she reached the light switch.

Flooded with fluorescence, the Institute's nerve center lay revealed. Triple banks of seismographs tracked Earth's pulse, their pens tracing a record of crustal motion at remote stations all over the Mountain West. In this day of computers, there was something satisfying about the old-fashioned drum with a strip chart tracing.

Inhaling the familiar ink smell, Kyle checked out the data for Yellowstone Park and nearby Hebgen Lake. Parallel rows of straight lines meant all was quiet, but her scalp prickled.

She chalked it up to Stanton's gray and disheveled appearance. He half-reclined on a faded plaid couch left behind by some graduate student, a cowlick in his faded umber hair. The furrows beside his mouth etched deeper than usual.

"What were you doing sitting in the dark?" She tried to keep alarm out of her voice.

"I'm . . . not sure. I believe I've been here . . . all night."

Stanton was indeed dressed in the same gray suit and

red tie he'd had on yesterday. Always a snappy dresser, he regularly gave Kyle a ration of grief over her workweek uniform, well-worn jeans and a pale blue cotton shirt rolled at the cuffs. Her excuse was that having grown to almost six feet, with her father's height and her mother's slender strength, her arms overshot most sleeves. With her dark hair pulled back from her oval face into a thick braid, she favored silver and turquoise accents that played up her exotic looks, a combination of Nez Perce, Tuscan, and central European ancestry.

This morning Stanton didn't look up to giving her a hard time about anything.

"Are you all right?" She went and knelt beside the sofa, putting a hand on his. His flesh felt chilled, and her heart beat faster as she wondered if she should call for help.

"Don't hover," he ordered.

With reluctance, she drew back and watched him draw himself together, pulling in bits and pieces, a lolling leg here, a lazy arm there. Finally, he stood and dragged on his smoke, exhaling a small wreath.

Kyle fanned the cloud. That part of her past she'd managed to kick, but had no doubt she could be back to a pack a day in no time.

"Coffee?" she suggested.

"Caffeine," Stanton said in a stronger voice.

Relieved, she walked with him toward the kitchen down a hall lined with maps of earthquake prone areas of the world. Once he was fully alert, they needed to talk about next Monday's annual funding meeting. Although having a Consortium of the Institute, the National Park Service, and the United States Geological Survey brought valuable resources to earthquake and volcano research, Kyle dreaded the budgeting chaos.

In the kitchen lounge where a bulletin board advertised used textbooks, pizza delivery, and 'roommates wanted,' she passed a steaming cup into Stanton's unsteady hands.

"Does Leila know where you've been all night?"

He looked confused, then brightened. "She called me on my cell. I told her I was too tired to drive safely."

"You should go home for a shower and breakfast."

"Soon as I finish my coffee." Stanton nodded. "Forty years and we've seldom spent a night apart."

As Kyle studied him with a worried eye, he flipped on the TV he usually kept tuned to the stock market. On-screen, Monty Muckleroy, a corpulent Los Angeles talk show host, sat on his signature, striped sofa. He faced a man with an aging hippie's halo of curly hair.

"Well, I'm damned," Kyle said. "It's Brock Hobart."

Fellow scientist Brock had developed a bit more salt than pepper in his hair in the years since she'd last seen him, but he looked as sure of himself as ever, going on national television in an academic uniform of tweed jacket over jeans. When she and Brock had worked together at USGS in Menlo Park, he'd seemed a regular guy. And though in recent years he had moved away from serious science toward the fringe, Kyle followed his earthquake predictions on the Web with the perverse fascination of a bird watching a cat approach.

"Come on, Brock," Monty urged. "The audience is waiting for your latest prediction."

The studio came alive with calls of "Yeah," "All right," and "What's shakin'?"

Brock shot the camera a conspiratorial look. "There's a reason I chose this morning to come on the show. With a full moon out there, we've got the earth, sun, and moon in alignment with Venus and Mars."

"What does that mean?" Monty played the straight man.

Kyle knew what it meant. Gravitation fields were at a maximum, making for the largest tides in years. Sometimes it did seem that more earthquakes happened under these conditions, but she wouldn't have stuck her neck out like she assumed Brock was about to do.

Sure enough, he jabbed a finger at Monty. "Earth tides set up the scenario for a quake waiting to happen."

"Ooh," from the audience.

"You mean today?" Monty gripped the couch's arm. "Like this morning?"

Brock nodded.

"Gutsy," Stanton observed, lighting another cigarette in defiance of university smoking regulations.

Her heart rate accelerating, Kyle mentally agreed it took brass balls to go on national television and declare an earthquake was about to take place.

"There you have it." Monty sounded subdued, as though his bluff as well as his guest's was about to be called. "Straight from Brock Hobart, a Stanford Ph.D. and former scientist at the United States Geological Survey."

In his typical fashion, Brock hadn't predicted where the quake would take place.

"When we come back," Monty enticed, "we'll talk to Laurie, who was kidnapped by aliens." Music swelled and the studio audience applauded.

"Little green men," Stanton mused, "and earthquakes on demand."

But, Kyle realized, though most geologists made fun of Brock with his website and quake predictions, didn't it strike a chord in her? Deep down, didn't she want to believe she could someday save some other little girl a lifetime of nightmares?

Stanton clicked off the TV. In the silence, she heard a buzzing from the lab.

Her fingers curled and she pushed away thoughts of the Wasatch Fault skirting the base of the hill the Institute sat upon. The zone of unstable earth was believed capable of producing a magnitude 7.5 earthquake, as strong as the one she'd survived at Hebgen Lake. Hoping their luck had not run out, she slid a hand onto the kitchen counter, the way a mother might check her child's forehead for fever.

Buoyed by the solid feel of the Formica, she turned to Stanton. "The alarm." His hearing wasn't what it once was.

In the same moment, the pager on her belt began to

vibrate, an electronic leash that connected her to the Institute 24/7. Whenever it went off, no matter where she was, a stab of anxiety pierced her.

She raced to the lab, where pens traced dark arcs on the strip charts. Taking a seat before one of the computer monitors, Kyle typed in quick commands, connecting to the National Earthquake Information Center in Boulder.

Stanton came up behind her carrying his coffee and a fresh cigarette.

Somewhere in the world, the quake continued. Kyle felt an ache in her chest for the little girl who must be crying for her parents. In Madison Canyon, her own voice had been small against the sifting and cracking of avalanches, while the earth heaved and shimmied like Jell-O.

Two minutes ticked toward three since the quake had begun. Sweat broke out down Kyle's sides, while at the same time she felt chilled. Though there was a chance the upheaval was in some remote area, people could also be hurt, dying, crushed beneath the rubble of homes where they had felt safe.

Finally, the amplitude of the oscillation began to dampen. Kyle and Stanton waited while the Earthquake Center calculated the location of the epicenter using triangulation of multiple stations. The first bulletin came up.

A major earthquake occurred near Yuzhno-Sakhalinsk on Sakhalin Island, Russia, 800 miles (1330 km) north of Tokyo, Japan, at 7:10 AM Mountain Daylight Time today, September 10th (September 11th at 12:10 AM local time.)

Sakhalin lay just off the east coast of Siberia, part of the 'ring of fire' encircling the Pacific. Just to the south lay Japan, with its populous coasts and its own unstable ground.

A preliminary magnitude of 7.3 was computed. This area has a history of large earthquakes. On August 4, 2000, a 7.0 struck 120 miles (200 km) north. In addition, on May 27, 1995, a magnitude 7.5 shook the Neftegorsk area 240 miles (400 km) north, killing 2,000 people and causing severe damage.

Kyle didn't want to feel relief that disaster struck faceless foreign victims, for she had lived the havoc wreaked by earthquakes and volcanoes . . . both as a child and as a scientist. Nevertheless, she was fiercely glad this morning's quake wasn't happening in Yellowstone where she would be forced to deal with it. Her love-hate relationship with the park region balanced uneasily at best.

Looking at a wall map showing the Pacific and the earthquake epicenters and volcanic terrains surrounding it, she knew it was too soon to feel relief. Sometimes, whether because of celestial alignments or seismic waves propagating through the planet, quakes tended to happen in widely varying locales in a sort of chain reaction.

Behind her, Stanton remained silent. Kyle assumed he was watching the monitor, but with a sudden jerky move, he seized her arm. Thinking he was about to say something about Brock Hobart's uncanny skill or blind dumb luck, she turned to him.

Instead of speaking, he gave a small gasp. His hand clutched her like a claw even as his body began to sag.

Leaping to cushion his fall, she found him a dead weight. His cup hit the floor with a clatter and rolled under a table. A trail of smoke curled from his cigarette, dropped from nerveless fingers.

❀ ❀ ❀

"Kyle, thank God you're here." Stanton's wife Leila entered the ER, her heels tapping on the tile. The sixty-five-year-old moved with the grace of a much younger woman.

"I was with him when he had the stroke," Kyle said.

Going into Leila's embrace, she was struck anew by how fine-boned her friend was, draped in the delicate softness of a gray silk dress. For the first time since Stanton's collapse, tears pricked Kyle's eyelids. She'd been too busy calling 911, screaming in vain down the hallway for anyone else there that early in the morning, and waiting by his side for the paramedics.

Leila must have felt the change in her, for her arms wrapped tighter. "God, Kyle, not Stanton."

Her anguish was all it took to set Kyle's dammed-up tears flowing. Though the age difference between the Jamesons and her was not so great that they could have been her parents, she had always treasured both Leila and Stanton as dearly as though they were bound to her by blood. Especially after losing her maternal grandmother, who had raised her after Hebgen Lake. Being in a hospital reminded her of Franny's last days and that ultimately, nobody got out alive.

"How is he?" Leila pulled back and wiped her wet face without shame.

"They're doing a CT scan." Kyle dashed at the salt tears on her own cheek. "After that, he'll be moved to a room."

The two women took seats in a small waiting area. A tattered copy of yesterday's newspaper littered the floor, but Kyle's focus was too shattered for her to read. She tried not to watch the wall clock as its hand leaped forward to mark each interminable minute. Though dry-mouthed, she did not dare leave for coffee.

After an hour's wait, she thought she was prepared. However, when she pushed open the door of Stanton's hospital room, she found out otherwise. He lay slumped on his side with his eyes closed, his skin as ghostlike as the transparent tubes connecting his IV bag.

Leila's gaze rested upon her husband. They had been friends first, or so the story went, but her look bespoke a deep and abiding love, one Kyle had always envied. After a disastrous relationship of her own when she was twenty, Kyle had believed up into her forties that she'd someday meet the right man.

"The doctor said he was awake," Leila murmured.

"Should we let him sleep . . . or maybe call somebody?"

Blue-veined eyelids flickered then opened. "Stop that infernal whispering." Stanton's voice, though weak, projected attitude.

Leila tugged Kyle along with her to his bedside. "Look

who's here?"

"I see who's whispering." He fixed them with a look composed half of iron will and half of melted wax where the left side of his face sagged.

When he reached out with his good right hand, Kyle met him. She kept her eyes on his, wondering if he could see out of them both. Part of her wanted to cry or run, but all they had been for each other kept her in place. Yet, as Stanton looked toward his wife, Kyle realized she should leave them. If, God forbid, he did not make it through this, he and Leila deserved their time together.

With an ostentatious look at her watch, she spun, "I was planning to cancel my afternoon seminar, but with you doing so much better, I think I'll go ahead and teach."

Stanton mumbled something she had to bend closer to hear.

"You and Hollis . . ." A bit of spittle escaped his mouth. "Now, no referee . . ."

How quickly he defined the animosity beneath the surface of every encounter she had with fellow scientist Hollis . . . or Dr. Delbert, as he insisted, though almost everyone he worked with had a Ph.D. The slight blond scientist peered at the world through wire-framed spectacles and pitched himself at the Institute as everybody's friend . . . except Kyle's. Although he was in his late thirties, he spoke in a breathless rush that people other than she interpreted as boyish enthusiasm.

"You'll be back and keep us from each other's throats,"

she assured.

Stanton gave a strained bark. "Not by Monday."

"Oh, God." In this morning's wake, she'd forgotten there were only six days to their funding meeting.

He gripped her hand. "Hollis came to me recently . . . asked me to make him . . . head of Institute . . . when I retire."

Her heart began a rapid pattering like she'd just searched her purse and found her wallet missing. If Hollis were in charge, she had an idea what would happen to her Yellowstone funding.

"Watch your back," Stanton warned. "Tell Hollis I said . . . you're to chair the meeting."

● ● ●

On the drive to the Institute, Kyle still couldn't believe Stanton had been struck down. From his unfailing energy, she had assumed he would work well into his seventies.

That didn't mean everyone else at the Institute was brain dead. Back in the nineties, when Stanton asked her to leave government bureaucracy and teach, she'd been re-reminded that academic funding was more about ass-kissing than science. It was especially difficult dealing with Hollis, who had joined the Institute two years ago from UCLA and seemed to think his prior credentials made him an instant shark in the Utah fishbowl.

This morning's crisis having shattered her habitual control, she strode into the geology building and found

Hollis in the seismograph lab before a computer terminal. The small-framed scientist turned toward the sound of her footsteps and hit a key that brought up his screen saver. A laughing Golden Retriever who looked a lot like Max filled the screen.

Kyle tried telling herself that if Hollis liked Goldens, he couldn't be all bad.

"I've just come from Stanton," she said coldly. "He's in bad shape, but was able to talk about Monday's meeting."

Though Hollis pushed back his chair and stood, she was able to look down on his head with its bad comb-over. Sparse blond stubble on his jaw suggested he might be growing a beard, but his thin moustache bespoke a difficult time ahead.

Taking off his wire frame glasses, Hollis rubbed the bridge of his nose. "What did Stanton tell you?"

"He told me about your going behind my back asking him to make you Director. And he said for me to take charge at the meeting Monday."

Hollis's complexion took on a splotchy flush. "I'll never be part of your inside track with Stanton . . ." His breath started to come fast. "All you have to watch is Yellowstone while I take care of the Wasatch where millions of people live. On Monday, I'm making a pitch for more support."

Kyle slammed her hand on the top of the nearest monitor. "You know millions of dollars were spent in Salt Lake setting up a real-time seismic network for the 2002 Winter Olympics." If the Wasatch Fault let go, reports from a network of sensors would arrive within seconds to guide rescue workers toward the worst damage.

"You've got all the resources you need, Hollis." She ignored his penchant for being addressed as 'Doctor.' Figuring a good offense would be her strongest defense, "I'm going to propose a number of new recording sites in Yellowstone."

"The Park Service needs to put their own people and money on it."

"That's for the Consortium to decide," she bit out. "As long as I can make my case on Monday, I think they'll agree inadequate resources are allocated to Yellowstone. You know perfectly well another eruption the size of the ones the park has seen in the past few million years would cause the equivalent of nuclear winter."

How many times had she lectured along these same lines without her pulse rate going ballistic? How often had she fielded questions from students and the press without feeling the sense of foreboding she did today? She glanced again at the map showing the 'Ring of Fire' and hoped the Sakhalin shake hadn't spawned others.

Turning back to Hollis, she went on, "Millions would die when crops failed around the world." She'd parroted those words before too, but today she imagined a hungry little girl watching snow fall from a leaden summer sky.

"What's got into you?" Hollis replaced his glasses and glared at her. "Stop being dramatic."

He squared narrow shoulders and marched away down the aisle between computer terminals. The oscilloscope hooked to a portable seismograph on the table showed a small excursion, a dutiful record of him slamming the door.

● ● ●

At 4 PM Kyle finished teaching her Earthquake Risk seminar and headed for her office. Passing Hollis's door, she heard him on the phone, ". . . talking about ridiculous things like nuclear winter . . ."

Her face went hot. Torn between eavesdropping further and walking away, she decided on neither. Instead, she stepped to his door and leaned against it, her arms folded across her chest. She cocked one of her brows in an expression of disdain.

Hollis flushed. "I'll have to phone you back." He fumbled the receiver and almost dropped it.

"To whom were you talking about me?"

He shook his head.

"More behind the back stuff?" She pointed her slender index finger at Hollis. "Whoever it was, you know what I said was not the least ridiculous. Even the park rangers tell the tourists about the possibilities."

She went on down the hall, trying to believe her sense of impending disaster stemmed from Stanton's collapse.

"Any calls?" she asked Xi Hong, as she passed his open door next to hers. She and the Chinese postdoctoral researcher shared a phone line in a triumph of bureaucratic false economy.

Xi shook his head. All the while, he maintained a squint at vertical rows of characters on his computer monitor. In one of his trademark moments, Hollis had suggested Xi was a spy for Mainland China.

As she started to go into her office, Xi roused. "There is a note here from the department secretary." He passed it to her with a grave look. "Leila says the CT scan shows area of damage in Stanton's brain from stroke."

Kyle took the message and scanned it, but there was no more than he had said.

She went into her small cluttered space and sank into the swivel chair. Raising her long legs, she propped feet clad in slim black flats on the desk, crossed her ankles, and leaned back. In the familiar, rewarding hubbub of teaching, she had managed to set aside thoughts of Stanton's misfortune, but now, with her eyes stinging, she crumpled the note and threw it at the wall.

Why him? And why *now* for his good fortune to run out?

On her office credenza rested what Kyle liked to think of as her lucky piece, a colorful chunk of the bright green copper mineral malachite. When she was growing up under the watchful eye of her grandmother near the great open pits of Globe, Arizona, Franny's second husband, Zeke, worked in the mines. He had learned early on that bringing a sample of deep-blue azurite or soft, turquoise-hued chrysocolla from the tailings piles outside the mine brought delight to Kyle's young eyes. By the time she was in junior high, her rock collection outstripped his capacity to identify samples. The malachite was the first specimen Zeke had given her; the mass of emerald hue striped with deeper green was worn smooth from touching.

As she worried the stone with her thumb, her thoughts returned to Stanton and the people who needed to know what had happened to him. Though the thought of telling others made her feel hollow, and served to make his collapse all too real, she lifted the phone.

For the next hour, she tried to swallow her sorrow and placed calls all over the world: California, Hawaii, Massachusetts, Bolivia, Japan, and the Philippines. She spoke in a controlled voice to Consortium members at the USGS Cascades Volcano Observatory in Washington State, researchers at a number of universities, and some of Stanton's contacts in foreign governments.

In the home stretch, she realized she had saved the hardest task for last, that of informing former Utah student Wyatt Ellison, now a Yellowstone Ranger. Perhaps because he was older than most graduates, fortysomething Wyatt was a friend to both her and Stanton.

Imagining the crestfallen look on Wyatt's lean and craggy face, she tried his office in the Resource Center near Park Headquarters in Mammoth Hot Springs. As it was after five, she also tried his park housing. Getting no answer and nothing on his cell phone, she decided not to break the news by email.

As she replaced the phone, Kyle picked up her lucky

malachite again.   Turning it in her hands, she figured Stanton needed it more than she did.

CHAPTER TWO
SEPTEMBER 11

Ranger Wyatt Ellison crawled through golden reeds along Yellowstone's Lamar River. Though the ground was cold in the northern range, he didn't mind. Time spent in the field was always good, especially on a fall day when the summer tourists had retreated from the park like a receding tide. It didn't even matter that a heavy-looking gray cloud sailed toward the valley, trailing a gauzy scarf of precipitation.

From his position in the river bottom, Wyatt could see mountains rising on both sides. To the southwest was the long shoulder of Specimen Ridge, crowned by Amethyst Mountain. On the slopes was a fossil forest of upright stone trees.

Though Wyatt had come late to the study of the earth, he liked to say he got there as fast as he could, arriving in the park a year ago at age forty-four to become their oldest rookie geologist. Today's excursion wasn't about rocks, though.

Ahead of him in an abandoned chute of the Lamar, Alicia Alvarez with the Wolf Advocates wriggled through scrubby vegetation. He appreciated the way her parka rode up over rounded hips, revealing designer jeans streaked with dirt. Following her lead, Wyatt crawled up a gravel bank and peered over the river-rounded cobbles.

There they were, five darker specks contrasting with golden autumn grass. The Specimen Ridge Pack trotted across the sage-dotted slope below the treed ridge where they'd denned last spring. Though Wyatt had watched them before from up by the highway at Yellowstone Institute's Buffalo Ranch, Alicia's association with the non-profit organization allowed her to work in closer. Her father, a South Texas banker and cattleman, made regular contributions to the wolf's cause.

In 1923, rangers had deliberately destroyed the last known den in Yellowstone, to leave the park without its most significant predator. Without a mechanism to take out the weak and sick, the winterkills became cruel. Fortunately, because of the hard work of people like Alicia, the 1995 reintroduction of wolves had begun to change the balance.

Beside Wyatt on the bank, the transplanted Texan's chocolate eyes looked out forthrightly from a bronzed face framed with midnight hair. Her wide, generous mouth wore a smile as she pointed a manicured finger. "See the alpha male," she whispered.

The largest member of the pack, with a coat so dark he looked black, held his tail high. The other wolves indicated subordinate status by adopting a slouching posture.

While Alicia set up her Bausch & Lomb spotting scope on a tripod, Wyatt reckoned the cost of her optics at more than he brought home in two weeks. Next, she reached for the Nikon slung over her back and uncapped her 1000-mm lens. Wyatt moved to man the scope, adjusting the focus for his nearsighted eyes.

Once the image sharpened, his first impression was of the alpha male's smoky ruff. Such a coat this early in the fall might mean they were in for a tough winter. A scattering of snow already spotted the talus beneath the cliffs on Specimen Ridge and pale hoarfrost coated the trees below.

As the wolf's quick gait carried him out of the scope's range, Wyatt drew back and studied the terrain. Several hundred yards upwind from the canines, a herd of elk grazed. Separated from the rest, a single cow stood alone at the top of a thirty-foot drop to the sagebrush flat.

Wyatt put his eye back to the lens. The Specimen Ridge pack moved as one, downslope toward the hapless loner. When they got closer, they stopped and spread out into a semicircular pattern to cover all escape routes.

The cow looked out at the river with apparent unconcern.

The wolves began their stalk, slinking behind cover of vegetation or topography. When they were within seventy-five feet of their prey, her head jerked and Wyatt saw the whites of her wide brown eyes. Although this was nature's way, he still rooted for her.

The circle of wolves drew tighter and Wyatt heard Alicia's quick breathing.

The cow glanced over the cliff and appeared to weigh her odds. With a tentative step out onto treacherous ground, the cornered animal began to slide toward the lip. At the last moment, she twisted with surprising agility and managed to leap to the side. Landing on an isolated block, she stood trapped and panting in her precarious sanctuary.

Wyatt focused back on the alpha male. Well fed this time of year, the wolf stalked with assurance.

However, as the first cold gust hit ahead of the lowering squall the male's ears pricked. Zooming out, Wyatt noticed that all of the pack listened intently and tasted the wind.

All at once, as if someone had blown a whistle they spooked, running with their tails flat out, legs pumping. The elk herd also took flight, the trapped cow watching them go.

"I wonder what scared them," Alicia said in a normal voice.

Thinking it might be the squall, Wyatt nodded at the cloud sweeping toward them. The first drops of rain stung his cheeks and Specimen Ridge dissolved into the mist. Now that the wolves had gone, he became aware of his knees covered in cold mud and his soaked shirtfront.

"What say we go start a fire?" he asked with a shiver.

"If this blows over." Alicia flashed a grin that promised more than sticks and kindling.

Before he could get out a bawdy suggestion, the ground jerked beneath him.

"What the . . . ?" Her eyes widened to dark pools in a face gone pale.

"Earthquake." Hunkering on hands and knees, his sensation was of being rocked in a boat. It went on for a number of seconds, and then all went so still he wondered for a moment if he had imagined it.

But no. Across the river, the elk no longer stood on the bluff.

● ● ●

Earthquakes too small to be felt by humans were standard operating procedure in Yellowstone. For the past fifteen million years the North American continent had been sliding west, while a hotspot in the earth's upper mantle traced a line of fire from Hell's Canyon on the Oregon border, through the cinder cones of Idaho's Craters of the Moon, and on to Nez Perce Peak in eastern Yellowstone.

The park itself had suffered three great eruptions, occurring respectively 2.0 million, 1.3 million, and 630,000 years ago. Each time hundreds of cubic miles of real estate were thrown into the stratosphere the collapse created a crater known as a caldera.

Wyatt routinely related these facts to some of the three

million tourists who visited Yellowstone each year. A seismograph at Old Faithful Visitor Center showed how the ground shuddered and shook with regularity.

Today, lying on damp earth that once more felt solid, Wyatt felt an unaccountable sense of dread. It was Alicia's unease about the quake transmitting itself to him, he figured, as he pushed his tall frame up and headed toward his Park Service Bronco.

Ranger Helen Chou answered the radio in the Yellowstone Resource Center in Mammoth. "You feel that?"

"Oh, yeah." He glanced at Alicia, who still looked unsettled. "Actually, I ordered that up to get my gal in a pliant mood."

Alicia rewarded him with the ghost of a grin.

"Right," Helen said crisply. "Magnitude 3.5." Her impeccable credentials of a Ph.D. from Cal Tech, earned at twenty-three, trumped Wyatt's Utah degrees. Wiry and tough, with black hair that brushed her waist, she was his right hand in park geology. "Epicenter is the eastern shore of Yellowstone Lake."

"No surprise there." The current hotspot was centered near the lake, where the most recent great eruption had taken place.

"The frequency of small tremors has increased since you left yesterday to go wolf watching," Helen added.

Wyatt tugged off his itchy wool cap, a gift from Alicia, and ruffled his thick hair. "Speaking of wolves, before the quake the Specimen Ridge pack bolted for the hills."

"The animals know," Helen agreed. "Did you hear about the big one?"

His alarms set off. If the Wasatch Fault in Salt Lake broke loose, Stanton and Kyle might get caught in the Institute basement. "Big one?"

"Sakhalin had a 7.3."

"No kidding."

"Brock Hobart was on *Mornings with Monty* and predicted it. Just before it hit." A note of excitement penetrated Helen's professional delivery.

"Be still my heart. Another sideshow courtesy of the self-appointed seer of the seismic community." Despite his flippancy, a frown creased Wyatt's forehead.

"You coming by to look at the chart?"

Wyatt considered. The squall was almost past, the clouds breaking up in the west to let through shafts of golden light. He'd been anticipating a nice campfire, along with the succulent aroma of beef stew on the night air.

Alicia came up behind him and slipped her arms around his waist.

"I'll be camping out again tonight at Slough Creek," he told Helen.

● ● ●

The patter of rain on a tent always made Wyatt feel sad. This night was no different, as the brief sunset clearing was followed by another storm. Lying in a cocoon of cozy warmth reminded him of the simplicity of childhood campouts.

Born and raised in Bozeman, he grew up feeling blessed by each day spent in the Mountain West. A high-school rodeo champion, he'd planned on college until his father's declining health dumped the family steel fabricating business onto his youthful shoulders. A brief and turbulent courtship ended in marriage to Marie Marvell, a local Pizza Hut waitress.

The note she left said *I need more* in slanting blue ink, along with the salient point that she was headed east on I-90 with a long distance trucker. Shell-shocked at thirty, Wyatt decided he wanted more, too. He got off his ass, sold the business, and went to the University.

The tempo of the rain increased. A long rumble rolled through the Absaroka Peaks.

Alicia turned toward Wyatt in her sleep. The instinctive gesture managed to hearten him, although he thought she read more into their relationship than he did. They'd been seeing each other since June, sometimes staying at each other's places or camping out, yet he had not suggested a more permanent arrangement. Perhaps it was undue caution on his part, but after Marie, he always kept some distance between him and any woman.

Alicia burrowed into Wyatt's shoulder, her long black hair spread over his chest. Capturing a strand that curled around his finger, he shifted in the zipped bed of down and brought her warmth against the length of him. It was colder than usual for September.

Thunder rolled again over the Lamar Valley. Snow showers on the peaks, while autumn rain fell at lower elevation. As if the earth was in concert with the sky, the rumbling seemed to send a shudder beneath the tent.

With this afternoon's magnitude 3.5, Wyatt didn't think he imagined the new tremors. He'd been in one big quake in his life, a 6.1 right here in the park.

In July 1975, he and his high-school buddies had been lunching on a ridge above the broad smoking plain of Norris Geyser Basin, the spot with the highest heat flow in the park. Wyatt had just popped the top on a beer when the ground beneath him leaped. He dropped his can and watched it roll away in a spreading puddle of suds. An instant later, he was knocked onto his stomach, his cheek scraped by gravel. For an incredulous moment, he couldn't figure out what was happening, but snapped to when a fissure opened like a zipper.

"Wyatt," cried a thin voice.

He turned to see Jules Feinstein, helpless without his glasses. Horn-rimmed spectacles danced in the dirt. As Wyatt scrabbled toward him, the glasses disappeared into the trench.

Grabbing Jules by the jacket, he braced his feet against a tree, fighting to keep them both out of the yawning chasm. Together, they hung on while the ground bucked and jerked like one of the rodeo broncos Wyatt rode on the Friday night circuit.

When it was over, they decided to get out of the park.

Since Jules couldn't see, Wyatt drove, only to be stopped by a roadblock in a few miles. A great slide of boulders covered the road south from Norris to Madison Campground, forcing the young men to spread their sleeping bags by the roadside that night.

The storm at Slough Creek grew more intense, the tent's rain fly flapping. Another tremor struck, stronger than the one before. Because Alicia had been alarmed this afternoon, Wyatt was glad this one did not wake her. She wouldn't understand that after years of studying the facets of this violent planet he found the sensation of feeling the ground move fascinating.

With his back flat to the earth, he imagined his body as a stethoscope, a listening device pressed to a living organism.

Another growl reverberated, a guttural warning from the land.

CHAPTER THREE
SEPTEMBER 12

Thursday evening, Kyle guided her 1984 Mercedes 380SL east on I-80, winding up into the Wasatch Range. She counted herself fortunate she preferred the older models, for a consequence of teaching life was that she couldn't afford a new one.

For two days, Stanton had 'rested comfortably' in University Hospital, although Kyle could see nothing comfortable about his situation. Every time she managed to find a break in her workload, or plain neglect it to stop by, she could hardly manage a cheerful face. Though she usually tried to get home before dark, this evening she'd stayed late because she believed Leila needed her.

Their vigil reminded her of the days when she was eighteen and had joined her grandmother in sitting Zeke's deathwatch. Franny, still slender and energetic at seventy-one, and standing nearly as tall as Kyle, had fought with everything in her to infuse her own strength into her husband's failing heart . . . to no avail.

To imagine what Leila's life would be like if Stanton did not survive, Kyle had only to recall how Franny's remaining six years on earth had been marked by a succession of days she described as having no meaning and no end.

As she left the lights of Salt Lake City behind, Kyle became aware of the dark forest and rugged red sandstone and limestone cliffs that loomed on either side of the road. Switching on the radio for company, she heard a newswoman on public broadcast. "After yesterday's major earthquake at Sakhalin Island, the death toll is counted in the thousands and climbing."

Kyle shuddered and turned up the volume.

"The quake was predicted by scientist Brock Hobart on the L.A. talk show *Mornings with Monty*. No one at the National Earthquake Information Center was available for comment."

NEIC had a public information officer on call 24/7. Apparently, they wouldn't touch this.

Kyle took the exit for her subdivision in a broad high valley. She'd looked carefully at the topography, evaluating it for landslide risk in the event of an earthquake.

It would be cheaper and an easier commute to live in Salt Lake, but her reasons had nothing to do with mountain charm. People in the valley built their houses, schools, and hospitals upon the sand; sediment laid down 10,000 years ago in Lake Bonneville. The freshwater glacial lake had covered vast portions of what would become Utah, Idaho, and Nevada, with Great Salt Lake a hypersaline remnant of former grandeur. The problem was that when shaken, loose sand saturated below the water table would liquefy . . . like in the Marina District of San Francisco, where the 1989 "World Series" quake had reduced unconsolidated landfill to the consistency of a milkshake.

Although she'd downplayed the Wasatch Fault to Hollis this afternoon for effect, Kyle knew all too well the USGS gave the probability of it spawning a large earthquake in the next fifty years as one in four. With two million people living within fifteen miles of the fault, studies had placed the potential death toll at over 2,000, with 30,000 homeless.

Rather than live in the valley, Kyle chose mountains cored by 200-million-year-old sediment. Though there was ongoing debate whether a Wasatch earthquake would be felt more severely in the heights or the valley, she slept better knowing she was grounded on solid rock.

Kyle turned in at the complex where she owned a modest townhouse, parked, and used her key-ring flashlight to augment the streetlight. Once inside, she began with the living room where overstuffed armchairs metamorphosed to crouching beasts in the shadows.

Preceding her entry with the flashlight beam, she switched on Franny's porcelain lamps that flanked her couch. In the dining room, she lit the fixture over a glass-topped rectangle of deep-green labradorite she'd saved a long time to purchase. Feldspar crystals in the stone winked.

Moving from room to room, Kyle turned on every light in her house.

From the point of view of escape, it would be preferable

to have the master bedroom on the ground floor. Yet, that was balanced by the fact that upper floors could pancake like they had in Northridge, California, where TV had brought a collapsed apartment house's image into the living rooms of the world.

Upstairs, beneath Kyle's bedroom windowsill, her climbing rope waited rigged and ready. Her earthquake clothes lay folded on the chair beside the bed, clean underwear to make any mother proud, socks, jeans, a sweatshirt, raincoat, and well-worn running shoes. In case the lights went out, a lantern powered by a six-volt battery rested on the floor.

Ready to face the night, she decided to try calling Wyatt again. After half a dozen tries today, she had not yet reached him.

Back downstairs in the kitchen, she dialed the number for Wyatt's employee housing in Mammoth. Just when she thought he wasn't going to pick up, a sleepy female voice answered.

Kyle kept her tone even. "I'm calling for Wyatt."

"It's a woman," she heard.

"Hello?" Wyatt said a moment later.

"It's Kyle. I'm sorry to call so late, but . . ." Her voice broke. "Stanton is in the hospital. He's had a stroke."

"Oh, no."

"His left side is pretty weak. He can talk."

"Are you and Leila holding up?"

The warmth in his tone made Kyle wanted to pour out

every detail of the past two days, beg him to get into his truck and come straight to Salt Lake . . .

"Do you want your robe?" the background woman asked.

"Hold a sec?" Wyatt said.

The moment for dumping her troubles on a man sleeping with another woman passed, as a rustling might have been the robe going on. The sound of metal against a hard surface was probably him ferreting out his glasses on the nightstand. Kyle imagined him standing beside the bed, his long feet pale against the dark wood floors she'd seen in his housing the one time she'd stopped by. He'd be settling his titanium frames on the bridge of his nose, his dark brows knitted with concern.

He was back. "Ah damn. Stanton."

"It happened the morning before yesterday in the lab. I've tried to call you."

"I was in the field." He paused. "Have you seen the seismic pattern up here for the past forty-eight hours?"

"I've been so caught up with Stanton and trying to keep a class schedule . . ." She knew she should have taken the time to check the signals from Yellowstone.

"We're having a swarm of quakes."

Her heartbeat accelerated. "That's the last thing I need right now."

"Me, too. If it weren't going on, I'd drive down to see Stanton. Buy you a beer."

"I could use one." Her mind raced. "We need the GPS data." Satellite receivers planted in over fifty park locations triangulated their position so that the smallest elevation change was detectable.

"I ran some numbers today," Wyatt said. "The caldera is on the rise."

Usually a spate of increased activity in the park piqued her interest. Tonight, it just seemed an additional, overwhelming burden.

"It's always up and down," she bargained.

"Six inches since last week?"

"Impossible." Between 1923 and 1984, the caldera had risen a mere three feet. Then, accompanied by thousands of tremors, it dropped eight inches by 1995; it has since started again to rise. "We've never recorded movement this rapid."

"Mount St. Helens rose a meter a day. Right before it erupted."

Kyle folded down onto the floor next to the phone. The 1980 eruption of Mount St. Helens, the worst in the human history of the United States, might have taken the country by surprise but not the men and women who studied volcanoes. They had known the deadly potential coiled beneath the smoking crater. Miles of forest turned to ash-deep wasteland, millions of trees mowed down like toothpicks, the Toutle River a rampaging flood that swept away bridges and everything else in its path . . . not to mention fifty-seven people dead or missing.

"Kyle?"

"I'm here."

"I wonder if you might bring some portable seismographs

up tomorrow."

She couldn't leave Stanton . . . but even as she formed the thought, she knew the danger from an awakening Yellowstone could spell disaster for so many that her problems didn't amount to anything in the balance.

"I can be there by afternoon."

"Good. Meet me at Earthquake Lake Visitor Center on the Madison slide."

Kyle gasped and put a hand onto the cool floor tile. She had never been to the Earthquake Lake Visitor Center, a few miles from where Rock Creek Campground had been. The idea of people putting a scene of death and devastation on a vacation agenda turned her stomach, not to mention her personal reluctance to stir up ghosts.

"We ought to check for renewed activity west of the park," Wyatt said.

After a second of silence, "You there, Kyle?"

He'd been a friend for years, but on policy, she never told anybody.

"Can I let you know in the morning? I've . . . got some things to work out."

Climbing the stairs toward bed, her thoughts roiled. She had succumbed to her uncanny fascination with the Yellowstone region several times in her life. First, when she was an undergraduate and attended geology field camp south of the park; next when she came to Utah for her Ph.D.; lastly upon coming to work at the Institute. Yet, she tended to watch from arm's length due to a lesson learned when she got too close.

During her first year at Utah, she had joined a student fieldtrip to Hebgen Lake. Twenty-three years old, with a B.S. and M.S. in geology from the University of Arizona, she figured it was a good time to put the past behind her.

All went well as the group loaded onto vans in Salt Lake and caravanned north. Pizza, beer and field stories carried her through to bed, but at 4 AM, she awakened in her sleeping bag on the floor of an overcrowded West Yellowstone motel room. Slick with nightmare sweat, she fought off her covers. The room's black ceiling lowered like the sky when dust had blotted out moon and stars seventeen years ago.

Breathe, she ordered. Her tight chest barely responded. She should never have let herself be peer-pressured into sleeping in the dark. Reaching by her side, she switched on a flashlight beneath her covers.

It didn't calm her racing heart.

Dragging the sleeping bag into the john, she closed the door and turned on the light. Stark green-blue eyes like her father's stared back from the mirrored medicine cabinet, her dark brows startled wings. "Jesus," she muttered, running a hand through her disheveled hair, while she tried to tell herself she was being ridiculous.

It didn't work. With shaking hands, she spread the bedding in the tub and spent the rest of the night in the garish reflection off white tile.

In the morning, Stanton approached. "Kyle? One of the guys thought you might be sick."

She kept her gaze on the wheel stops in the motel parking lot. "Maybe a stomach virus. Since we're staying here again tonight, would it be okay if I crashed today?"

He let her stay behind, but something in her quavering voice or averted eyes must have tipped him. The day they got back to school, Stanton asked Kyle into his office and closed the door. Wordlessly, he passed across a newspaper account of the Hebgen Lake catastrophe. The list of victims included Rachel and Daniel Stone.

It hurt somehow that there was no mention of Max.

"Are you sure you want to study earthquakes?" Stanton asked.

"There's no better place for me," Kyle's younger self had told him. As much as she loathed her memories, it was in and near Yellowstone that she might find the key to warn others.

Seeming to understand her inability to discuss the past, Stanton had set the matter aside.

Still going to bed with her light on after so many years, Kyle thought how Franny had accepted her grandchild's fears, making sure her room had an extra lamp and a backup nightlight. Moreover, as there were things in Franny's life that she had refused to discuss with Kyle, she had never pressed for details about that awful night. Perhaps Franny had not wanted to know too much about how her only daughter died.

Celebrities might go to shrinks; might even think it fashionable, but Kyle had never gone for counseling. Her reading told her psychologists forced you to relive bad experiences, to go through them relentlessly until you were too worn down to get excited.

Kyle preferred her method, erecting a wall and putting disaster behind it.

Yet, she felt sure that if Stanton knew what Wyatt had told her, he'd want everything checked out, including the area near the defunct Rock Creek Campground. And there was no gracious way of refusing without attracting attention. Wyatt might start probing for answers she wasn't prepared to give.

No, it was clear that with Stanton out of commission and Hollis gunning for her funding, Kyle had no choice. She must face the danger gathering beneath Yellowstone.

CHAPTER FOUR

SEPTEMBER 13

The next afternoon, Kyle drove the Institute van along the Hebgen Lake shore. The fifteen-mile length of dammed reservoir ran east-west, a few miles outside Yellowstone's western boundary. Looking out over the gray expanse, she questioned the shreds of what she regarded as her sanity.

With a jerk of the wheel, she pulled into an overlook.

This was ridiculous. A single peek behind her wall and the bogeyman was still there.

Deep breaths of the crisp fall air, in and out until she calmed.

There was some time before she was supposed to meet Wyatt, so she opened the door and stepped out with a crunch of gravel beneath her boots. A sign indicated a walk down to the lake would take her to the site of summer homes flooded during the 1959 earthquake. Determined to treat this like any other fieldtrip, she reached behind the seat for her Canon and brought along a field notebook and pen.

As she looked around, she realized Dad had stopped the Rambler here on the drive west to Madison Canyon.

That August day had been a bright gem, the lake shimmering beneath a faultless sky. Today was cold and cloudy bright with a sprinkling of snow capping the trees on Coffin Mountain to the southwest.

Kyle set out on a narrow footpath through waist-high brush. Evidently, based on the poorly marked trail, not many people cared about the ancient ruins anymore.

After a few hundred feet of steep incline, she came to a weathered log cabin without windows or doors. Going down to the shore, she photographed a house that had sunk to its roofline when the bank collapsed and dropped twenty feet. Waves lapped at fragments of green tarpaper where the shingles had weathered away. Had the place been empty that August night, its owners blessedly away? Not likely during the high season for vacation and fishing.

Kyle imagined being shaken awake and kicking open the jammed door, leaping a crevice that had opened in the earth, while her house fell away behind her into turbulent waters.

Taking no pictures or notes, she stared at the wreck before retreating on foot back to the road.

A few miles farther, the lake narrowed into a neck, where a seven-hundred-foot-long, ninety-foot-high wall of earth held back the reservoir. In the twelve hours after the initial shock, the lake had sloshed back and forth like water in a bathtub, sending three-foot surges over the dam's crest at least four times. Kyle photographed the sign that proclaimed: THE DAM THAT HELD, an impressive feat since the construction dated back to 1915.

The highway began to wind downhill beside the un-impounded river. At her next stop, a twenty-foot scarp followed the trace of the Hebgen Fault. Although softened by years, the earthen wall was still an impressive monument to the upheaval. A vision of her father on the high side of a similar scarp sent a shaft of pain through her.

Farther on, the Madison began to widen into Earthquake Lake, the remnants of the flood. Kyle closed her eyes and rode another wave of anguish as she imagined a black wall of water rushing toward Rock Creek Campground.

For several weeks after the quake, the Madison had been dammed completely. Although the Army Corps of Engineers cut a channel that permitted the river to renew its flow, the slide had flattened the configuration of the valley floor. Even now, drowned trees stood with their tops sticking out of the water.

Along the shore, the original highway remained as violently tilted pavement blocks. The rebuilt route lay higher on the hillside, the new construction smoother and straighter than the road Kyle had watched from the Rambler's rear window.

Seven miles downriver, she came to the edge of the massive slide. The shock wave ahead of eighty million tons of falling mountain had created the hurricane force wind that swept into Rock Creek Campground.

Her mouth went dry and she gripped the wheel. Thankfully, what remained of the campsite was on the opposite side of Earthquake Lake. She drove past and began the winding climb up and over the massive treeless mound. In a few minutes, she caught sight of the round building of the visitor center perched like a flying saucer on the north rim of the valley.

Kyle parked and got out. From this high vantage point, the impact of what had happened took shape.

On the afternoon when she and her father had fished for trout, Sheep Mountain had formed the south wall of Madison Canyon, a pristine north-facing slope covered in dense forest.

Until the magnitude 7.5 quake tore it in half.

At over one hundred miles per hour, trees, earth, and solid rock had shot over a thousand feet down the canyon and up more than four hundred on the opposite side of a river thrown from its bed by the shock. The great scoop-shaped scar loomed above the visitor center.

Faced with the awesome sight, Kyle's nerves frayed like a worn rope. She tried more deep breaths of the crisp fall air and saw the emotion on her face reflected when an approaching father drew a child closer and gave her a wide berth on the sidewalk.

In Rock Creek Campground, she had seen terror in her father's gaze across the widening crevasse. Only now did she understand what he must have seen behind her.

When the landslide had crashed into the Madison River, it sent a thirty-foot wall of water racing upstream, breaking and toppling trees in its path. Before Kyle could turn away from her father's stricken gaze toward the sound, a colossal force caught the Rambler. Shoved sideways across the clearing with her inside, the car broadsided against a pine. A great thud on the roof was another tree falling.

An ominous rush surrounded the station wagon and she leaped onto the open tailgate. Bark scraped her palms as she found a foothold on a branch and blindly dragged herself up. Below, the black tide rose almost as swiftly as she scrambled ahead of it. Higher in the tree, the limbs grew smaller and the trunk whipped back and forth.

A terrible roaring increased, as though mountains ground together.

If Dad would come, he'd swim her to safety, like when she jumped off the diving board. Mom would be waiting, ready to dry her with a thick towel and ruffle her hair.

Kyle strained to make out the Rambler in the gray shadows. The picnic table and her parents' tent were gone . . . beneath this rising flood.

"Daddy!" she shrieked. "Mommy!"

Darkness and the shuddering earth mocked her.

● ● ●

Wyatt pulled his Park Service Bronco in at the Earthquake Lake Visitor Center. As always, the wound that had not yet begun to heal struck him. On both sides of the channel dug through the slide by the Corps, bare rock and earth lay dissected by great ravines. Only at the edges had reforestation begun, revealing small patches of what looked like Christmas trees.

Kyle sat on a bench with her back to him wearing well-fitting jeans and a red down vest over a plaid flannel shirt. Her hair was braided at the back of her head; turquoise and silver dangled from her earlobes. As he approached, she did not turn but seemed absorbed in looking toward the ruined site of Rock Creek Campground.

Wyatt came up behind her. "What hell it must have been for those poor bastards caught down there."

Kyle started.

She turned on him, red-eyed, and he realized with a small shock that she was crying.

"Sorry I scared you." Shoving his hands into his pockets, he turned away. But though he studied the vista, he saw her face superimposed on the pale sky. Usually strikingly attractive, with prominent cheekbones, a high-bridged nose and clean line of jaw, today her features had twisted into a mask of tragedy. Awkward moments passed, while he wondered whether to say something or just give her time. The decision made through default, he leaned against a nearby rail and waited.

Finally, she said in an almost normal voice, "Let's put out some equipment."

With the sense he'd somehow failed her, Wyatt led the way back to their parked vehicles.

Together, they drove in caravan down over the huge landslide and turned south on Highway 287. The Old

Madison Valley Fault parallel to the road was not believed to be as active as the Hebgen Lake and Red Canyon Faults farther east, but they wanted to check that theory.

Coming to a dirt road, Wyatt signaled a turn. In the Bronco's rearview mirror, he saw Kyle follow him. Forest punctuated by patches of golden meadow unfolded on either side as they drove deeper into the wilderness. It was difficult to believe desolation lay just on the north side of the ridge.

When Kyle signaled him with a tap of her horn, he pulled up beside a thick pine.

Getting out, he agreed, "This looks like a good spot." The scarp of another small fault ran along the right side of the track.

He got out one of the portable seismographs. In contrast to the older models that had weighed an unwieldy amount, the newer technology had created lightweight sensors of only a few pounds. Inside the metal casing was a pendulum that would remain steady while the rest of the instrument moved with the earth.

Kyle pointed out a relatively flat area a little distance from the road. Wyatt lifted the seismograph and carried it to the chosen spot. After digging a hole to ground the instrument and insulate it from wind or vehicle noise, they opened the solar panels that would power the battery for the detached drive.

"We're going to need extra help to gather all this data," Wyatt said.

"After I chair the Monday Consortium meeting, I'll

get Xi Hong to take my seminar so I can come back."

"I can count on Helen Chou."

Kyle plugged in her laptop and ran through some tests to be sure the seismograph functioned. As they prepared to leave, Wyatt patted the unit. "I hope we don't need you, little fella."

❋ ❋ ❋

"I'll have a stout," Wyatt told the waitress, anticipating the rich, molasses-tasting brew. He and Kyle shared a booth in the Red Wolf Saloon in West Yellowstone, Montana. The small town located ten miles south of Hebgen Lake served as the western gateway community on the park boundary.

"Light beer," Kyle added. Beneath the glow of a brass mine lamp, she traced the scars of myriad initials carved into the wooden table.

Wyatt watched the movement of her long, expressive fingers. Since leaving Utah, he'd missed their working late and adjourning for a brew . . . although they'd never been in quite this situation before, alone in the field and sitting in an intimate booth that would have been perfect had they been lovers. Tonight, she'd let her hair free from her habitual braid and let it flow in shining waves over her shoulders. It made her look younger and in his mind erased that she was somewhat older than he.

When the waitress brought their drinks, he raised a toast. "To Stanton."

Kyle clanked her mug against his and took a long swallow.

"And to you getting the bucks for Yellowstone," he finished.

They each drank again.

"I'd rather be lucky than smart at this Consortium." Kyle drummed the tabletop. "I found out that even before Stanton collapsed, Hollis Delbert has been circling like a vulture."

Wyatt raised an inquiring brow.

"Asked Stanton to put him in charge"—she mimed quotation marks in the air—"when he retired."

"Like Stanton was ever going to quit." Wyatt grimaced. "I've never liked that SOB Delbert."

Kyle flashed a grin. "You're just hacked off because he gave you a B in Tectonophysics."

Wyatt laughed.

She pushed back a stray lock of hair and her oval face settled into serious lines. "What worries me is that Hollis is planning a frontal attack at the Consortium."

"You mean his Salt Lake project deserves all the money because nobody lives in Yellowstone?"

She nodded. "You know, if Rockefeller hadn't gotten the Grand Teton National Park started, there'd be a city like Denver or Salt Lake in Jackson Hole . . . folks driving to office buildings, trying to see the mountains through a smog inversion. Yellowstone would probably have ended up in Disney's hands."

"Since that didn't happen, Hollis may get our funding."

"I hope you're wrong," Kyle said, "but what really worries me is something I don't even want to think about."

Wyatt studied her. "You mean what if Stanton doesn't come back?"

She nodded again.

He considered the impact Stanton's loss would have on both the Institute and the lives of people who cared for him. For his own part, Wyatt felt the older man was family. When he'd decided to start college, Stanton had been the catalyst to his choosing geology as his major.

Struggling through his first mineralogy exam, Wyatt had wondered what he'd been thinking when he signed up. Just then, Professor Stanton passed through the lab.

Wyatt fiddled with the bright yellow specimen he'd been examining. It looked like a piece of colored glass, but this was mineralogy.

The professor peered at him through tortoise shell reading glasses and barked, "Hardness?"

"Softer than the porcelain plate," Wyatt said. "I'm not sure whether it's harder or softer than glass."

Wyatt detected a gleam in Stanton's pale blue eyes.

He looked at the specimen one more time. "This really is a piece of manmade glass."

As Stanton smiled conspiratorially, Wyatt decided a guy with a sense of humor would be a nice place to start for a major professor.

He'd never been disappointed.

"If he doesn't make it back," Wyatt told Kyle, "you'll

carry on as the new head of the Institute." Even as he said it, he realized she'd never expressed a desire to run the place.

"It's not up to Stanton," she argued. "If he has to retire, he gets one vote as to who takes his place. That's assuming he's considered competent by the committee. Volcano Hazards or the National Park Service could come up with their own candidate."

"Then on Monday, you'll have to convince them you can pour from the proverbial boot more neatly and spill less than anybody."

Kyle smiled. In the lamplight, her eyes reminded him of a tourmaline in a ring his mother had when he was young. A deep-green stone, but when you held it up and looked though the side of the long crystal you could see blue shining from its depths.

Memory he had repressed stirred. Of a time or two when he'd found himself considering Kyle as a woman and not just a friend. He reckoned that happened every now and then whenever a man and woman spent a lot of time together, especially colleagues with similar interests. They might be well suited for each other, except neither he nor Kyle seemed to be looking for a long-term relationship. Better they be friends and not spoil it.

Yet, the part of him that liked the color of her eyes and the way she brushed her hair back from her rounded brow . . . That part of him had hated to see her crying this afternoon.

"Want to tell me what you were upset about earlier?" he asked.

As Wyatt watched, her eyes changed from tourmaline to black onyx.

● ● ●

The first time the tree stopped shaking, six-year-old Kyle thought it was over.

Her wet clothes clung nastily. Below, in the blackness, water rushed and gurgled.

Within moments, aftershocks erupted, though as a child she had no name for them. Each time the slender trunk whipped from side to side, she screamed and knotted her arms and legs tighter until blood ran down them. Continued grumbling came from the surrounding mountains as avalanches rearranged the debris. The wind lifted and lightning spawned a jagged streak.

At home, Kyle and Max always waited out storms beneath the stairs. She'd press her face into his golden fur so she couldn't see the flashes.

"Max," she called without conviction from her perch in the pine. "Here, boy."

As the storm approached, she closed her eyes. Without her dog to burrow against, violet daggers of light penetrated her lids. Once, she looked and saw in the eerie light a brand new mountain smack in the middle of Madison Canyon. Trunks of trees, tossed like matchsticks, protruded from the face of the slide.

The rain continued to soak her. Her teeth chattered and

she trembled so much she feared falling into the floodwaters. Mom, Dad, and Max, too, could all swim better than she, but what did that count for when rivers flowed uphill, mountains collapsed, and the moon was blotted out?

● ● ●

"Kyle?" Wyatt's sharp tone brought her back to the present. In the Red Wolf's cozy amber light, he looked solid and friendly, a man she could trust with anything.

"There's nothing to tell," she lied reflexively. How easy it would be to give in to the entreaty in his eyes.

"Christ, Kyle. This is me, remember." He bent forward beneath the mine lamp, looking determined. Though she was not a small woman, Wyatt's size and sheer intensity made her feel delicate. "You were crying this afternoon. About Stanton, or some guy?"

She shook her head, her hands clenched beneath the table.

A shuttered look replaced Wyatt's caring expression.

With a sigh, she mourned the distance between her and the rest of the world. She particularly hated for her past to drive a wedge into her and Wyatt's friendship. Back when they had worked together, she'd thought a time or two about revealing that dreadful night. Usually in a similar situation when the beer was cold and the bar cozy. Each time, she came to the same conclusion she did now.

Never looking back was her best defense. Especially

now, for she feared the swelling caldera was only the beginning of their troubles.

CHAPTER FIVE

SEPTEMBER 14

Saturday afternoon, Kyle rode the bow while Wyatt guided a Park Service cabin cruiser across Yellowstone Lake. Though the damp wind tugged at her braid she stayed on deck, feeling the unaccustomed distance between them. Ordinarily, they'd be laughing together, focused on the splendor of the world's largest high altitude lake. Surrounded by mountains above 8,000 feet, the pristine water filled the deepest depression in the 630,000-year-old caldera. The Yellowstone River flowed north out of the lake and east to join the Missouri and Mississippi.

The sky's reflection deepened mysteriously to cobalt in the mirrored surface. On the western horizon, wispy horsetails materialized. The first Arctic front of the season was sweeping down from the northern Pacific, but was supposed to hold off at least through Sunday.

Shoving her hands into the pockets of her field parka, Kyle raised her face to the sun. The pleasant drone of the boat's engine underscored how peaceful everything seemed. Yet, the average tourist never suspected that nearly three hundred feet down in the lake, probes measured temperatures in the boiling range while remote cameras captured mineral spires around submerged hot springs.

Visitors tended to view things as static, or thought they changed slowly, the way erosion washed mountains to the sea. Yet, when the Hebgen Lake quake had struck, geysers erupted all over the park. New springs started to churn and boil. Near Old Faithful, Giantess Geyser went off for one hundred hours instead of its usual thirty. Fountain Paint Pots overran the paved parking lot, and a geyser called "Steady" wasn't anymore.

The cruiser steered toward Dot Island, an isolated patch of earth that in the late 1800s had been a zoo, complete with buffalo and elk. Now it was deserted except for nesting osprey.

When they were a hundred yards offshore, Wyatt stuck his head out the cabin door. "Ready with the anchor?"

Kyle moved forward to the chain locker.

Fifty yards out, he killed the engine and she splashed the anchor.

Quiet descended.

Wyatt ducked his head to get out the cabin door. "You should have stayed inside with me where it's warm."

"I don't spend enough time out in the park," she equivocated.

"Come more often." Though his eyes were hidden behind prescription sunglasses, she sensed tautness in his apparent small talk.

"The workload at the Institute . . . the students . . ."

She would not tell him she had a superstitious sense that lightning did strike more than once in the same place.

With his tall frame propped against the cabin wall, Wyatt went on, "I'd be glad to have you help out, especially since Helen's been spending a lot of time in Seattle."

"What's there?" She hoped he'd take her cue and stop dwelling on the fact that there were questions she couldn't bring herself to answer.

"Helen's boyfriend is an Associate Professor at the University of Washington."

"Any chance of her leaving you?"

"Lord, I hope not. We're going to need all the help we can get."

He turned his attention to the dinghy. "Give me a hand with this."

Together, they lowered the small boat. Once free of the cruiser, it looked like a plump toy bobbing. Nonetheless, Kyle handed down the seismograph and a pair of lifejackets and joined Wyatt aboard. As they headed toward shore, she told herself the lake seemed rougher because she was in a small vessel.

Yet, by the time they were near the island, she was certain something was amiss. Though the wind was not any stronger, the lake churned with whitecaps that had definitely not been there before.

A nasty wave slapped the side of the boat, sending her equilibrium haywire.

She reached to grab the gunwale and missed. It reminded

her of when she was a kid and misjudged a leap from one tree limb to another. Almost in slow motion, she fell forward.

Though Wyatt caught a handful of her parka, he couldn't stop her. Her hand plunged into cold water and her sunglasses splashed into the lake. Then she crashed into the boat's side, taking the impact on her chest beneath her right arm.

Pain exploded.

"You okay?" He still had hold of her coat.

"Damn." She squinted against broken diamonds of light and wished her glasses hadn't sunk.

Though the first sharpness of hurt began to dull, an experimental breath sent a stab through her chest. "I hope I haven't broken a rib," she managed. In a moment, she'd try and sit upright.

Another wave smacked the engine, causing it to shift and turn the boat broadside.

Wyatt let Kyle go and scrambled for the tiller. The engine sputtered and died, the dinghy tilted at a sickening angle, lake and sky seemed to spin.

A bigger wave broke, leaving Kyle and Wyatt thigh-deep in the overturning boat as their personal flotation gear washed into the lake. If she'd thought the water frosty when she stuck her hand in, she'd severely underestimated.

Wyatt abandoned ship. His angular face set in concentration as he fought to stand in the surf and drag the boat the remaining two yards to the sand. Trying to ignore her pain, Kyle scrambled out chest-deep and floundered toward the bow. Another comber washed in and she found herself swimming in waterlogged clothing.

Over the slap and crash of waves, she heard Wyatt shout for her to try and grab the boat. The next deluge broke on top her shoulders and shoved her down like a huge hand.

Kyle kept her eyes open to dispel the suffocating darkness, but the clear lake had turned turbid. She windmilled, imagining darker and dirtier waters.

Another wave crashed, rolling her over. Her boot brushed gravel and she staggered to stand. Wyatt's hand stretched toward her.

Before she could reach it, the next swell lifted her to the foundering dinghy. The one after helped her and Wyatt push the boat onto the beach.

As if a pack of hounds pursued her, she clambered out. Her parka must weigh a hundred pounds, water pouring out of its pockets and folds onto the gray pumice sand.

"What in hell?" Wyatt said, just as she realized she was still off kilter, like riding an elevator that traveled in small jerks.

"Earthquake," she gasped.

● ● ●

The first thing Wyatt heard when the ground stopped shaking was Kyle's laughter.

Not a merry sound, but the raucous guffaw that had

seized him and his buddies in the old Bozeman neighborhood when Jules Feinstein fell off his bike. The kind of laugh you didn't intend, yet, it was out there with an edge that bordered hysteria.

"You okay?" he asked. He'd never thought of Kyle as anything but tough.

It took her a few moments, but she finally swallowed her laughter with a gulp that sounded like a hiccup. "Fine."

She didn't look fine. The rap on her side explained a lot, but there seemed to be more. She looked scared.

"Kyle?"

She seemed to shake herself mentally. "How big do you think that was?"

He considered. "3.5 or maybe a bit more. Stronger than the one I felt the other day."

"A 3.5 shouldn't cause that much lake turbulence."

"Underwater landslides," he suggested. "Tsunami effect." The creeping cold started him shaking. "We've gotta move." He put a hand on the boat's bow.

"Not before we do what we came for." She nodded toward the seismograph in its metal case, sitting in the boat bottom in eight inches of water. "Good thing it's all-weather."

"No," Wyatt decided. "If we take the time to dig a proper hole, we'll both have hypothermia."

"I hate to have come all this way for nothing." Kyle was shivering and her lips and fingernails had gone from healthy pink to blue.

"Too bad." The shaking had hold of Wyatt in earnest as he took her arm and urged her toward the dinghy. He wanted to get her . . . and him, someplace warm.

She grabbed the seismograph and he thought she still meant to deploy it. Fortunately, she set it on the ground a little ways off and helped him grab the boat and tip it up on its side. Water poured onto the sand.

He climbed in and waited for her to retrieve the instrument and shove the bow off. A wave broke over the stern and his boots were once more in the water.

"Here goes nothing." He pulled the rope starter and willed the engine to turn over without a hitch. Park Service maintenance tended to be variable.

On the first try, the rope dragged at his hand. He pulled again, trying to steady his grip. The fifty yards to the cruiser would not be a tough swim in a warm pool.

The afternoon sun shone mockingly.

On the third try, the motor sputtered and died.

The chop of the lake had not subsided with the earth's shaking. It continued to roil the way water sloshes in a bowl long after the hand that shook it is withdrawn.

Four tries, five. Wyatt closed his eyes and tried to forget the cold.

The next pull on the rope starter rewarded him with a cloud of blue exhaust.

As he guided the dinghy toward the cruiser, each cresting wave smacked the bow. Kyle hunkered down and pulled up the hood of her parka, while in order to steer he was forced to take each biting splash square in the face.

When they reached the larger boat, Kyle gathered the painter and leaped aboard.

Once he was on the cruiser, Wyatt started the main engine. In the short time they'd been gone, the motor had cooled and the heater's flow felt like air conditioning.

"We've got to get out of these wet things." Kyle stripped off her parka, opened a bench locker, and looked inside. "Blankets?"

"Aft."

Wyatt heard the rustle of her taking off her clothes and dumping them in a sopping heap on the metal deck. They'd been on a lot of fieldtrips together, coed treks to the Moenkopi Desert where there were no bushes and a potty stop consisted of boys on one side of the bus and girls on the other. He and Kyle had even shared a tent, waking to a frosty Colorado morning and slithering into jeans inside their separate sleeping bags.

He checked the heater and found the flow warming.

Kyle came up beside Wyatt with a faded red blanket wrapped sarong fashion and tucked beneath her armpits. Another draped her shoulders like a serape. She'd taken apart her fraying braid; strands of wet hair left darker spots where they dripped onto the wool.

He'd seen the sprinkling of freckles that adorned her bare chest before, too. Fieldtrip skinny dipping in motel hot tubs had more than once resulted in the rowdy students being thrown out by irate proprietors, or passively forced by the less assertive who simply turned off the gas. Come to think, Kyle had been the only one who always wore a swimsuit, a long, slender black tank.

Then how come seeing her half-dressed today set up a thudding in his pulse?

"You go and change," she ordered. Her strong fingers gripped his shaking arm. "I'll take the wheel."

"I'll be all right," he said through teeth that chattered despite the heater's effort. "We'll be at the dock in fifteen minutes."

She made a move to shoulder him aside, and he caught a glimpse of scraped skin and swelling starting beneath her armpit. That was going to be a humdinger of a bruise.

As she readjusted her blanket, something in him was disappointed at the aborted glimpse of her small yet well-formed breast. For distraction, he studied the rough fabric with distaste.

"I'm allergic to wool," he carped.

"Allergic to wool?" she whined back at him.

"All right," he chuckled, "I broke the cardinal rule of the fieldtrip."

"First one to bitch is a sissy." She raised a sardonic brow and prodded him with her elbow. "If I'm going to dock dressed in this high style, you're going to also."

Wyatt stepped back and let her drive. Aft, the rough ride forced him to sit on a locker to take off his boots. It took longer than he expected, his fingers fumbling wet leather laces. Finally, he got them off and followed with his parka and uniform. Wrapping a folded blanket around his waist, he put another layer of wool around his shoulders and went forward.

He leaned against the dash, warming his hands and feeling the blanket scratchy on his skin. As Kyle drove competently, he saw no need to take back the wheel.

After a while, he pointed out the newly pink patches on his chest. "I really am allergic." He gestured toward the blanket around his waist. "It's all I can do to keep this on."

She didn't miss a beat. "I'm sure a naked ranger would be a hit at the marina."

He laughed, both because he found the image preposterous and because they had finally broken the ice between them after last night. Despite his wool irritation, he felt good as he gazed out through the spattered windshield.

The view was of Gull Point, where wave-cut bluffs scarred the dense forest. On the north shore, the majestic structure of the Lake Hotel stood out, its pale yellow a contrast to the backdrop of green woods. Near the entrance to Bridge Bay marina, the highway crossing marked the opening into the sheltered cove. Wyatt could not remember when he'd been happier to end an outing on the lake.

Kyle pulled off throttle for the no-wake zone and the cruiser settled in the water. In a few minutes, they would be on their way to the hotel's cabins. He planned on showering until the hot water heater drained, lying beneath blankets until it reheated, and doing it again.

Only a few nights ago, lying in his tent feeling tremors,

he'd been excited about being on the scene for this latest chapter in Yellowstone's seismic history. Today, he realized if the quake had kicked up a bit stronger, he and Kyle would have been swamped.

From there, it was a small reach to think of being dragged down by their sodden clothing and drowned.

CHAPTER SIX
SEPTEMBER 14

Two hours later, Kyle felt warm again, but was still shaky inside. And hungry, a deep insistent longing for red meat or some other fatty delight. As she crossed the lawn from her small wooden cabin toward the three-story Lake Hotel clad in yellow-painted lumber, she noted a pair of buffalo lazing in the long golden grass. In the balmy afternoon, it was difficult to believe the wilderness had turned from menacing back to benign.

She entered the hotel through a side door and spotted a pay phone in the hallway. As her cell had drowned this afternoon, she took a moment to set down her leather portfolio of maps and called Stanton's hospital room. Leila answered faintly.

"How's our patient?" Kyle twisted the wire that connected receiver to phone.

"Sleeping."

"Hope I didn't wake him."

"Actually, he's sedated," Leila confessed. "This afternoon he tore out his IVs, threw that green rock you gave him off his bed tray, and smashed it. The doctors say he'll need to stay in the hospital longer."

Kyle closed her eyes and leaned against the edge of the phone box. A pain in her injured side demanded she take the news standing straight. "I'm sure he'll get through this stage."

"They're going to keep him sedated for twenty-four hours, then see."

If Kyle were at the hospital, she'd put her arms around Leila; cry with her, but it was out of the question for her to break down with a busload of chattering retirees filing into the hall.

"Are you taking care of yourself?" Kyle raised her voice.

"Yes." Leila didn't sound convincing. "How are you doing?"

"Fine." Kyle did not intend mentioning her and Wyatt's dip in the lake.

"You don't sound fine."

"I'm all right," she insisted. Then, because it was Leila, "No, I'm not. Wyatt and I had a hell of an afternoon. There was a pretty significant quake."

"Oh, dear." Leila had never indicated she knew about Kyle's past, but the warmth in her tone suggested Stanton had told and sworn her to secrecy.

Pressing her lips together to keep her secrets inside, Kyle changed the subject. "I'll be back in town tomorrow, probably too late to visit. I'll come Monday after the Consortium meets."

After hanging up, she walked toward the lobby to

meet Wyatt and passed a vending alcove. Appetite born of years of addiction seized her, not for a cola or chocolate bar despite her hunger, but for the heated swirl of tobacco smoke. The way things were going this week, she would no doubt have pulled out some cash and bought a pack but was saved by whatever Surgeon General had wiped out cigarette machines.

Entering the main lobby, she paused before the fireplace. Ceramic tile fired in the 1920s formed a lovely frame for a hollow promise. Since 1959, when the Hebgen Lake quake had weakened the chimney, the fireplace had remained cold and dark.

Crossing in front of the antique wooden bar, Kyle smelled spilled liquor. Broken glass littered the floor; the cleanup crew must have been overtaxed by damage from today's quake.

In the middle of the lobby, a display of old-time photos demonstrated that the wide room, with its tulip light fixtures, columns, and polished hardwood floors had not changed much since the hotel opened in 1892. The sunroom, where she and Wyatt planned to meet, was a 1920s addition to the original lobby. The bright space formed a half circle with wide windows fronting the expanse of lake, mountains, and sky. People sat on couches and chairs, reading, or playing one of the board games set out for amusement.

Wyatt was seated in a cushioned wicker chair near the center-most window, his gaze on the cobalt water. Kyle looked and saw whitecaps roiling in all directions, peaking in points that shot up startlingly high. It looked odd, considering no appreciable wind ruffled the grass and trees. Although the earth movement seemed to have ceased, she suspected it had merely subsided to a level below which a human observer could detect.

Coming up behind Wyatt, she was struck by how nice he looked in the afternoon light. His jaw line was tight; he had good hair, too, wavy and full. She touched his shoulder, not a thing she would normally do, but today her frame of reference felt upside down. Still feeling shaky, she let her fingers rest a moment, feeling muscle and sinew beneath his well-washed red pullover.

He turned and gave a coconspirators smile that brought back shared danger. "You warm enough?"

She nodded at his glass of stout. "Enough to drink a cold one."

He motioned to a waiter and ordered Kyle a light beer. "Sorry, I just assumed. You want something else?"

"That much you do know about me."

"I also suspect you're as starved as I am."

She glanced over her shoulder toward the dining room entrance beside the bar.

Wyatt smiled. "Dinner starts in half an hour. We're on the list."

Sinking into the chair beside him, Kyle savored the view. Memories of having a drink here with Stanton after a day of fieldwork made her throat tight.

"You all right?" Wyatt asked.

She swallowed. "I called Leila. The doctors believe Stanton will be in the hospital longer than they thought."

Wyatt pulled his jeans-clad legs in and straightened from his slouch. "What's going on?"

"She said he was violent."

He nodded. "My dad . . . He had a stroke when he was only fifty-seven. They had to tie him down."

"Did he get better?" Kyle hoped so, though she knew Wyatt had gone into the family business after his father's sudden death.

He shook his head. "He was trapped on the rim of the world . . . on life support for weeks."

A lump thickened Kyle's throat as he went on, "I took the night shift at the hospital so I could keep up work. Sitting there with machines humming, I'd study Dad's hands, watching them get thinner and paler each day." Wyatt stretched out his own hands, brown and strong-looking.

She reached and placed her palms over his. "That must have been difficult to watch."

"I remember his hands when they were like mine now." His expansive gesture broke their contact. "Threading line, teaching me to fly-fish the Yellowstone, steadying me on a log to bridge a stream."

Tears stood in her eyes, for she knew Wyatt as a man of few words.

"Dad taught me to ride when I was no bigger than an ant on a huge hill of horse. He trained me to rodeo when I was thirteen, picking me up off the dusty dirt of the corral and setting me on my feet. 'Good try,' he'd say no matter how poor the ride. Then he'd point me back toward the wall-eyed horse and say, 'Do it again'."

"He sounds wonderful," she said. "I lost my mom and dad when I was six." She stopped, for he'd heard that fact before, and she didn't care to embellish. "Franny's Zeke died when I was eighteen. I guess Stanton is the closest to a father I have."

"God, I hope he gets through this." Wyatt lifted his hand as though to touch hers, but the waitress arrived with her beer and he reached to drain the last of his.

She took a bracing drink.

He ordered another stout and gave her a long look. "You were mighty young to lose both your folks." The question he'd never asked before hung in the air.

"A terrible accident," she tempered with her eyes on her glass. "My mother's mother, Francesca di Paoli from Tuscany, I was the only one who ever called her Franny . . . She and Zeke raised me. You remember me telling you stories?"

As though he understood she didn't want to discuss her parents' deaths, Wyatt nodded. "Seems I recall she was one tough broad."

"She worked on a dude ranch in Jackson Hole back in the 1920s, taught me to ride the way your dad did you. Her first husband, a Wyoming cowboy, was something like one-eighth Nez Perce."

Wyatt settled in his chair and gave her an easy smile. "Know any smoke signals?"

She gave a soft laugh and flicked one of her turquoise earrings, setting it swinging. "At maybe one thirty-second Nez Perce, I think I'd be better with a signal flare."

A piano player began his first tune of the evening, a haunting rendition of "Clair de Lune." The moon was waning now, after being full the day of the Sakhalin event. Outside, the lake continued to dance in the fading afternoon light.

It was so nice that Wyatt seemed at ease with her again that it was a shame to disturb the mood with work. Nonetheless, the sight of plaster dust on the floor, which had no doubt fallen during today's quake, made her point to the portfolio. "Shall we look at tomorrow?"

"That would be a trick," Wyatt chuckled. "Isn't Brock Hobart the one with the crystal ball?"

"He gets lucky." Nevertheless, his aim had been troubling her for years, especially since she and Stanton saw Brock on TV.

Wyatt gave her a serious look. "Everybody says predictions are so much bunkum, but don't you still hope to warn the innocent before nature goes on a rampage?"

She'd figured he shared her dream, but hearing him speak it made her chest swell. "I suspect it's the dirty little secret of most seismologists."

His eyes were on a level with hers. "It's always been mine."

"And mine, since I was a child." She turned her attention to rummaging in her portfolio. "Have you found out the magnitude of this afternoon's quake?"

"I phoned Helen. She said 4.0."

"Epicenter?"

"Nez Perce Peak."

Kyle drew out a geologic map of Yellowstone and Wyatt moved his wicker chair closer to hers. Behind them in the main lobby, some woman's heels made a hollow tapping on the hardwood floor.

"Here." Kyle put a fingertip onto Nez Perce on the map.

East of the lake, the Absaroka Range where Nez Perce Peak was could be seen from the sunroom window. Green and peaceful looking, the mountains were born of fire fifty million years ago. The exception that pierced the range's heart was Nez Perce; a volcano that Stanton and his graduate students had discovered was only 10,000 years old.

"It escaped notice for a long time," Kyle reminded Wyatt. In an age of satellite telemetry, with NASA bragging that everything from foliage to mineral content could be detected from space, lots of people lost sight of the fact that remote sensing was limited.

Wyatt leaned forward, their heads closer together. "Following the trajectory of the hotspot all the way from Oregon, it's always made sense that the newest volcanic events should be northeast of the lake."

Kyle clanked her beer bottle against his. "Here's to it being another 10,000 years before anything new happens."

Wyatt's expression suggested the chances of that were slim.

Thinking how rapidly the ground beneath the lake was rising gave Kyle a shiver, as though something wicked approached.

The tapping heels came closer and a feminine cry came from behind them, almost making Kyle drop her drink.

"Alicia!" Wyatt got to his feet and headed with a long-legged stride to meet the woman rushing at him.

Kyle had a fleeting impression of huge dark eyes in a tanned face before Alicia buried her head against Wyatt's shoulder. Whereas most tourists sported casual clothing, she wore a little black dress that looked expensive, as did her high-heeled sandals and the simple yet heavy gold chain around her slender neck.

This must have been the woman in Wyatt's bed Thursday evening.

CHAPTER SEVEN
SEPTEMBER 14

"M eet Alicia Alvarez with Wolf Advocates," Wyatt introduced, his arm around her yielding waist.

"It's a pleasure to meet you," Kyle's hand extended to Alicia, though she did not smile. "Your group had a major influence in getting the wolf back into the park." Her voice sounded a little stiff.

Wyatt smiled at Alicia. "You remember I told you about my dissertation advisor, Dr. Kyle Stone of the Utah Institute of Seismology."

As the two women shook hands, Wyatt marveled at the differences between them. Though many would have judged Alicia more feminine, Kyle's combination of confidence and handsome carriage carried a powerful punch, as evidenced by a passing male who took in the way her jeans fit before checking Alicia out. Come to think, the distinction between the women went deeper than the physical. Kyle was the person he'd most like to have a beer with and talk about what made Yellowstone tick.

Alicia's eyes, rimmed in something that made them look larger than usual, continued to dart from Kyle to

Wyatt. "What are you two doing at the hotel?"

Her implied accusation set him on edge.

"Fieldwork," he replied. "We're staying in the cabins." He glanced at her fancy dress and sandals. "You?"

"I'm meeting some people for dinner . . . staying here tonight . . ." Her look suggested an invitation to her room. "Tomorrow I'm taking them wolf watching in Hayden Valley."

"Do you have time to join us for a drink?" It might smooth things over.

"I've got a few minutes," Alicia allowed.

As they settled into chairs, she continued to eye Kyle. "Have you ever modeled?"

"Goodness, no." Kyle looked as if the idea was preposterous. "I was in one university or another for eleven years, and after that I did research and taught."

"Very well, I might add," Wyatt interjected.

A strained silence fell.

Reaching for her beer, Kyle winced and lowered her arm gingerly.

"Are you okay?" Wyatt leaned forward.

"What's the matter?" Alicia asked.

"We were out on the lake this afternoon during that quake," Kyle said. "I slipped and banged myself on the side of the boat. It's nothing."

"It didn't look like nothing," Wyatt disagreed. "You have a bad bruise under your arm."

"How did you see her naked side?" Alicia asked tartly.

● ● ●

Kyle met the challenge in the thirtysomething woman's snapping eyes. In the academic environment where both sexes worked together on as equal a footing as possible, she wasn't used to dealing with insecurity. For that was clearly the root of Alicia's animosity, along with an apparent fantasy that there was something between Kyle and Wyatt.

As the silence lengthened without her or Wyatt explaining how he had seen her bruise, she decided to change the subject. Figuring women liked compliments, she nodded at the collar of gold that lay heavily around Alicia's neck. "That's a lovely necklace."

Alicia's gaze took in Kyle's earrings, along with the ring of fine webbed turquoise from the Kingman mine in Arizona. Kyle had selected it because it reminded her of one her mother wore on her sixth birthday. That ring had not been recovered.

"I understand academia doesn't pay," Alicia observed, evidently finding the silver jewelry wanting.

"Oh, for God's sake," Wyatt said. "Being a ranger doesn't either."

Kyle had had enough. She rose to her full height, suppressed another wince at her injured side, and looked down at Alicia. "I disagree about the pay. Teaching is the most rewarding thing I've ever done, turning out fine students like Wyatt, who take jobs that pay not in dollars but in quality of life and helping others."

Someone called Wyatt's name from the entrance to the dining room.

"There's dinner," Kyle said. She walked away toward the podium where the dining room manager waited.

● ● ●

After a hearty steak dinner alone, while Wyatt remained with Alicia and joined her and her clients in the dining room, Kyle walked beside Yellowstone Lake. The darkening water was still unsettled, but now she could blame the brisk wind that had blown up in the past hour. The temperature was dropping rapidly, clouds rolling in from the southwest. She'd not checked the forecast since morning, but the unmistakable smell of snow emanated from the thick-bellied bank as it approached.

Despite the cold, she was still steaming at the scene in the sunroom. She and Wyatt were here to work, as Alicia was supposed to be. The very suggestion that Kyle and he . . . her face warmed even with the lake wind buffeting her cheeks.

She turned her attention to the road rimming the shore. A lobby exhibit informed that the present hotel drive was once part of the Grand Loop Road, back in the stagecoach days.

Franny had told Kyle that her first husband's parents met at the Lake Hotel at the turn of the twentieth century.

She tried to imagine the Chicago heiress and the Westerner, a man a lot closer to the family's Nez Perce roots due to his mother being a half-breed. That must have been an even more brow-raising combination than Francesca di Paoli turning up to wed a Wyoming dude rancher.

Kyle envisioned the old days; the hotel drive lined with carriages, the lobby alight with electric bulbs. Each evening an orchestra had played after dinner, now echoed in the piano player or sometimes a string quartet in the lounge. She found it interesting that people thought of the 1890s as a long time ago. When your focus measured geologic time, man's tenure in the park seemed the blink of an eye.

Watching the sun sink over the trees behind the hotel, Kyle reflected that the period after sunset and before dark always fascinated her. It was as though each evening presented a dare, to watch the light fade minute by minute and see how long she could remain indifferent.

Using the excuse that she was getting chilled without the parka she'd left dripping over the shower rod in her bath, she walked briskly through twilight toward her cabin.

Once there, she unlocked the door and entered the spare and chilly room. Some fiddling with the electric heater set in the wall revealed it was on a fifteen-minute timer so she anticipated a fitful night of sleeping and waking to reset the dial.

Kyle undressed, took a hot shower, and donned a soft flannel shirt to keep her warmer. Then she lay back on the too-short bed. With her rangy build, she felt the polar opposite of Alicia with her full breasts and rounded behind. Thank God, she'd always been comfortable with the way she looked and at ease with her own company, like having dinner alone in the dining room.

She had been fine with Wyatt staying with his girl . . . the yearning centered in her chest tonight was not for him. It was much more basic.

Being reminded of a world designed for couples made her ache for her own vanished youth and the man she had loved and lost.

● ● ●

Twenty-year-old Kyle rode shotgun in Nick Darden's Chevy as he pulled away from the Calico Palace Pizza Parlor in Jackson, Wyoming. A typical Wednesday evening at geology field camp, except for the miraculous fact that Kyle had Nick to herself.

Back in June, the students had assembled at a 4-H camp near Alpine, forty miles south of Jackson. For the first three nights, the food was okay, wholesome and filling, if not exciting. Roast beef, mashed potatoes, and green beans; then chicken, rice, and salad; followed by ham, slaw, and red Jell-O. On the fourth day, the kids they shared camp with changed and the cycle began again.

Kyle and some of the others had fallen into the habit of driving up the Snake River Canyon to Jackson for dinner, never mind that the monotonous camp fare had been paid for. Somehow, tonight she and Nick had been the only ones who wanted to go.

It was funny. The first time Kyle had seen him, she'd not been impressed. With sun-streaked brown hair about the same color as his eyes and summer tan, he looked monochrome. Then he smiled and the gimlet glint of his irises suggested she was included in an excellent joke.

Evenings, Nick played his guitar in the barracks and the students sang along. The high point of camp so far had been his performance at The Golden Horseshoe Bar in Alpine. Before an eclectic mix of RV campers, sheepherders from surrounding ranches, and geologists, Nick took the stage almost shyly, situating himself with care on a bar stool. He made it all the way through the first verse and half the refrain before the assembled company realized he was singing the praises of "Charlotte the Harlot, the Cowpunchers' Whore."

This evening, Nick drove through the town of Jackson and south. Mountains loomed on either side of the road, made visible by a full August moon. Kyle tried to ignore its baleful eye and focused on their approach to Astoria Hot Springs, an ancient resort with tourist cabins separated from the main highway by a bridge across the Snake River. The camp was the last outpost of light before they headed into the steep-walled canyon.

Watching the ragged outcrops of limestone, Kyle told herself that going to dinner with Nick didn't mean anything. He treated everybody in camp to the same brand of disrespectful banter that made him seem a friend until she realized it kept him at a distance.

She studied his profile in the dash lights. His nose wasn't large, but it had a little bump as though he'd broken it. It gave him a little boy quality that seemed to match his can't-take-it-seriously attitude. His lashes were long for a man's, dark whispers against his cheek.

Kyle turned away so he wouldn't notice her looking too long. A steep embankment whizzed by.

Without warning, a sudden flash of motion caught her eye. Headed straight for the passenger door, a huge boulder rolled and bounced down the road cut. She had no time to think or speak before the rock smashed into the pavement scant inches behind the Chevy, blasting apart with a crack that shot shrapnel against the rear bumper.

Nick swerved. "Holy shit!"

Kyle looked back in time to see the largest broken chunks bound over the edge and disappear into the gorge.

The Chevy fishtailed and came back under Nick's control. He put his arm around Kyle's shoulders and drove one-armed while her fingers clutched his shirt.

"Hey, hey," he soothed. "We cheated death." But rather than stop to look at his car for damage, he accelerated. "I'm getting out of this canyon. That rockfall might have been caused by an earth tremor."

Kyle felt as though a hand reached inside her chest and clenched off her breath. She'd been doing all right with field camp, steering clear of other students' weekend excursions to Yellowstone and Earthquake Lake. Another ten miles of steep-walled gorge unfolded interminably as she pressed her head against Nick's shoulder and willed the boulders above to remain in place.

Finally, moonlight revealed the mountains receding and being replaced by the blessed broad flats along the Palisades Reservoir. Once in the open she felt better and became aware the drive would be over soon. With Nick's arm around her, it was easy to want more.

The final half-mile was on the 4-H camp's dirt road. The Chevy drifted a bit on the curves, gravel pinging the undercarriage.

Nick pulled up in front of the barracks and stopped with a jerk. "The eagle has landed."

They separated, he toward the men's head, an ancient railroad car in the woods, while Kyle went down the hill to the ladies'. The cinderblock box was a damp attraction for mosquitoes.

In the mirror above the sink, her eyes looked enormous in a face pale despite her summer tan. Raising her hand, she touched the places where her hair was tousled from Nick's shoulder. She carried a brush in her daypack but didn't want to smooth it. Rather, she wished Nick's hands would muss it further . . .

A moan escaped her. Midnight had passed on her evening with Nick and she'd come home from the ball.

Wrinkling her nose at the faint insecticide smell of a

No-Pest Strip someone had hung in the shower, she abandoned its protection and started her solitary walk back up the hill. Although the moon was still high, casting double shadows where pole lights illuminated the camp, she used her flashlight. The barracks windows were dark, everyone stocking up on sleep before a 5 AM call. Kyle had rigged a battery-powered light above her bunk, not too bright to disturb her two roommates. To be on the safe side, she changed the AA batteries every other day.

As she reached for the handle to open the barracks door, she caught a movement out of the corner of her eye. Turning, she saw Nick balanced in a handstand on the split log fence.

"You're still up," she said.

Deftly, he lowered his feet to the ground and faced her. His hand came up to fend off her flashlight beam. "You should have known I would wait for you."

He came closer. Jeans and a flannel shirt fit him in a way that seemed to accentuate his body. He wasn't tall or broad-shouldered, but he walked toward her with a catlike tread.

"Douse the light," he said.

Without thinking, she snapped it off.

Nick caught her wrists and slid his warm hands inside her sleeves.

"We had a shock tonight," he murmured. "And I couldn't quite see us bunking with the guys and gals."

He didn't kiss her, just pulled her against him. This

couldn't happen, because she was taller than he by a good three inches and refused to slouch to make short men feel better.

But it was happening.

Beneath the full moon's light, she stood with her face against the softness of his shirt, thinking that anybody could look out of the barracks and see them. Her hands rested awkwardly on his sides because she wasn't sure what to do with them.

Gently, he tipped up her chin. At first, his lips felt chilly, but they warmed like his hands. Kyle didn't close her eyes; rather she watched the silver sheen of a snowfield on the mountain above camp. It contrasted with the heat consuming her insides.

"Come on," Nick urged against her ear. "While you were gone, I put up my tent in the woods." He nodded toward the shadows where moon glow did not reach.

She felt a tug of apprehension. "It's dark." Yet, how she wanted to . . .

"You've got a flashlight," Nick said.

❋ ❋ ❋

She went with him, that night and all the nights of summer, another three weeks.

For the last camp project, Kyle and Nick worked together on the mountain above Astoria Hot Springs tracking a surface called an unconformity. The rocks on top were millions of years younger than those beneath, with no record preserved between. The upper strata were slanted, or dipped, at a completely different angle, indicating that the surface of the earth had been tilted to a new place before the next layers were laid down.

Those final weeks of summer were like that for Kyle, as she metamorphosed into a woman she'd never imagined she could be. Learning the contours of a man's naked form, not simply with her eyes, but with fingertips so sensitized she might have been reading Braille . . . laughing in the early morning, their mingled breath coming out in puffs in the chilly tent, feeling the hair-roughened skin of his chest moving over the smoothness of her breasts, sharing a single apple, biting off bits in turn until there was nothing left of the juicy pleasure but a stripped-down core . . .

After all these years, she'd yet to forget a single word of the letter she'd pulled from her student mailbox a week after camp ended.

What we had was beautiful, but I can't see you transferring to UCLA or me to Arizona. Too many things can happen before we get out of school. Even then, we probably couldn't get jobs together. But I'll always remember the gal who sleeps with the light on.

In her cabin behind the Lake Hotel, Kyle rolled over and got off the bed, gasping at the pain of her bruised side. She went into the bath and reeled off toilet paper to wipe her eyes.

It had been a long time since she'd cried over Nick Darden.

Once he had persuaded her to unlock doors that she'd never even peeked out and walked away with her heart. Over the years, when she thought of loving again, she always concluded that Nick's leaving had turned her to a woman who did not want to settle for less.

It wasn't as if there'd been no men in her life. She had dated a fellow graduate student at Arizona for several years and here at Utah she'd kept company with a research associate for four years until he went home to Greece.

Tonight, that did not seem nearly enough. She looked through the bathroom door at the single imprint her body had made on the bedcovers and longed for the quickened breath, the pounding pulse, for flesh on flesh.

Blowing her nose, she told herself she was just being sentimental because Wyatt had found somebody. Or because a stroke had separated Leila and Stanton after forty years.

Whatever the reasons, she was alone, her secrets intact.

CHAPTER EIGHT
SEPTEMBER 15

Snowflakes drifted through the dawn. Their white blanket draped the grass and flocked the pines outside Kyle's cabin near the Lake Hotel. She had awakened cold, but not realized the significance of muffled silence until opening the door.

Through the shadowless light, she trudged toward Wyatt's cabin. By the time she got there, her hands were so chilled it hurt to knock. Thrusting them in the pockets of her down vest, she waited. Her still-soggy parka hung in her cabin.

After a minute, she knocked again.

A snow squall approached over the lake, a gray haze sweeping toward shore. The whirling front obscured her view of the water, then the meadow, and finally swallowed the cluster of cabins. She ducked around the corner into the lee and beat on Wyatt's window.

Even as she pounded, she expected she knew where he was. In a heated hotel room with Alicia, whose budget appeared larger than that of the Institute or the Park Service.

Snow swirled and eddied into the sheltered space, cold

burning Kyle's nose and ears. Why had she left her hat and gloves on the top shelf of her closet at home when she knew perfectly well it could drop below freezing any day of the year in Yellowstone?

"Kyle!" Wyatt called from across the white expanse of lawn. He was walking from the hotel carrying two Styrofoam cups with covers. Coatless, he wore the same pullover he'd had on at dinner, and when he gestured toward her cabin, she wondered if he didn't want her to see his bed had not been slept in.

The thought sent another stab of loneliness through her. It had taken a long time to get to sleep last night, with only her memories and the inadequate electric heater for company.

"Java?" Against dimensionless white, Wyatt's eyes were dark pools.

She reached to take a cup from him, and their gloveless hands brushed. "Thanks."

"Is that the best you can do?" he chided. "I slept like the devil, waking up a dozen times to reset the damned heater. Then I get up, throw on my clothes, and go on a fieldtrip in the snow to bring you coffee . . ."

Kyle burst out laughing. Even the icy flakes attacking her eyelashes ceased to matter as she processed that Wyatt hadn't spent the night with Alicia.

Not that it mattered.

Wyatt slung an arm around her shoulders and turned her toward her cabin. "By the way, after you told Alicia off about teaching and being a ranger, she was all apologies. You don't know, but she left a considerably soft life on her father's Texas ranch to come up here and work for the wolves."

"Hmmm." Kyle failed to commit.

She led the way to her cabin, stomped snow from her boots, and reset the panel heater for another fifteen minutes. Then she tossed up the spread to cover the twisted sheets, aware of Wyatt seeing the evidence she had slept poorly. Sitting diagonally across the narrow double mattress from him, she stripped the plastic cover off coffee with just a touch a cream, the way she liked it.

Although the wire heater coils began to glow cherry red, Wyatt hunched his shoulders and kept his arms crossed. Wordlessly, Kyle tossed him the flannel shirt she'd slept in.

He caught it and pulled it on over his light sweater. To her surprise, it fit, just a trifle snug across his chest.

"We could share clothes," Wyatt said. "Save money."

She knew she dressed casually, in the office and the field, but somehow this stung. Maybe it was the memory of Alicia in her little black dress and high-heels that Kyle, proud as she was of her height, would not have chosen.

"Alicia is lovely," she said, without planning to.

Wyatt's eyes were steady on hers. "Yes, she is."

The heater ticked away. A gust of wind rattled a windowpane.

Wyatt looked toward the whirling whiteness. "I

checked the forecast. Snow, sleet, and freezing rain all over the region."

Kyle took another gulp of coffee and set it aside. "I'd planned to leave at midday, but if I want to make it to the Consortium tomorrow, I need to go right away."

Shoving up off her bed, Wyatt gave her a grave look. "After the size of yesterday's quake, we need to keep a close eye on things here."

There, again, a stomach clutch that set her mind awhirl with images. Of broken rock and fissured earth, of people waiting for news of loved ones, and a little girl clinging to her grandmother's hand.

Wyatt's touch on her shoulder brought her back. "You okay?"

Kyle forced a nod.

"I'll hold the fort until you can get back with more monitoring equipment," he promised.

● ● ●

Driving to the west entrance of the park took five hours, twice the normal time. Once she got to lower elevation, Kyle expected the snow to give way to a cold, soaking rain. Instead, the eddy of flakes continued to whiten the pavement and obscure the center stripe. At an Exxon station in Rexburg, Idaho, she got a soft drink and a chocolate bar with almonds and drove on. With a good ten miles to Pocatello, the van's heater gave up.

Impatience drilled her as the snow came down faster. If she had this weather all the way to Salt Lake, she'd have to chair the Consortium without preparation. She fiddled in vain with the heater's control, while she tried to think of some opening remarks for the morning welcome and not to dwell upon her lack of a good slide presentation. At best, she'd have to throw together some bits and pieces from past talks.

How odd it would be for the Consortium to meet without Stanton. The last piece of business was sure to be the consideration of officially appointing an interim successor. She'd never thought of herself as ambitious, but Hollis Delbert's grasping at the prize made her want it.

And that made her feel like a greedy child.

Nonetheless, since Hollis's dislike for her apparently blinded him to the potential hazards in Yellowstone, she intended to buttonhole Colin Gruy, senior scientist with USGS Volcano Hazards Program before the meeting. If she let him know Stanton's wishes, he could make the motion to leave her in charge until things sorted out.

Low-hanging clouds permitted only a filtered glimpse of white hills on either side of Interstate 15. At least five inches of snow covered the right of way. Seeing a shell of ice coating stalled cars on the shoulder, Kyle wondered for the first time if she would make it home tonight. Digital numerals on the dash clock revealed it was after four and she had at least two hundred miles to go.

As the cold seeped into the van's interior, Kyle's toes first stung, then began to numb. She took turns steering with one hand, warming the other on her stomach. It would be nice to stop and get her coat, but she feared she couldn't get back into the tracks of the eighteen-wheelers. When she got to Pocatello, she'd stop at Wal-Mart, buy a hat and gloves, and some of those thermal hand and boot warmers.

The ringing of sleet joined the mopping of wipers, and she slowed from thirty to twenty miles per hour. At this rate, it would take another six hours.

Ahead, she saw brake lights along with flashing blue and red beacons.

Coming to a standstill, she climbed into the rear of the van. Her parka was still too damp to wear, but she put on her down vest. Still longing for hat and gloves, she listened to the radio with her hands shoved in her pockets.

And tried not to think of the hours between now and tomorrow in terms of sand and hourglasses.

Ten minutes passed, then twenty, until the wait turned into an hour. As the pale light began to leach from the sky, the line showed signs of beginning to move. Kyle jumped out to scrape her ice-streaked windshield but before she was half-finished, the flimsy plastic scraper she'd found in the glove box snapped in her hand.

A horn blew and she threw the broken pieces into the snow.

Back behind the wheel, she pressed the accelerator. The van slewed sideways until the front wheels took hold. Backing off the bumper ahead, she tried to maintain a careful distance.

On the shoulder was a green and-white sign for an exit, half-covered with snow. **_ORT _ALL: 1/2 MILE**, it said.

From her knowledge of the area, Kyle knew it was the turnoff for Fort Hall, still a good seven miles out of Pocatello. In half an hour, she got to the ramp and found a sign directing all traffic to exit.

She lowered her icy window.

A red-nosed policeman shouted, "Everybody off! We've got two jack-knifed eighteen wheelers."

Something seized inside Kyle's chest. Highway 91 paralleled I-15 down to Pocatello, but there were no major alternate routes through the Caribou National Forest south of town. "I've got to get to Salt Lake," she called.

"Not tonight."

"But I have an important meeting . . ."

The policeman blew his whistle and waved her on.

CHAPTER NINE
SEPTEMBER 16

At 2:41 Monday afternoon, Kyle slipped in the back door of the Institute auditorium. The lights were dimmed for Xi Hong's PowerPoint presentation, but she could see the roomful of students invited to the Consortium's afternoon session.

The funding meeting had been scheduled for nine, in a small conference room down the hall. She had marked the hour in a Pocatello high-school gymnasium. Once the blizzard had stopped and the plows had been through, she'd been able to drive no more than fifty.

It was tempting to shout out that she had arrived, find out immediately what plans had been made for postponing the funding talks, but Xi had worked hard on his research and Kyle did not want to steal his show.

Taking a seat in the back row, she let her eyes adjust. She wondered how they had handled her absence this morning. She'd called before she got on the road and Xi had agreed to pass the word she was held up.

The audience burst into applause, alerting her that he had completed his talk. She clapped woodenly.

Hollis Delbert rose from the front row and went to the podium. With his blond hair sprayed down darkly and wearing a navy suit, he looked out of place among the casual academics. "I'd like to thank you all for coming to our public session of Consortium Research. I think I can speak for everybody at USGS and NPS in saying we had an excellent crop of papers this year." He characteristically ran out of air.

His audience interpreted it as a place for applause.

Hollis ducked his head.

Kyle frowned. In her absence, she'd expected Colin Gruy to take the chair. Instead, he sat in the front row looking attentive.

Hollis gulped and went on, "Of course, the sad note is that Director Stanton Jameson can't be with us today. I know we all wish him a speedy recovery."

More applause. For Stanton, Kyle joined in.

A student turned off the projector and switched on the room lights. From thirty feet away, Kyle was sure Hollis saw her.

Bending forward, he said in a satisfied tone, "As Acting Director of the Utah Seismology Institute, I hereby adjourn this Consortium."

Kyle scrambled to her feet. Swimming against the throng, she saw Hollis go out the front door with Yellowstone's Chief Scientist, Radford Bullis. A big burly man, Radford looked as though he might have a Harley stashed behind his park housing. His stride was even longer than hers, and Hollis was probably panting to keep up.

In the interest of speed, she exited the rear. Hollis and Radford were nowhere in sight.

In the hallway, she caught up with Colin Gruy. With his silver hair swept back, he looked the quintessential aging British hippie, except for his fringed leather jacket. He had taken fervently to the American West.

She touched his arm, and he turned with a swing of buckskin and a surprised look on his narrow, patrician features. "Kyle! We didn't expect you today."

"It was rough going, but I made it. Let's get Radford and the rest of the committee together."

A puzzled expression on Colin's face gave her a chill. "Did you hear the funding requests without me?"

He put out a hand and patted her shoulder. "You should get some rest, Kyle. I know it's been hard on you, worrying about Stanton."

She brushed that and his hovering hand aside, wishing she'd had time to go home, shower, and put on decent clothes. "Yes, it's terrible, but we've got work to do."

Colin shook his head. "Hollis stood in for you."

"How can that be?" Kyle asked. "Stanton asked me to take charge while he's out."

A frown appeared between Colin's thick silver brows. "Beg pardon?"

"When I visited him in the hospital, Stanton asked me to take his place." Remembering Hollis's claim to be Acting Director, she looked at Colin incredulously. "Hollis didn't tell you."

"No," Colin admitted. "He did say he's been worried about you, the way you dropped all your preparations for the meeting and rushed off to Yellowstone."

Before she could tell him about the seismic activity surge, he went on, "This morning when you didn't show up, Hollis stepped in and made a most favorable impression on the committee."

"Look," she said in a tight tone, "last time I saw Stanton his mind was perfectly sound. Let's go talk to him."

Colin agreed.

Kyle suggested she drive, and he asked her to take him from the hospital on to the airport. Still keeping an eye out for Radford and Hollis, she helped Colin secure his bags and stow them in her Mercedes trunk alongside her own gear from the van. Then she guided her car uphill past the golf course toward University Hospital. Though the day had warmed into the upper forties and most of the snow on the roads and lawns had melted, the foothills above were still white.

Colin busied himself lighting a thin, foul-smelling brown cheroot.

Kyle put down her window. "Don't do that in my car."

"Quite." He extended his long arm across her and flicked the cheroot out the open window.

She pulled into the hospital parking lot and cut the engine. Turning to Colin, she kept her hands on the steering wheel. "Have you seen the swarm of activity that caused me to go to Yellowstone?"

"You know better than anybody how the caldera respires, a shake here, a rattle there." Colin flicked ash from his sleeve. "You need to stop worrying about worst case scenarios."

Kyle suddenly knew who had been listening to Hollis's phone gossip. Grimly, she went on, "Wyatt Ellison has discovered the caldera rose six inches last week."

"Why, that's remarkable!" He met her eyes for the first time. "In fact, it's fantastic. Are you sure?"

"Quite." She mocked his British inflection. "I'm worried about pressure building beneath Nez Perce Peak. I had planned to ask for more equipment this morning instead of being stranded by a storm."

To his credit, Colin looked appropriately thoughtful. He opened the Mercedes door, got out, and lit another cheroot. The aromatic tobacco scent drove Kyle to an upwind site so she wouldn't ask for one.

Leaning against her fender, he dragged deeply on his smoke. "This business in Yellowstone is disturbing, but I'm afraid I can't help you right now. I'm leaving for Sakhalin tomorrow on a joint excursion of USGS and the Russian, Chinese, and Japanese surveys."

She hugged herself against the brisk wind. "Since Hollis is taking care of things here, I'll assign my seminar to Xi and go back to Yellowstone. Wyatt and I will put something together."

"I'm sorry, Kyle, but Xi is coming with me. Being invited on an expedition like this will give him a lot of clout when he goes home to China next year." He finished his cheroot and ground the butt with his heel.

Hot words boiled to her lips, but she knew if offered a choice between the trip and monitoring Yellowstone, Xi would certainly accept the honor. In fact, she could not try and deny him, though she felt certain something was brewing beneath the park.

As they walked into the hospital, Kyle turned on Colin. "If you're taking Xi, send me some help from USGS."

While they waited for an elevator, he frowned. "Funding, manpower, it's tight all over."

"Come on, Colin." She raised her voice and drew some stares in the hospital hallway. "You owe me."

The elevator doors slid open, and they got inside with a crush of other people.

Upon arriving at the room Stanton had been in, Kyle shoved open the door to find a woman in a striped gown watching TV. "Sorry."

Colin beat her to the information desk. "Critical Care Unit," he told her when she caught up. He looked anxious, reminding her that he and Stanton went back further than she and her professor did. More than forty years ago, the two men were fellow students at UCLA.

With her pulse racing, it seemed to take a long time to walk to the CCU. There they found Leila sitting with bowed head in the cubicle where Stanton lay with closed eyes. Equipment surrounded his bed, and a monitor displayed his heartbeat and respiration.

Leila rose, her lovely face drawn, and embraced Kyle. Her shoulders felt even more delicate than on the day of her husband's collapse, and she quaked like a leaf in the wind. Yet, despite the circumstance, she wore an elegant suit and a string of pearls with a rich patina, a marked contrast to the doctors and nurses in casual uniforms and sneakers.

With a trembling hand, she gestured Kyle and Colin toward the waiting room. Once outside, she turned to them woodenly. "He had another stroke."

Kyle's throat closed.

"What do his doctors say?" Colin asked.

Looking more fragile than Kyle had ever seen her, blue veins prominent in her porcelain forehead, Leila cast a longing gaze back toward Stanton. "They're not sure he'll live."

● ⁕ ●

Kyle held it together enough to drive Colin to the airport, though her hands were unsteady on the wheel. After his remark about her needing rest, she was determined not to let him see the depth of her despair at Stanton's turn for the worse. With Xi leaving, Hollis free to throw his weight around, and the seismic upheaval in Yellowstone, she had to retain the professional respect of the USGS representative to the Consortium.

As she pulled off the Interstate at the airport exit, blue-black rain clouds hung over Great Salt Lake, its mirrored surface reflecting lightning bolts.

"Thanks for driving." Colin looked around the curb-side check-in. "Xi is on my flight."

Kyle scanned the crowded sidewalk, but didn't see her post-doc assistant.

Colin shifted his laptop bag to his other shoulder. "Hell of a thing . . . Stanton."

Tears sprang to her eyes and she tried to blink them away. "I'll go, then . . . before it rains." She extended her hand and realized with horror that she was still shaking.

"You've got a lot on your plate, Kyle." Colin's voice was gentle. "Let Hollis handle the Institute red tape."

"Right." She gave him a direct look. "I'm counting on you to send help for Yellowstone."

CHAPTER TEN
SEPTEMBER 18

By Wednesday morning, Kyle had heard nothing from Colin or anyone at USGS. On her way to see Stanton before work, she determined that today she would find someone to handle her seminars, pack up the department seismic equipment, and be ready to leave for Yellowstone early tomorrow.

Over a week after his collapse, Stanton was still in critical care. Kyle's 6 AM visit found him asleep and alone. She hoped Leila was at home getting some rest.

Standing beside his bed, Kyle thought he looked smaller lying down than he had at the Institute. About the same height as her, they'd stood eye-to-eye most of the time. This morning, she wished he could advise her about the swarm of activity in Yellowstone, but when she tried relating some information about it in a soft voice, his face took on a pained look. With a sigh, she found herself staring at the monitor displaying his vital signs.

He couldn't die. There was still so much to be done . . . together.

Yet, she had no choice but to carry on without him.

Finding a fragment of malachite on the bedside tray beside a water pitcher and cup, Kyle picked it up and rubbed it between her fingers. Then, reluctantly, she replaced it where Stanton might reach it with his good hand when he awakened. Bending close, she promised to return soon, but did not want to be too specific since she planned to leave for the park.

On the short drive to the Institute, she drove with her convertible top down, enjoying the air. The rest of the snow from Sunday's storm had melted with yesterday's rain and the smog that usually lay in the valley had blown out. Above the university, sunrise silhouetted the peaks and painted their tops with hues of coral as she parked near the Wasatch Fault.

Once in the building, Kyle stopped by the seismograph lab. Since the light was on, she went in and checked the Yellowstone stations. The blotchy seismic pattern typifying an earthquake swarm seemed more intense than the day before.

With a frown, she went down the hall to the equipment storeroom. The shelves and floor were bare.

Hollis Delbert sat behind his office desk, dressed in a suit again.

"Where are the seismographs?" Kyle demanded.

Hollis took a deliberate moment before looking away from his computer. In two days of being in charge, he'd rearranged his office furniture so supplicants stood on the far side of his desk. A single guest chair sat against the wall.

"Kyle," he said vaguely.

"Pleased to meet you. What happened to the equipment in the storeroom?"

Hollis remained seated but pulled himself up behind the desk as though conducting a formal interview. "I have earmarked it for use on the Wasatch Project."

"You can't have put everything in the field."

"Let's just say I've put things where they can't be misappropriated."

Kyle's face got hot. "We need that equipment in Yellowstone. The caldera has come up six inches in the past week. Even you know that means magma is on the rise."

"That damned caldera pants like a dog," Hollis scoffed.

"You know we've never seen anything like this. And there's no evidence the Wasatch is anything but quiet."

"My students' work has shown that the Snowbird Branch of the fault, not ten miles from here, has been locked up for the past decade. I'm hoping to God we detect some movement that might relieve the tension before we have a massive earthquake."

"So we're damned if the faults move and damned if they don't." She reached for the guest chair and swung her leg across the top. Straddling it backward, she leaned her chin on her hands. "I know there's work to do along the Wasatch, but the threat at Yellowstone is real, too. Think of the park full of tourists, of Mammoth, West Yellowstone, Cody."

He shoved his glasses up where they'd slid down his

nose, but did not reply.

"Come on, Hollis. I'm not taking anything off you with the caldera coming up this fast. Think what we've learned about the eruption of Toba in Sumatra 75,000 years ago. Based on DNA studies of human remains found both before and after, the earth's population was nearly wiped out by ash clouds causing climate change."

Hollis sneered. "If something like that happens in Yellowstone, we're both dead."

"Dammit! Of course, we'd be dead this close to ground zero." Suffocated by ash, or killed in the collapse of roofs overwhelmed by the weight. "Is death toll just words to you, like passed on, succumbed, and the other tidy euphemisms?"

She rose and kicked aside the chair; it went sprawling on its side with a clatter. "Dead! We'd be dead like my folks . . ."

Something in Hollis's eyes stopped her. A look that said her outburst would be reported to Colin and anybody else who would listen.

Kyle took a shuddering breath and tried to get calm. "If Stanton were running things, he'd divide our resources between the projects, get on the phone, and find more. What say we split what we've got here right now?"

Hollis stared at her across the desk.

"All right." She went to the door. "You play your game of hide and seek. I'll get what I need elsewhere."

First, Kyle dialed Cass Grain, a fellow seismologist at USGS in Menlo Park. Kyle had met red-haired, ruddy-faced Cass on a plane to Bogotá in November 1985, when the Nevado del Ruiz volcano had erupted in Colombia. The cataclysm had killed 23,000 people in lahars, landslides composed of rock and soil mixed with melted snow and ice. Expecting to fulfill their roles as scientists, the young women found themselves overwhelmed by human need. Going without sleep for days, they toiled alongside desperate villagers, searching for survivors beneath the moonscape of debris flows. Their small field shovels, usually used for gathering samples, dug to uncover men, women, and children. Each time Kyle's blade struck something yielding, she felt a surge of hope that faded as ash-painted flesh came up lifeless.

After excavating the dead, they reversed the process, assisting the locals in digging graves in the hard soil of a country churchyard. Open trenches were placed beyond the rusting wrought-iron fence, for the plot was now far too small.

As Kyle waited for Cass to answer the phone, she studied a photo on her credenza, of the two of them in front of the sloping fuselage of a DC-3. Cass had managed a brave smile in defiance of the horrors they'd witnessed. Kyle had been too shaken to muster a pleasant expression.

Cass answered in a hearty voice that became subdued as soon as she learned who it was. "I heard about Stanton. How soon do you think he'll be back?"

Kyle had been lying to herself about that, but because it was Cass, she was able to say, "He won't be back anytime soon . . . maybe ever."

The line went silent for a beat.

"You knew he'd retire," Cass said. "You just didn't expect to take his place under circumstances like these."

"Hollis Delbert is in charge." Kyle spoke over the hard feeling in the back of her throat.

"How in hell did that happen?"

"It's a long story. Colin Gruy had a hand in it."

"Doesn't Stanton have a say?"

"Since they moved him to the CCU, he's not talking."

It turned quiet again.

With an effort, Kyle got to business. "What I'm calling about is I need some portable seismographs for Yellowstone. There's a swarm of activity and Hollis is holding the Institute's supply hostage for the Wasatch."

"I saw the Yellowstone action on the Web," Cass said. Even when she and Kyle weren't in touch they kept up with each other through the little tracks and traces of their projects.

"What you didn't see," Kyle told her, "is the vertical motion on the caldera. It's coming up like an active volcano rather than a dormant thermal area."

"Where's the fire?"

"I'm afraid it may be Nez Perce Peak."

"I've been worried about that mountain ever since we learned it was such a young volcano," Cass said. "Honest to God, I wish I could help, but we've got everything in the field." Kyle heard a sound like a fist striking a metal desk.

"If there was anything in storage, I'd overnight it."

Did Cass's sense of urgency make her feel better or worse? At Nevado del Ruiz, they'd learned together the meaning of "death toll" in a way neither Hollis nor Colin seemed to grasp. On the other hand, as Kyle preferred to believe, the men did know such things at a gut level and refused to let it out.

At least Wyatt seemed to understand.

"I guess I'll try Volcano Hazards." Kyle skipped to her next line of backup, the USGS Cascades Volcanic Observatory where Colin worked. "I can check what Colin did about sending me some help."

Cass hesitated. "Do you know about the new group in Volcano Hazards?"

"No."

Volcanologists had the same toys as seismologists; maybe they could help. Kyle snugged the phone against her neck and reached for a piece of paper. "Wait till I get a pen, and give me a name."

"You won't need a pen," Cass said slowly. "The new group leader is Nicholas Darden."

● ● ●

Her luck had run out. Nick was only a call away, and she had the best excuse on the planet to make it.

Slumping forward, Kyle put her head onto her crossed arms. Over the years, she had kept up with Nick's career so she'd know how not to run into him. After he became a volcano junkie and was out of the country for most of the year, she continued to attend professional meetings with antennae out, ready to turn on her heel if she so much as saw him.

She never had . . . but in her imagination, in dreams when he came to her, he was always the same shining youth who had wakened at dawn and scaled the highest peak before noon.

Lying with her head on her desk, Kyle felt like a fool for being hung up over a thirty-year-old affair. If she saw Nick again, she would simply meet a fellow traveler, someone else whose bright hair had faded and whose lips had thinned.

Surely, she could find equipment elsewhere.

The IRIS/PASSCAL Instrumentation Center in New Mexico provided field equipment for people with grant money, but you couldn't just call and order seismographs like carryout pizza. The National Earthquake Center in Boulder was an option, but they indicated Hollis had already requested assistance and it was being taken care of. The same thing happened at other research centers, where they politely assumed she was helping Hollis with his calls.

When she got to the end of her list, Kyle hung up and stared at a geologic map of Yellowstone on her office wall. Though the surface had been mapped and even the floor of the lake, there was no truly reliable picture of what went on beneath the earth. Everything geoscientists did—seismic, gravity-oriented, and magnetic surveys—all were forms of remote sensing. Each piece of data was only an inexact piece of a larger puzzle.

Kyle feared time was running out to solve it.

CHAPTER ELEVEN
SEPTEMBER 18

Wyatt looked at the laptop display from the portable seismograph he and Helen Chou had just placed in Mist Creek Canyon. "Looks like we've got tremors now."

The snowy creek bottom was cold where the mid-morning sun did not reach. Helen brushed a lock of black hair back under her knitted cap, unzipped her pack and pulled out a thermos of coffee. Her nose cherry red, she poured for herself, and pulled out another stainless steel cup for Wyatt.

"Is Kyle coming back with more equipment?" she asked in her characteristic direct manner.

"When she left Sunday, there wasn't time to make plans."

"Speaking of plans," Helen's voice softened. "I guess this is as good a time as any to tell you."

Wyatt was hunkered down on his heels, but some nuance in her tone made him straighten up. "What's that?"

She studied the steam off her coffee. "I've given my notice."

Wyatt felt that little shift he always felt when the world changed. Helen was one hell of a partner. Brilliant, as well as a hard worker, she was the kind who came to Yellowstone to intern, then moved on. "Where to?"

"The University of Seattle."

"Where Bill . . . ?"

"Yes. I hate to let you down."

Wyatt tried to swallow his disappointment. "People move," he said. "We'll manage."

"I'd stick around and help you out with"—she gestured at the seismograph—"all this, but Bill insists I get out of here right away."

Maybe that wasn't such a bad idea. If Wyatt had a family, he'd probably find an excuse to send them to the in-laws until things settled down.

While they finished their coffee, Wyatt tried to tell himself Helen's loss would be somewhat offset by Xi Hong, but even so, her absence was one more blow at a time he and Kyle could ill afford it. Come to think of Kyle, she had suspected this might happen when he mentioned Helen's relationship with Bill. Maybe woman's intuition was better.

Wyatt and Helen hiked back to the Park Service Bronco they'd left at dawn in Pelican Valley. In the sunny meadow, the day was warming, droning insects the only sound in the silence.

However, when they climbed into the vehicle, the dispatcher broadcast a message to all units. "We need a wilderness first response in the Pelican Creek basin, up the flank of Mount Chittenden from Turbid Springs."

Wyatt opened the channel. "Ellison and Chou here.

We're parked on the Pelican Creek service road next to Turbid Lake."

"Proceed up the trail along Bear Creek toward Jones Pass," the dispatcher instructed.

"What are we looking for?"

"We've got a report of a burn victim. His wife called 911 from a cell phone and said he fell into a hot pool."

Wyatt shot a look at Helen. "There aren't any thermal features in that area."

The dispatcher came back. "The operator said the woman was clear on their location."

"Have them ask again. They're probably up the other side of the valley at the Mushpots."

"They lost the signal."

"We'll search where they said," Wyatt agreed, "but you'd better send somebody up the north side, where the hot pools are."

Slamming the driver's side door, he drove the Bronco as far as he could on the dirt track, jouncing over ruts. At the trailhead to Jones Pass, Helen pulled out the first aid kit while he grabbed a signal flare from the truck and stowed it in his pack.

For over a mile, they hiked beside Bear Creek, gaining four hundred feet of elevation. As they got closer to where the campers were supposed to be they shouted and blew a whistle.

Wyatt wondered about the hot spring. The park was full of thermal features, and who was to say they'd all been mapped? He particularly hoped this report was incorrect for he'd seen firsthand what scalding water could do.

Last June he'd been walking on Old Faithful's main trail near Castle Geyser, instructing one of the summer student rangers, when a woman on a bicycle hailed them. She braked to a sharp halt and pointed back the way she'd come. "A little girl. She fell in!"

"Where, ma'am?" Wyatt asked.

"Morning Glory Pool."

Radioing for the local ambulance, he commandeered the bicycle and left the student to calm the woman. It wasn't a strenuous trail, wide and paved, but his heart pounded as he rode.

In a few minutes, he covered the mile and found a crowd beside Morning Glory Pool. Once of the hottest springs in the park, it had been named for its blue-white appearance and trumpet shape. Over the years, park visitors had thrown in things that blocked its neck and cooled it enough for algae to dull its sheen.

By the pool, a man bent over oddly, holding his arms to his chest. When Wyatt saw a woman in a lavender dress kneeling beside something on the white rocks, he realized the man must have burned his arms pulling the girl from the pool. "She slipped through the fence," he moaned.

Wyatt found it odd that the mother wasn't holding her daughter until he saw the bright, boiled look of the child's skin. In places, it had peeled off, leaving bare flesh and muscle that looked like when you skinned a deer.

From the somber way people parted to let him through, Wyatt knew he was too late.

When he and Helen had walked for half an hour, he began to notice wisps of steam rising in places along the trail. That was odd, for he'd hiked this stretch with Alicia back in July and hadn't noticed any. Of course, it was a lot warmer then, so he might not have seen them.

Another hundred feet, and he definitely saw a small field of fumaroles, vents like chipmunk burrows, except they blew steam like teakettles.

"Something new?" Helen asked cautiously.

"We'll have to check them out later." He kept up the pace.

A few minutes later, she stopped and held up a hand.

Wyatt listened. The wind tossed the tops of the pines, and a crow gave a raucous warning.

Then he heard a high-pitched call that sounded like a human voice.

He blew his whistle, cupped his hands, and shouted, "Halloo."

"Over there." Helen started down the hill at a right angle to the trail.

Wyatt followed, sliding in slippery evergreen needles. As they approached Bear Creek he could hear it rushing, normally a soothing sound.

Another cry, this one louder, helped them home in on a yellow tent beside the stream. Someone in jeans and a brown hooded parka knelt beside another person in a sleeping bag. A red North Face jacket lay on the ground near the remnants of a campfire.

"Hello, we're with the Park Service," Helen said.

The kneeling person turned, a slender woman of perhaps sixty years with the tanned and weathered look of the inveterate sportswoman.

"Gretchen!" Wyatt blurted. He'd had drinks with Gretchen and her husband only a few days ago in Mammoth.

She leaped to her feet. "Wyatt, thank God!" She cast a swift glance over her shoulder. "David doesn't know how bad . . ."

"We'll have a look." Helen headed in.

Wyatt hung back, having trouble with the fact that the victim was one of the park's own. David Mowry, a longtime naturalist and resident of Mammoth, was the renowned author of over a dozen books on the Yellowstone region. He worked across the hall from Wyatt in the Resource Center.

"What happened?" Wyatt asked.

Gretchen twisted her hands together and looked confused. As Wyatt knew her to be a bright and determined woman who never minced words, he wondered if she might be going into shock.

"Wyatt," Helen said, in a calm voice he recognized as forced.

"Right here." He moved closer.

David's face and neck bore a parboiled look with the skin peeling away from the flesh. His eyes were wide open and their strange whiteness made Wyatt wonder if he was dead.

The fallen man writhed. "Christ Jesus, it hurts!" He waved an arm and connected with Helen's shoulder.

She recoiled as his hand brushed her parka and left a patch of skin on the rough material.

Wyatt realized David was blind, his eyes cooked along with the rest of his flesh.

Helen pulled back the sleeping bag with care, exposing his bare torso. In places, his skin had sloughed to reveal weeping raw flesh. Wyatt made a guess at ninety percent/third-degree, which made it tough to imagine him surviving. Especially as he and Helen could not start an IV.

"I've been making him drink water," Gretchen offered.

"That's good," said Helen.

Numbly, Wyatt reached for his radio and called the base. "We need a chopper *stat*! Victim is David Mowry, Caucasian male around sixty years, third-degree burns over most of his body. Conscious . . . at this time." He gauged the small clearing. "With the trees in here, the stretcher will have to be roped up into the chopper."

Helen poured water from her bottle over David's torso and he seemed to become calmer.

"We'll have you in the hospital in no time," Wyatt said loudly.

"It doesn't matter." David's voice was faint.

Wyatt drew Gretchen aside. "He's going to have to go to Burn and Trauma in Salt Lake."

Gretchen picked at her sleeve and nodded. She was shivering.

David went into another fit of screaming. Helen moved back a few feet.

Wyatt decided to examine the scene. He and Alicia had actually been right here two months ago, dropping down off the trail to hike the creek bottom. That big fir with the moss on it leaned a little farther out over the cut bank now. On the sandy beach below, where the bank sloped gently, they had taken off boots and socks and cooled their feet.

He'd mentioned at the time that this would make a nice campsite.

"Where was David when he got burned?" he asked.

"Just there." Gretchen pointed to the place where Wyatt had gone wading two months ago. He didn't see anything that looked like a thermal spring, none of the usual white or buff-colored mineral deposits, no colored algae.

He walked closer and stopped. Faint wisps of steam rose from the edge of Bear Creek. Another step forward and he saw the boiling, where sand spun in hundreds of tiny caldrons. Mindful that many visitors got an unpleasant surprise when they couldn't resist testing the water temperature, he put out a careful hand.

An inch or so from the surface, he felt the heat.

"Did David fall in?" The footing looked solid enough.

"We both swam there yesterday," Gretchen said. "The water was so cold that we sat by the fire when we got out. This morning, he decided to go skinny-dipping and dove straight in."

Wyatt let himself down and sat on the creek bank.

Gretchen spoke slowly, "When he staggered out, he kept saying, 'I've killed myself'."

On the one hand, David Mowry had done something stupid, but the signs were so very subtle. Who was Wyatt to say he might not have done the same? The first time he and Alicia had hiked into the backcountry, they'd made love on a sun-warmed rock beside a sparkling stream and dived in naked without testing the waters.

Wyatt pushed to his feet and moved upstream. He knelt and refilled his canteen with cold water to ferry to Helen.

Gretchen went to her husband's side and spoke words of encouragement that Wyatt felt rang hollow. He squatted on his heels near David. "Hang in there, buddy."

Over the burned man's head, he met Helen's serious dark eyes. She gave a barely perceptible shake of her head.

Minutes passed and David thrashed less. His respiration became labored, making Wyatt suspect fluid buildup in lungs seared by boiling water.

Finally the chop of an approaching helicopter sounded. As it came into view, Wyatt recognized a Bell 206, the kind he'd done some fieldwork out of in the park interior. He dug in his pack and sent up a flare, then stood in the center of the clearing and waved. Dark clouds scudded across the patch of sky and the chopper danced and shuddered as it lowered.

Shielding his eyes from flying grit, Wyatt watched a man descend a cable carrying a folded stretcher and an equipment bag. Once he got to the ground, Wyatt led the way.

Helen had her back to them, hugging herself as if she felt cold. Gretchen Mowry knelt beside her husband, cradling his red jacket instead of his disfigured body.

The dead man looked smaller somehow, as though more than breath had left his body.

CHAPTER TWELVE
SEPTEMBER 18

YELLOWSTONE CAMPER DIES AFTER DIVING INTO HOT SPRING.

Kyle's blood surged as she stared at the tagline on the breaking news page of her Internet provider. Sitting up straighter in her office chair, she clicked on the story.

YELLOWSTONE NATIONAL PARK, Wyo.
Sixty-one-year-old David Mowry died in Yellowstone Park this morning after jumping into a stream and finding it to be a hot spring. The noted author and naturalist was pronounced dead on arrival at the Intermountain Burn and Trauma Center in Salt Lake City after being taken from Yellowstone by helicopter.

Lord, not David Mowry. She hadn't known him personally, just read his books, but . . .

First on the scene, Park Rangers Helen Chou and Wyatt Ellison told reporters waiting in Salt Lake that Mowry was so thoroughly scalded he never stood a chance of surviving. The

search and rescue helicopter pilot, Chris Deering, a veteran
Vietnam and many western fire seasons, said the pickup w.
routine, Mowry having passed away just before he arrived.

Mowry, who lived in Clancy, Montana, was campir
with his wife Gretchen east of Yellowstone Lake. She told do
tors he got up early for a swim in Bear Creek and dove into tr
same pool they'd been swimming in the day before.

This time it was boiling.

Kyle's heartbeat slowed, yet deepened to a steady thuc
ding.

It remains to be determined whether Mrs. Mowry we
mistaken about the hot spring appearing overnight.

Carefully, Kyle placed the printout on her desk atop
pink slip that said Wyatt had called at noon. It was aft
five now; she'd been busy advising graduate students aft
making her useless spate of calls for seismic equipment an
picking up a new cell phone.

She dialed his cell. He answered in a tired voice.

"Where are you?" she asked.

"You heard." Her tone must have tipped him.

"Read it on the Internet."

"With no one there to pronounce David . . . Helen an
I carried out the rescue effort and flew down with him t
Salt Lake."

"Are you still in town?"

"We're at the airport in West Yellowstone." He sounde
distant. "Caught a ride back up with the pilot."

"Are you all right?"

"I've been better." She knew Wyatt and David had been close.

Something twisted inside her. "If you'd stayed in Salt Lake, I could have bought you dinner."

"Rain check." His voice brightened a little.

"What's this about a new hot spring? Did you get a chance to ask David about it?"

"He was beyond that."

She felt a dry spot in her throat as she waited.

"I did talk to his wife Gretchen . . . She's certain the spring went from cold to hot overnight. Even if she's wrong, I was there two months ago with . . . we waded in that very spot."

"You're sure?"

"Yes. And this morning walking in, Helen and I saw a dozen fumaroles along the trail. I'd swear they weren't there in July."

"I'm coming up," Kyle said.

"We're losing Helen to Bill in Washington, so be sure to bring Xi."

"Double damn. Colin took Xi on the Sakhalin tour."

"Just you and I, then. Bring more equipment."

"One way or another, I'll get what we need," she promised.

As she replaced the receiver, her bruised side gave a twinge. The echo of what could happen with nature on a rampage, along with the still indigestible knowledge that David Mowry had lost his life, made her stare at the telephone after she'd set it down.

She'd assured Wyatt she would come through, yet she'd called everybody she could think of this morning.

Except for one man.

There must be some way other than calling Nick. After all, Hollis had probably already reached him and poached whatever spare hardware there was in his group.

She wouldn't know unless she asked.

Still, she hesitated, a fluttery feeling in her stomach at the thought of speaking to Nick. Would he be all business, or would his manner grow warm and teasing when he recognized her voice?

This was ridiculous. Behaving like a college kid when lives were at stake . . . there was no excuse not to follow up the lead Cass had given her.

With a sigh, Kyle dialed the Cascades Observatory main number and asked for him.

His extension began to ring. She gripped the phone.

"Hello," he said in his cheery distinctive tone.

"Nick, I . . ."

". . . I'm not available right now, but leave a message and I'll get back to you."

Sweat gathered on her palms and she slammed the phone down. "Goddamn answering machines!"

Though he might be out of the country or merely down the hall, Kyle decided to call him tomorrow from Yellowstone. With Wyatt there, she'd be better able to handle her end.

Between stuffing her portfolio with maps and checking email, she telephoned a professor in the Geology Department who agreed to take her seminar. Next, she packed her laptop, auxiliary solar power pack, and looked at the empty place on the credenza where her lucky malachite had rested.

Down the hall, she scribbled her name on the sign-out sheet for the van and took the keys off the nail. She'd leave her Mercedes in the lot; ask a friend in campus security to keep an eye on it.

She went looking for Hollis, intent on convincing him a dead man was reason enough to free the hidden equipment. Unfortunately, a check of the office and labs found him gone. No doubt he was at the Faculty Club sitting at the table Stanton always used for after-hours visiting with fellow professors.

She thought of calling Hollis's cell, but decided two could play his game. If she discovered and removed his hidden equipment cache, she could imagine his astonishment when he found it gone.

Moving through the Institute's cool fluorescent corridors, she felt a shiver, the way she had when she was a kid playing hide and seek. But this was no game.

Trying to appear nonchalant, she opened doors and looked into laboratories and graduate offices. Some were blessedly empty. Twice, she blundered into a study group and had to exit after a quick scan of the space. In a small closet between classrooms, used for chemical storage, she surprised a young man and woman embracing.

There was no sign of the seismographs, not even in the storage sheds behind the building.

After half an hour of searching, she became certain Hollis would return and catch her. It was sweet to think of snatching the equipment from beneath his nose, but another to imagine his ire. He was taking this being in charge altogether too righteously.

As she made a third pass by Stanton's locked office she paused and stared at the door. She had a key, but since he'd been gone she'd had no occasion to go in.

Looking up and down the hall, she waited until some mineralogy students exited the lab and entered a stairwell. Sneaking around in a place she'd always been comfortable was crazy.

When she opened Stanton's door, darkness within exuded a breath of basement air, redolent with the must of paper and an earthy scent. She groped for the light switch.

Stanton's desk and credenza were piled with papers. His file drawers gaped to reveal overstuffed folders. It looked a mess, but Kyle knew Stanton could go straight to what he had been working on last week, or find the raw data for her own twenty-five-year-old dissertation project.

Without pausing in the outer office, she went through a rear door. Here stacks of rocks were piled on open metal shelving. Another door led into a darkroom, long unused since the advent of digital cameras. The last she remembered it had stored army-surplus sleeping bags for student fieldtrips.

Kyle opened the door and let in a wedge of light. As her eyes adjusted to the dimness, she made out the shapes on the slate counters and tile floor . . . seven portable seismographs made the darkroom look like the luggage-storage area of a hotel.

"Bingo," she said.

● ● ●

"What do you think you're doing?"

Hollis Delbert's grim voice made Kyle jump, but she loaded the sixth seismograph into the rear of the Institute van with assurance.

"What does it look like I'm doing?"

Hollis waved his arm. "It looks like insubordination." He cast about for the ultimate slur. "It's theft!"

"Don't be tiresome." Kyle bent and lifted the last seismograph.

"You had no right to go into the office of the director in his absence. Not without my permission."

He really was serious about this. Not only serious, but she didn't have anybody here to back her up.

"Did you locate more equipment?" Kyle asked.

A shadow passed across his face. He glanced sideways and didn't answer.

"The National Earthquake Information Center told me they were sending you something."

"Nothing definite. Take those seismographs back inside."

Adrenaline flushed through her in a hot wave that left her fingertips stinging. "This is the second time in a week I've caught you lying."

Hollis's pale skin reddened.

"You twisted the truth on Monday when you knew perfectly well Stanton left me in charge."

"The Consortium chose me."

"And you just lied about not locating any seismographs. NEIC said they were going to send you some." Even as she spoke, she realized how petty she and Hollis sounded, arguing in a public place like kids over a ball glove.

He planted his feet and put his fists on his hips. "Put the equipment back and give me the van keys."

"No." Kyle felt completely outside the box she'd built and lived inside. "When the equipment arrives from Boulder you can use it on the Wasatch." She slammed the rear door of the van and headed around to the driver's seat.

Hollis dogged her and she thought for a moment he was going to grab her or throw a punch. "I'm calling security." He yanked his cell phone from his belt.

Kyle was in place, starting the engine. "Knock yourself out."

As she drove away, she saw Hollis in the rearview mirror, waving a fist and shouting.

CHAPTER THIRTEEN
SEPTEMBER 18

"Heard you had an even rougher day than the rest of us." Chief Scientist Radford Bullis stood on the threshold of Wyatt's park housing wearing full dress uniform. The expression on his broad face conveyed his own grief for David Mowry.

"You might say that." Aware of his worn jeans and Wolf Advocates T-shirt, Wyatt invited Radford in. Behind his unexpected visitor, a crimson rim of sky shone above Sepulcher Mountain above Mammoth Hot Springs.

"I figured you'd forget Janet Bolido's reception this evening," Radford said mildly.

Though their new boss was not the first woman Superintendent in Yellowstone, she came from the Department of the Interior in Washington amid flying rumors she was everything from a nurturing coach to a harridan. "Isn't the reception cancelled after David . . . ?"

"I'd have thought so, but I spoke with Ms. Bolido myself. She suggested a memorial service in the park chapel tomorrow afternoon, but as for tonight, she believed it would give her a chance to personally convey her sympathy to the staff."

"Easy for her to throw a party," Wyatt groused. "She never met David."

Radford nodded but went on, "If you like, I can wait while you dress. Drive us both up."

Wyatt knew the pecking order well enough to get his dress uniform on in record time. Without further griping, he got into his boss's truck.

Radford negotiated the hairpin turn up the hill toward park headquarters. "Tell me what happened today."

Keeping his eyes on the campground across the highway, Wyatt noted several RVs with TV satellite antennas. An elderly couple in matching jogging suits was the only people outside.

"Hello," Radford prompted.

"Helen and I rushed in to the Mowrys' camp and administered first aid. Even if we'd had a saline IV, morphine . . ." The sense of helplessness Wyatt had felt came rushing back.

Radford slowed to avoid a bull elk defying a **ONE WAY** sign where the road entered Mammoth proper.

"We were too late."

After a little silence, Radford said, "The news reported something about this spring being mysterious?"

"Mysterious enough. It wasn't there yesterday afternoon."

Radford raised a brow. "Is that what Gretchen says?" His tone conveyed that she might have been too distraught to tell a straight story.

"Yes, and I think she's probably right. I was up along Bear Creek two months ago. Cooled my feet in the same spot."

Radford seemed to consider as he drove into the eclectic small village that was the nerve center of Yellowstone. Past the older buildings of frame and stone that had once been an Army installation was the abandoned parade ground. The vintage, 1920s-constructed Mammoth Hotel, covered in pale siding, sat near modern dormitories built for concession employees. On the side of Terrace Mountain, the stair-step levels of the hot springs dominated the landscape.

Radford pulled into the hotel parking lot. "Keep your eyes and ears open tonight. You'll see why it would be wise to keep your story to yourself."

Wyatt got out and slammed the car door.

Inside the hotel lobby, a sign on an easel proclaimed, "Park Service Staff welcomes Superintendent Janet Bolido." The party was well under way in the Map Room, named for a large wooden wall mosaic of the United States. In the high-ceilinged space with a wall of glass overlooking the lawn, at least fifty uniformed rangers mingled with support staff in cocktail attire and business suits.

Wyatt walked away from Radford.

"Tough about David, buddy," said a fellow scientist.

A clap on the shoulder. "Hell of a thing."

An outstretched hand.

The park historian and coauthor of several of David's books stopped him. "Sorry you and Helen . . . but if somebody had to be there, I'm glad it was folks he knew."

Though Wyatt had been keeping it together since this morning, he suddenly lost it. Things were changing too fast, big irrevocable things that were taking people he cared for out of his life. How he longed to turn back the clock to last week.

"Helen's left town," he told the historian. "I'm looking for a drink."

Taking a glass of red wine from a caterer's tray, he took a huge swallow and tried to compose himself. It was difficult with all the people around who had known David, so he walked over toward the food alone.

"This looks wonderful," said a feminine voice beside Wyatt.

The petite woman's close-cropped black hair held a sprinkling of gray. She had a good tan, or it could be that she had naturally golden skin, set off by a black velvet dress. Only the faint lines around her eyes suggested she was in her fifties.

Trying to appear a casual partygoer to this stranger, he tapped the crystal of his wineglass and noted its ring. Something special on the buffet also, an ice sculpture of the Gateway Arch constructed at the park's north entrance in 1903. The elegant touch, coupled with the sumptuous spread, told him this was clearly catered by Firehole Inn in the small town of Gardiner, five miles north down the

Gardner River Canyon.

Wyatt had not had any food since breakfast, and though he wondered if he would be able to eat, he followed the woman's lead down the long laden table. He placed a crostini topped with goat cheese and basil onto his plate, along with an asparagus spear wrapped in prosciutto. As he reached to sample a small sandwich made with medallion of elk, Chief Ranger Joseph Kuni tapped the microphone that was set up in the center of the floor-to-ceiling bay window. A hush spread at the sight of the tall and elegant Native American.

"Good evening, everybody." Though the sound system took a moment to kick in, Kuni's voice needed no amplification. Wyatt had never been on the receiving end of one of his famous come-to-Jesus lectures, but he'd heard plenty about them. "I'm sure I speak for everyone here when I extend a hearty welcome to tonight's guest of honor, Ms. Janet Bolido."

An obligatory wave of applause swelled.

The woman in black turned to Wyatt and shoved her plate at him. Reflexively, he took it. Without so much as a thank you, she walked through the crowd that parted before her.

When she got to the microphone, Janet thanked Joseph for the 'warm welcome.' Wyatt shook his head. If he'd not been so preoccupied over David, he would have picked up who she was sooner. Her publicity photo didn't do her any favors.

"Tonight is about getting acquainted," Janet said, "and I want to tell you how pleased I am with the opportunity to serve as Superintendent of our nation's first National Park."

More applause.

Her face sobered. "There may be some of you here, especially those in the Resource Center, who find it difficult to enjoy the evening after learning of a colleague's tragic death."

A morsel of elk went dry in Wyatt's mouth, and he set his plate on a tray.

"I want to take the opportunity to express my deepest sympathy to all the friends of David Mowry. Though I did not have a chance to know him before coming to the park, I read several of his books and was looking forward to meeting him. His loss is a great blow to our community and the world."

After a moment of silence, Janet made what looked like a practiced sweep with her eyes. "This evening, I'd like to give you an idea of what I'm about."

Radford Bullis came to stand beside Wyatt. "Check this," he murmured.

"The National Park Service stands for preservation," Janet said, "and I'm in favor of that as much as any person in this room."

Wyatt took a long swallow of wine.

"However," her voice firmed, "the Department of the Interior cannot be a money sink. Yellowstone is a wilderness of over two million acres, a hundred miles in any direction.

With the exception of Grant Village in the late 1980s, and the newer Snow Lodge and planned Visitor Center at Old Faithful, most facilities in the park are ancient."

She waved toward the historic frame buildings of Fort Yellowstone beyond the window. Over a hundred years old, they were still in service with rusting metal roofs and leaking steam radiators. "I've been sent here to encourage the building of newer and better tourist facilities. To do this with the budget constraints in today's difficult economy will require that we promote increased traffic and boost revenue through soliciting financial contributions." She smiled. "We're about to embark on an international public relations campaign, reviving a promotion the Northern Pacific Railroad once used for Yellowstone."

Pausing, she raised both arms and invited, "Ladies and gentlemen, welcome to Wonderland!"

People started to laugh, but the wave of mirth was swiftly stifled as the Superintendent's audience realized she was serious. Chief Ranger Kuni led a round of applause, his iron gaze holding control.

As the reception began to break up, Wyatt and Radford headed out beneath the porte-cochere in front of the hotel. It was full dark and the half moon shone on the white stone of the hot springs.

Wyatt shook his head. "Wonderland."

"It worked for the railroads." Radford buttoned his coat against the evening chill. "Had tourists coming in droves for stagecoach tours. For a while it looked like the

Northern Pacific might get their wish to build a spur line into the heart of Yellowstone."

"Maybe it was okay then," Wyatt argued, "but in the twenty-first century it's hokey."

"I don't know. There's Disneyland, Sea World . . ."

"Pure fantasy. Built from scratch. You can't do that to Yellowstone."

Radford pointed at a busload of Asian tourists headed for the restaurant. "People already come from all over the world. We've got boat rides on the lake, theaters in our visitor centers."

"So why not make 'em IMAX?" Wyatt let his sarcasm fly.

"There's been an IMAX at the Grizzly Center in West Yellowstone for years," Radford countered. "Why not one inside the park where the American taxpayer gets the revenue?"

"Sounds like your boss has sold you."

"As your boss, let me make one thing clear," Radford said. "It doesn't matter if I'm for it or not and that goes double for you. Our new Superintendent says 'Wonderland,' we jump-start printing posters and T-shirts."

Wyatt bit the inside of his cheek.

Radford stopped beside his Park Service car. "And to be sure we understand one another, the Wonderland campaign is not compatible with scaring the tourists about earthquakes."

CHAPTER FOURTEEN
SEPTEMBER 19

After a check with a friend in campus security revealed Hollis had not called, Kyle felt safe spending the night at home rather than driving through the dark to Yellowstone.

Though she went to bed exhausted, each time she got close to drifting off, her conscience woke her. Then an internal argument would ensue. Surely, the reason Hollis had not reported her was that he recognized her right to the department equipment. With her seniority at the Institute and Stanton's endorsement of her as his successor, what she'd done did not even constitute insubordination.

Punching her pillow, she noted it was past midnight. If it were not so late, she would phone Wyatt for reassurance . . . and to comfort him in the loss of David.

She settled on her side and stared at the phone in the glow of her bedside lamp. A lonely pang had her hand halfway to the receiver, but the memory of Alicia's sleep-drugged voice answering for Wyatt made her lower her arm back to the bed.

Time passed and she avoided looking at her clock.

Then, despite her belief she'd never fall asleep, she suddenly jerked awake to total blackness.

Above her bed, the mirror shuddered in its frame. She struggled with the covers; the headboard knocked against the wall. An amethyst geode fell from a shelf above and glanced off her head. It crashed to the floor, smashing her pager, and rolled.

She made it out of bed and crouched, straining to hear as though the suffocating darkness had plugged her ears as well as blinded her.

A long rumble resonated through the high valley.

Fumbling with frantic fingers, she found her lantern and sent its beam stabbing into blackness. Despite the light, shadows loomed in the corners.

Though she'd drilled for this, it took a while to fight her way into her clothes. When she reached for the window, she hoped it hadn't jammed in the sash.

Thankfully, it slid up. Outside there were no lights; the power was out for as far as she could see.

Kyle gathered her climbing rope and tossed it, bending to watch it unfurl into darkness. The near end was attached to one of the wall studs where she'd broken out a bit of Sheetrock. Her hands shook and her heart was pounding so fast she thought her knees would collapse.

Practice, she told herself, makes the difference; though in recent years she hadn't climbed down a cliff or a building.

Lightning strobed, revealing towering thunderheads. Kyle's stomach tightened. A storm, now of all times, reminding her of a scrawny girl trapped up a tree while wind-driven rain whipped her face.

Another jagged streak illuminated a line of rain sweeping down from the mountains.

She leashed her lantern to her belt with a clip, glad she'd recently replaced the battery. As she put her leg over the sill, the first stinging drops lashed her.

Warily, she straddled the rope and backed out the window, bracing both feet against the cedar siding. The lantern dangled, sending erratic beams over the wall and the ground below.

The rain came in earnest, obscuring the shapes of even the nearest buildings. Combined with the darkness surrounding her, the deluge conspired to rob her of breath.

In fits and starts, she worked her way down the side of the building. Her running shoes slipped and slid on the wet wall. She felt herself speeding up, the rope heating her downhill hand that controlled the speed.

One foot lost contact and she crashed into the cedar siding with her shoulder. A fresh wave of pain attacked from her boat bruise while her lantern smashed the wall and went out.

For a long moment, she dangled in darkness. Her compact metal flashlight was in the pocket of her jeans and she couldn't let go the rope to reach it.

Carefully, she braced her feet against the wall and started lowering again. Although her bedroom was on the second floor, the townhouses were built on the hillside, making her descent a three-story drop.

Lightning flared again. Her feet touched grass.

Quickly, she moved away from the building in case the first shock had merely foreshadowed something larger. She pulled out her small flashlight and turned it on, a lonely circlet on the lawn. The wind came up, sweeping the rain against her. Thunder rumbled again, setting her on edge for another jolt.

She played the light over the side of the building, looking for structural damage. Nothing showed on this side.

Kyle looked for her neighbor Christine, an energetic widow in her late sixties. Though they'd talked numerous times about what to do in an earthquake and planned to meet where Kyle waited, there was no sign of her . . . or of anybody.

Christine's doorbell was electric; its little gold light extinguished, so Kyle knocked.

More thunder rolled.

She pounded and called, "Christine!" Shivering now, she hugged herself. Her jacket that had been billed as water-resistant was soaked; another failed aspect of her preparations.

The door opened a crack on the security chain and Christine peeked around the door edge. "Kyle?"

The chain rattled and the door opened to reveal a big woman in a purple caftan that clashed with her unnatural red hair. "What are you doing running around in the rain?"

Kyle's drenched clothing stuck to her skin and she

became aware of her hair straggling around her shoulders. "Grab a jacket and get out," she warned. "Didn't you feel the earthquake?"

Christine's eyes widened. "Why, no."

"I'm afraid the Wasatch Fault has let go." Saying it made her stomach hurt.

"I don't think so." Christine peered out into the storm, looking reluctant to give up shelter.

"Come on, you've got to get outside," Kyle insisted. "These townhouses could be a death trap."

At that instant, the lights came on.

● ● ●

Kyle's dining room was brightly lit as she used her laptop to access the Website of the National Earthquake Information Center. Christine stood behind her at the glass-topped stone table.

It took up to twenty minutes for earthquake waves to propagate all the way through the earth, but only a few minutes to pinpoint the region.

"What do you see?" Christine asked.

"There should be a bulletin on the seismic warning system by now."

Kyle frowned and switched to the Institute site. There she could see the local seismograph with no delay, provided the auxiliary power was on and the telephones were working.

A moment later, she stared in disbelief. The local trace

was undisturbed.

It took another full second of confusion for Kyle to realize no disaster unfolded in Salt Lake . . . no collapsed buildings or broken water mains, no children lost in the night. Her mirror had rattled, but she must have disturbed it herself, knocked the geode and her pager off from her own startled reaction. She would never have panicked had there been light.

"I'm sorry." She pushed to her feet. "I was wrong." Her cheeks felt hot.

Christine looked at the computer and at Kyle. "I didn't think I felt anything."

Kyle walked into the downstairs bath, switched on the light, and closed the door. Clutching the edge of the pedestal sink with both hands, she listened to Christine let herself out.

In the mirror, her eyes were almost all dark pupil; her face a frozen mask, as another strand of her life unraveled.

Without waiting for daylight, she packed and left for Yellowstone.

CHAPTER FIFTEEN
SEPTEMBER 19

When Kyle drove into Mammoth Hot Springs on Thursday afternoon she still felt on edge. Driving into the usually quiet town, she was surprised to see a line of media vehicles in front of Headquarters. Though parking was at a premium, she got the last space next to the Resource Center. The long wooden building, fronted with a wide porch, had once been a Fort Yellowstone troop barracks. A maintenance shed behind had stabled the cavalry's horses.

As she got out of the van, Wyatt came toward her wearing the dress version of his ranger's uniform, jacket buttoned to his chin and a wide-brimmed hat level over his brows. He looked so sad that she walked forward with open arms.

They embraced. She bent her cheek against his shoulder and felt the itchy wool he probably hated. "I'm so sorry about David."

"I'm glad you're here." Wyatt sounded infinitely weary and her heart ached for him.

His arms tightened around her and her throat felt

thick. David Mowry would never again know the power of a human touch, the magic that comforted both her and Wyatt. It was a long moment before they broke apart.

She looked around the lawn. "What's with the press?"

"There's a memorial service before Gretchen takes David home."

Chief Scientist Radford Bullis joined them. Also wearing dress uniform, he bore a serious look on his broad face. "Dr. Stone." He shook his head. "Last night I had a disturbing call from Hollis Delbert. Most disturbing."

Beside Kyle, Wyatt raised an inquiring brow.

"Hollis told me you drove off with the Institute vehicle and the seismographs earmarked for his Wasatch research." Barrel-chested and ham-handed, Radford had a voice so soft that Kyle had to lean closer to hear him.

Wyatt burst out laughing. "And she carried them across several state lines."

Radford scowled. "Hollis says he made it clear you were not to take that equipment."

"I imagine he didn't tell you about his game of hide and seek," she came back. "With the quakes this past week, the situation here is a lot more unstable than along the Wasatch."

Radford interrupted. "I live in the park. It's always shaking and rattling, but nothing bad ever happens."

"But, nothing, Radford," she snapped. "What about Hebgen Lake?"

"That was a long time ago. Technically, it's not in the park."

"Close enough," Wyatt interjected.

"At any rate," Radford said, "Hollis wants you to return to Salt Lake immediately."

"I can't do that."

The Chief Scientist's composure frayed. "We've all been trying to cut you slack because of Stanton, but frankly, I'm surprised at you."

"Surprised at me? I'm sure Wyatt has briefed you about the hot spring where David Mowry died. You must see the situation is more serious than Hollis thinks."

Radford shot a glance at Wyatt. "You're sticking by your story about it heating up overnight?"

"It's no story," Wyatt replied. "Something bad is happening in the park . . . look at David. God knows what's next."

Radford looked uncertain a moment longer. Then he looked away from their united front, surveyed the gathering crowd around the chapel, and nodded. "I'll let you and Hollis settle your own disputes."

"Look out," Wyatt said to both her and Radford.

A female reporter with faded red hair spilling over the shoulders of her denim jacket bore down on them. "Carol Leeds, *Billings Live Eye*." A videographer, tall and lanky with a graying hank of ponytail, trailed behind her.

Lining herself up beside Radford, Carol told the camera, "I'm here in Mammoth with Dr. Radford Bullis, Yellowstone's Chief Scientist, and," she quickly read his badge, "Ranger Wyatt Ellison." Extending the microphone to Kyle, Carol smiled cordially. "You are?"

"Dr. Kyle Stone," she said grudgingly, "of the Utah Institute of Seismology."

Carol brightened. "I'm here to ask about the reports that David Mowry drowned in a hot spring heated to boiling overnight. Perhaps you would care to comment, Dr. Stone?"

Before she could demur, Wyatt stepped forward. "She was in Salt Lake when this happened. I'm with the park's geology section, so I'd be better able to answer your questions."

"Could you tell us about the spring . . . is it *Dr.* Ellison?" Carol Leeds asked.

"I was first on the scene," Wyatt said. "Mowry's wife Gretchen told me he dived into a portion of the creek that was cool yesterday."

"How could that be?"

"Theoretically speaking, in an area of high heat flow, a new fissure in the earth might permit the release of steam or hot water in an area previously cool . . ."

"Wouldn't this be dangerous?" Carol broke in.

Wyatt's tone remained even. "I think David Mowry's wife would agree that it's dangerous."

The reporter looked momentarily abashed, but pressed on. "How many more of these fissures could there be?"

His smile looked forced. "I was going to say that we have not had a chance to look into the story. The banks of Bear Creek have several areas that look similar."

"I'm told that none of the park maps show a hot spring

in that area," Carol persisted.

"That's correct," Wyatt said. "Yellowstone is the world's most active hydrothermal system; with more than 10,000 hot springs, pools, and geysers. We don't put out any maps with all of them."

Radford looked into the camera. "Be vigilant in watching for all kinds of danger, from wildlife to boiling springs. Don't let what happened to David Mowry happen to you."

Despite her persistence, the reporter seemed to know the interview was over. Thanking them, she moved on toward the crowd gathering at the chapel.

As soon as she was gone, Kyle turned on Wyatt. "Why did you evade her question about the spring? You had a chance to warn people."

"Radford warned them," Wyatt said evenly.

"I'm going over to the service." Radford walked away through rows of staff housing toward the small stone chapel.

Kyle studied Wyatt's expression and made a guess. "You were told to keep things quiet?"

Wyatt nodded. "The park's new Superintendent wants things sunshine and roses. She's got an idea to revitalize the old Wonderland campaign and thinks earthquakes"— he gestured toward the gathering mourners—"and cold springs turned scalding overnight might frighten Joe American."

"You can't just go along," she challenged.

He looked chagrined. "Radford made it clear that with this woman exposed pegs will be hammered. Look at you . . . with Stanton gone, Hollis is after your head. None of us will be any use if we get kicked off the project."

"Politics." Kyle crossed her arms over her chest. "What a crock of bull."

"Think about it." Wyatt waved a hand at the breeze ruffling the cottonwoods and drifting golden leaves onto the lawn. "Who's going to believe something's going on underneath all this peaceful beauty unless we bide our time and gather evidence? Even with David's death, everyone figures Gretchen might have gotten the story wrong about the spring. We've got the classic dilemma . . ."

She sighed. "Are we warning people or crying wolf?"

Wyatt checked his watch. "Time to head over. You coming?"

Church bells spread rich tones on the autumn air. Kyle almost told him she couldn't bear to attend, but the pain in his eyes suggested he could use her support.

"Let's go," she agreed.

Several hundred people had arrived, with law enforcement rangers directing parking to keep the road in front of the chapel clear. As Kyle watched, another press vehicle was given a prominent spot at the curb.

With a grimace at the circus atmosphere, she followed Wyatt and joined the line of mourners. The sun on the stone buttresses that flanked the church's walls brightened myriad colors of lichen on the native rock. Near the door, a young man comforted a slim gray-haired woman in black. Kyle presumed them to be David Mowry's wife and son. It was confirmed when the woman greeted Wyatt with a hard hug and whispered, "Thank you for doing what you could."

Wyatt led Kyle inside. A chill met them, as the stone insulated the sanctuary from the day's warmth. After a moment for her eyes to adjust to the dimness, she looked around the simple house of worship. Pale, painted walls contrasted with dark trim; a large and plain wooden cross adorned the front wall beneath the arch of ceiling.

The altar was decorated with banked floral arrangements. Orchids bent on emerald stems, carnations spread a cluster of pompoms, and blue stars of agapanthus rose on thick stalks. As Kyle and Wyatt advanced into the sanctuary, the flowers' mingled scent smelled like the viewing room in a funeral parlor.

She was glad there was no casket in evidence.

Wyatt directed her toward a seat in the third row behind the Yellowstone brass. The small woman in a black dress suit had to be Janet Bolido, the new Superintendent.

As David Mowry's family seated themselves in the front pew, a hush fell over the murmuring crowd. From the side of the altar, a man in crimson robes entered. He went to the organ and began to play "Nearer My God to Thee."

Kyle had not been to church since Dad had driven them each Sunday in the Rambler wagon. Pastor White had exhorted them from the pulpit. When she'd spent the night clinging to a tree in stormy darkness she'd wondered if the earthquake happened because she'd let her attention wander during the sermon to the myriad colors in the stained glass, like rubies, emeralds, and sapphires.

Near the end of August 1959, there had been a memorial for the victims of Hebgen Lake, just inside the mouth of Madison Canyon. The local sheriff had vetoed a plan to meet directly on the slide and moved the site a mile west. A child psychologist who had evaluated Kyle while Franny and Zeke drove up from Arizona suggested they attend.

The mourners sang hymns and prayed, and The Bishop of the Montana Episcopal Diocese spoke. "Unto God's gracious mercy and protection we commit you."

She didn't understand. Her parents must have been saved. They just hadn't yet been located.

The Bishop intoned, "Lord, accept these prayers on behalf of the souls of Thy servants departed. Grant them an entrance into the land of life and joy in the fellowship of Thy saints."

Kyle closed her eyes. "Dear Lord, please send Mommy and Daddy back." Tears stung her lids. "If you do this, I won't ever ask for anything, I promise."

On the day of the service, there were still forty people missing. Ten of them were found alive.

Kyle never did ask God for anything else.

In the Yellowstone chapel, a woman in black robes came in bearing a large color photograph of David Mowry, one that Kyle recognized from his latest book jacket. The smiling, sturdy, bald man wore a red North Face parka.

The clergywoman arranged the photo against the back of a chair facing the congregation and went to the podium. When the last notes of the organ faded, she permitted a moment of silence before saying, "Let us pray."

The chamber seemed to rustle as people settled themselves in their pews and bowed their heads.

"Our Father, Who art in heaven, hallowed be Thy name."

The assembly joined in, their murmurs forming a communal growl.

Wyatt's low baritone rumbled beside Kyle's ear. "On earth as it is in heaven."

She pressed her lips together. For an instant, she thought she saw the suspended chandelier move, but that had to be her imagination.

"Give us this day our daily bread," came the never-forgotten cadence.

Kyle's father had a saying. "All things cometh to he who waiteth." He'd always stopped there for effect and broken into a grin. "If he worketh like hell while he waiteth."

"Forgive us our trespasses."

Any human trespass she could imagine paled in comparison to the night God had turned His spotlight of full moon on the Madison Valley, to better illuminate His shaking loose a mountain.

"As we forgive those who trespass against us."

She realized she was crying in the same instant she saw the suspended chandelier really was on the move. Ever so gently, it swayed in an increasing arc while the mourners prayed on. After the colossal mistake she'd made last night, she was suspicious, but the telltale motion continued.

Kyle leaped to her feet, stumbled over peoples' legs, and ran out of the chapel.

● ● ●

She was halfway across the lawn before Wyatt managed to snag her arm, realizing too late that it was her injured side.

He heard her gasp. She stopped.

"I'm sorry." He touched Kyle's other shoulder, gently this time. "What's the matter?"

He'd wanted to leave the church the moment he'd seen the picture of David, hale and smiling in the red parka his wife had embraced in the clearing where he died.

Kyle rounded on him, wild-eyed, as he'd never known her. "Didn't you see it?"

"See what?"

"The chandelier. Another quake."

"I didn't feel anything."

He felt her trembling beneath his hand. A brisk breeze rattled the cottonwoods and sent more leaves spiraling. Night frosts had begun to fade the green of the irrigated lawns. "It's cooling off out here. Let me get you some coffee."

Placing a hand at the small of her back, he urged her toward the Resource Center.

Inside, at the receptionist's desk, Iniki Kuni raised her head. Chief Ranger Joseph Kuni's daughter, just eighteen and reed-thin, sported multiple piercings of ears, nose, and even her navel, visible in her waist-skimming top.

"The service over already?" she asked.

"Not yet," Wyatt replied. "Iniki, this is Dr. Kyle Stone from the Institute in Salt Lake. She just drove in."

His office door stood open, the desk piled with papers threatening avalanche. He showed Kyle inside and crossed the hall, trying not to look at David's nameplate and vacant office.

In the kitchen, he checked the pots for coffee. Iniki pampered the staff, buying beans at a coffee shop in Gardiner and grinding them fresh. Today's selection was featured in purple calligraphy on a lavender index card. *Viennese Cinnamon*, David's favorite.

Wyatt pulled down the nice guest cups, thick white mugs with the Yellowstone Park logo, a mountain peak above the boast *Oldest and Best*. How long before it was superseded by *Wonderland*?

Automatically, he stirred in a touch of cream the way Kyle liked it.

Back in his office, she stood where he'd left her. He moved a paper pile and slid a hip onto the corner of his desk. This erased his slight advantage of height and put them on the level. "So why is a tiny tremor such a big deal?"

Her lips moved in a bitter twist. "Believe me, you haven't got the time."

He was reminded of the evening in the Red Wolf when she'd refused to explain her tears. At the time, he'd felt rebuffed. Today, he determined to break down her defenses. "I've got all the time you need."

Her eyes reflected a deep pain. "Last night I woke up and panicked, thinking the Wasatch Fault had let go a huge quake."

"That doesn't sound so terrible."

She shook her head. "I climbed out the window into a terrific rainstorm and roped down the side of the building."

The image almost made him smile.

"Don't you dare laugh at me," she threatened.

He maintained a solemn expression. "I'm not."

"Your eyes are smiling."

"Maybe." He grinned.

Kyle gulped her coffee. "I scared my neighbor pounding on her door, telling her to get outside."

Wyatt kept his tone reasonable. "Maybe I did feel like smiling. It sounds to me like you overreacted to a bad dream."

"And again today."

"Maybe." She bowed her head. Her sleek hair was divided by a part above a faint widow's peak.

"Tell me the rest," he urged.

When she did not speak, he started putting things together on his own. Her panic attack last night and again when the chandelier swung, the hysterical note to her laughter after the earthquake on Dot Island, the odd way she'd acted at the Earthquake Lake Visitor Center, as though she thought the mountain might begin shaking again.

"Kyle," he said, "if you're afraid of quakes, why do you put yourself in places where they happen?" He propped his hands on the desk on either side of her, suddenly aware that mere inches separated their bodies.

She looked at him; her eyes clear green-blue. "Wyatt . . ."

With a pounding heart, he lifted his hand and cradled her cheek. Gently, he moved his thumb over the silky skin beneath her eye. A bluish shadow there bespoke her night terrors.

Someone rapped the office door in sharp staccato.

"Yee haw," a man said jovially. "Am I interrupting anything?"

CHAPTER SIXTEEN
SEPTEMBER 19

The intruder laughed lightly, the sound of a man who seldom took things seriously. Kyle's view of the entry was blocked by Wyatt, but she'd have known that voice anywhere.

Already unnerved by the tenderness in Wyatt's touch, she vowed not to drop her cup.

Wyatt backed away, his face flushing, and turned toward his guest.

In jeans and a blue work shirt, tanned, with sun-streaked tousled hair, the ghost from her past stood in the doorway.

"Hello, I'm Nick Darden."

Kyle's heart started to race.

Nick took a few steps closer with a compact catlike grace that still set him apart. His tawny-greenish eyes glinted with what could only be termed polite interest. "I'm looking for a Dr. Ellison."

A dreadful suspicion seized her. "I'm Dr. Stone of the Utah Institute." She ignored Nick's outstretched hand.

"Pleased to meet you," he said without a trace of

recognition.

Through the years, Kyle had played a hundred scenarios. Perhaps they would meet at a convention icebreaker and trade banalities while half a dozen colleagues looked on. It might be more public, as she announced the speakers' awards at a banquet and found his name on the list.

She had never considered he might not remember her.

"This is Dr. Wyatt Ellison," she introduced. Feeling cold all over, she watched the two men shake hands, Wyatt taller and leaner.

Nick gave an easy smile. "Colin Gruy sent me from Volcano Hazards at USGS. I've brought some seismographs, extra GPS receivers, you name it."

Kyle remained standing while Nick took a seat and pulled his foot in a scuffed hiking boot up onto his thigh. Somehow, it underscored his casual air, especially with Wyatt sitting across from him in dress uniform.

How was it possible for Nick to have changed so little? Sure, there were crinkles around his eyes, his hair wasn't as shiny, but the attitude was still that of field camp court jester. His eyes darted around the office, skipped over Wyatt's rock collection on the windowsill, and lit briefly on a rodeo trophy with a gold bronco rider spurring his kicking mount. The plaque proclaimed Wyatt Ellison *All-Around Cowboy at the Bozeman Summer Roundup, 1979.*

Nick turned back to Wyatt. "Colin sent me alone rather than calling a full deployment team alert. He and I are sure there's nothing unusual going on."

Wyatt glanced out the window toward the Yellowstone Chapel, where the friends of David Mowry were beginning to disperse, and then back to Nick. "We all know about opinions. Now, are you here to help or tell us our business?"

Nick settled back and crossed his arms. "A bit of both, I imagine."

He was even cockier than he'd been as a student, but considering his position in Volcano Hazards, Kyle wasn't too surprised. Although career advancement within the USGS and academic halls was traditionally based on the principle of 'publish or perish,' the mavericks accepted their upward mobility as stagnant. They asked only to be called to the next hotspot around the world.

Kyle decided it was time she used her vocal cords, lest Nick conclude Wyatt had the only brain in the operation. "We need to get up into the backcountry as soon as possible."

"By helicopter?" Nick asked, his eyes once more passing over her without expression.

Wyatt snorted. "You kidding? On our budget, I was planning to pack in with horses."

"Horses?" Nick's voice rose.

"Unless you've got the money for a chopper?" Kyle suggested hopefully.

"No," Nick said. A little silence fell.

"I fucking hate horses," he went on after a moment.

Wyatt raised a dark brow.

Nick nodded toward the rodeo trophy. "I take it you're a pretty good rider?"

"In Bozeman, I used to compete every Friday night."

"Barrel racing?"

Wyatt crossed his arms, matching Nick's pose. "Bronco riding, bulldogging, a bit of everything."

"Real cowboy, eh?"

The two men stared at each other.

Wyatt broke the standoff. "What do you know about Yellowstone, Darden?"

"I did geology field camp down the road at Alpine."

"So did Dr. Stone."

From the corner of her eye Kyle saw Nick swivel his head toward her.

"What year were you there?" His pleasant tone exempted her from his clash with Wyatt.

"A long time ago." She looked directly at him for the first time, her expression even.

The impact of his eyes sent a shaft of longing through her. Despite, no, because he was no longer youthful and untried, he seemed even more aware of his power to interest a female. He might not remember her, but she decided he was damn well going to. "The 4-H camp's bunkhouse was pretty spare, but I actually spent the last three weeks sleeping in a tent."

Nick's green gaze froze. A beat of silence passed while he digested her words. Then his expression sharpened.

"My God!" He shook his head. "Kyle."

The familiar warmth of his voice, one she'd never wanted to hear again, made something twist inside her.

Her mouth went dry.

"I feel like a damned fool." His eyes, formerly pale chips of glass, upon meeting a stranger lighted. He studied her with an intensity that embarrassed her.

"Don't." She lifted a hand to tuck in a stray strand of her hair. "I've changed a lot." Nick hadn't, though. He still reminded her of Southern California sunshine.

She turned to Wyatt. "We went to camp together."

"Small world," he said flatly.

Nick's voice shifted to his old familiar banter. "So how the hell are you? Married? Kids?"

"Fine, and no." She twisted her hands. "You?"

"I took a swing at being married. Twice. Now I'm afraid of striking out."

"Why don't we take a look at the equipment you've brought?" she suggested coolly.

"Sounds good." Wyatt pushed back his chair. Before they headed out, he took off his dress jacket and hung it on the back of his door, replacing it with a fleece one with Park Service insignia.

Behind the Resource Center sat a white panel truck labeled *United States Geological Survey*. Nick opened the back and displayed a wealth of equipment. "What's your pleasure, Ma'am? GPS receivers, portable seismographs, electronic tiltmeters? Doctor Nicolas has brought 'em all."

Kyle laughed. Sliding open the door of the Institute van, she revealed her own cache of seven seismographs.

"I thought you were out of equipment." Nick sounded

surprised. "Colin said it was all dedicated to the Wasatch Fault."

"There was a custody battle."

Her euphoria evaporated as she caught sight of the last traffic leaving the memorial service. Out on the main road there were still some press vans.

"What's with all the action?" Nick asked jovially. "I remember this place as pretty quiet."

"A colleague, David Mowry," Wyatt said, "whom you may know from his books, dove into a hot spring that wasn't supposed to be hot. I got there just in time to watch him die."

Nick's smile disappeared like a conjurer's handkerchief. "That's tough. I heard about him on the news when I was driving over."

"His memorial service was in the chapel today," Kyle explained.

Nick shifted his weight from one foot to the other. "Is it true the spring was cold the day before?"

"It is." Wyatt folded his arms over his chest. "You want to think again about there being nothing going on here?"

Nick slammed the back of the truck, dusted off his hands, and looked at Kyle. "I'm starving. How 'bout some chow?"

To her surprise, it was after five. She tried to think of when she'd last eaten and realized it had been dinner last night. After her predawn panic, she'd driven to Yellowstone on a single Coke.

"You two go ahead." Wyatt turned away. "I'm heading home."

"No," Kyle said quickly. "Come with us." Too late, she realized he might be meeting Alicia.

Wyatt demurred, his hands shoved deep in jacket pockets. "It sounds as though you and Nick have a lot to catch up on." He walked toward his Park Service Bronco.

"We'll come by your office in the morning," Kyle called after him. She waved, but he wasn't looking back.

Nick's grin flashed familiar. "I don't think the cowboy likes me."

As the Bronco drove past, they walked together across the parking lot, then between the stone headquarters building and the Chief Ranger's historic quarters next door. With the sun dipping toward the mountains, the chill began to settle in earnest. Fallen leaves made small tearing sounds beneath their feet.

When they reached the street, three television crews were filming a man with a halo of curly hair. Behind him was the backdrop of Mammoth Hot Spring's terraces.

"Here's trouble." Nick's familiar tone suggested he knew Brock Hobart well.

The freelance earthquake predictor, dressed casually in jeans and a light jacket, sat on a picnic table surrounded by press. When he'd gotten lucky with Sakhalin, his cult following had swelled.

Carol Leeds of *Billings Live Eye*, who'd interviewed Radford, Wyatt, and Kyle earlier, was at the forefront. "I understand you predicted the earthquake in Sakhalin last week, right before it happened."

Brock smiled. "Yes. If Monty Muckleroy hadn't invited me on his show, I would have been a lone voice making predictions on the Internet."

"What a PR hound Brock's turned into." Nick leaned his shoulder against a tree and watched.

"Fishing for a return engagement on *Mornings with Monty*," Kyle agreed.

"I understand your prediction at Sakhalin had to do with some alignment of the planets," Carol prompted.

"Actually, it's the sun, moon, and earth that were in alignment. This happens twice a month with the new and full moon. At this time, the ocean and solid earth tides are at maximum," Brock lectured. "Quakes that have occurred during alignment include Bishop, California in 1912; Anchorage, Alaska in 1964; and Kobe, Japan in 1995."

Everyone listened, including the pony-tailed cameraman.

"And last, but certainly not least," Brock spread his hands. "Your own Hebgen Lake in 1959."

Nick moved closer and bent to Kyle's ear. "That was a nasty one, killed thirty people in the landslide and flood."

Thankfully, she'd never told him. That was one more vulnerability she didn't need. It was bad enough to see him again and wish they'd never crossed the line into intimacy.

The reporter continued to question Brock. "What brings you to Yellowstone now?"

He put on a grave look. "During last week's align-ment, I noticed the park experiencing an unusual swarm of quakes."

Kyle's heart began to thud and she moved closer to Nick. "Wyatt has measured six inches of vertical move-ment on the caldera in the past week."

"Six inches isn't much," Nick murmured.

"Not for a Cascade Range volcano. Here it's pretty significant."

"So what are you predicting?" Carol asked.

"I'd say . . ." Brock looked around at the mountains that ringed the high valley, as though searching for a sign. Finally, he placed his fingertips together. "Certainly with the new moon we could easily see an event in the 6.0 mag-nitude range."

Nick whistled.

Kyle's stomach clenched. As the reporters wrapped, and Brock slung his legs down and got off the picnic table, she started toward him with a determined stride.

Nick snagged her arm. "Hey."

It was too late. In front of Carol Leeds and the other members of the press, she faced off Brock. "It's been a while since USGS."

"Kyle." A smile broke over his features, a man recog-nizing a former colleague.

Though she'd once liked Brock, today she wasn't hav-ing any. "I can't believe how irresponsible you've become."

Brock made a gesture of bewilderment.

"Every one of us in the field would love to predict when and where disaster will strike." She pointed a finger at his chest. "But you're going too far."

Video and still cameras captured the moment.

Brock apparently noticed they were back on stage and shrugged. "Okay, then. When it turns out I'm right about the park becoming a powder keg, you and Darden here"—his look included Nick—"can buy the beer."

"We'll be in the backcountry, as soon as we can get there," Kyle told Brock.

He sobered. "Maybe you ought not . . ."

Before he could echo the thoughts she'd been having about the wisdom of going to Nez Perce Peak, Kyle started away with Nick at her heels. He caught up and took her arm.

Carol Leeds followed them to the edge of the lawn. "Dr. Stone, was it . . . ? Would you care to comment . . . ?"

●　●　●

Nick chuckled as he walked with Kyle under the portico outside the Mammoth Hot Springs Hotel. "Even if you didn't comment, they'll make hay of your telling Brock off."

She swung to face him, hands on hips, color flushing her prominent high cheekbones. "I shouldn't have done that, but damn it, it felt good."

As he held the door for Kyle, the lobby welcomed Nick. He didn't mind roughing it in the field, but he liked comfort as well. The polished wood floor shone and a huckleberry scent mixed with chocolate wafted from the gift shop to sharpen his hunger.

"You got a place to stay?" he asked.

"I need to register," Kyle replied.

Nick followed her toward the desk on the lobby's back wall, taking the opportunity to look her over. The years had been kind, reflected in her athletic build and quick movements he had to hustle to keep up with. He realized he'd never forgotten her scent, a mix of forest freshness and a jasmine-like musk. He did not think it was perfume.

There were changes, though. This woman bore only a fleeting resemblance to the youthful Kyle Stone. That girl had been quiet and content to sit on the sideline while others played a rowdy game of Hearts on somebody's, usually his, bunk. It had taken more than a few tries to convince her to sing along when he played guitar. Now, when she looked at him, her eyes bore the determination of a powerful woman.

While they waited for check-in, he sensed she didn't want him staring at her so he perused the lobby. Off to the right was a circular staircase to the upper floors, nestled in the curve of a huge bay window.

"Oh, shit," he muttered.

He'd stood with Kyle in exactly this spot before. Though he'd had a devil of a time convincing her to come to Yellowstone, something he'd never figured out, she'd finally agreed.

Back in the seventies, you didn't just pop into a hotel with a woman like you could today, so she had turned her grandmother's opal ring around to look like a gold band, while he signed the register, "Mr. and Mrs. Nicholas Darden." That evening, he had thought about going up those steps with her to a big carpeted room with a private bath, but all they could afford was one of the spare little cabins lined up in rows at the base of a sage-covered slope.

This evening, though his USGS per diem would cover a hotel room, Nick decided he wanted to stay in a cabin. He wondered if he would be able to recognize the one he and Kyle had shared.

The clerk looked their way. "Ladies first," he said.

"Go ahead." Kyle glanced at him and their eyes met for the barest moment. It made him aware of how her silver-buckled belt defined a waist his hands might almost span. "You had farther to drive than I," she insisted.

Nick dragged his focus to the front desk.

After he secured the key to a cabin, Kyle spoke briskly to the clerk, "I'd like a room in the hotel with a queen bed and private bath. Ground floor."

Drifting nearby, Nick waited for her. If he were alone, he'd probably just hit the snack bar for a burger, but this evening he wanted to buy Kyle dinner. It had nothing to do with being on expenses . . . it was because a single look into her enigmatic chameleon eyes had him prepared to spend a week's wages on the best entrees and fine wine.

Maybe it was just nostalgia for a simpler time in his life

. . . What if he had not been a coward and taken a powder? The passage of time and his experiences with other women had cast that long-ago summer in ripe and golden hues.

What an ass he'd made of himself, not recognizing Kyle.

"How about dinner?" he asked with a grin.

In that instant, he saw the toughness she'd shown to both him and Brock evaporate. Her unguarded gaze, that had not changed even as her face had matured, connected with his . . . This time for more than a moment . . . revealing she remembered everything.

Yet, she turned toward the hall, key in hand. "You go ahead. I'm getting room service."

Nick watched her go, already planning to locate Brock and find out what made him so certain something big was breaking in the park.

CHAPTER SEVENTEEN
SEPTEMBER 20

Wyatt heard the rain begin; first, a few pings on the metal roof of his Park Service housing. A moment later, it resolved into a steady thrumming. His bedside clock said seven past midnight.

He found himself inexplicably awake, something that had happened to him before in the park, a sensation usually corroborated by the seismograph when he saw it the next morning.

He'd come home this afternoon and turned on the TV just in time to see Brock Hobart predict a 6.0 event. Letters on the screen had proclaimed the coverage live. Next, Wyatt had seen himself on tape with a voiceover. "Here is what Park Service geologist, Dr. Wyatt Ellison, said about noted Yellowstone author David Mowry's death in a brand new hot spring."

He'd been put out when the reporter interrupted his explanation with, "Wouldn't this be dangerous?"

Wyatt waited for his disclaimer, but the TV image shifted to Radford Bullis looking self-conscious.

"Yellowstone's Chief Scientist also gave a warning,"

said the voiceover.

Jesus, thought Wyatt. The new superintendent was not only going to wonder what kind of stupid interview they had given, she'd be livid.

As if that weren't bad enough, he next heard, "Immediately after our interview with Dr. Hobart, Dr. Kyle Stone of the Utah Institute questioned his credibility."

She looks magnificent, Wyatt thought, with her shoulders back, pointing the finger and telling Brock off with increasingly rosy cheeks. But when Dr. Nicholas Darden took her arm on camera, Wyatt frowned.

Lying in his bed, he listened to the rain. It was good to be inside and warm on an inclement night, but the cadence brought back the melancholy he'd felt in his tent when camping with Alicia. Tonight it had an edge to it.

Wyatt pushed back his covers. Alicia would not expect him to drive down to her place in Gardiner this late, but he expected it would be a nice surprise.

After dressing, he went into the kitchen, grabbed his parka, and plucked his keys off the counter. He first considered his Park Service truck then decided he was on personal business this evening.

A few minutes later, he guided his pickup into Gardner Canyon, a steep-walled section where signs warned of falling rock. He sensed rather than saw the vertical amphitheater of thinly bedded sand and shale looming on the right side, where he'd often seen bighorn sheep defy the edge.

Headlights swept around a curve and into Wyatt's

eyes; a big RV, probably heading up to the campground. He was happy to be on the cliff side rather than next to the drop-off. As the two vehicles drew closer to each other, he heard something over the truck engine and the wet slap of his windshield wipers. For a moment, he thought the RV had engine trouble.

An instant later, he pinpointed the sound as coming from above in the rock amphitheater. A gathering roar shot adrenaline down his arms.

He stomped his accelerator and blew the horn to warn the RV. The driver responded by swerving toward the roadway's outer edge. Still blowing his horn, Wyatt sped downhill. The RV passed and he saw a white haired man with glasses behind the wheel.

"Go back!" Wyatt shouted, waving a hand.

The RV continued up.

In the red glow of his taillights, Wyatt watched a jumbled mass of mountain roil across the road. A rush of compressed air ahead of the slide shoved the truck sideways like an invisible road grader. He fought the wheel, expecting any second to be caught and crushed.

Ahead, the road curved to the right, out of the avalanche chute. Wyatt clutched the wheel and fought the pressure wave. A hail of rocks smashed his pickup's panels and the passenger side window took a hit and broke.

He wondered if he was going to make it.

● ● ●

Kyle lay in her hotel bed beneath a lamp's glow, unable to go back to sleep after believing she felt an earth tremor. Her watch said it was seven past twelve.

Maybe she was imagining things, for there was a rainstorm again like last night. She got up and went to the window, peeking around the curtain to keep from being a nude silhouette against the room light. Outside, rain slanted beneath the streetlamp's glow, breaking up the reflections on the pavement. A lone light burned in one of the cabins behind the hotel.

Maybe Nick was awake, too.

She stabbed her hands through her sleep-mussed hair. Working with him was going to be tricky. Although she'd turned down his offer of dinner, she wouldn't be able to avoid him forever. Thank goodness Wyatt was going into the backcountry with them.

Her stomach rumbled, protesting that her room service supper had been too light. Unfortunately, a quick mental inventory brought up nothing open in the park at this hour.

Five miles down to Gardiner, her hunger bargained. There was at least one twenty-four-hour gas-and-convenience store.

She dressed and left the hotel, driving the van past unlit office buildings, the post office and clinic. Down the hill around the hairpin turn, the campground was also dark as were most of the houses on the right side of the road.

Kyle recognized Wyatt's place. His porch light was on and though his Park Service Bronco was in the carport, his pickup was not there.

A Coke and one of the big chocolate bars with almonds drew her on toward town. One thing she wouldn't do anymore is chicken out because it was dark. Not after last night.

A sign welcomed her to Montana and she headed into Gardner Canyon. No cars were coming into the park at this hour. As she drove, she reconsidered . . . perhaps a loaf of bread and a jar of peanut butter.

Around the next curve, all thought of food was forgotten. Sound, sudden, a rumble rising into a roar. The primal note of landslide, a sound deeply embedded in her psyche, was enough to strike terror as she clenched the steering wheel.

The van seemed to be in awful slow motion and she froze with her foot poised between the accelerator and the brake. She didn't know if the danger was behind, in front, or about to strike her dead on as the cacophony filled the night.

Headlights appeared from around a curve, an RV coming up from below.

In the van's high beams, a mass of mud and rock tore across the road directly in front of her. Kyle watched the RV caught and bulldozed, lifted up onto its side, and shoved over the drop.

She jammed on the brakes, and the rear wheels lost

traction. The back end came around, swung sideways, and slid on the sheen of mud coating the pavement. The edge of the drop was close, too close.

Holding tight to the wheel, she watched the headlights arc through the night, expecting at any second to go past the point of no return.

With a jolt, the van came to rest against the mound of earth. Kyle's head jerked and she narrowly missed cracking it against the window. She expected the air bag to deploy, but it did not, probably because of the side impact.

A vision of telling Hollis the Institute's vehicle had been buried made her want to spin the wheel and accelerate away from the slide, but she cut the engine and left the headlights on as she leaped out. Her running shoes gave little traction on the slippery pavement and she nearly went down.

From her pocket, she pulled out her flashlight and played it over the irregular mound of mud, boulders, and felled trees. The RV must be under tons of rock, but she had to hope it might be lying somewhere down near the Gardner River.

The wind-driven rain renewed its assault and she pulled up the hood of her parka. She drew out her new cell phone and punched in 911, holding her other hand with the flashlight over the instrument to keep it from getting wet.

The dispatcher answered.

"There's been a landslide in Gardner Canyon," Kyle reported, finding it hard to talk and breathe at the same time.

"Someone else has just reported that."

Kyle looked around, but as there was no one in sight, she assumed the call came from down the canyon. "I'm on the upslope side where an RV went over the edge. No rescue vehicles can get up from Gardiner, so contact the Park Service to send help down."

"What is your exact location?"

"North of the Montana line, still inside the park. For God's sake, I've got to go check on some people." With a wet shiver, Kyle broke the connection. She decided to call Wyatt in case he was home for help, but her cell phone gave three sharp beeps and died.

Studying the broken landscape, she could see the slide blocked at least two thirds of the river. Water ponded behind the earthen dam, dark water that would be even blacker without her flashlight. The quick torrent already ate at the loose material.

She continued to play her light around. Then she gasped.

The rain-scattered glow revealed the wheels and chassis of the RV tilted toward the sky. It lay in an eerily unstable position, almost on its back. One headlight was buried, the other pointed into the heavens. The vehicle's rear end was in the river.

"Help!" Kyle heard thinly on the wind.

Sidestepping to avoid a fall, she hurried downslope. Her mind spun with things she wished she had with her, starting with the sturdy climbing rope she'd left in her bedroom at home.

As she drew nearer to the RV, someone cried out again.

Kyle slid to a stop on the downstream side. The engine still ran, giving off diesel fumes. The front of the passenger side was embedded in the slide, the window and part of the windshield buried. Through the driver's window at knee height, she saw two people crumpled on the ceiling that was now the floor.

She scrambled closer and saw the door about halfway back. It appeared to be clear, but she would have to climb over a huge boulder to get to it.

The rock was slippery and covered in sharp sand that tore at her hands. The traction of her running shoes was the only thing that got her to the top. About to make the four-foot drop that would put her in front of the door, she felt a little shift and went still, not sure whether to go or stay.

Slowly at first, then with gathering momentum, the rock started to roll. Kyle leaped and grabbed the metal panel on the side of the RV. The raw bottom edge, now at the top, felt like it would cut her fingers off as she dangled from it. Her dropped flashlight shined a half circle on glistening earth.

The boulder smashed the light, tumbled end over end, and landed with a splash fifteen feet below. From where she hung, Kyle couldn't see what else might be coming down the hill. The sharp edge of metal dug deeper into her palms.

She opened her hands.

When she landed, her legs sank calf-deep into muck. She struggled to free her uphill foot. When she tried to lift it, her other leg went in to the knee. Stretching up, she just missed being able to reach the door handle.

Kyle listened to the growl of the diesel and the river's rush. Transferring her weight from one foot to the other, she wriggled to try and free them. First one and then the other shoe and sock were sucked off in the mud as, inch by inch, she drew her legs and feet out.

The RV shifted, slipping farther down the hill. Praying it didn't roll and crush her beneath it, she grabbed for the door handle. Her stinging hands gritty on the metal, she yanked and it gave in her hand.

Kyle tumbled inside and smelled styrene from the paneling and carpet. She dragged herself up using a captain's chair hanging from what was now the ceiling. The RV sloped at a high angle, and in the light from the dash, she made out an elderly couple in matching jogging suits, kept from rolling back by the ceiling box containing the air conditioner. A dark smear in the man's silver hair might be blood.

"Hello!" Kyle called.

The woman gasped, "Thank God."

"Can you slide down to me?" Kyle called over the engine noise. "We can get out the door."

Before she finished speaking, the RV gave another shudder and lost at least five feet of freeboard. She wondered if this was it, but the vehicle hit another sticking point and stabilized with her up to her waist in cold river water.

The engine died.

"Come on," Kyle urged. "It may go any second."

Slowly, the vehicle began a sickening roll downhill onto the passenger side. The woman screamed. Kyle braced herself and went with the movement, realizing they would not be able to get out the door that had just been buried in the slide.

Now on its side, the RV stabilized once more.

"Halloo!" someone called from the front. A flashlight beamed in.

"Kick in the windshield," Kyle called.

She heard a sharp thud, then another. Nothing happened.

"I think you can push 'em out, but not in," said the RV's owner.

Kyle realized that the window behind the driver's seat was an option. She used the seatback to drag herself up and managed to shove up and out a two by two foot section of glass. Then she hung back and motioned to the trapped couple.

The woman shook her head, and Kyle realized that neither she nor her husband likely had the strength to pull up through the opening. As she cast about for an idea, Kyle recognized that the person outside was unfurling a rope and tossing it through the window.

The woman grabbed it and held on while her rescuer pulled. First her body and then her legs disappeared through the window. The pitch of the vehicle grew sharper, as it continued its slide into the river. Her husband managed to hold on to the frame and get out the window.

Another shift of the RV and Kyle lost her grip. She fell back down the steeply sloping ceiling into black water that was over her head . . .

❀ ❀ ❀

Dawn had not brought relief to six-year-old Kyle. Trapped in the tree by the Madison's floodwaters, she could see no sign of the Rambler, not even its roof. Tatters of yellow nylon decorated a nearby tree, suggesting the rush of wind ahead of the landslide had blasted her parents' tent from its moorings. The only familiar thing was the Coleman Lantern dangling from a rope in a tree canted at an extreme angle. As she watched, rising water covered it.

Despite the surrounding silence, she screamed and screamed until her throat was raw.

All night she'd held on, just like Mommy and Daddy would have wanted her to, knowing they would find her with the promise of light.

The waters touched her toes. She clutched the high thin trunk that already bent beneath her weight. Holding her breath as though that would make her lighter, she tried to shinny up a few more feet.

With a lurch, the tree bowed and deposited Kyle in the flood.

Never had she been in water this swift or foul, filled with boughs that brushed like writhing snakes, and tasting of earth when a great mouthful washed down her throat.

The current caught and carried her tumbling. The awful desperation for air forced her mouth open and she gasped in water. Choking, she drew in more and flailed wildly for the light.

Something solid hit her back and she came to a stop, pinned against something by the water's force. It shoved at her shoulders and dragged at her legs. Scrambling, clawing, sobbing, she flailed until she found purchase.

Gasping and fighting for every inch, she emerged from the flood onto the jumbled mass of landslide, where she lay on her stomach coughing and spitting up water. Morning became a lighter gray as she shrieked once more for Mom and Dad, Max, for somebody . . . anybody.

CHAPTER EIGHTEEN
SEPTEMBER 20

When Kyle surfaced inside the drowned RV, her chest muscles seized. Splashing ineffectively in her soaked clothing, she fended off floating sofa cushions that refused to support her weight and tried without success to find a handhold. A big mouthful washed down her windpipe.

A shout from above. "Grab the line!"

A wet splash. She floundered until her fingers found a rough coil. "I've got it," she gasped.

Slowly the rope went taut. One tedious inch at a time, Kyle began to come out of the water. Her sore and stinging hands protested, but she was not going to let go.

Just another foot to get purchase on the lip of the opening and she pulled herself painfully through to slide down the windshield.

She landed hard on rocks and mud. Barefoot, she hobbled onto the rocky slope away from the slide. Just as she was thinking of dropping and kissing the solid earth, the RV gave a final shudder and slid into the river.

Kyle did go down then, onto hands and knees. Nausea

came in hard waves, and she bent forward while a gush of river water poured from her mouth. The night spun around her.

A hand touched her shoulder. "You all right, ma'am?"

The uniformed Park Ranger who had answered her distress call helped her to her feet.

Though she wanted nothing more than to lean on him, she saw the shell-shocked look of the older couple. "I'm okay, but those folks . . ."

As the ranger assisted the RV's owners up the hill, the rain's pounding renewed. Kyle managed to make her way slowly back up to the road and retreated inside the van. Her khakis were soaked to a dark brown. Beneath her jacket, she was a candidate for a wet T-shirt contest.

After thanking the ranger and telling him she was staying at the hotel, she started the van and backed away from the slide. Up the hill at Wyatt's house, she stopped and picked her way carefully across the rocky lawn to the front door.

But though she rang his bell, knocked politely at first and then beat with her fist, no one came to the door. For good measure, she went around the darkened back of the house to the window she thought might be his bedroom. Using her keys, she rapped on the glass.

"Wyatt," she called through chattering teeth.

"Help you?" yelled an angry male from the front yard. His torch's beam was as bright as a headlight.

Thankful she hadn't been caught trying to open the

window, Kyle turned to him. "There's been a big landslide in the canyon. I was trying to wake Wyatt to tell him."

The man took a few steps closer.

"I'm Dr. Kyle Stone of the Utah Institute, in the park to do some fieldwork with Wyatt."

The interrogation light lowered and she made out a heavyset man, barefoot and wearing a plaid robe. He carried an umbrella she would gladly have wrestled him for.

"You look like you've got the field all over you." He gestured at her sopping, muddy clothes. His expression softened to one that seemed more kindly. "I live in the other side of the duplex. Guess Wyatt's not here."

"Do you know what time he left?"

"I don't keep track. I was asleep when you started up a racket."

With her cell phone DOA, she drove as fast as she could back to the hotel. There were no telephones in the rooms, part of the 'charming ambiance', but there was a pay kiosk in the lobby.

Her feet leaving a blood-tinged trail on the polished floor, she went to the phone in a hall at the rear near the hotel desk. She drew a credit card from her wallet and dialed directory assistance, getting more blood from her cut hands on both the card and the phone. "In Gardiner, Montana, please. I need the number for an Alicia Alvarez."

After a moment, the operator came back, "I'm sorry, but that number is unlisted."

Hanging up, Kyle backed against the opposite wall of

the deserted hall and tried to stem the rising tide of panic. Wyatt could be buried under tons of rock and not be discovered for days. She had to sound an alarm, get the road equipment out there in the middle of the night . . . she needed . . .

Behind the registration desk, a lone young woman in jeans and a crocheted top played Solitaire on the computer.

"Nicholas Darden," Kyle said. "Give me his cabin number."

"I'm sorry, ma'am, but . . ."

"Look, this is an emergency. I'm going to have to insist."

The clerk took in Kyle's disheveled state and wet clothes. "I guess I can get one of the guards to walk over there with you."

● ● ●

Nick couldn't sleep. He'd awakened around twelve-thirty, thinking maybe he felt an earth tremor. He'd also heard some kind of sound after he sat up, like a dump truck dropping a load somewhere in the Mammoth area.

Now that he was awake and thinking about quakes, he couldn't help but recall Brock Hobart and his press conference. Both earthquake seismology and volcanology had their folks that nobody seemed to take seriously. Yet, over beers and dinner that Nick had bought even though Brock's new moon was almost a week away, he had to admit that he had been intrigued.

Brock was correct in his observation of the large quakes

he had listed for the press, including Hebgen Lake. It was a fact that the gravitational and tidal forces he claimed as a catalyst profoundly affected all manner of earthly phenomena.

Nick himself believed in the reports of animal disturbances before humans detected a quake. He also knew tidal forces caused people to act strangely, when there was a full moon. ERs were always full that night with the victims of everything from cars running off the road to incidents of domestic violence.

One thing Nick had argued with Brock was his prediction of a quake as large as a 6.0 in the park. The movement of magma in most volcanic terrains did not spawn quakes that large unless there were some unusual circumstances like a superimposed active fault system.

Even so, after talking with Brock, the possibilities in Yellowstone looked exciting. The seismic records showed a definite ramping up of activity, enough that Colin had decided to send him here. And the unfortunate death of David Mowry, whose books Nick had devoured, made it somehow personal.

Seeing Kyle again after all these years brought it damned close to home.

The last week of field camp, he and she had been mapping partners. With over ten square miles of mountain to cover, they set out to identify the geological formations. On their second day out, Nick discovered a small overhang of pink quartzite cliff in the Jurassic Nugget Formation, where a small spring had encouraged aspen. It started out as just a shady place to rest, until he tugged at the knot of Kyle's halter-top.

For the rest of the season, they took their lunch break in the cool privacy.

Nick stared at the dark wood ceiling. Could this cabin be the very one where he and Kyle had stayed? It seemed to him that the rustic box had been on the end of row like this was.

A nostalgic ache spread through him. He'd been smitten enough to carry her across the threshold, and at that perfect moment in space and time, he'd meant everything the gesture implied.

Someone knocked on his door. Nick sat up in bed, thinking nobody could get his room number . . . unless Kyle had eavesdropped when he checked in. Warmed by that possibility, he shoved back the covers and headed for the door.

❋ ❋ ❋

As the hotel security guard paused with his hand raised to knock again, Kyle heard Nick's voice through the cabin door. "Who's there?"

"It's me." She spoke to the wooden panel.

The outside light came on and Nick opened the door wearing a pair of boxers. His body was as compact and muscular as Kyle remembered, his nipples tight against the night chill.

"There's been a landslide in Gardner Canyon," she said. "The highway is blocked. I think there must have been an earthquake, maybe several."

With a gesture, Nick dismissed the guard and drew her in out of the weather. "I thought I heard something a while ago."

When he failed to turn on an inside light, she limped over and switched on a lamp.

"My God." His green eyes darted from her wet hair to her bare feet. "Are you all right?"

"I think so. I was on my way to Gardiner for a snack when . . . the mountain came down."

Nick started toward her and seemed to realize he was less than dressed. Turning away, he scooped up a pair of sweat pants and drew them on.

She spoke to his back. "I helped get some people out of their RV after it got swept into the river. Lost my shoes in the mud."

Still bare-chested, Nick turned and stared at her. "No wonder you look like that. Get out of those wet clothes and into my shower before you catch your death."

Kyle wasn't deterred from the reason she'd come. "Wyatt's not at his house . . ."

Nick's jaw set. "You make a habit of dropping by in the middle of the night?"

"After I left the slide, I came back up to his place."

Nick picked up a shirt and slid his arms into the sleeves.

His brusque motions suggested he was irked at not being the first person she sought after such a close call. "From what I saw when I got here," he said, "you two are pretty tight."

Though something had felt different today in Wyatt's office, especially when he'd touched her cheek, an automatic denial rose to her lips. "He's got a gal. A lady who works with Wolf Advocates."

"That's where he is, then." Nick walked toward her, smiling once more.

"He must be with Alicia," she said, "but I tried to call and her number's unlisted."

"Think," Nick urged. "What are the chances you and Wyatt were both on the canyon road at the exact moment of the slide?"

Considering how she'd overreacted during the storm at her home last night and again during the earth tremor when she was in the chapel, Kyle nodded reluctant agreement.

With his shirt unbuttoned, Nick stood before her. In the lamp's glow, he looked impossibly young as he gestured to the rustic wood walls. "Think this might be the same cabin?"

"Don't know."

He moved forward, and despite her sodden condition, he slipped his hands inside her jacket to barely graze the sides of her waist. "There's nothing we can do about Wyatt or the landslide tonight."

Nick's touch resonated along her nerves the way his voice had when she'd first heard it again this afternoon.

How tempting it would be to go into his arms, but some deeper instinct warned she couldn't simply start up where they'd left off.

She raised her hands to gesture him away.

"You're bleeding," Nick said sharply, grabbing her wrists and turning her palms up.

She stepped back. If he started ministering to her wounds, she'd still be in this room at dawn. "I've got first aid supplies in my bag . . . I shouldn't have awakened you."

"Kyle . . . wait . . ."

Before she could change her mind, she let herself out into the night. The wind had picked up, colder and dryer as the clouds began to break apart. As she walked away from Nick's cabin, and she did believe it was the same one they'd shared so long ago, a little voice told her he was right. Wyatt was warm and secure in bed with Alicia.

And she was playing the fool to walk away from Nick's offer of the same thing.

For a moment, she almost turned back, but reason said it would be like jumping into black and icy water, with no sense how far down the bottom lay.

Kyle started toward the hotel. With her feet already wet and achingly tender, she slogged despondently through freezing puddles in the parking lot.

From somewhere up on Sepulcher Mountain above the hot springs came a howl that prickled her skin into goose bumps. She'd heard a lot of coyotes, but this full-throated call sounded as though it came from a larger animal. One of those wolves Alicia and her fellow workers had brought in from Canada to repopulate the predator system.

An answering howl from behind the hotel reminded Kyle that as soon as they were provisioned, she, Nick, and Wyatt would be on their way into the Yellowstone back-country.

All her muscles knotted in anticipation. Going back to Earthquake Lake had not had the desired effect of laying her ghosts. Rather, they had risen up to taunt her, turning her into a crazy woman who climbed out windows into rainstorms and tried to call Wyatt's girlfriend in the middle of the night.

A wolf bayed again. A quarter-moon shone in the clearing sky, each day shrinking toward Brock Hobart's next alignment.

● ● ●

Wyatt rapped his knuckles on the door of Alicia's townhouse beside the Yellowstone River in Gardiner. He was still sopping, though the rain had let up. The point was driven home when she opened her door and gasped, "What happened?"

"Landslide at the canyon bend."

"You could have been killed."

"Baby, for a minute I thought I had been." He stepped inside, his rain-soaked clothes dripping onto the tile floor. Running his truck heater full blast on the way down hadn't chased away the cold, or the edginess at realizing how close to disaster he'd been.

As soon as he was in the clear, he'd stopped and used his cell to call 911 and report the slide. Then he waited for the emergency crews, standing in the road with his flashlight to stop anyone coming up, before they rounded a blind curve and crashed into the dam across the highway.

"Come into the kitchen." Alicia wore a leopard print robe gathered at her waist with a black satin sash. It gapped to permit a glimpse of her breasts while she pushed Wyatt's parka from his shoulders and hung it over a kitchen chair. Turning back to him, she struggled his T-shirt out of his waistband and up over his chest. He raised his arms to let her draw it over his head.

"Take off those wet jeans and get straight in the shower." The wind had soaked his pant legs to the crotch.

When he finally came out of the bath, replete from the blessed solace of hot water, she waited with a steaming mug of something to drink. He laid his glasses on the nightstand and the candles giving off a sandalwood aroma became wavering points of light.

Alicia fussed over him and gave him sips of green tea he determined was laced with brandy. He got naked beneath the smooth covers and drank tea again, thinking of asking for more brandy.

Before he could, Alicia walked out of the room and came back with the bottle. She poured for them both and slid in beside him, her warm flesh slippery through silk.

She kissed him and her lips clung in a way that pushed back the danger and the cold night.

She raised her head and looked into his eyes. "I love you," she whispered.

Wyatt ran both hands through his hair, parting its damp waves. He swallowed and resisted the impulse to clear his throat. The last time he'd told Marie he loved her, it had been the rote habit of the long married. He hadn't really listened to himself, and neither, apparently, had she. Less than two days later he came home from the fabricating company and found his wife and her clothes gone.

Alicia waited, the air seeming to thicken between them. Her dark eyes shone with hope.

It would be so easy to go with the flow, but long habit kept him from committing without thinking things through. There was one thing, though, that she might appreciate.

He pushed himself upright in bed, jostling her. "Could you find my keys?"

Her eyes narrowed and she flounced out of bed, shoving the bedroom door open a little harder than necessary. "Need your wallet, too?" she called. "It's pretty wet."

"Just the keys."

Alicia came back and sat on the edge of the bed as he sorted the jangling mass. Hoping she'd understand there were words he couldn't say, he twisted the ring and removed the extra house key. "You should have one of these. Look out for the place while I'm gone."

Wyatt drew her down in bed and snuggled her against

his side, feeling fortunate at tonight's narrow escape. Considering he, Kyle, and Nick were going into the back-country for the new moon, he had to hope Brock Hobart was a head case.

CHAPTER NINETEEN
SEPTEMBER 20

Early in the morning, Wyatt drove his pickup around the vehicles queued at Yellowstone's north entrance. "Morning, Teri," he greeted the female ranger who waved him through the employee gate and returned to turning away tourists in the traffic line.

With the main road from Gardiner to Mammoth closed by the slide, only Park Service workers would be permitted to take a dirt track up through the hills, a route that had been the historic access into the park. As Wyatt turned his truck onto the road usually reserved for one-way downhill, he checked his rearview mirror for Alicia in her Navigator. She was meeting some clients at the hotel for a wolf watching tour.

This morning he'd awakened to find her pressed against him, her arm twined across his chest. When she told him again that she loved him, eyes gleaming, he had smothered her words with a kiss.

As for why he was holding back, he reminded himself she was used to Dior while he led a simple ranger's life. Though both of them were originally raised on ranches, hers was a broad expanse of South Texas scrub, home to her father's collection of purebred Angus and exotic imported Axis and Fallow deer. Wyatt came from hardscrabble acreage in a valley north of Bozeman where his father and he had taken care of chores morning and evening.

Yet, while he drove over the sage covered hills, he decided his reluctance to commit had nothing to do with their diverse backgrounds. Alicia was a trouper who enjoyed fieldwork. Her neat townhouse in Gardiner wasn't ostentatious, and her outdoor clothing came from the same catalogs he shopped.

They could make things work. There was no reason not to . . . except for the vague yearning that stirred in his chest at the memory of Kyle's troubled eyes, and her recent refusal to talk freely to him.

Wyatt pressed the accelerator. The final leg of the uphill track wound back down above Mammoth. From this elevated vantage point, it looked like a toy town thrown together from different game sets, ancient buildings mixed with modern.

As he emerged from the dirt road onto the paved parking lot, he passed the hotel where Kyle and her old flame had spent the night.

❋ ❋ ❋

Kyle greeted the ranger raising the United States flag outside Park Headquarters. With last night's rain a memory, the sun had risen over the tabular top of Mt. Everts. A rime of predawn ice was melting from rooftops and parked vehicles.

At her side, Nick moved lithely through the frosted grass, his boots making crunching noises. He raised his arms over his head and stretched like a cat, expanding his chest to inhale deeply. Following his lead, Kyle took in the bracing air, though she walked more gingerly, her feet sore from the stone bruises she'd gotten on the slide.

"You still worried about Wyatt?" he asked.

Before she could reply, she followed his gaze across the lawns to the Resource Center. In front of the building, Wyatt was getting out of the Bronco.

She shouted his name. He turned and she waved, resisting the impulse to run over and hug him.

Wyatt waited for them outside the entry. With a glance at Nick, he said, "I trust you passed a pleasant evening."

"And an even better night," Nick rejoined.

"That's more than I can say for myself." Wyatt thrust his thumbs into his jacket pockets and leaned against a porch post. "After midnight I was driving down to see Alicia"—did Kyle imagine a faint emphasis on his girl's name?—"when the side of the mountain came down into Gardner Canyon."

Kyle gasped. "I was driving down, too, and almost got wiped out by the slide."

Wyatt's dark eyes held hers. "Are you all right?"

She kept her bandaged hands in her pockets. "For some reason I was scared for you. As though I knew you were out there too."

She became aware of Nick scrutinizing them.

Suddenly, Wyatt pushed off the post and nodded at something behind her. "Company."

Kyle turned to see the *Billings Live Eye* van pulling up.

Wyatt started toward the outer doors of the arctic entry. "After the way they twisted my words yesterday, I think I'll let someone else handle them."

Reporter Carol Leeds jumped out the van's passenger door at the same time Brock Hobart stepped onto the north end of the porch. "There you are," she called to him.

"Guess if you won't oblige her, cowboy, old Brock'll have to do." Nick gave a theatrical sigh. "And here I thought they were looking for me."

Brock moved to stand in front of the Resource Center sign, making it look like the freelance earthquake predictor was sanctioned. In casual clothes and thick-soled boots, he posed as every inch the field geologist.

"Chop, chop, Larry," Carol called and waited while her ponytailed cameraman brought out his equipment. As soon as he signaled ready, she began, "I'm here this morning in Yellowstone with scientist Brock Hobart, talking about last night's landslide that blocked the main northern road into the park. Apparently, no one was hurt, but the highway will require extensive repair before reopening." She put the microphone in front of Brock.

He looked appropriately grave. "I've checked the Yellowstone Seismic Network and determined an earthquake of magnitude 2.7 happened last night at 12:07 AM local time with a 3.1 following at 12:29. The first report of the landslide came in from a motorist with a cell phone just minutes later."

Carol broke in. "Could this have been the quake you predicted?"

Brock shook his head. "The new moon's not for another five days."

Kyle felt a chill that wasn't entirely from the brisk wind. "I've had enough of this."

Nick snagged her wrist. "Come on," he murmured. "See the rest of the circus."

She stayed in place and noted that Wyatt did, too. A few moments later, she regretted it, for Carol Leeds spotted them watching and lost interest in Brock. "Ranger Ellison," she called. "I understand you were first on the scene last night."

"How in hell do they do that?" Wyatt asked as he opened the Resource Center's front door.

"They managed to miss that I was there," Kyle told him.

Cameraman Larry filmed their retreat into the building, getting footage of Iniki Kuni at her desk. The Chief Ranger's daughter looked pale as she gestured with ringed fingers adorned with chipped black nail polish. She wore a half a dozen earrings and one in her nose, which Kyle thought would go a long way for Yellowstone PR.

"Dr. Ellison!" Carol's voice was shrill. "If I may?"

"You may not." Wyatt ushered Kyle and Nick into his

office and closed the door in her face.

As soon as it shut, Nick began to laugh.

Wyatt went behind his desk and checked the seismic records. He reported that, of course, Brock had pulled the correct information off the website. "Looks like the first tremor loosened the hillside and the second sent it down the canyon," he concluded.

"Let's talk about getting into the field." Nick tapped his foot.

Wyatt reached for a yellow legal pad and a pen. "It's going to take at least today and tomorrow to get provisions ready for the backcountry. One mule can carry two of the plastic, weather-resistant boxes with components of the seismic stations. We'll need ten or twelve mules . . . our wrangler will drive them up and back. I'll set up horses for me and the two of you."

"I thought we got that straight yesterday," Nick said.

Wyatt grinned at Kyle. "You mean Dr. Nicholas Darden fucking hates horses?" To Nick, "It's tamer than surfing."

Kyle figured Wyatt wanted Nick in the saddle to even the playing field a bit. After all, Nick's disdain for a lowly park ranger, even one with a freshly minted Ph.D., was obvious.

"Come on, guys," she interjected. "Without a helicopter . . ."

A muscle jumped in the side of Nick's jaw. He looked at her. "Do you ride?"

"Passably," she allowed.

There was a short silence as Nick seemed to digest that there was no way he could get into the field without playing along. "Bring on the bridle," he said. "I'll ride whatever you've got."

Next, they made a list: solar generator to run the computer, fuel, food, and camping gear. Kyle made a mental note to get a new climbing rope to replace the one she'd left home.

"Winter weather is setting in at elevation," Wyatt warned. "We'll make base camp at the Nez Perce patrol cabin, a log structure without much insulation. When the fire burns down at night, it'll be cold near 10,000 feet."

"What about the horses?" Nick put in.

"Lucky for you, the cabin has a little horse barn and corral."

Wyatt tore off a page from the pad that was thick with writing. "Kyle, how about if you and Nick shop for provisions? I'll make arrangements for the pack train and the seismic equipment."

Before she could take the paper from his hand, the office door banged open.

"What in the world were you thinking?" demanded a wiry, black-haired woman wearing a Park Service uniform of dark trousers and gray shirt. "Slamming the door in a reporter's face?"

Wyatt shoved back his chair and stood with a glance at his still shuddering door. "It happens I was careful not to slam it, Superintendent Bolido. But after the way they twisted our interview yesterday, I didn't want to risk letting anything out that might scare the tourists . . ." He extended a hand. "Wyatt Ellison, by the way."

She ignored his gesture of introduction and Wyatt gestured to Kyle and Nick who remained seated. "Dr. Kyle Stone of the Utah Institute and Dr. Nicholas Darden of USGS."

The Superintendent barely nodded in their direction. "Just now, *Billings Live Eye* came to my office. They wanted to know what the geology department is covering up after Brock Hobart's prediction of a 6.0."

"I'm not hiding a thing," Wyatt replied. "Ask whatever you want."

She stared at him for a long moment and then seemed to decide on a different management approach. Ruffling her hair, she inhaled deeply. "Okay."

Nick rose gracefully and offered his chair in a manner Kyle thought bordered on caricature.

The Superintendent appeared to be charmed by him. "Sorry, I'm Janet Bolido."

"I gathered as much," he replied with a grin.

Janet responded to Nick with an answering lift of her lips and sank into the chair beside Kyle.

"Dr. Stone," she said. "Dr. Ellison. I'm pleased to meet you all."

"We're mounting a geologic expedition into the park interior . . ."

Janet broke in. "Can we start with this big quake Brock Hobart says is coming?"

"I used to work with Brock at USGS," Kyle said, "but now he's considered beyond the pale by most serious scientists."

Wyatt nodded. "The publicity surrounding David Mowry's death probably attracted him here."

Kyle bent forward. "But nobody can do what he is claiming."

Nick, watching them volley over tented fingers, put in, "All we can say is we've had a swarm of activity. Some caldera swelling."

Janet held up a hand. "Speak English."

Briefly, Kyle gave a thumbnail sketch of Yellowstone geology, which she thought Janet should have been up on before coming to the park. She concluded with, "An increase in seismic activity might lead to a large earthquake or even a magma explosion."

"You mean an eruption?" Janet shrilled. "As in a volcano?"

"The park is virtually the planet's largest volcano. There have been many eruptions before and will certainly be again."

Nick cleared his throat. "When people like Hobart say a 6.0 is coming, we can't say it's not. Usually the deadline passes and the predictor goes home, but who can say?"

"What do you think is going to happen?" Janet's sun-weathered brow furrowed.

"I don't know." Nick shook his head. "A quake of over magnitude 5.0 would be unusual in volcanic terrain, but who's to say with the park's complex geology?"

Since Wyatt had told her of Janet's reluctance to frighten tourists, Kyle now sensed the Superintendent was hearing what she wanted in their uncertainty. So she said, "Something you should be aware of. Last night's Gardner Canyon landslide happened at the time of a 3.1 magnitude earthquake."

"The press told me," Janet said. "And asked whether the slide was connected to the quake. I said I didn't know."

"You don't," Nick agreed. "It was raining to beat hell, wet enough to destabilize any steep slope."

Janet tapped a square-tipped nail on the desk. "I'm beginning to think you don't know much."

Kyle felt a flush of heat and saw a dull red appear on Wyatt's cheekbones.

"Not you folks in particular," Janet tempered. "But geology doesn't sound like a very exact science. Why should I pay for fieldwork when you can get funding from"—she pointed at Nick—"USGS."

He looked regretful. "I wasn't authorized to bring Volcano Hazards' checkbook."

"Just the thing to kick off our Wonderland campaign," Janet said glumly. "Volcano Hazards."

With his sacred cow being gored, Nick became animated. "Scientists tend to monitor areas of unrest from a distance, like Kyle's network of seismic stations. Pilots run traverses measuring gravity and magnetics."

He pointed at the Superintendent. "But Lady, when earthquake zones or volcanoes wake from slumber, you go to the field."

CHAPTER TWENTY
SEPTEMBER 22

"Aren't there service roads in the park?" Nick groused.

Kyle suppressed a smile and watched him stand well back as Wyatt unloaded a horse from one of the trailers. In the low meadow near Pelican Creek, last night's frost had melted to dewdrops on the grass.

"There are some roads." Wyatt patted the russet rump of a black-maned stallion. "I thought you'd rather rough it."

Nick turned away, drew his Volcano Hazards ball cap lower over his eyes and said no more. Evidently, he recalled the cardinal rule of not bitching in the field.

"Actually, where we're going there are only trails," Wyatt relented with a sidelong glance from under his uniform hat. "Okay, boy," he murmured, as the horse's hooves clattered down the trailer ramp. "Meet Thunder."

The big bay tossed his head and Wyatt let him dance on his slack lead. Thunder surged past, flicked his tail at a fly, and swished Nick's face.

The muleteer chuckled. His remuda of twelve long-eared animals stood patiently, each bearing several hundred pounds of equipment and supplies.

"Thunder isn't for Nick?" Kyle hoped Wyatt wouldn't have pulled such a stunt.

"Course not. Got a smoky gelding out of the stables, one they use for greenhorn lessons. Gray's his name." He gestured toward the sedate-looking animal. "Matches his personality."

From where he stood a respectable ten feet from Gray, Nick said, "Yeah, but what'll I do if this guy spooks?"

"I'd say old Gray's almost guaranteed not to." Wyatt chewed a piece of straw. "Almost, because with horses there's never a sure thing."

The muleteer laughed again. "I'll stick with my plodding girls."

Despite Gray's reputed passive nature, Nick gave him cautious looks all through the short and not-so-sweet riding instruction from Wyatt.

Kyle spent the time getting familiar with the gait of Strawberry, a sweet roan filly with a bit of spunk. Though Franny had taught her to ride when she was seven, she had not been on a horse in some years. Fortunately, it wasn't something easily forgotten.

As they got under way on the gentle terrain, their pace was easy. Flocks of migratory ducks and geese were on the wing, their calls punctuating the rhythmic thud of hooves. Where the horses' passage crushed the sage, a pungent scent rose from silver-green leaves.

Despite Kyle's reluctance at heading into the backcountry, she enjoyed the crystalline blue of morning sky.

As they rode into the forest, she caught a glimpse of Mary's Bay through the trees. At the northeast end of Yellowstone Lake, the smooth curve of shore marked where the reaction of hot rock with cold ground water had produced a steam explosion only 14,000 years ago.

As the trail steepened on the incline to Mist Creek Pass, Kyle rode between the two men. Wyatt sat tall in the saddle, looking official in his uniform. Tourists did not carry firearms in the park, but he wore a holstered pistol on his hip.

Nick rode more sloppily, alternately holding himself up in the saddle and slumping over Gray. After a while, he began to cover his unease with bravado, one exotic story following another from his field career.

"So there I was at Kilauea next to this molten river of lava," he said when they got back on the horses after a lunch stop. "The levee broke and spilled a flood right toward me."

Kyle smiled, for the thick Hawaiian lava was usually easy to avoid.

"I was a goner, for sure," Nick spun, "until I made it onto a little rise. Stood there and watched the stuff run around my private island, all the time wondering if my boots would catch fire."

"Guess it all worked out." Wyatt effectively cut off the tale.

They drew up in a clearing to rest the horses. Though Kyle and Wyatt dismounted, Nick remained on Gray's back with one hand on the saddle horn. Squinting up at him in the midday light, Kyle noted that aside from being a bit more sun-beaten, his once-familiar hands had not changed; square nails cut short, a little scar on the left wrist. He'd told her it came from teasing the neighborhood tomcat when he was nine.

Deliberately, she looked away. When he'd spanned her waist in his cabin and she'd run, he'd let the matter drop. Now, she didn't know whether to be glad or sad that he gone back to treating her with the teasing manner he'd used on everyone at field camp . . . no matter whether they were provision shopping, packing, or sharing two night's unromantic hamburger dinners in the Mammoth grill.

They traveled deeper into the wilderness. The trail, a corridor through tall trees, became hypnotic as Indian summer sun cast shadow stripes. In another half-hour, the caravan reached the crest of Mist Creek Pass.

After another rest, they wound down to the confluence of Cold Creek with the Lamar River, eleven miles out from the trailhead. The skyline on the valley's opposite wall was dominated by Nez Perce Peak, looking peaceful in the golden light. The side facing them sported enormous blocks of talus, tumbled rocks as big as houses. The crown of the peak, clearly a cinder cone, was bare and smooth, already snowcapped. It dropped away rapidly into three sharp spines of ridges. The great radial dikes of dark rock had been emplaced while liquid, oozing along zones of geologic weakness.

While Kyle and the others paused to appreciate the tranquil yet majestic beauty, there came the clacking of stone against stone, an avalanche of boulders rearranging the mountain's west slope.

● ● ●

Three hours later, Kyle released the rope that held her duffel bag behind Strawberry's saddle. Tired and sore, she was dismayed by her first sight of the Nez Perce Patrol Cabin.

"It looks ancient," she said to Wyatt.

He chuckled. "The system of backcountry cabins dates to the late 1800s. The Army set up 'snowshoe cabins' for winter anti-poaching patrols."

Accepting that she'd stayed in a more rustic accommodation, Kyle studied the high valley. The cabin sat in a meadow above the Saddle Valley separating Nez Perce Peak from the Little Saddle and Saddle Mountain complex to the north. They'd come up through a steep-walled canyon, but at higher elevation, the terrain smoothed out. Behind the cabin rose a steep and forested slope, while above towered the terminal end of the easternmost dike.

Wyatt and the muleteer dismounted and started carrying boxes though the cabin door. Nick sat atop Gray as though gauging the distance to the ground.

"You getting off here or making the round trip?" Kyle asked.

"Not sure."

She dumped her duffel and extended a hand. "Come on, I'll help you."

Wyatt's laugh rang out from the split log front porch.

Nick ignored Kyle's offer and slid to the ground. "The eagle has landed."

Wyatt helped the muleteer ease the load off another of the pack animals. "You just gonna stand around looking pretty?" he asked Nick, shouldering his burden.

As afternoon shadows lengthened and the gear was unloaded, the muleteer said his goodbyes. "You folks be careful with that big quake coming."

Kyle's spine prickled as the mules moved off compliantly downhill.

Wyatt saw to the horses, bringing out picket pins from the load and staking the animals out to forage. They'd brought pellets and grain to supplement the autumn grasses.

While Nick chopped firewood, Kyle set up the kitchen and threw a blanket over the ancient sprung sofa that was the cabin's token attempt at luxury. She checked the supplies that remained with the place full time. Canned food, bottled water with a skim of ice from last night's freeze, blankets, windproof matches, and a signal flare kit.

Kyle opened the plastic weatherproof bag and drew out the red pistol with a black handgrip. The aerial flares were 12-gauge and looked like shotgun shells. The label promised the red distress flares to be 15,000 candlepower with a burn time of six seconds.

Thoughtfully, she put everything back where she'd

found it, recalling her conversation with Wyatt about flares and smoke signals. Nez Perce Peak had been named, along with Nez Perce Creek farther west in the park because a portion of the tribe had passed this way in 1877. Pursued by the U.S. Army, they fled across three states after refusing to go on to a reservation. According to Franny, Kyle's great-grandfather had ridden with the tribe as a child and somehow escaped their capture and subsequent incarceration in the equivalent of concentration camps.

When it started to get dark, Kyle went back out to help Wyatt. Together, they put the horses into the small stable where they'd be safe from bears, filled their feed buckets, and gave them a drink from one of the plastic water barrels they'd packed in.

When she and Wyatt returned to the cabin where Nick was stacking wood on the porch, she asked, "Shall we fire the generator?" The portable electric plant put out 1,500 watts, enough to power their computer and light the cabin's main room from a utility light.

Wyatt, in charge of logistics, shook his head. "Need to conserve fuel."

Kyle went to the bunkroom and transferred one of her flashlights from her duffel to the pocket of her pants. When darkness deepened, she did not ask, but fueled and lit a Coleman lantern to hang above the table.

Nick had drawn the short straw and had to cook the first meal. While he opened cans of pork and beans and set out store-bought bread that would go stale in a few days,

Kyle worked on an equipment inventory.

Each of the new permanent field stations would consist of the seismograph, to be placed in a hole about three feet deep to isolate it from surface disturbances and wind noise. The foam used to pack the equipment would be used to line the hole to further reduce signals from the wind. Wired to the seismograph was the digital acquisition system, or DAS. A GPS clock synchronized systems around the world to the exact time, and solar panels charged auto batteries to provide power. All the components would be packed into the weatherproof chests that had been used to transport them, strapped on the mules.

Her inventory complete, Kyle used the satellite phone to check email.

A note from Leila said Stanton's condition had stabilized and he'd been moved to a less critical care status. He had been briefly conscious and Leila was certain he recognized her. With her throat feeling thick and her eyes stinging, Kyle composed a reply.

So glad to hear Stanton has improved. Wyatt and I are pulling for him. We arrived today at the Nez Perce Patrol cabin in the Absarokas east of Yellowstone Lake. The ride up was beautiful. Hope the weather holds.

Her fingers paused over the laptop keyboard.

Nick Darden . . . you remember me telling you about him over too many glasses of wine? You won't believe this, but Colin Gruy sent him to help us out. The cocky you-know-what didn't even recognize me at first . . .

Kyle stopped typing and looked at what she'd written. She could well imagine all the questions Leila would come back with on this one. And if Nick happened to be looking at the computer when a message about him came in . . .

She backspaced and erased the last paragraph.

Xi Hong reported in from an Internet café in Yuzhno-Sakhalinsk, but said he would be out of touch when he went into the field. She sent a newsy message about their project, telling him about everything including Nick's arrival, omitting only their past relationship.

Finally, there was an incoherent rant from Hollis Delbert, damning both her ethics for stealing his equipment and casting aspersions on Radford Bullis for not forcing her to return it.

Her fingers poised over the keyboard to compose a scathing reply, but instinct told her to choose her battles.

Next, Kyle checked the seismic patterns for the park stations already in place. To her surprise, things had quieted since the day before.

"Nick," she said.

"Yo." He turned from where he was stirring beans in a cast-iron Dutch oven over the fire.

"Look at this."

With a graceful motion, he rose and came to study first one and then another of ten stations. "There's the event that sent those rocks down the mountain earlier." He pointed to a sharp excursion on the chart from Pelican Cone, a mountain they had passed on the trail a few miles east. "Other than that, things look pretty still."

There was no concrete reason to argue, but Kyle felt as if she could sense the unsettled pulse of the earth. Though she tried telling herself she had overreacted before, it didn't help.

Leaving her at the laptop, Nick went back to dinner prep. A few minutes later, she had to move the computer off the table for chow call. Although the steaming plates of beans appeared appetizing, there was no butter, salt, or pepper, nor anything set out to drink. Nick sat and started to eat while Kyle poured bottled water and Wyatt collected condiments from a cardboard box.

After forking up a mouthful of beans, Wyatt reached for the salt. "Cook much?"

Nick scowled. "You a *cordon bleu* chef, as well as the consummate horseman?"

"That's enough!" Kyle said.

Wyatt's expression went dark. "What's enough?"

"It's going to be a long goddamn field season if you two keep at each other's throats." Although she was hungry, she shoved back her chair. The definitive firmness with which she shut the cabin door behind her was not quite a bang.

In the stable, the horses nickered softly. Ignoring their invitation for company, or more likely a plea for extra oats, she studied the night. The sky, that had been clear earlier, was overcast. Toward the Nez Perce summit, the towering dike was blacker than the rest of the sky.

Kyle pulled out her flashlight and turned it on. From inside, she heard Nick and Wyatt's voices continue to mingle in acrimony.

A moment later, boots clomped toward the door. She placed her light on the rail with the beam pointed outward and hugged herself against the chill.

The door behind her creaked the way it had when she'd come out. With her back to it, she felt the feathery cloud of her down coat settle over her shoulders. Not knowing which man was behind her, she inhaled the sharpness of impending weather. "I smell snow."

"That time of year." Wyatt moved in front of her and glanced at her flashlight. "Think that'll keep the bears away?"

"Something like that."

He eased onto the porch rail, crossed his long legs at the ankles, and nodded toward the closed cabin door. "Seriously, what are we going to do with Dr. Nicholas?"

Thinking this was about turf or resenting outside interference, she tried to set him straight. "Colin sent Nick to help. He was doing us a favor."

"Do you always have to be so damned reasonable?"

Something Stanton had told her when she was a student came back. "You don't go to work to make your friends."

Wyatt's easy posture dissolved, and he came to his feet. "You and Nick were more than friends."

The sting of accusation surprised her, starting an unsettled feeling in her chest. To hide it, she studied the clouds, billowy bellies pregnant with snow. "When Nick saw me in your office, he didn't even recognize me."

Wyatt's look was steady. "You sure as hell remember him."

The first flakes swirled.

Wyatt went back inside, shutting the door with crisp deliberation.

Kyle slammed her hand against the log wall and immediately regretted it. She'd taken the bandages off her cuts only this morning and now the deepest one started bleeding again. She also managed to get a wood splinter near the base of her thumb. Sucking her palm and biting at it only served to push the sliver in deeper.

It was unlike Wyatt to take such an active dislike to someone, and in her past experience, most men liked Nick's pleasant mix of banter and bullshit. Though she heard no voices inside, she stayed out a while longer watching the snowfall.

Someone clattered dishes and she figured her ill manners had been punished by missing the rest of her dinner. It couldn't be helped, though. She needed to cool off so she wouldn't be angry with Wyatt for pointing out the unvarnished truth.

Yes, she remembered Nick. For all these years, each summer rainstorm had made her imagine him on a Wyoming mountain, soaking wet and trying to struggle a poncho out of his pack, yet laughing. On every camping trip she took, the unique waxy smell of a tent's interior took her back to their hideout in the woods. Year by year, September brought the memory of her heartbreak upon reading his final letter.

When she went back in, the Coleman lantern gave a rasping low fuel warning. The dishes were stacked in the drainer. Wyatt stood in front of the fire, his rangy legs apart. He'd changed from his uniform into black sweats that emphasized his lean body.

Nick was not in sight.

Wordlessly, she tossed her jacket onto the couch and went to the kitchen where she made and ate a peanut-but-ter-and-jelly fold-over. In the light from the lantern, she poked again at the splinter and grimaced.

Wyatt glanced over his shoulder and came to her. Peering through his glasses at the small wound, he extracted a Swiss Army Knife from his pocket, pulled out the tweezers and went to work. As he concentrated, a line appeared between his dark brows.

After a minute of prodding that burned and stung, he said, "There." With the fragment of wood out, she thought he studied her palm longer than necessary.

"Thank you," she said.

The lantern sputtered out.

Standing in the dimness with Wyatt still holding her hand, she forgot to be alarmed at the lack of light. The dying fire's illumination accentuated his cheekbones and she became aware that with both of them barefoot, he was several inches taller than she.

With his free hand, he drew off his glasses and perched them on top his head. Her stomach fluttered with a disconcerting feeling foreign to their prior easy friendship.

He let her fingers go. "You need to get a fresh bandage on that cut."

From the first aid box in the kitchen, he pulled out a flesh-toned strip and helped her position it over her wound. Then they went back to standing side by side before the hearth. When the front of her legs grew uncomfortable, she turned around to cook the other side.

Though she'd been on dozens of fieldtrips, sleeping ten to a motel room in her school days, sharing cabins and tents in close quarters, this was different. She felt a deep reluctance to climb into her sleeping bag in the bunk above Nick's and only a few feet away from Wyatt. There was an intimacy to the arrangement that almost made her want to drag her bag out and sleep on the sofa. Already unsettled by Wyatt's attitude, she both feared and anticipated that she might catch the scent of Nick's skin, a mix of musk and spice that wasn't soap or aftershave. From the next room came the distinct sound of him clearing his throat.

Wyatt looked toward the door. "I think I'll turn in."

Kyle watched the embers until she heard the two men's mingled deep breathing. Even then, it was a long time before she lit her candle lantern, suspended it from the bed frame, and slid into her sleeping bag. Sure enough, she smelled the essence of Nick.

Wyatt threw out his arm in a restless motion.

Difficult as the chemistry was between the three of them, she was glad she wasn't alone on the mountain.

CHAPTER TWENTY-ONE

SEPTEMBER 23

"Where's Nick wandered off to?" Wyatt asked Kyle the next afternoon in the field.

"Don't know." She scanned the rocky talus on the west slope of Nez Perce. Last night's snow had not amounted to anything, melting away before 9 AM.

She and Wyatt worked on a ridge, preparing a permanent seismic station with a line of sight to a receiver on Mount Washburn. Its radio signal would transmit to the Institute automatically.

Wyatt tossed aside the shovel he'd been digging with, lay on his stomach and extended his arm into the hole. Placing the digital sensor experimentally onto solid rock, he checked its position and pulled it back out. "Ready for plaster of Paris."

Kyle mixed white powder with water in a plastic bucket.

"This would go a lot faster if Nick pulled his weight," Wyatt observed.

"He's probably found something interesting."

Wyatt fiddled with the sensor, frowning at it. "Next you'll be telling me Dr. Darden has studied volcanoes all over the world, while I'm just a lowly Ph.D. out of the Mountain West."

"If that's what you are, then I am, too." She turned her face away to avoid the plaster dust as she mixed. "Stanton taught us both what we know."

"You've seen Nick's attitude toward me."

She stopped stirring and let the silence go on until Wyatt pushed up on the lip of the excavation and looked at her.

"I've seen yours toward him," she said.

He sat for a moment looking irritated. "So, I haven't been all over the world. I'm content to be who I am."

Once she remembered commenting on that when they were in the rock lab. "It's peaceful working with you, Wyatt," she had said while she emptied a ball mill that crushed samples. "You know when to talk and when to be quiet." He'd leaned against the slate-topped counter looking comfortable inside his skin.

With Nick around, Wyatt no longer seemed to feel at ease.

"No fancy trips to Tibet or South America for me," he went on. "I've just lived this region. That should entitle me to some respect."

"You have mine."

Something searching in the way his eyes met hers made her look away to the northwest toward Mount Washburn. "I could never make Nick do anything, not even when . . ." she broke off.

"You sound bitter." He sat up, his long-fingered hands draped over his knees. "Want to tell me about it?"

Kyle didn't want to talk about Nick, but something softened inside her at Wyatt's gentle tone.

Crouched on her heels, she stirred the plaster for a moment while she thought of how to explain her feelings. When she raised her head, he was studying her with a waiting expression.

"Remember the first time you fell in love?" she tried. "The world looked freshly minted like a coin, the images on it you and your other half. It was molded, meant to be."

Wyatt's angular jaw set, but she went on, "You couldn't imagine not growing closer and closer until you became one."

"Since I've been single, love isn't something I've given a lot of thought to." He inhaled deeply.

In an effort to get the spotlight off her and Nick, Kyle met Wyatt's troubled regard. "You've never told me what happened to your marriage."

He picked up a pebble and turned it in his hands. "Marie ran out on me. Took all her clothes and left a note."

"Oh, no." A shaft of pain went through her at the image of him coming home, perhaps whistling as he came through the door. Then stopping at the sight of a lone slip of paper where the table ought to be set for supper. "From the few times you spoke of her, or rather failed to speak of her, I was afraid it was something like that." She paused and took a breath. "Nick sent me a letter. After field camp was over."

As though speaking of Nick conjured him, he came into view, hiking slowly up the mountain's spine. He wore no hat; his hair glinted in the sun.

Wyatt followed her gaze. "Have you two taken up where you left off?"

"Left is the operative phrase, as in he left me." She poked around in the bucket. "This plaster is about to set up."

He picked it up and poured some slurry into the hole. Kyle handed him the seismic sensor. Bent with her head close to his, she watched him place it in the plaster and level the bubble on top of the case.

The scrape of boots on gravel announced Nick. His face was animated, his eyes a little bloodshot without sunglasses. "Come see what I've found."

Wyatt got up, brushed off his pants and gave Nick a hard look. "After you give us a hand with the solar panels."

Nick returned his glare. "I've been working as hard as you, cowboy."

"Come on, gentlemen." Kyle took the pole and the two men the business end, lifting the iridescent blue panel covered with circular cells into place on a five-foot aluminum mast.

Fifteen minutes later, the station was in operation. One of the plastic chests contained the batteries, the digital drive and the clock, covered with a tarp weighted down by stones. A few feet away, more rocks stabilized a square of plywood over the pit sheltering the DAS. Wires connected the sensor to the data drive.

Kyle and Wyatt followed Nick down the ridge to a thick cliff of gray sandy material, studded liberally with rocks from pea-sized to several feet in diameter.

"What do you see?" Nick asked.

She studied the outcrop. "Pyroclastic flow?"

He nodded. Those roiling volcanic landslides could spread over wide areas, depending on eruption volume and topography. Any hapless animal or human in the path of one with clasts this size would be bulldozed.

Kyle pointed downslope to another outcrop fifty yards below. "What about that?"

"Part of the same event."

A stunned silence fell over both her and Wyatt. A flow that size would have to indicate a vent or source far larger than the mountain upon which they stood today.

She and Wyatt walked a little way down the trail, agreeing with Nick as they went that there did not seem to be a break in the deposition of the flow.

"How long ago?" she wondered.

Nick patted his pack. "I've taken samples we can send in for age dating once we get home. But you already said there were radiocarbon dates from wood fragments found in the flows here that indicated an eruption date around 10,000 years ago."

"A geologic eye blink," said Wyatt.

Nick cleared his throat. "Let's walk up to the summit." His tone and the way he looked at Kyle suggested he was inviting only her.

"Yes, let's," she agreed, including Wyatt with a smile.

He checked his watch. "Coming up on four. I need to schlep these tools back, check on the horses."

"Come on," Kyle urged.

"It's my night to cook." His head bent and he scooped up the dusty plaster bag.

Aware that Nick wasn't supporting her argument, she urged Wyatt, "We can have a late supper."

Without a reply, he retrieved the mixing bucket, collected the shovel and walked away.

Kyle and Nick climbed.

Though her feet were still tender, she appreciated placing her feet on rock rather than the tile floors at the Institute. Though she got into the field occasionally, she envied Nick that aspect of his nomad life. Along the way, he pointed out aspects of the stacked flows that made up the mountain, and stopped now and then to knock off a rock sample and study it with a ten-power hand lens.

As the ascent became more difficult, even his patter died. Kyle breathed deeply and evenly through her nose and paused for frequent sips from her water bottle. When the spine of rock disappeared into the smoother slope above tree line they slowed further to account for the waist-high brush.

When they reached bare scree above, their boots crunched on dark porous cinders. The going was tough in the loose and gravelly material, but finally they reached the top of the mountain.

Kyle bent over and put her hands on her thighs, letting the breeze cool her. After a moment, she lifted her gaze from her footing to the limitless horizon.

"My God."

"I thought you'd like it." Nick lifted both arms in a football referee's signal for a touchdown. "I climbed up here this morning to start my traverse."

Beneath an azure sky marked by cotton ball cumulous, the long valley of the Lamar stretched to the northwest. Mountains lined either side. To the south were the twin peaks of Castor and Pollux, rising to over 11,000 feet. Formed of layered sediments, they reminded Kyle of the Precambrian Belt Series exposed in Glacier Park and the Canadian Rockies.

West across the Lamar rose Pelican Cone, topped by both a fire lookout and one of the seismic stations whose pattern she had studied yesterday.

Beyond, sunlight sparkled on a glimpse of Yellowstone Lake, making it look like a signal mirror. A hundred miles to the southwest, the air was clear enough to see the bluish spires of the Tetons.

Nick gestured at the mountain they stood upon. "From up here, you can read the volcano's history in its shape."

A frisson of foreboding touched a nerve when he called Nez Perce a volcano. Of course, that was the correct terminology, but hadn't she been thinking in terms of past events in a context of geologic time.

Using his hands, Nick mimed the sequence. "First,

a series of big ash flows pulsed from the vent, gradually building the shield-shaped mountain." With its broad smooth sides, it would have looked benign, except for the three black basaltic spines spreading from the peak, steep-sided buttresses with sheer drops on either side.

"Then the vertical dikes were emplaced, where molten rock squeezed up through the softer welded tuffs formed from the hot ash." Later erosion uncovered the dikes, making treacherous footing for man or beast. "The most recent event was the extrusion of the cinder cone."

Nick slung off his pack and threw himself down onto the ground. Kyle followed suit more slowly. Though she looked out at the view, she sensed his gaze on her.

"It's been a long time since we climbed a mountain together," he said.

Feeling like a kid again, she found her eyes darting from the stunning vista to her hands, to the laces of her boots. Finally, she realized that was silly and looked directly into familiar green eyes. "A very long time."

"It feels good." All trace of teasing was gone from his tone.

"It does," she admitted. Though they sat at least five feet apart, it seemed closer.

They studied each other a moment longer, then Nick bent and picked up a handful of cinders, sifting them through his fingers. "Notice anything funny about this stuff?"

His abrupt change of subject both surprised and relieved her. For something to do, she scraped up some gravel and studied it.

Nearly as lightweight as pumice, this scoria might float in water. Small vesicles showed that it had been frothy with air bubbles when extruded from the volcano. As iron leached out and oxidized, it had weathered to shades from vermilion to ochre. Kyle broke a fragment crisply in half and saw the original dark surface beneath a rind no more than a millimeter thick.

"Think this is 10,000 years old?" Nick asked.

She stared at the freshly broken surface. "It reminds me of material from Craters of the Moon over in the Snake River Plain . . ." Idaho's broad volcanic expanse had been dissected by a fissure so recently that it gave the effect of a broken asphalt parking lot.

"Craters is dated at 2,000 years, give or take," Nick estimated.

"Sunset Crater north of Flagstaff . . ." A classic cinder cone named for the oxidized colors they were seeing here.

"1064 A.D.," Nick said. "Precisely dated from tree rings."

"Some of the stuff in Hawaii . . ."

"Stanton's students age-dated this mountain," Nick mused. "Do you know where they took their samples?"

Kyle broke another piece of scoria. "I can find out."

Nick pulled a cloth sample bag from his pack and labeled it "Nez Perce Summit-2."

"I grabbed some on the other side this morning," he explained. After putting a generous handful of cinders in the bag, he drew out his folded topographic map and hand-held GPS. It took only a moment to take a reading, mark an 'X' on the approximate spot, and write the coordinates on both the map and the sample bag's label.

While Nick worked, Kyle recalled that she carried a map of the Nez Perce area, drawn by a Master's candidate several years ago. She dug around in her pack and found it beneath her notebook.

When she tried to unfold the map, the wind made it snap and billow in her hands. Nick slid on his behind across the loose surface, took one side of it, and settled in beside her. Shoulder to shoulder, they bent their heads together.

Though the map bore dirt stains from other trips to the field, the tough, tear-resistant material was intact, the black ink notations legible.

Kyle located Nez Perce.

The students had sampled stream and river drainages, as per standard procedure. They had grabbed a piece of some of the pyroclastic flows Nick had shown her and Wyatt down the valley. In addition, they had brought back chunks of the great dikes radiating outward from the base of the cinder cone.

No markings were apparent near the summit.

"Kids," said Nick.

"We were young once."

Nick dropped his side of the map and let her struggle to fold it. "You and I were never so young not to climb to the top of the mountain and check it out."

"Come on." She focused on cramming the map into her pack. "We made our own mistakes."

"Guess I deserve that one." He pushed to his feet. "At any rate, I think we're seeing evidence that this mountain was born yesterday."

Once more, her spine prickled. "The plumbing's still down there . . . waiting to be used again."

CHAPTER TWENTY-TWO
SEPTEMBER 24

At midafternoon the next day, Kyle rode Strawberry out of a narrow canyon onto a wider, brush-covered slope above seismic station two. She dismounted and took a replacement data drive from one of the weather-resistant bags behind the saddle.

The little roan nickered and nudged Kyle's shoulder, sending a gust of warm alfalfa breath down her neck. Kyle set the equipment down and stroked Strawberry's horsy-smelling nose. "You think so?" she murmured.

The horse pawed the ground.

"Well . . ." Kyle dragged out the word. "Okay." Digging out a carrot from a plastic bag, she offered it.

Strawberry tossed her head and neighed, her strong white teeth crunching the slightly withered vegetable as though it were ambrosia. "You're a good girl," Kyle enthused.

Turning her attention to the seismic station, she pulled back the tarp and opened the weather-resistant box. After activating the quick release on the cables, she disconnected them from the working drive and replaced it with the substitute.

A closer look at the solar array revealed a few rips in the plastic coating, but it had been that way when deployed. As long as they were seventy percent effective, the panels remained in use. A problem she did see was a healthy dose of bird droppings on the cells. Using a cloth from her saddlebag, she scrubbed away the material that would keep sunlight from the panels.

Putting the data drive into the saddlebag, Kyle checked the sun angle. If she didn't want to be caught by darkness, it was time to head up the trail.

With a flick of the reins, she urged Strawberry toward the patrol cabin. Once in the canyon, the path wound among tall trees, and the earth was spongy beneath the horse's hooves. Afternoon shadows lay deep.

As Kyle drew closer to the cabin, she wondered if Nick would get back before Wyatt. If he did, would he keep up his artful distance, or had yesterday's time alone on the mountain broken the ice once more?

Though the thought of Nick made her pulse accelerate, shouldn't Wyatt's angry and protective reaction be a warning about jumping back into a relationship with a man of Nick's track record?

Last night, during one of his field tales, Nick had said that in the course of his two failed marriages he'd been careful not to tell his wives how much fun he had in the field. And this right after a story of his being in a small plane headed for one of the Aleutian volcanoes. In near zero visibility, past the point of no return on fuel, he admitted to writing a farewell note to his current spouse, then crumpling it and burning it upon a safe landing.

Deep in the canyon, Strawberry picked her way daintily, but just before the trail wound down into a hollow, she stopped without warning, ears cocked.

Kyle tensed, while not even birdsong broke the quiet. As she scanned the woods, Strawberry pawed the earth and tossed her head toward a five-foot high outcrop of black basalt.

There. Kyle spied a deer, lying on its side with the unmistakable boneless look of recent death. The buck's rack would have pleased some hunter.

Strawberry snorted.

Perhaps a poacher waited in the rocks for them to go away. On the other hand, there was no sign of a bullet wound. No marks of a predator's teeth or claws, but Kyle needed to dismount to be sure.

A gentle nudge sent Strawberry forward. Perhaps the buck had broken its leg on the rocks and died of dehydration. But wouldn't she have noticed it when she came down the canyon earlier?

Strawberry stopped and refused to move into the low area.

Then Kyle caught the stench of rotten eggs. Hydrogen sulfide, a deadly poison heavier than air, tended to pool in topographic depressions. Colorless, the gas's only warning was the few seconds in which its victim could smell before the scent receptors in the nose burned out.

Less than thirty feet away Kyle spied another dead deer, this one a doe.

Choking, she jerked the reins.

Strawberry wheeled and ran up the rise. Though she hated to do it, Kyle dug in her heels, spurred and yelled.

Once over the rise and again on the downhill, they galloped around a curve, where a deadfall they'd circumvented earlier lay across the path.

Forced to rein in, Kyle inhaled carefully. The air bore the moldy aroma of moss and autumn leaf litter. Two breaths, three, and she didn't feel dizzy or nauseous. Strawberry stood steady.

Yet, as the sunless chill in the canyon deepened, Kyle wondered what to do. The narrow trail through steep rock walls was made impassible by the gas.

On the south side was the boulder field. Even if Kyle could climb it, she would have to leave Strawberry behind. That would spell certain doom if the sweet animal tried to follow and broke a leg.

She tried repeatedly to radio Wyatt or Nick, but the canyon ramparts interfered with the signal. Though Nick had said he would be on the east side of the mountain, Wyatt had gone down the canyon.

The thought seized her that if the gas had been there this morning, he and Thunder would have died like the deer. This was further proof that the seep had begun only a few hours ago. It reminded her ominously of David Mowry diving into a spring turned scalding overnight.

Checking her watch and the sky, Kyle figured Wyatt and Thunder should be headed back this way. Though it would be dark soon, she decided she must backtrack to the canyon mouth and wait to warn him. Together they'd try circling up over the smoother face of Little Saddle and down to the cabin.

Fifteen minutes later, she was on the open slope. Wyatt still did not answer his radio. Neither did Nick. On the next try, her batteries gave up.

Two hours later, Kyle watched the light fade over the broad bowl of the Yellowstone caldera. The stack of firewood she'd gathered ranged from kindling to stout branches. Now she looked with dismay at the size of the pile and calculated it might last a few hours at most. She had two flashlights, but she'd not brought extra batteries for what was supposed to be a day hike.

Despair washed over her. Oh, to be a normal person who enjoyed touring caverns, who laughed when they turned out the lights to show total darkness. With mounting dread at the gathering twilight, she looked around for more wood.

In the canyon, deadfalls lay at haphazard angles, some propped up by others, but there was too much danger of starting a forest fire if she lit off a blaze in so much dry wood.

On the grassy slope, she located a likely length of pine, sun-bleached silver white. It was about a foot in diameter and ten feet long, and with some wrestling, she got a rope around it. With the horizon dimming from scarlet to ultramarine, Strawberry dragged the log to Kyle's makeshift camp.

In the last light, she spread her sleeping bag and ground cloth, thankful that the team always took bedding as a precaution when they rode out. From her daypack, she pulled high calorie trail munchies.

She scraped away the grass to bare soil in a circular area and ringed it with chunks of rhyolite. Tearing a few blank pages from her field notebook, she crumpled them, put on small sticks of kindling and applied a wooden match from her kit.

She felt foolish. Wyatt had probably circled around and was already back at the cabin. Right now, he and Nick were no doubt bickering over who should take her turn at cooking while she sat alone. Though she didn't want to think about it, tonight was the dark of the moon, a night when only stars cast illumination.

Her small smoky fire was a nice touch, but it couldn't hold back the vast ink of sky. She raised her eyes to blacker shadows of mountains that were always thrusting up and eroding away. In the canyon, gas must still be seeping.

Strawberry nickered from where she was tethered.

"Sorry, girl, I haven't any food for you." Or water. Her canteen contained less than a pint.

Out in the darkness, a coyote howled.

With a struggle, Kyle got the pine trunk almost to her fire. Then it hung up on a stub of branch and refused to budge. She sat on the ground and tried to use the power of her thighs.

The approaching clop of hooves came from the trail. "Need help?" Wyatt asked gruffly.

She turned and saw a dark shape on an even darker horse. The brimmed hat made it a scene from a Western movie.

Urging Thunder into the ring of firelight, Wyatt slid easily out of the saddle. "You're the last thing I expected to find out here."

"The canyon's off limits." She pointed uphill. "H^2S killed two deer right on the trail."

He looked thoughtful. "You could have died if you'd ridden too close."

"Lucky for me, Strawberry smelled it and we turned back. I was afraid you would come along in the dark."

Wyatt looked at her little fire and the bigger log she was trying to burn. "You waited here for me? At night?"

"You could have died," she echoed.

He slung an arm around her shoulders and gave her a hard squeeze. "Come on, let's build a blaze we can read by."

● ● ●

Half an hour later, by the light of a bonfire, Kyle sat on her sleeping bag and watched Wyatt radio Nick. After explaining tersely about the gas seep, he listened for a few minutes and then signed off. "Nick wasn't surprised about the gas . . . said it goes along with a volcano awakening."

Kyle hugged her knees and shivered despite the flames that had her front side baking. "Yesterday, when we climbed to the top, he talked about this being a volcano. I guess I'd been thinking of it in more passive terms, like volcanic terrain, or dormant."

"I have, too." Wyatt set aside his radio. "But there's a reason this expedition includes a volcanologist."

"I wonder how extensive the gas seeps are. How many more . . . ?"

He put out his hand in a stop gesture. "Don't go there. We need to get through this night without giving ourselves the heebie-jeebies."

Kyle took a bracing breath of smoky mountain air. "You're right."

Wyatt spread his sleeping bag on the opposite side of the fire and took a seat. "Nick didn't sound pleased about our being out here together."

Wyatt didn't sound happy either.

She leaned forward and felt the fire's heat further warm her cheeks. "Look, about Nick and I . . ."

"I don't need to know your business." Wyatt spoke stiffly, but the expression in his eyes gave away some essential vulnerability.

"I want you to." Maybe if she could make him understand, he'd settle back into being the friend she needed.

A line appeared between his brows. "If you have to say something, I'm listening."

Now that she'd waded out this deep, she had to think a moment for the right words.

"Let's say your wife Marie dropped back into your life without warning. Wouldn't you feel something? Nostalgia, curiosity, the old what-if?"

Wyatt shook his head. "Bringing up Marie is not the way to make me understand."

"All right then, Alicia . . . somebody you care for a lot."

Wyatt looked at her for a long moment, and his expression softened. "I imagine this is tough on you . . . but I think I'd be clear on who dumped who. And make damned sure not to play the fool a second time."

Their eyes locked across the flames.

Wyatt's gaze broke away and he got up to put more wood on the fire.

"You go on to sleep," he said. "I'll make sure you don't wake up in the cold . . . or dark."

CHAPTER TWENTY-THREE

SEPTEMBER 25

Near noon the next day, Kyle and Wyatt rode into sight of the cabin.

When they drew closer, she caught sight of a beard-stubbled, tousle-haired Nick at the corral fence offering Gray a feed bucket.

Wyatt clucked to Thunder. Kyle nudged Strawberry into a trot to keep up with the longer-legged stallion.

Nick met them; his eyes flicked from one to the other. "You two keep warm last night?"

"Snug as bugs," Wyatt retorted.

He'd been as good as his word, keeping the fire stoked so Kyle never opened her eyes to darkness.

Wyatt got off Thunder and began to unload the data drives.

To Kyle's surprise, Nick did not escalate a confrontation. Instead, he led the other two horses into the pen and offered food. Both animals bypassed the bin for a drink from the trough.

Nick headed toward the cabin, pausing to pick up some of Kyle's gear. He stopped about halfway there and pointed to a nearby rock. Atop it lay two dead ground squirrels and one of the usually vibrant gray and black birds known as the Clark's Nutcracker.

Kyle looked at the carcasses. "Where did you pick those up?"

"Not close by or we'd be leaving." Nick gestured east along the valley between Little Saddle and Nez Perce. "Found them over there when I was mapping a fault this morning."

Kyle frowned. "None of the geologic maps show a fault in this area."

"Come inside and I'll lay it out."

As they entered the cabin, Wyatt spoke softly to Kyle. "I've been all over this area and didn't recognize a fault." He sounded as though he didn't believe Nick.

Kyle poured her and Wyatt a cup of coffee while Nick spread his field map on the table. Superimposed on a published topographic quadrangle, he had sketched and made notes in red ink.

He pointed to an east-west line cutting by the cabin. "Here the edge of the Nez Perce flow is abrupt, against a fault that's part of the older range." Block letters indicated he had named it the Saddle Valley Fault.

Kyle caught his inference and felt her breath come faster. "You mean we're seeing an ancient fault, reactivated when Nez Perce erupted."

Nick had made a notation of where he found the asphyxiated squirrels and birds. Kyle put her finger on the spot and ran it west past the cabin until she came to the canyon where the deer had died.

"It all lines up," she said. "The son of a bitch is active again."

● ● ●

"I'm going out with you guys," Kyle told Nick and Wyatt after they'd spent an uneasy half an hour over lunch.

Wyatt demurred. "We need you monitoring the stations. It may seem dull, but I, for one, am counting on you to let us know if we need to get out of here."

Kyle's chest clutched. After their deduction that the Nez Perce vent was so much larger and younger than previously thought, Nick had seemed both edgier and more exhilarated. With the discovery of the active fault, he had become more so.

He turned to her. "I was intrigued by Brock Hobart predicting a quake as large as a 6.0, but discounted it because volcanic areas usually don't experience large shakes. But with this fault, and the new moon tonight, we'd be foolish not to have you on alert here."

For several hours, she monitored the stations, surprised to find them transmitting a continuous signal of quiet. Nonetheless, she watched the computer screen with distrust.

Finally, for something to distract her, she checked email. Another nastygram from Hollis suggested her 'unauthorized leave of absence' should be unpaid.

Adrenaline shot down her arms, leaving her tingling the way she had when the van jolted to a stop against the Gardner Canyon slide. Her breath coming fast, fingers flying, she fired back:

Before Colin left for Asia, he appreciated the gravity of the Yellowstone situation enough to send us Dr. Nicholas Darden of the Volcano Hazards Group. We are currently at the Nez Perce Patrol Cabin monitoring a situation that Dr. Darden believes could result in a sudden need for evacuation.

It took at least an hour to calm down, as she kept checking for another salvo from Salt Lake. When none came, she alternatively studied the seismic patterns and stirred an iron pot of beef stew hanging from a hook in the fireplace. The recipe was one from Franny, who had been quite the chef.

The contrast between twenty-first century technology and nineteenth century living made Kyle think of Franny's life in Jackson Hole during the 1920s. Then, most roads were unpaved, though the late nineteenth century advent of the bicycle had brought some macadam to the West. Horseback and wagons were still common modes of transportation alongside the automobile.

Though the land was wilder than her native Tuscany, and a far cry from New York, where Franny had worked briefly as a cook, the Italian immigrant had found her soul in the West.

As she replaced the lid on the stewpot, Kyle recalled that on her family's last trip together, Mom and Dad had stopped by the old dude ranch near Jackson. Kyle's memory was of rail fences falling into disrepair and abandoned buildings that had begun their return to the land, as the Park Service intended.

The Nez Perce cabin, although newer, was fashioned of the same rustic log construction. Running a hand along the rough wooden wall, she walked to the door. Outside, nature's gift of Indian summer beckoned.

Today's sky was almost indigo. Flaxen grasses rippled in a zephyr of breeze. Though the last of the season's goldenrod had dried on the stalks, bees droned around it. Stalks of the camas plant bowed nearby, their blue summer flowers' history; like the Nez Perce who had camped in these meadows in the high summer of 1877.

According to some stories, believing the pursuing Army to be far behind them, the refugees had stopped to rest their horses and gather camas roots, a staple food they enjoyed in all seasons, boiled, mashed, and ground into flour long after the first snows flew. And with that group had traveled a small orphan boy.

Kyle hunkered down on the cabin's front stoop and imagined her great-grandfather, not quite part of any culture due to his mixed blood. She had no idea whether he had been an outcast or accepted by the tribe. Perhaps he had put up barriers between himself and the world the way she had, albeit for different reasons.

From inside the cabin, she heard a male voice on the radio.

Startled from her reverie, she went in and answered.

"What's shakin'?" Nick asked.

"Nada. The latest data says the quake swarm has completely subsided."

He chuckled. "Brock Hobart won't care for that. According to him, tonight is show time."

Another jolt shot through Kyle. "He'll have to be disappointed."

"Time will tell."

"Where are you?"

"I've found a lava cave a ways up from the cabin. Not far from the ridge along the dike. If there hadn't been a forest fire here in '88, I might not have seen it."

"Did you go inside?" She imagined a dark opening in the hillside, one she would not care to approach.

"The entrance drops down a hole. There was a cone of last season's snow in there, insulated by the lava, but I figured if I skied down I might not be able to get back up."

Pleased that for once Nick had avoided danger, Kyle said, "Wise choice. When are you coming back here?"

"Depends what's for dinner."

"Homemade beef stew."

"Well, hell, honey, I'll just hang up my rock hammer and rush right over." Nick stopped transmitting without any kind of radio protocol.

An instant later, he said again, "Come in, Nez Perce?"

"Nick?"

Wyatt drawled, "Sorry to disappoint you."

Kyle bit her lip. "He just called in from a lava cave on the east ridge."

"He should be back to the cabin by dark then?"

"I suppose. Why?"

A moment of silence had Kyle thinking they'd been cut off. Then Wyatt said, "I got the idea you didn't much care for the dark." Tonight really would be black, with the new moon rising in the middle of the night.

"There's the generator and the lantern." She tried for casual.

"I know." He sounded a little embarrassed. "The thing is, I'm down the Lamar at site seven and may not get back until tomorrow."

Nick had said he was coming to the cabin soon, but the reminder of impending nightfall made her say, "Wyatt, if you're not here you'll miss my best beef stew."

"Damn. You don't know how sick I am of the dog food Dr. Darden throws together."

"Try and make it?" she said. "Even if you get in late?"

After signing off, Kyle checked the seismic charts again. Continued quiet made her wonder what Brock Hobart was thinking, for she was certain he must be following the signals today.

If only they knew more about Nez Perce Peak. Their study of the layered thickness of flows used the geologist's first principle: "The present is the key to the past." The problem was that more and more scientific studies lead to: "The present is the key to the present."

What went on in the past didn't always look like today's world. In fact, it seldom did.

During the Cretaceous, marine dinosaurs and flying reptiles inhabited seas that spread over the North American continent. In the Pennsylvanian, great swamps harbored dragonflies the size of Cessnas and spawned coalfields that stretched over thousands of square miles.

If, deep within the earth, molten rock now pressed toward the surface, what path would it take? Might the earthquakes be a sign of magma moving up the preexisting and reactivated fault line? Or was it gathering beneath the high peak of Nez Perce as it had less than 10,000 years ago?

Another check of the passive seismic response, and her restlessness increased. Feeling field-grubby after last night's campout, she decided Nick and Wyatt's absence was an excellent opportunity to use the shower.

The black plastic bag full of solar heated water suspended from a tree a few yards away from the cabin. No curtain, just *au naturel* in a perfect afternoon.

Yet, as she lathered her lean flanks, rinsed, and dressed in a pair of clean black fleece pants and a matching top, she could not forget the hours ticking away to the new moon.

Despite Nick's jovial threat to throw down his rock hammer and return to the cabin right away, it was several hours before he arrived. At the sound of his footfalls on the porch, she looked up and was startled to find it had gotten dark. The light from her computer was the only illumination save the cook fire.

Nick looked as grimy and field weary as she had been, shrugging out of his daypack and unlacing his boots to place them side-by-side near the door. With an appreciative sniff, he went to the fireplace and grabbed a rag to lift the stewpot lid. "This definitely shows a woman's touch."

He put another log on and used the poker to bring the blaze to brightness. "Where's the cowboy?"

"Down the Lamar Valley. He may not make it back this evening."

Nick gave a low whistle and padded in sock feet to her side. "All still quiet on the Nez Perce front?"

Kyle nodded. "It's creeping me out."

Bending, he inhaled close to her hair. "You took a shower." So lightly that she scarcely felt it, he lifted a strand and twirled it round his finger. "Think I'll clean up, too."

Left alone with her heart thudding while he went into the bunkroom, Kyle shut down the computer and turned on the utility light.

When he passed through the main room carrying a towel and fresh clothes, Nick shielded his eyes with his arm. A moment after he went outside, she heard the rhythmic cough of the generator go silent. In the same instant, the bulb over the table went dark.

Kyle took a calming breath. She tried not to hurry as she reached for the Coleman lantern, pumped up the pressure in the fuel reservoir, and applied a match to the delicate mantle of ash. Going to check on the stew, she sniffed the mingled aromas of beef, potatoes, carrots, and onions, while she tried not to imagine that just outside Nick was naked.

This was too much. His voice floated in a cappella, a concert of bawdy drinking songs including his old field camp standard "Charlotte the Harlot."

He came in a few minutes later dressed in sweats. "Still too bright."

With a glance at the shadowy corners, she left the lantern on.

He sauntered toward the bunkroom. "With any other woman, I'd think the glare was a brush-off, but you've always insisted on a night light."

It was his first allusion to her penchant for 24/7 illumination. Following him to the bunkroom door, she hesitated over what to say.

As he bent over his bed beneath hers, putting down his dirty clothes and hanging his towel on the bed frame, she realized he didn't know she was behind him. When he raised his head, she saw him pause and stare at her twisted sleeping bag on the top bunk.

Very slowly, he bowed his head and put his nose to the fabric as though detecting her scent. In profile, she saw him close his eyes while he crushed a handful of nylon-covered down in his fist.

"Nick?"

He stepped back, the movement stirring up a clean

soap smell that mingled with his own distinctive essence. For a moment, their eyes met, then he gave a little 'you caught me' kind of shrug and bent to drag something from his bag from under the bed.

"To complement dinner." He displayed a bottle of brandy.

Though Kyle didn't usually drink hard liquor, she thought it might stave off her awareness of the impending new moon.

❀ ❀ ❀

Wyatt drew his hat lower against the wind sweeping down the canyon and strained to detect the trail's pale track. Between Nez Perce Peak and Little Saddle Mountain, the moonless night was deep as velvet. As he emerged into the high valley, he saw the faraway glow of cabin windows. Though it was certainly his imagination, he could swear he caught a whiff of aromatic beef stew on the wind.

Kyle's original recipe was one he'd sampled before, during a party at her mountain townhouse. Although the memory was repressed so deeply Freud would have been proud, it broke through the way a river rafted winter ice.

That night, as Kyle's gathering wound down, Wyatt stayed behind to help her police the area. He was on the deck picking up beer cans when she came out through the sliding glass doors. No doubt because of the hot August day she wore a loose-fitting white cotton dress, a startling departure from her usual khakis and tailored shirts.

Though the evening air had cooled, she raised her hands and lifted her hair off her slender corded neck. "Leave that, Wyatt."

He finished the task, twisted up the trash bag and carried it out to the curb.

Kyle followed.

Lightning split the sky, and wind ruffled her hair and dress. They stood beside his truck, talking of nothing, the way people bargain with an evening's end. A choker of silver lay just below where the pulse beat in her throat.

Wyatt ran out of small talk and reached for his keys.

Kyle put her hand on his forearm. "Are you sure you're okay to drive? The last thing you need is to have an accident when the rain comes."

He stood not a foot away from the woman he'd always thought of as one of the boys.

Was it because of the soft way she was dressed, or perhaps the shine of her eyes with their fascinating blend of blue and green? All he knew was he was shaking with the need to make a move forward, a simple adjustment that would not be simple at all.

"I'll be fine," he lied, getting into the truck and slamming the door.

He really had been okay. After a few days of telling himself that professors and students slept together all the time, he concluded that even bringing up the subject would ruin their relationship. Her friendship and their easy way of working together were too valuable to risk for a few minutes pleasure.

Yet, watching her with Nick Darden gave him second thoughts. If he had been forthright about his feelings for her after he'd finished his degree, perhaps he wouldn't be in this foul mood tonight.

Last evening, alone with her beside the raging bonfire, he'd been hard pressed to keep his secret. With the firelight casting her features in relief, she'd looked more beautiful than he could ever recall seeing her.

It might be foolhardy to press on, but Kyle had asked him to.

He also had a superstitious desire not to be alone for the witching hour of Brock Hobart's prediction.

CHAPTER TWENTY-FOUR

SEPTEMBER 26

Kyle reached a languorous hand and poured more brandy for her and Nick. They'd moved from the dinner table to the tired sofa, and she was startled to note that by her watch it was past midnight. The cabin was getting chilly as they let the fire burn down to diminish the hazard of sparks when they turned in.

The thought of bed made her raise her glass and take another ample swallow. It delayed the moment when she and Nick would go into the bunkroom. In the half-light of the dying fire and her candle lantern that he'd accepted as compromise when he turned off the Coleman, he looked as young as when they'd first known each other. All the details were there, down to the scruffy beard from not shaving in the field.

Kyle tipped her cup and found it empty. "Oops."

Nick smiled. "I think you must be drunk."

She giggled.

He placed both hands on hers and leaned in. "I'll bet you're so wasted you can't beat me at Hearts."

With deliberate enunciation, she challenged, "I could

never get so drunk that I couldn't whip your ass at Hearts." Her hands felt hot where he touched them.

She got up and stirred the embers. Trying for nonchalance, she grabbed her candle lantern to take to the bedroom. Nick followed, plucked her sleeping bag off the top bunk, and dumped it below with his.

Kyle felt a flush of awareness the way she had earlier when he sniffed at her hair. No, this tide flowed warmer, as they stood together before the narrow mattress. Flashes of a field camp Sunday afternoon when they were alone in the 4-H barracks naked atop a sleeping bag.

Nick set the brandy bottle and their cups on the floor beside the bed and rummaged in his bag for cards and a pack of Marlboros.

She climbed into the far end of the bunk against the wall and spread her sleeping bag over her legs. "I haven't seen you smoke."

"When I drink." Taking a position at the opposite end of the bed, Nick covered his own legs, struck a match, and applied it to a cigarette. The end of the white paper curled into ash and the smell of tobacco smoke surrounded them. He tossed her the cards. "Deal."

She shuffled. He cut. She dealt them each thirteen and placed the rest on the bedding between them. Nick took a deep drag and held it in.

Kyle gathered her cards and began to sort them. The candle shed barely enough light to tell the spades from the clubs.

Across from her, Nick exhaled a smoke cloud. "At least you still play Hearts."

She gave him an even look. "Some things you don't forget."

A grin crinkled the corners of his eyes. At field camp, the nightly game had begun about the time most students went to bed. Once the barracks got dark and quiet, a small cadre of serious partiers played until drowsiness overtook at least one of the players. Kyle had been a latecomer to the game, joining only after the night she and Nick went to his tent.

In the dim light beneath the upper bunk at the Nez Perce cabin, Nick arranged his cards. His foot brushed hers as he led with the two of clubs. Kyle followed suit with a six, gathered up the hand and played the eight. His foot was back while their eyes stayed on the cards.

Another few tricks and most of the clubs were cleaned up. Pondering his next lead, Nick raised his eyes to Kyle's. Holding out the cigarette, he kneaded her calf with his toes.

As if from a distance, she watched her hand float up. Relaxed from the brandy, she opened her mind and her mouth and drew in the smoke. The first drag choked, the second smoothed the rough edges.

"More." He leaned to hold the Marlboro to her lips.

More was what she wanted. Like Alice through the looking glass, she passed from her existence as Dr. Kyle Stone to the girl who'd won Nick Darden's heart.

If only for summer's end.

His foot inched higher. As though she was outside herself, she saw them facing each other. It would only take the smallest move by either of them.

Nick made it, slicking his undershirt over his head.

If she said no, she felt certain he would put away the party and let her climb into the narrow top bunk. He'd dutifully crawl into his sleeping bag, and she could listen to him breathe the way she had each night they'd been on the mountain, the cadence punctuated by the soft snoring she'd once imagined would become her nightly music.

Kyle leaned against the wall and watched Nick's progress toward her.

She didn't want to say no. She wanted it the way it used to be, the quick breath and pounding of the blood. To forget the miles and the years that had separated them. To desire him the way she did when she awoke sometimes before dawn, heart racing. In dreams, he was always youthful and brilliant, captured in sunshine.

Now, in the candlelit bunk, Nick's sparkling eyes promised it could all be true again. His hands were sure when he captured the hem of her fleece top and drew it up to cup her breast.

Kyle raised her lips to meet his.

❀   ❀   ❀

Wyatt had the cabin in close sight, a dark shape against

starlight. The windows no longer glowed and he did not believe he could smell the stew anymore. Of course, by this hour, Kyle would have given up keeping a hot meal for him. She and Nick would have gone to bed.

With a nudge to Thunder, he indicated he wished to go faster.

To his surprise, the horse shied as though he'd seen a snake on the trail.

"Easy, boy." Wyatt smoothed the stallion's neck with his hand.

Thunder reared with a snort and flare of nostrils.

Wyatt kept his seat with the ease of long practice as his mount threw up his head repeatedly. When a soothing tone failed, he said sharply, "Settle down."

Thunder whinnied, a high shrill cry.

Wyatt released the reins and slid to the ground. There was no point in putting a tight lead on a frightened animal, especially when shades of charcoal prevented him seeing what was wrong. Bears were seldom nocturnal with a new moon, but he gave a sharp look at each of the hulking boulders. Human activity in their range might have pressured them into night hunting. From his belt, Wyatt removed his can of pepper spray repellent.

"What is it, Thunder?" he asked. "What's out there?"

As the big horse continued to paw and stomp, the ground gave a sudden leap.

Wyatt sat down hard.

In the instant that Nick's lips met Kyle's, her lantern gave a jerk. The flame fluttered and the bed frame jumped and crashed. Her dreamy sense shattered as her and Nick's teeth clashed together, and she tasted blood from her lip.

"Get down." He was off the mattress, grabbing her arm and dragging her to the floor.

The beds walked across the bouncing boards. Bark rained from the log walls and bits of dried mud from the chinking landed in Kyle's hair. She lifted a hand to knock them away, feeling stupid with drink.

"Out of here," Nick shouted. He crawled toward the door.

Kyle stared at her light and was reminded of a swinging lantern casting weird and dizzying shadows over a ruined picnic table. She froze, crouched on hands and knees.

The candle went out, plunging the bunkroom into blackness. A scream built in the back of her throat, but she couldn't make a sound.

She remembered that, too. After shrieking for hours into the darkness, there had come a time when she opened her mouth and nothing came out. All the while, she heard the screaming inside her head.

Nick was back, tugging her shoulders to draw her across the shuddering floor. In the other room, half-burned logs spilled from the fireplace. The rag rug smoldered, sending out acrid dusty smoke.

"Make it stop!" She clapped her hands over her ears to shut out the din.

The floor bucked again, and a hail of chimney stones crashed through the roof.

Kyle tried to crawl, but she couldn't. A sour rush of brandy filled her mouth.

In the hideous light of the now burning rug, she saw Nick sprawled bare-chested.

Wyatt vaulted into the cabin. He grabbed the rug by an edge and pulled the thick pile through the doorway.

Blackness, barely relieved by pulsating ruby embers, smothered her like thick cloth. In that instant, the earthquake stopped.

Nick's laughter broke the sudden silence like someone switched on a radio. Not a bray of mild hysteria like her own on Dot Island, but the joyous peal of a person truly enjoying himself. Someone who tried the newest and wildest roller coasters, down-hilled double black diamonds, and chased volcanoes for the pure adrenaline shock.

"Outside," Wyatt ordered, his silhouette darker than the sky in the doorway.

Kyle realized with dismay that her top was rolled around her chest, exposing her bare waist where Nick had shoved it up. She dragged it down.

Though she heard Nick shuffling toward the front door, Kyle swiveled her head toward the bunkroom. Her duffel held at least three flashlights and a supply of batteries, so she crawled toward the ebony maw. Christ, why had she drunk so much?

After the brilliance of the burning rug, the bunkroom seemed darker than before. She felt around blindly for her bag, her hand striking several metal bars arranged at crazy angles.

A beam flashed into the room's depths, revealing that the bunk beds had come apart. The upper frame and mattress hung canted like the collapsed sections of the Bay Bridge in San Francisco's 1989 earthquake.

A hand gripped her shoulder from behind.

"Nick." It came out a sob.

"Sorry to keep disappointing you," Wyatt gritted.

An aftershock jolted, and the bed frame came down in a clatter. Kyle grabbed Wyatt's knees with both arms. "Why doesn't it stop?"

In a few seconds, the ground movement ceased.

Wyatt pried her hands from around him. "Get outside."

Another shock brought a piece of heavy metal down in a blow to her ankle. The scrape sent a wave of nausea through her, one so strong that she gagged. Only by an effort of will did she keep from vomiting on Wyatt's boots.

"You're drunk," he accused, stepping back.

Giving up the search for her lights, she followed his flashlight through the front room and onto the porch. Nick was already outside, his face and bare chest pale in the starlight, arms crossed against the cold. Kyle went down the steps in sock feet; gravel underfoot reminding her that her soles had not yet recovered from losing her shoes while trying to get into the swamped RV.

She sat on a boulder, put her head in her hands, and shivered in her inadequate fleece, feeling both sick to her stomach and ashamed that Wyatt was seeing her this way.

Inside the cabin, she heard him kicking the remains of the embers back onto the hearth. She should have done that.

In a moment, he emerged carrying an armload of sleeping bags, which he dumped at the base of the porch steps.

Something else she should have thought of.

"You want this?" She looked up in the dimness to find Wyatt with her jacket extended at arm's length. Carefully, she took it. He made another trip for her and Nick's boots, throwing them to the ground. Last, he brought out one of Kyle's flashlights, turned it on, and placed it in her hand.

In the glow, she saw Nick sneer. "Kyle's a big girl. I think she can take care of herself."

"Looks like you were taking care of her all right." Wyatt's tone dripped disgust.

"Want to mind your own business while you toss me my jacket?"

For a moment, she thought Wyatt would refuse, but he bent, snagged Nick's coat off the earth, and flung it short. "You're drunk, too."

Nick lunged, missed the catch, and had to retrieve the garment from the ground.

"You're drunk all right," Wyatt drilled. "Both of you half-naked . . ."

"Naked's how it's done, cowboy."

Disbelief penetrated her brandy haze. If anyone had told her a week ago that two men would be fighting over her, she would have told them they were crazy.

Nick drawled on, his voice affected by the booze. "You need some lessons on how to get a gal in the sack . . ."

Kyle's trouble was that she didn't know whom to root for. Neither Wyatt nor Nick sounded like themselves, or at least, the selves she imagined she knew.

"Stop it," she ordered.

"If I need lessons," Wyatt came back, "I'll get them from somebody who has the guts to stick around after he gets a woman to fall for him."

She heard the hurt in his voice, a reminder that Marie had dumped him the way Nick had her.

Nick dropped his coat and advanced on Wyatt.

Kyle pushed up off the cold rock. "I said for you guys to cut it out!"

Bare-chested and barefoot, his hair disheveled as though he and Kyle really had been in bed going at it, Nick swung a right hand roundhouse.

Wyatt threw up his arm but Nick missed. "Look, I'm sober and I don't need . . ."

"No, you don't need anything here." Nick drew back and wound up to strike again. "Kyle and I go way back."

Wyatt parried another blow, catching this one on his forearm.

"Damn it!" Kyle shrieked. "Will you stop?"

In the instant Wyatt's attention shifted to her, Nick

brought up his left. It connected with Wyatt's cheekbone, just below the eye. The sound wasn't like in the Old West movies when John Wayne hit with a satisfying punch; this dull thud sounded sickening.

"Nick, no!" Kyle dropped her light and it landed to shed a half circle of illumination on the surreal scene.

Wyatt's eyes flashed and she could see his clenched teeth. "All right, you sonnuvabitch." He brought up his hands and thrust at Nick's chest, sending him sprawling amid the grass tufts on the rocky slope.

Lying on his back, Nick spread his hands at his sides in a gesture of surrender. But it was mock, for he raised his head and glared at Wyatt. "Okay, cowboy, we can't settle this 'cause she's the one who decides."

Suddenly, both men were staring at her. Kyle had never felt so inelegant in her disheveled state, so helpless at watching two men she cared for fight . . . but at Nick's words, she had also never felt so powerful.

Nick, no matter that he had left her long ago, wanted her once more. Wyatt, bless his heart, was defending her honor against the man who had broken her heart.

Her gaze darted from Nick to Wyatt and back. "This is ridiculous . . ."

"Hey, look at that!" Lying on his back, Nick pointed to the rising new moon. "Old Brock would be proud."

CHAPTER TWENTY-FIVE
SEPTEMBER 26

Hours later, Kyle lay in her sleeping bag beneath the sky. The fingernail of pale moon reminded her of when she was five, looking through her father's telescope at the brilliant pockmarked surface. He'd shown her Saturn's gauzy rings and the big red spot on Jupiter that glared like a baleful eye.

Once Dad had pointed out a little spark moving fast against the black of beyond and told her it was a Russian Sputnik.

Tonight, as the bright bead of another satellite fell between the stars, she was in a different sort of cold war. Ten feet from her, Nick snored evenly, while Wyatt had spread his bedding farther away. The wind bore the stench of burned rug.

She'd never been able to sleep when she drank. Oh, she'd fall into a stupor for a while and then awaken feeling like hammered rat shit. With a cottony mouth and throbbing temples, the iceberg peak of a huge submerged hangover, she realized that even though her sleeping bag had good insulation, the cold was seeping through.

Reality was insinuating itself back into her consciousness, as well. Brock's prediction had come true. And if the new moon quake's focus plotted on the plane of the fault running through the Saddle Valley what did that mean? Could her suspicion of this afternoon be correct, and the gas seeps along the valley really be evidence that magma was rising along the fault? She would have to talk with Nick about it in the morning.

She looked at him, his forehead a pale shape against the darkness. If there had been no earthquake, what would have happened between them? She thought she knew, something naked, raw . . . and needful, for she'd been alone too long. Yet, how did he view what they'd been about to embrace, with the passion she thought she'd seen in his eyes, or with the kind of crass male indifference he'd thrown in Wyatt's face?

Twisting her head toward Wyatt, she saw that he lay with his hands clasped behind his head, staring at the heavens. She had an idea how much more virulent his anger would have been had he walked in on her and Nick in *flagrante delicto*.

Something surged inside her. Whether it was anger at Wyatt for not joining the Nick Darden fan club or hurt at his continued betrayal of their prior closeness, she didn't know. Maybe she'd brought this on herself by refusing to tell Wyatt the reason for her tears at Earthquake Lake, or not recounting enough details of her and Nick's past when Wyatt asked the other day, but that didn't make her sense of loss less painful.

She didn't expect to fall back to sleep, but the next thing she knew her eyes stung in the relentless morning light. The generator rattled and coughed. Her headache was a horror, and her head stung in the cold.

When she raised it, she saw that at least four inches of powdery snow covered her sleeping bag. Nick's was still mounded nearby and his frosty hair stood up in disheveled little peaks. Wyatt was gone. Over by the stable, the three horses munched breakfast from the bin he must have filled.

Kyle worked the zipper and slid out of her cloth cocoon. Retrieving her jacket, she brushed it off, and found her boots stiff from the cold. Carrying them, she headed toward the cabin. Wood smoke poured from the leaning chimney. At the door, she stumbled and wondered if she might still be drunk. Then she realized the jamb was askew.

Inside, the pungent aroma of coffee greeted her. Last night she would have sworn they'd have to abandon the cabin, yet now the cheery fire made a mockery of last night's terror. Clean-shaven, save for his moustache, Wyatt was intent on the computer screen. A steaming mug sat beside him.

"Morning," Kyle muttered.

"Coffee's ready." He did not look up, but she saw the livid bruise beginning to form, a bona fide black eye. Its colors were likely to rival those of her bruise from the dinghy when they'd swamped in Yellowstone Lake.

A brief war waged between hot caffeine and cold feet. She dropped her boots by the fire, picked her way across the boards for a mug and poured. As she did, she realized Wyatt had piled the fallen rock, pulled down the loose timbers and swept. "You've been busy."

"Um."

She stood by the hearth and drank.

Wyatt raised his head. "Nick still sleeping it off?"

Something sharp in his tone brought back her anger. "I don't have to defend myself to you. At least Nick was drunk when he hit you, what's your excuse?"

"I seem to recall you asked me to hurry back here last night. Christ, if you'd told me you had other plans, I'd have camped on the trail."

"Maybe you should have," she returned. "What in hell's the matter with you?"

He slowly flattened his palms on the table. "You're a smart woman, Kyle. You figure it out."

The intensity of his gaze combined fury and something passionate. The fire toasted the back of her thighs while the morning chill nipped her front. Her coffee mug began to tremble.

She cradled it with her other hand, while holding eye contact with Wyatt. Somehow, she had trouble breathing.

"Darden's a player," he went on. "He lights where the volcano blows."

"So what?" Nick stood in the doorway.

Kyle turned toward him.

"I'm a guy who drives fast and does handsprings on fence rails." He walked to her and plucked the cup from her hand. His Adam's apple bobbed beneath his stubbled jaw as he swallowed and made a toasting motion toward Wyatt. "Kyle's a big girl, as I vaguely recall telling you last night."

Kyle felt heat rush to her face and prepared to tell them both to stand down.

Before she could, Wyatt glared at Nick. "Let's not go there again. We have to work together, at least until we get off this keg of dynamite."

Nick shrugged. "Come on, Kyle. What say we make breakfast?"

If she had to face food, she'd probably throw up. Still seething, she went out onto the porch and resisted risking another splinter in her palm. When Nick followed, she put out her hand in a stop gesture. "Not now. Just not now, okay? Let me be a few minutes and then I'll help you cook."

He opened his mouth, but appeared to change his mind and went back inside. Though she listened to see if he and Wyatt had words, it stayed quiet.

A hard wave of nausea rose. She deep-breathed until it passed.

After a few minutes she went in and helped Nick with breakfast. He worked by her side with uncharacteristic quiet, but knowing him, she likened it to the seismic lull that had preceded the earthquake. She was less able to hold things in, breaking eggs into the skillet so viciously that they were peppered with shell and the yolks broke.

As they sat to eat, an aftershock rattled the dishes. Wyatt sat quietly through the tremors while Nick rode them with a surfer's grin.

"That was the first I've felt this morning," she said. "I would have expected more."

Nick took on a thoughtful look. "Scientists in Japan often use a period of relative inactivity along a fault system to predict a sharp release of stored energy. Maybe the period of quiet we observed led to last night's event?"

"I thought those periods of quiet were measured in months and years," Wyatt said. "We're talking about too short a time period here."

"I would have thought so, but things seem to be happening here on an accelerated timetable."

Kyle was glad that speaking of their mission brought the two men to a truce.

Nick went on, "We know for a fact from Wyatt passing safely through the canyon the other morning that the gas seeps popped up within a matter of hours."

A mouthful of pancakes grew bigger and dryer as Kyle chewed and forced them down.

Wyatt pushed back his plate. "You guys should look at the quake records from the remote stations. Unless I miss my interpretation, the focus of last night's quake was right under us at Nez Perce Peak."

"Uh-oh," Nick said.

Kyle got up and paced. Charring marked the floor from the burned rug. "We need to gather the quake data from the stations we've set out near here."

Wyatt agreed. "We'll go on horseback and split up to save time."

"Whoa." Nick held out his hands. "I'm walking, especially with the snow."

Wyatt looked exasperated. "I'll take Thunder down the Lamar Valley. He can cover more ground in a day than Kyle on Strawberry or Nick on shank's mare."

"Whoa," said Nick again. "Kyle stays here."

"This is going to take all three of us," Wyatt argued.

"I'm going with you guys," Kyle insisted, while Nick and Wyatt left their dishes on the table and started putting their gear together.

Nick stopped rummaging in his pack and gave her a level gaze. "You need to monitor the stations."

Wyatt went to the computer.

Kyle looked at the machine. "We need to email Mammoth and tell them how bad the quake was up here."

"I sent Radford a message earlier." He glanced at Kyle. "Now I'm letting Alicia know I'm all right up here."

❊ ❊ ❊

Sleeping at Wyatt's house, as she had been since he left, usually gave Alicia a good feeling upon awakening.

This morning she was uneasy.

In the night, she'd been shocked awake by a quake that went on for many seconds, sending her heart into her throat while she waited for it to stop.

In Wyatt's terry robe that dwarfed her, she moved rest-lessly around his kitchen making tea. She turned on the TV and found out that last night's shake was bigger than she'd imagined.

A still photo of earthquake predictor Brock Hobart was in split-screen with host Monty Muckleroy.

Monty smiled. "Folks, our friend Dr. Hobart has done it again. Brock, tell us what happened in Yellowstone last night."

"With the new moon rising," Brock's voice sounded a little thin, "Yellowstone experienced an earthquake of magnitude 6.1, as I predicted last Friday."

"I believe you said 6.0." Monty looked coy.

The audience laughed.

"Monty, if you don't think a 6.1 was close enough, I'll have to find another talk show."

"Oooh," went the audience.

"As far as I've heard," Brock went on, "there were no casualties. Most of the energy hit the park interior."

"What do you predict next?" Monty asked.

"My preliminary analysis, based on public information on the Internet from the Yellowstone Seismic Network, makes me suspect there is a lot of energy still in the ground."

Brock's casual prediction of more trouble infuriated Alicia. There he sat far from harm's way while Wyatt and the real scientists were treated as nobodies.

After Monty promised to keep the nation informed

through more chats with Brock, Alicia headed up to Mammoth. Two news crews waited in the lot outside Headquarters. Inside the Resource Center, Iniki Kuni had a rumpled look to her spiky hair.

"Did you feel that earthquake last night?" Iniki asked.

"It was tough not to," Alicia allowed, realizing that the young woman was more frightened than she had been. "But, didn't you grow up here? Aren't you used to it?"

Iniki got up, revealing a thigh-high skirt. "It's never been this bad. First that landslide, then last night . . ." Her voice went shrill. "Brock Hobart says it isn't over."

Alicia said kindly, "Maybe we ought to wait and see what Wyatt and the scientists have to say. Wouldn't you rather rely on them?"

Iniki subsided back into her chair. "Okay, but I haven't heard from them."

"I came to send email to Wyatt," Alicia said. She vowed that after Wyatt's absence this time she'd stop being computer illiterate and get her own account.

With a glance over her shoulder at the large corner office, Iniki said, "Radford's always freaking out about security. He doesn't even let me into his email, but since he's not here, why don't you use Wyatt's computer?"

"Password?" Alicia asked.

Iniki pulled open a drawer and pointed a dagger-like nail at a sticky note. "It rotates every week. Thunder for his favorite horse, stone, like rocks, get it? Or," she grinned, "Alicia."

As she moved down the hallway, Alicia smiled to herself. Inside Wyatt's office with the door closed behind her, she smelled heat from the radiators and could swear she caught the scent of him, a subtle mix of deodorant soap and evergreen. Finding his dress jacket hanging, she buried her face in woolen folds. She wanted to cry, for staying at his house was a poor substitute for being with him. Even his office felt abandoned.

She moved behind his desk and sat, trying to hold on to her sense of him.

After booting up Wyatt's computer, and finding his password was 'stone', she opened his email. Not checking up on him, she did scroll through his inbox. He must have cleaned house recently, for he'd deleted almost everything except a long list of messages from kstone@ut.edu.

Frowning, Alicia opened the oldest one that dated back over a year.

Congratulations, Wyatt! I'm so happy you decided on the Yellowstone job instead of going for the oil company money. At least you won't be far, for I'm going to miss my favorite student. I look forward to our working together in the future.

In the next half hour, Alicia learned that Salt Lake City was at risk for a major earthquake, that Wyatt and Dr. Stone communicated at least once a week, and that the professor's favorite color was blue.

Alicia closed the folder. She brought up a new message box, but whatever had been in her head to tell him had gone. As for his password, *Stone*, yeah, she got it.

Leaving the Resource Center, she found Superintendent Janet Bolido in her uniform and badge, fielding questions from reporters on the lawn.

"Last night's earthquake measured magnitude 6.1. The last time we had one that strong was in 1975," called Carol Leeds of *Billings Live Eye*. Her faded mass of red hair made her look like Medusa in a jeans jacket. "What about damage?"

"The Lake Hotel got a good shake," Janet said, "but in the morning light we're finding harm was minimal. Glassware, souvenirs, and the round glass window in the main stairwell were broken."

"Aftershocks?" another reporter asked.

"They haven't been too bad," Janet said with evident satisfaction.

Carol Leeds broke back in, "The main road was clear yesterday, but last night's quake rained more rock and dirt into Gardner Canyon."

"Is that a question?" Janet countered.

Alicia leaned against a porch post and found she was checking to see if it felt solid or whether there were more tremors.

Carol went on, "What do you think about Brock Hobart predicting last night's quake?"

Janet's voice stayed even, but Alicia thought she looked infuriated. "I take my information from park scientists. They tell me that earthquake prediction, as to the specific time, place, and magnitude, is impossible. Brock may have made a lucky guess. So did psychic Jeanne Dixon with the Kennedy assassination."

"What do your scientists tell you is going to happen next?"

"There is a team in the field even as we speak, adding more seismographs to our already extensive network. If they come up with anything, you'll be the first to know."

CHAPTER TWENTY-SIX

SEPTEMBER 26

After Wyatt and Nick had gone into the field, Kyle studied the seismic data. As she worked, the information coming from the stations corroborated their suspicions.

The focus of most of the recent earthquakes, including the 6.1 magnitude they had dubbed the New Moon Earthquake, made an accurate map of the Saddle Valley fault plane, dipping down into the earth at about seventy degrees. A shiver ran down her back as she looked at the time and intensity of the previous shocks. Small tremors had stopped a few days before the New Moon Earthquake, the period of relative quiet a potential indicator of stress building in the ground. Noting the continued lack of post-quake aftershocks, her fingers went still on the keyboard.

No, she told herself, it wasn't time to start thinking like Brock Hobart.

Yet, she decided to access his website. To the right of his publicity photo, shot in a rustic field setting, blared the headline:

YELLOWSTONE QUAKE FAILS TO EASE BUILDING PRESSURE.

Pressure, the kind that sent gas to the surface . . .

Grabbing a gas detector, she went outside to check on the area around the cabin to make sure it was safe. Too high a concentration and she'd be forced to start climbing to avoid the heavier-than-air hydrogen sulfide.

Once she'd gotten a negative reading, she decided to risk a quick check on the progress of melting snow for the horses' drinking water. Down the hill in the sunny Saddle Valley, she and Wyatt had spread a black plastic sheet and scooped a thin layer of snow over it. The edge of the sheet was draped over a rock and folded to funnel melt water into a PVC bucket. Around the black expanse, bare earth glistened, with sparse areas of frost propping up little castles in the dirt.

Although the wind cut coldly at Kyle's face and neck, even those ice palaces were collapsing in the sun. Certain they had laid the tarp out on snow a few hours ago, she looked around and found that across the hillside, the hummocky blanket of white renewed.

If she had not been so concerned with checking her gas detector, she realized she might have seen it sooner. The area of barren ground was perhaps twenty yards wide, the melt line roughly linear. It followed the slash of Nick's red pen across the map, as heat from below the ground escaped along the Saddle Valley Fault.

●　●　●

When dusk fell with no sign of Wyatt or Nick, Kyle began to imagine the worst. Wyatt had gotten into a pocket of poison gas, or wandered onto a thin crust and fallen through. Nick had gone into the lava cave he had found up the mountain and been unable to find his way out.

Just before full dark, she walked outside and used her gas detector again to be sure all was still clear. Coming back, she checked on the horses. Gray fell eagerly upon the fresh food she put in the buckets, while Strawberry sniffed at Kyle's pockets for the expected sugar treat. "Good girl," Kyle whispered, petting her velvet nose.

Next came fueling the generator, building a roaring fire on the hearth, and lighting the Coleman lantern. Finally, she decided to make dinner. It was supposed to be Wyatt's turn, but the guys would be hungry when they got in. With their food stores nearly down to canned and dried items, she chopped an onion and mixed in cans of beans, tomatoes, and chili. As she was stirring the pot, she heard the sound of boots on the porch.

"Yo, Kyle!" Nick opened the door with a grin, his nose red from the cold wind, his jacket and pants smeared with dirt. "That chili I smell?"

"You bet." Feeling some butterflies at being alone with him after last night's debacle, she blurted, "Have you seen Wyatt?"

Nick sobered. "He's right behind me, seeing to Thunder." He went to the fire and put his back to her, holding his hands toward the flames.

A moment later Wyatt paused in the doorway and took in the cooking pot. His eyes sought hers. "Thanks. I wasn't looking forward to cooking."

"You're welcome," she murmured. "I'm glad you're back safe."

"In addition to bringing the data drives from the west, I found traces of H_2S all along the Saddle Valley." Wyatt took a few long strides and intimidated Nick into making room for him to get warm.

Ignoring Wyatt, Nick looked at Kyle. "Did you see the snow has melted all along the fault?"

She nodded. "Based on your experience with live volcanoes, what do you think's going on here?"

He frowned. "Volcanoes can throw off a lot more gas and heat than this and not hurt anybody . . ." he trailed off.

"But?" Wyatt asked.

"In 1993," Nick said, "at Galeras in southern Colombia, volcanologists took a fieldtrip to the crater. They believed it was safe because the fumaroles were quiet and the earth tremors calm." In a grim voice, he finished, "It erupted without warning. Killed nine and injured six."

CHAPTER TWENTY-SEVEN

SEPTEMBER 27

The next afternoon Kyle kept checking the seismic traces. Nick's warning about Galeras only served to renew her suspicion that the quiet after the New Moon's storm might be the calm before the next one.

She rose and went out onto the porch to stretch her legs. This sitting around waiting for something to happen was driving her crazy to be out in the field.

At just past two, she saw Nick walking up from the valley.

"You're back early," she called when he was within ear-shot.

"Thought I'd beat the cowboy's time." His light-hearted banter was back, a sign she interpreted to mean he wasn't going to speak of the other night, at least not in a serious manner. "Where is he, by the way?" Something in Nick's expression said he was turning the tables on her for asking where Wyatt was the afternoon before.

"Should be just down the way, putting a new cable on seismic station four."

He nodded toward her boots at the doorway. "Get

your shoes on."

"What for?"

"Thought we'd check for gas readings in that lava cave I told you about. If you bring your climbing rope you can help us get in and out."

The last thing she wanted was to go into a cave. "Don't I need to stay here and watch the signals?" she said, though only moments before she'd been eager for an excursion.

"It's not far up to the cave mouth, and I got to thinking. Gas readings from a lava tube could be another valuable early-warning tool." She heard that he didn't mind risking their lives for information.

Well, weren't they all gambling by simply being here? If something happened as swiftly as it had at Galeras, there would be no time to even call for a helicopter.

Nick took her silence for assent. "Did I see your climbing rope in the stable?"

"It's there on a nail," she replied evenly.

He headed out for the small log building, but once alone, she hesitated. The mere idea of total darkness made her breath come shallow. What if they got underground and got lost?

When Nick came back, she was still sitting before the computer.

"Daylight's wasting," he said.

"I don't . . ."

Nick grinned. "You don't like the dark . . . I know." With a flourish, he dipped into two of his pockets and brought out flashlights. "Extra backup." He nodded toward the bunkroom. "Bring some of yours."

Moving quickly before she could change her mind, she geared up, putting extra lights in her pack as he suggested. Then she grabbed her jacket and put on her boots. If she got to the cave and couldn't manage it, she'd tell him she should stay outside to be sure the rope didn't come untied or something.

"It's not far," Nick said. "We'll hike the spine and then drop down on the east side."

The trail was rugged and so steep that they had to climb more than halfway to the summit before the mountaintop came into view. When Nick came to a sudden stop, Kyle trod on his heel.

"Sorry."

Nick didn't answer as he stared up the slope.

She looked. Above the tree line, up on the rusty looking cinder cone, steam poured from hundreds of places. The brisk breeze drew eddies and currents in the smoke-like vapors.

Nick slung off his pack, pulled out his map and marked the broad field of vents onto it. "They may be just water vapor, but without any silica tubes to collect a gas sample, we don't know."

Kyle's heart started to beat faster. According to studies in Central America and the Kamchatka Peninsula, there was a definite order to the gases released by rising magma. First water, then carbon dioxide, hydrogen sulfide, and finally hydrogen chloride was the last to be emitted before an eruption.

"There may be HCl in the gas." He confirmed what she'd been thinking.

Though Kyle half-expected him to want to walk up to and sniff around the steamers, he turned to her. "I had a clear view of the summit from down the valley a few hours ago."

"No steam then?"

"Not a trace." He wiped sweat from his forehead with the back of his hand. "Let's go back and check the seismic."

● ● ●

At the cabin, Nick sat on the porch steps and drew a pack of Marlboros from his coat pocket. When she sat down beside him to remove her boots, she caught the slightly sweet aroma of cured tobacco.

"I thought you only smoked when you drank."

He shook his head as he cupped his hands and used a lighter. "I also smoke when the shit hits . . . although this situation may soon call for a drink as well."

Something in his tone suggested he was thinking of them trying to find the bottom of a brandy bottle. Her cheeks flushed.

Though they needed to go inside and check the seismic, they sat a few moments in silence. Their shoulders did not touch, but Kyle imagined she could feel warmth from his.

And a moment later, "Hey, here's Wyatt," Nick said unnecessarily.

Wyatt reined in Thunder at the corral, dismounted, and unloaded three data drives from the seismic stations. He stopped and looked into the pen where Strawberry was trotting in fits and starts, her mane tossing. Even Gray looked wall-eyed.

With a scratch of his head, Wyatt brought the drives up and set them on the porch.

"Horses are spooked," he said with a glare at Nick's cigarette. "Maybe a bear."

He went back toward the barn.

Rather than follow Wyatt into bear territory, Nick rose and lifted two of the drives to take inside. Kyle followed with the third.

She started up the laptop and hooked one of the drives to it for downloading. It was from the closest portable station to the peak, with data that should cover the time when the steamers had erupted.

Nick pulled out his cigarettes and lit another with the leisurely style he lent to the smallest action. The smoke made her nostrils flare.

"For God's sake," she snapped. "Take that outside."

Nick stubbed it out on the wooden tabletop, leaving a circlet of char. "There." The cabin door opened again and he said, "See a bear, cowboy?"

As Wyatt fanned his hand at the leftover smoke, the cabin floor leaped. The computer bounced up and smashed back onto the tabletop. Pots and pans clattered to the floor.

"Guess there wasn't a bear," Nick said cheerfully. "Just the animal earthquake alarm."

Kyle grabbed the table's scarred pine boards, her heart rate in overdrive.

She'd asked for this, through every geology class, fieldtrip, or conference with Stanton in which she had insisted earthquake seismology was right for her. The thumps and bumps went on for less than ten seconds and then subsided. Wyatt went back out, probably to calm the horses again.

"Nick," she said. "Give me a cigarette."

He tapped one out with maddening slowness, making a production of placing it between her lips and lighting it. The first drag stung.

Fifteen minutes later, staring at the seismic records, Kyle inhaled the smoke from her third cigarette. It was just as she'd imagined, back in the groove as though she'd never left.

"Take it easy," Nick cautioned. "You're not used to it."

He was right. The nicotine had gone to her head as surely as the brandy had the other night. A little lightheaded, she looked at her laptop screen though a soft focus.

Wyatt came in and sloughed off his coat. He removed his boots with a glance at Nick, who was still wearing his muddy ones.

"Horses okay?" Nick asked to Kyle's surprise.

"They settled after the shake."

She hoped their calm meant there would be no more action this evening.

Wyatt sniffed and made a distasteful face. "Come on, Darden, take the cigarette outside."

Nick straightened from where he was laying logs for the evening fire and spread his empty hands. Caught with a Marlboro halfway from her mouth to the saucer she had used as an ashtray, Kyle said, "I'll put it out." She was getting nauseous, anyway.

Wyatt dropped his boots with a thud. "I've never seen you smoke."

"I quit." She ground out the butt. "Ten years ago."

He looked from her to Nick and back. "I don't think I understand you anymore."

Nick's head was down as he placed a match to kindling. Kyle's face flamed.

She gave her attention to a first look at the new seismic patterns.

Her hand went to her throat. "Guys."

Both men must have heard her urgency for they crossed the boards in record time. She pointed to the screen, where instead of the usual random pattern of noise, or even a normal earthquake signature that peaked and dampened over time . . . here was a constant oscillating sine wave. Kyle had seen it in books and in sample signals from volcanoes.

"Harmonic tremors," Nick confirmed with that secret edge of excitement she'd come to recognize in his voice.

"Magma's definitely on the move."

Kyle could feel the pulse in her neck. "Isn't there some other explanation?"

Wyatt frowned. "It wouldn't matter even if there were. We've got gas seeps that kill wildlife, steam vents . . ." He ticked them on his fingers. "A big earthquake along a rejuvenated fault."

"What do you think is next?" Kyle asked Nick.

"What's next?" He rubbed the back of his neck. "I heard that in the Philippines from the brass at Clark Air Force Base before Pinatubo went off. At Mount St. Helens, the USGS got Washington Governor Dixy Lee Ray to evacuate people up to eight miles from the crater. After nearly two months of nothing, local authorities let them go back to their cabins at Spirit Lake to retrieve belongings. Narrowly missed getting them all killed."

Nick paced, his booted feet jarring the boards. Bits of mud flew off the lug soles. "At Long Valley Caldera in northern California, all the signs were there. Harmonic tremors clearly showed magma heading for the surface. I staked my reputation on an eruption that's yet to happen. And when local business and real estate values plummeted, guess who got blamed?"

● ● ●

Wyatt lay in his bunk listening to Nick's snoring and Kyle's even respirations. After the New Moon quake, they had put the beds back together the same as before, with her on the top shelf above Nick and Wyatt across. She was no closer to Nick, but it seemed so.

Kyle's candle lantern cast flickering shadows on the dark logs.

Not many people her age were afraid of the dark, but he'd decided she was. At the Institute, she always waited for somebody else to traverse the shadows to the seismograph lab's light switch. Casual, the way she dragged her feet a little, or turned back to check on something in her office. As for her fear of earthquakes, he recalled how high strung she became whenever the seismic alarm went off. In a rush to check out the signals, she stared at the screen so tensely that sometimes he didn't even think she saw it.

It all seemed odd in a woman he'd always thought was tough as asbestos.

As Wyatt's gut told him to get off the mountain, he thought it must be worse on Kyle.

● ● ●

The rough bark ceiling hung a few feet above Kyle's head in her wavering light. She lay and thought of the dead deer, small rodents, and birds overcome by gas. And the fault that ran through the lowest point of Saddle Valley, just a short way downslope. Deadly fumes could even now be pouring from fissures, filling the local topographic bowl, and rising in darkness toward the horse stable and cabin.

Knowing she'd never sleep, Kyle unzipped her sleeping bag and climbed down. She was careful not to step on Nick, who continued to snore. Through her socks, she felt the chill in the floorboards.

With her lantern in one hand, she padded into the front room. There, where the brighter light would not disturb Nick and Wyatt, she turned on a powerful torch and slipped on her jacket and cold boots. With a gas detector in hand, she went out into the night.

Her breath steamed and her nose stung from the chill, making her realize how much residual warmth there was from the coals on the hearth.

Upon nearing the stable and hearing the horses soft whickering, she paused to open the top half of the door and give all three a handful of feed pellets. Bold Thunder kept trying to shove Strawberry and Gray aside.

"Go on, you big galoot. Let the others have some, too."

Moving on, she checked and rechecked the detector, trying to protect it from the strong east wind, all the way to the low point where the fault line was. There, for the first time, there was a concentration of a few parts per million, barely enough to measure. Yet, as fast as things were changing on the mountain, she knew it could be only a short time before toxic levels were released.

She started back up the hill on swift feet. The moon was noticeably larger this evening, reminding her of Brock Hobart's tidal theories. With a 6.1 logged on the new moon, she began to wonder what the next full moon might portend.

Back in the cabin, she considered waking Wyatt and Nick, but with the wind dispersing the gas, it was safe enough to let them sleep while she thought things through.

As expedition leader, it was her call on whether to pull out. If they left, they wouldn't have access to information from the portable seismic network, but over half of the stations now relayed signals to the Institute computers.

She turned off the torch and curled up on the worn sofa in the candle lantern's glow. A pack of Nick's cigarettes lay on a wooden spool that served as end table, along with his lighter. The woman who'd been smoke-free for ten years waged a brief war with old habit and lost once again.

Fire at her fingertips in the shadowy room reminded her of finding Stanton alone in the seismic lab before his stroke. She wondered what he would think if faced with the information they had gathered. The harmonic waves, gas seeps, and heat flow with steam vents popping up like pressure cookers were all signs that historically pointed to eruptions.

Except when they had not.

Back in 1975, an evacuation order was issued the day before a magnitude 7.3 quake struck Haicheng in China. The precursors included changes in land elevation and ground water levels, foreshocks, and reports of strange animal behavior. It was believed that many thousands of people were saved by the evacuation. On the other hand, only a year later, China suffered a magnitude 7.6 in Tangshan. Without any warning, 250,000 people died.

In California, the Parkfield area had suffered large earthquakes in 1857, 1881, 1901, 1922, 1934, and 1966. USGS and other scientists regularly monitored the faults and had made a prediction of a magnitude 6.0 between 1988 and 1992.

It didn't happen.

At Mount St. Helens, the public had been officially warned that the mountain might erupt within a few months.

It hadn't taken that long.

Her head spinning with the conflicting stories, she took another drag on the Marlboro. It didn't please her.

Wyatt appeared in the bunkroom doorway. His feet looked pale against black fleece long johns like hers. His chest was bare. "Can't sleep?" he asked softly.

"No." Knowing his aversion to smoke, she stubbed out her cigarette.

He went back into the dark bunkroom. Upon his return, he wore a pullover and carried his sleeping bag that he used to cover them both. In the light of the single candle, his face looked tanned and gaunt while a trace of midnight shadow stubbled his jaw.

"I can't stop running scenarios." He ruffled his sleep-tossed hair. "Guess there's something to be said for surfing with no fear." He nodded toward the bunkroom. As if on cue, Nick snuffled in his sleep.

"I've been thinking about what we should do," she said.

They sat for a moment in silence.

"Me, too," Wyatt admitted. "If Nick's right about magma

pushing up the fault or under the peak, this is no ordinary situation where strain will be released. Each larger quake might buy a little time before the next, but who knows?"

"I went out a while ago and detected gas below the cabin. It's blowing away right now, but . . ." She envisioned red-hot melted rock pushing its relentless way toward the surface. Upon reaching a narrow conduit like the Saddle Valley fault, it would build heat and pressure until a fissure broke through to release lava . . .

Or the mountain could explode, blasting down the forest and crushing the cabin walls.

As if the earth could read her thoughts, a jolt shook the cabin.

At the shock, Kyle's own walls, the ones she had built inside her, broke down. Fragments of memory formed into sharp shards. Incoherent shades of black and gray were accompanied by a shower of sound and earth.

Her fists clenched on the sleeping bag and she closed her eyes. Pain stabbed at her, the awful sense of loss, flashing her back again to memories so ancient they should have been long buried.

"Kyle." Wyatt's voice was soft yet intent.

Small sparks of light exploded like fireworks as she lifted her fists and rubbed them against her eyelids. She didn't want to see, but . . .

She opened her eyes and took a jagged breath.

From across the length of sofa, Wyatt reassured her with his dark eyes. His free hand shushed across the sleeping bag and settled over her cold fingers. "You going to tell me about it this time?"

She acted on long-established instinct. "Tell you what? That any thinking human being would be scared sitting on this powder keg?"

"I am," he agreed.

Though no further tremors shook them, a shudder went through her.

"Would it help if I built a fire?" Wyatt asked.

She looked at the hearth and nodded. Not wanting to think, she focused on him bringing in firewood along with a gust of chill.

"This'll fix you right up," he promised, laying the kindling with care and piling on a small log.

She had the presence of mind to toss him Nick's lighter. As the flames caught and shadows brightened, he came back, slid under the sleeping bag and tucked it snugly around them. Sitting thigh to thigh, his warmth seeped into her.

It seemed the most natural thing in the world when he put his arm around her and drew her against him. Together, they watched the flames while his question remained between them.

"Wyatt . . ."

"Right here."

Yet, after being alone with her secret for nearly a lifetime, she pressed her lips together.

He squeezed her shoulders. "You're the strongest

woman I know. You can do anything you want."

"No . . . no." Darkness, black water, and a dead moon stifled her.

"Kyle." Wyatt pulled her head down so her ear rested over his heart. "For God's sake, talk to me."

Held warm and solid against him, feeling his pulse, she actually began to consider letting someone into her private nightmare. If she shared her burden, perhaps it might weigh less.

"It's bad," she warned.

"We can take it." He bent his head. Something that might have been his lips brushed her temple.

She took the plunge. "I was in Rock Creek Campground the night the mountain fell. Both my parents died."

From the back room, Nick's soft snoring continued.

"My dog Max . . . he was the sweetest Golden. I've never had another dog." She felt tears rising. "I spent the night in a tree. Climbing higher and higher to keep from drowning. The lantern went out . . . the moon was covered by dust clouds."

Once she started, she found she wanted to talk about that long-ago night. About the ground roll, the strange sensation of near weightlessness when the earth lifted, and the constant battering of aftershocks. For a long time, she talked and Wyatt listened.

"When you think about what happened," he asked, "what scares you the most?"

Was it the first shock that had torn through the earth

and dropped the Rambler? The sight of her father seized by the shock wave and tossed like a straw man? Max's frantic barking silenced by an avalanche of sound?

"When I couldn't hold on to the tree anymore, I fell into the black water. I managed to make it onto the slide, and I was taken to a hospital. Franny and Zeke drove up from Arizona to get me. Ever since then, what scares me the most is the nightmares I have of finding my family dead . . . and the fact that I have no idea if they are real."

"Anything I could say," Wyatt pressed his cheek to hers, "would be inadequate." He gestured toward the bunkroom. "Does Nick know?"

She shook her head. "Stanton figured it out, back when I first came to Utah and refused to take a fieldtrip to the slide. I've never told anyone else."

With his free hand, Wyatt smoothed her tousled hair. "I'm the first?"

"I haven't talked about it because I couldn't bear to think about it. Even though I've worked on Yellowstone, I'd never been back to Earthquake Lake or Madison Canyon . . . until I met you there. I tried to put it all away in a corner of my mind as dark as that night, and I've always kept the lights on."

Wyatt glanced at her candle lantern.

She looked toward the bunkroom. "I once thought I loved Nick with everything in me, but I could never imagine telling him. He's such an adrenaline junkie he'd probably tell me to buck up or some other jolly cliché."

Wyatt touched the purpling skin below his eye that was forming into a real shiner. "Is there anybody really home?"

"He's in there, all right. He just doesn't let people get close."

"A lot of us are like that . . . me, you . . ."

Kyle smiled and dashed at the tears on her cheek. "I guess with my secrets, I'm one to talk." Settling back into the sofa, she ignored a spring pressing her back. "When you asked me to meet you at the Visitor Center, I honestly thought if I went back, I'd see a weathering landslide and be able to tell myself it no longer frightened me." She scooted down and settled her head on his shoulder. "Since the trouble started up here, I'm like those Vietnam veterans flashing back, or a guy who stormed the beach at Normandy."

"In the last few weeks, you have been different." He waved his hand to indicate a progression of ups and downs.

"Crazy?" she asked bitterly.

His face changed to a look of determination. "I'll fight anybody who says you're crazy."

"Well, try this on. We all make fun of Brock Hobart making predictions. Yet, now I wonder if he isn't on the right track. He's certainly as serious in his beliefs as I am when I say we need to alert them at Headquarters about more big earthquakes. At the very least."

Wyatt nodded.

"Better be sure you want in on this," she advised. "If we put out a warning and nothing happens, for days or weeks or months, everyone will say we're nuts."

CHAPTER TWENTY-EIGHT
SEPTEMBER 28

"How domestic." Nick's voice startled Kyle awake. He stood in the door of the bunkroom, a cowlick in his hair. Morning light grayed the windows, and his breath steamed.

She was shocked to realize she was still in Wyatt's arms. A bad taste in her mouth from the cigarette and a crick in her neck warred with the languid sensation of waking up next to someone warm. Wyatt stirred, and when she would have leaped to her feet, he placed a restraining hand on her arm beneath the sleeping bag.

"Oops," he drawled, not sounding the least sorry. "Must have fallen asleep watching the fire."

As Kyle got up slowly and took the few steps to the bunkroom to dress, she wasn't sure she was sorry either. Fairy tale wisdom had it that one cared for one man at a time, the way she'd once wanted Nick with everything in her. In the field, things weren't that simple.

In one of her late-night talks with Franny, her grandmother had told Kyle of her own experience as a young woman in Wyoming. While she was working at the Jackson

Hole ranch, two men had courted her, brothers, and she'd confessed to the very real dilemma of loving them both. In fact, the outcome had been so difficult it had caused a family rift so deep that one branch had moved to Texas.

At least in Kyle's case, there was no question of having to choose between Nick and Wyatt. Nick's overtures must have originated in a brandy bottle, and as for Wyatt, he had Alicia.

Yet, as Kyle's hand mirror revealed her hair to be a rat's nest over her shoulders, she could still feel the soothing way Wyatt had smoothed it back from her face when she'd confided in him. Had he kissed her temple or had that been her imagination?

Breakfast was a strained affair. Nick set plates with such precision she wished he'd plunk them down. The silence went on so long, she finally couldn't stand it.

"Last night before we . . . fell asleep, Wyatt and I were talking about what to do."

Nick's head came up sharply and his eyes shifted from her to Wyatt and back. "I daresay." His voice was edged with the kind of violence that had already led to Wyatt's black eye.

Kyle slapped her hand on the table. "Oh, for God's sake! We were talking about the mountain." With all her heart, she wanted to suggest they go back to civilization, but wasn't that the coward's way?

Wyatt spoke. "I think we should leave this morning, before things get any worse."

She expected anger from Nick, derision at the very least. Instead, he pressed his lips into a line and nodded.

Wyatt cleared the table and started cleaning up. Nick had cooked, and though by their system he was technically exempt from doing dishes, to Kyle's surprise Wyatt helped with that task as well. They were to leave the patrol cabin as they'd found it: clean, blankets and rations in place, and a fire laid in case someone in need of warmth and food sought shelter there.

"I think we need to send a new message to Radford Bullis," Kyle suggested as she booted the laptop. "Wyatt and I talked about warning folks about what's happening up here."

Nick cast another measuring gaze at both her and Wyatt. "I guess you think I'm opposed to that after what I said about our false alarm at Long Valley Caldera."

"You're not?" Wyatt asked.

"Of course not." Nick dried a coffee mug. "I'm all in favor of keeping people abreast."

"Then let's do it." Wyatt polished a spoon.

Relieved that the two men were willing to accept a truce to discuss the work at hand, Kyle opened a mail file. Fingers poised, she tried to figure out her opening. Short and sweet, or long on jargon?

She began typing.

We are leaving Nez Perce Peak this morning due to high heat flow and the danger of hydrogen sulfide gas seeping up a fault along the north side of the mountain. Fields of new fumaroles have appeared on the summit for which we have no gas analysis. Our seismic readings indicate that the park will probably experience more and possibly stronger earthquakes before this cycle of activity subsides.

A low whistle came from Nick's pursed lips as he watched over her shoulder.

She couldn't read his mood. "What would you say?"

Nick set aside his dishtowel, pulled out a chair and sat down facing her. "You might have thought I was snoring the night away, but sometimes I do my best thinking by not thinking. This morning when I woke, I had a gut instinct something was even more wrong than we've thought." He gestured toward the computer. "Let's have a look at the GPS data."

While Kyle accessed the information, Nick went on, "I got to thinking about David Mowry being killed miles from here. We've been looking at the local GPS stations, but . . ."

Wyatt put the last dish into the cabinet and joined them at the table. "You mean what if this thing is bigger than just Nez Perce Peak?"

"Precisely."

Kyle plotted the differential data showing the elevation changes since the New Moon quake on a map. Staring at the large contoured bull's-eye that covered a quarter of the park and centered on Nez Perce, she said tersely, "You're right, Nick."

He looked at the screen. "About your message to Radford.

I think you'd better make it stronger."

● ● ●

Alicia entered the Resource Center at eight-thirty to find
a wide-eyed Iniki Kuni behind the reception desk. Black
bellbottoms and a matching cropped top looked out of place
against the scientists' Park Service uniforms and Alicia's
own jeans and flannel shirt. Before she could ask for news
of Wyatt, Iniki thrust a trembling sheet of paper at her.

*We are leaving Nez Perce Peak this morning due to high
heat flow and the danger of poisonous hydrogen sulfide gas.
Examples of dead wildlife have been found along a previously
unmapped active fault that is a conduit for rising magma. Our
seismic readings indicate that the park will undoubtedly experience more and stronger earthquakes, without warning and at
any time. There is also a definite possibility of a volcanic eruption with Nez Perce Peak as its focus.*

Along with Wyatt, Kyle Stone and a Nick Darden
were listed as senders.

"More earthquakes," Iniki wailed. "A volcano! Do we
need to get out of here?"

Alicia studied the message again, this time trying to
focus on something other than the fact that Wyatt was
coming out of the field, which was fine with her since he
wouldn't be spending nights around Kyle Stone anymore.
On the second reading, the words 'poisonous gas' and 'dead
wildlife' stuck out.

"If we needed to get out, they would tell us," said Alicia. Wouldn't they?

● ● ●

"More and stronger earthquakes. Without warning," Janet Bolido said to Radford Bullis. "What warning does an earthquake ever give?"

She slapped the printed email onto her cluttered desk. Somewhere in those piles of paper was the approval she was ready to sign for the Wonderland advertising campaign.

Radford shifted his broad body in the straight-backed wooden guest chair.

"What does their gibberish mean?" Janet crossed her arms. "A *definite* followed by *possibility* of a volcanic eruption? What am I supposed to do with this?"

Radford tented his fingers and studied them. "You get what the mountain gives you, Ms. Bolido."

Janet whacked the offending paper and her French manicured fingernail poked a hole in it. The Chief Scientist was another of those Ph.D.s, a dime a dozen around here. Doctor this and that.

Her office door opened without a knock and Chief Ranger Joseph Kuni's tall form filled the frame.

"Joseph, I need a head's up opinion instead of the wishy-washy crap the scientists are shoveling." She passed him the email. "Before he mounted this expedition, Wyatt Ellison told me geologists couldn't make this kind of prediction!"

Kuni glanced at the chair beside Radford's and stayed on his feet. He read, his brow creasing by the time he was done. "This doesn't look wishy-washy to me. Looks like something changed Ellison's mind."

Radford's chair squealed against the floor as he got up. "At the very least, we need to issue a press release."

Her gaze located the Wonderland campaign papers.

"I agree," Kuni said. "The season is winding down, but maybe we should consider closing the concessions in the center of the park early."

"No," Janet argued. "You remember . . . some guy predicted a big earthquake in Missouri on a certain day?"

"Iben Browning, New Madrid Fault Zone, December 3, 1990," Radford said.

"Scared a lot of folks and nothing happened," she remembered.

"We've learned a lot since 1990," Radford countered.

Kuni nodded.

Seconds ticked past while Janet considered. Before coming to Yellowstone, she'd known scientists carried more weight here than in an urban park setting.

She stood. "I didn't sign on to be a disaster manager, but go ahead and draft the release." Then, thinking better of giving away too much control, "I'll look it over before it goes out."

When Radford and Kuni were gone, she sat staring for a long time. A lot was riding on her ability to increase revenue at Yellowstone, most notably her rise to the top of the ladder at Interior. She'd never get a Cabinet post, those were political appointees, but she could be the one feeding the Secretary his or her cues.

Craving a jolt of caffeine, Janet pushed back her chair. She could ask somebody to bring coffee, but she decided to walk over for Kuni's daughter's gourmet selection. While she was there, she could look over Radford's shoulder as he composed the release.

When she shoved open the door of the Administration Building, the *Billings Live Eye* van was parked in front of the Resource Center. On the front porch, Iniki Kuni's hands fluttered as she talked to a reporter.

Wondering what the media folks wanted with a secretary, Janet decided to evade an interview and turned back toward her office.

At her desk, she sipped the bitter brew that passed for coffee in the Administration Building and flipped through snail mail with her eyes and ears pealed for the new email signal. Half a dozen false alarms later, the draft from Radford came through.

The purpose of this press release is to alert the public and employees of the National Park Service to the recent earthquake activity in Yellowstone. Historically, the most persistent earthquake swarms have been on the west side of the Park. This is where the 1959 Hebgen Lake Earthquake and landslide killed thirty people.

1959 sounded sufficiently long ago, if not far enough away.

Other swarms occurred in 1985 and 1986, as well as 1999. This fall's most recent two-week series culminated in the September 26th magnitude 6.1 event. Following the quake, there has been an unusual lack of aftershock activity. The Utah Institute of Seismology, the USGS, and the Park Service will continue to monitor the situation.

Janet smiled. No layman would take the time to finish reading this, much less find anything alarming about it.

Scientists in the field from the above agencies have reported reactivation of dormant faults, along with seepage of poisonous gas. It is their opinion that further earthquake activity will take place, along with the potential for a volcanic eruption in the vicinity of Nez Perce Peak. All park visitors and employees should educate themselves as to the emergency preparedness precautions in the attached file.

The list included storing water and food, inspecting for hazards like unsecured bookcases. She glanced up at six wide shelves of books towering behind her desk.

"Bullshit," she muttered. There was no way to predict earthquakes or volcanoes with any kind of precision. There were plenty of examples of people crying wolf; she'd seen some of the TV shows about false alarms in different parts of the world.

It would take only a year or so to see results from the Wonderland Campaign. Once it was rolling and she could take some credit, she'd angle for the next promotion back in Washington. All she needed was a little luck.

With a few clicks of her keyboard and mouse, Janet

deleted the paragraph with the warning, along with the emergency-precautions attachment.

She hit the send button.

● ● ●

Alicia prowled the aisle of the Pic and Sav Shopping Center in Gardiner. Wyatt was a meat-and-potatoes man, so she'd already picked up some bakers. Now she frowned at the steaks.

"Hey, Kelley," she called to the gray-haired mom of the family operation. "All your meat out?"

Kelley's age-spotted hand selected another golden apple from a box and added it to the pyramid she was building.

"Skinny New York strips aren't what I want for Wyatt's first night home," Alicia said. She planned to wait for him at his house, clean sheets on the bed, the salad ready to toss, steaks seasoned to grill. When he came in, tired and dirty from the trail, she'd draw a hot bath and pour him a drink. "No rib-eyes hidden out?"

Kelley smiled. "You might try up at the Firehole Inn. Edith bought all my rib-eye and filet, but she might sell you some."

"At a premium," Alicia grumbled.

She started to maneuver and found a traffic jam blocking the aisle. A baby started to squall as her mother's cart knocked cans off a piled up display. Above the cash registers, helium balloons began a gentle sway.

Alicia went still.

An elderly man in coveralls came into the store, looked with dismay at the empty cart bay, and stumped down the aisle to grab and balance three large jugs of water.

Kelley put down the apple and wiped her hands on her apron. "What's up, Harry? Didn't know there was a drought."

"Earthquakes coming. Gotta lay in emergency supplies in case we lose power or the water mains break."

Kelley raised an eyebrow. "You can't tell when an earthquake's coming." She stopped and mused, "Unless . . . did Brock Hobart make another prediction?"

"No, siree." Harry set the jugs on the floor beside the checkout. "These are mine," he told the pregnant woman in line.

Alicia glanced up at the corner TV tuned to *Billings Live Eye*. At this midmorning hour, they would normally be broadcasting some network talk extravaganza. Instead, the local anchor was speaking over a banner, "Breaking News in Yellowstone National Park."

"Kelley!" Alicia called. "Turn up the TV."

"That's what I saw," said Harry, as Kelley ran to her glass-fronted customer-service office and pointed a remote at the television.

". . . Startling news from Yellowstone this morning," said the spectacled Clark Kent type anchor. "In the wake of the 6.1 magnitude earthquake here, scientists have warned of," he consulted a paper, "more and stronger earthquakes and a volcanic eruption at Nez Perce Peak."

Alicia watched the expressions of the people in the store. Those who had already heard the news redoubled their determination to lay in supplies. The others wore a shocked look that gradually shifted to a mental assessment of the contents of their shopping carts.

The anchor went on, "After Carol Leeds, our roving reporter in the field, filmed an interview with Ms. Iniki Kuni of the Yellowstone Resource Center, the Park Service issued an official release." He smiled. "I won't read it to you in its entirety, but it does conclude with mention of September 26's magnitude 6.1 event." He consulted his copy again. "I quote, 'Following the quake, there has been an unusual lack of aftershock activity. The Utah Institute of Seismology, the USGS, and the Park Service will continue to monitor the situation'."

Though the official version was less ominous, no one in the store put anything back.

CHAPTER TWENTY-NINE
SEPTEMBER 28

Kyle, Wyatt, and Nick rode down the canyon from Nez Perce Peak. They'd skirted the area of poison gas where the deer had died and avoided the fault line in case of new seeps. Nobody had much to say.

She wondered if the others were as jumpy.

Probably not. Steady Wyatt wasn't above admitting to fear, but she had faith he'd never give in to it. Her view ahead was of his brimmed hat and the back of his jacket, as well as Thunder's broad flanks and flicking tail.

Nick, bringing up the rear atop docile Gray, no doubt thought leaving the mountain cramped his style. She wasn't happy about abandoning their fieldwork, either. Hollis Delbert was going to be livid that they'd left all the equipment that wasn't part of a permanent station.

Well, just because she was paranoid didn't mean the mountain wasn't a pressure cooker. She could hardly wait until they'd put some miles behind them.

Without warning, Thunder shied. Strawberry planted her feet. Gray lifted his front hooves in an uncharacteristic display of pique.

"Hey!" Nick sawed on the reins. Gray bucked.

"Earthquake." Wyatt's thigh muscles bunched beneath his jeans as he brought Thunder under control.

The rocking disorientation and Strawberry's unease transmitted through the horse's trembling flanks. Tamping down a suicidal impulse to spur her to a gallop, Kyle waited for the worst.

Instead, the shaking diminished and died. Fortunately for Nick, who had little control over Gray, all three horses settled. Against silence, the clacking of rocks marked small landslides in the canyon.

"At least a 4.0," Nick observed.

Kyle tried not to transmit her anxiety to Strawberry.

Wyatt turned in his saddle and looked at her. "Okay?"

Nick groused, "I'm all right, but old Gray's never showed that much spirit."

"Kyle?" Wyatt said.

"Let's go on." She tried to sound steady.

Wyatt gave Thunder a nudge and he moved along. Kyle and Nick followed, riding side by side where the trail widened.

"You doing all right with Gray now?" she asked.

Although the morning was still cool, Nick's coat was tied around his waist and his hair dark with sweat. He'd talked about walking back to their trucks and trailers at the Pelican Creek trailhead, but finally admitted it would take more than one day to hike the twenty-plus miles.

"Horses." Nick gave his once-more sedate mount a

wary look. "When I was a kid in Ventura, my father took me to a ranch in the mountains near Ojai. I was scared as soon as I saw the huge chestnut he expected me to ride."

A surprise; Nick's tales never featured fear.

"The big ox stepped on my foot. I bit my tongue and tried to shove him off. He leaned and put more weight on that hoof until I screamed for Dad."

"And that's kept you away from horses?"

"I tried again at a country birthday party when I was fifteen. An old nag like Wyatt gave me, not that Gray's a bad sort." Nick patted the horse's neck. "That one was startled by a rabbit in the brush. I tried to keep my seat and my pride . . . fell off and broke my nose."

"So that's how you got that bump." She remembered tracing its contour with a fingertip. "I'm surprised you didn't get back in the saddle."

"You mean because I work on active volcanoes?"

She nodded.

"I find volcanoes both irresistible and frightening. I'm never more alive than when I'm on a crater rim watching a hail of stones or a river of lava. I know I can't stay long because I'm gambling with death, but I can't help wanting to go again and again." His eyes glowed the way a man's might when speaking of a woman he loved or his children.

What must it have been like for his wives, left at home while he spent three quarters of the year in South America, the Philippines, or Japan? Waiting for letters and phone calls instead of sharing a life that included going to the grocery store, doing the dinner dishes, and snuggling together in bed.

As if he heard her thoughts, Nick lowered his voice. "Living the way I do plays hell on relationships."

"You were a free spirit before you ever set foot on your first volcano," she said evenly.

He looked away as though to check whether Wyatt was in earshot. "We all make choices, Kyle." He maneuvered Gray closer. "But you know, there was a lot more shaken up the night of the new moon than you might realize."

Her face grew warm at his declaration. Knowing his attentions had been more than liquor talking put her back in a quandary.

How simple it had been at twenty. Nick had only to crook his finger and she'd been all over him. The way she'd described that feeling of first infatuation to Wyatt, how she'd fallen for Nick with no doubt, no fear, and no concept that either could ever pull back from the other.

She wasn't twenty anymore.

When they rounded the next bend, Kyle caught a whiff of something foul, so faint that it took a moment to recognize the stink of rotten eggs. In the same instant she realized it, Nick shouted, "Gas."

From about ten yards ahead, Wyatt called, "I don't smell anything."

"Behind us," Kyle decided. This was different from the stench the other day, with an added acrid tang.

She nudged Strawberry forward and heard the shamble

of Gray's hooves as Nick got him moving. Wyatt cleared the way by directing Thunder ahead. Kyle held her breath until after she passed the place Wyatt had been. Then she sniffed and could no longer detect any aroma.

Nevertheless, they all rode as fast as the trail would permit until the seep was well behind. On the wide spot of another bend, the three drew rein.

Nick lit a cigarette with hands that looked unsteady and looked back toward the mountain. "We've come down quite a ways, but we're still along the east-west trend of the Saddle Valley Fault. That gas is probably part of the same plume over a magma column."

Wyatt touched Thunder's neck in a reassuring manner. "That confirms it is bigger, not some narrow neck under the peak."

Nick turned to Kyle. "Did you get a good whiff back there?"

Her pulse began a slow and deliberate thudding. "You mean the sour?"

"Along with the hydrogen sulfide rotten-egg odor, I caught some hydrogen chloride. Usually seen close to eruption time," Nick offered for Wyatt's benefit.

"I know that," Wyatt bristled.

"But what kind of eruption?" Kyle asked. "The map we made this morning showing a broad area of swelling's got me spooked."

Nick smoked and considered. "There was significant overlap between the last three great eruptions in the region.

If Nez Perce is hooked up to the last caldera, all the way back to Yellowstone Lake, such would measure nearly thirty miles . . . over a thousand times greater than Mount St. Helens."

Wyatt gathered Thunder's reins. "Then may I respectfully suggest we get the hell out of here?"

● ● ●

Ahead lay the worst part of the trip, a narrow canyon where the trail followed a shelf above a rushing stream.

"Just this little stretch, boy." Wyatt stroked Thunder's neck. "Then you're home free."

The footing looked treacherous. In places, the trail was no more than a few feet wide due to cave-ins. The hillside bore the scars of prior landslides with scattered islands of outcrop and trees.

Nick peered ahead. "I don't like the looks of this bastard any more than I did the other day."

Wyatt turned to Kyle. "Ready?"

Unease ate at her and made her feel too warm in the canyon shade, but she nodded.

Ten feet, fifty, a hundred, and they were out on the middle of the shelf. Thunder moved placidly, Strawberry with her customary care, and Gray was once more slow and stolid. Kyle tried not to grip the reins too hard with her sweat-slicked hands.

She could hear Nick's quick breathing behind her. A

glance over her shoulder, and their eyes met.

"Be careful, Nick." Her voice wasn't steady.

"Always." Gray stepped on a rock and Nick took a second to adjust his balance. "Thinking about volcanoes . . . I've lost friends to the beasts. When it happens, I . . . we all in the community remember that every one of us addicted to volcanoes would rather die on one than anywhere else."

"Throw some salt over your shoulder, quick," Kyle admonished. "To ward off bad luck."

"Sorry, babe. Fresh out." Nick gave her a sad smile.

"Halfway," Wyatt marked from ahead.

Suddenly Thunder lifted his muzzle and snorted. Strawberry stopped. Gray shuffled to a halt.

With a faint rattle, pebbles loosened and skittered down the slope.

Kyle watched the dancing grains, mesmerized. She'd never felt so vulnerable, stuck in the middle of an avalanche chute on a path too narrow to turn around on.

Before she could urge Wyatt to hurry, before she could have more than a hair-raising premonition, a huge jolt struck.

She slammed forward and jerked back, as though she'd been rear-ended by an eighteen-wheeler. The coppery taste of blood spread in her mouth.

Thunder went onto his knees. Wyatt slid off him. Kyle couldn't see where he landed. Strawberry danced and somehow managed to stay on her feet. Gray gave a shrill scream.

With the next shock, the horse and Nick fell into the canyon.

● ● ●

Cameraman Larry Norris drove while Carol Leeds rode shotgun in the *Billings Live Eye* van on their way from Yellowstone to Billings. The Paradise Valley unfolded on either side of the highway. Although flat and relatively treeless, the land was nonetheless surrounded by a ring of mountains and billed as the gateway to Yellowstone. After being discovered by the rich and famous, it sported multimillion-dollar retreats, resorts, and overpriced retirement homes.

This morning Larry was too preoccupied to enjoy the scenery. In order to keep up with Carol's schedule, he'd had to leave the house while his eight-year-old son Joey was in the middle of an asthma attack. His wife Donna was going to be late to her job again, and that wasn't fair.

Through his fog, he heard Carol. "This could be as big as the fires of '88. And right now, it's all ours."

She snapped and unsnapped her jeans jacket, and he figured she was scheming. Larry thought that at forty-seven she should give up hoping for an anchor slot, but this morning's exclusive story warning of earthquakes was a fine scoop. Maybe she was thinking the new station manager would consider a promotion.

Larry steered with one hand on the wheel and turned to look at her. That probably drove her nuts wanting him to keep his eyes on the road. "I keep thinking about our source," he said. "That little Goth at the Resource Center. You suppose we did the right thing breaking without hearing from Park Management?"

"We're never going to make everybody happy." Carol flipped back her thick hair. "Why don't you take the pictures and leave strategy to me?"

Her cell phone rang. The voice of station manager Sonny Fiero sounded loud enough for Larry to hear. "Bad news. Seems the latest Park Service release doesn't mention doom and gloom."

Larry smiled as Carol said, "What time did it come out?"

"Right when we went on the air with your video. Look, I hate to say this, but that gal with the pierced nose and black fingernails isn't exactly an official source."

"Hindsight, Fiero," Carol blustered. "If you didn't think email straight from scientists in the field was reliable, you should have killed the story."

There was a little silence from the other end.

"So what do you want us to do?" Carol asked.

"Get back to the park and find out who's right on this," Sonny ordered.

"U-turn, Clyde," Carol told Larry.

"Roger." Covering the park required a lot of road miles; recently they'd been back and forth more than once some days.

Larry braked and found that the van began to swerve. "Uh-oh."

"For God's sake, do I have to drive, too?"

"It's not me." Larry fought the wheel with both hands.

Carol grabbed the chicken bar above the passenger door and braced on the dash. The van left the highway and bounced into the ditch.

● ● ●

Superintendent Janet Bolido's desk leaped up and landed with a thud.

What in the name . . . ?

She watched her computer monitor go over backward and heard it smash. A rising rumble came from all around her. With a white-knuckle grip on the arms of her chair, she managed to stay seated and upright.

From the hall outside, she heard someone shout, "Get outside!"

The floor continued to roll, and she wondered if she could walk.

A book fell from the shelves and hit the floor beside her. And another. Then one hit a glancing blow to her shoulder. An ancient copy of *How to Lie with Statistics* that she'd kept because she liked the concept.

Janet struggled to her feet. If you couldn't get out, a doorframe was supposed to be safer than the middle of the room. A book hit her elbow, square on the funny bone. The corner of another crashed into her cheek. She brought her hand up and rubbed the place where it smarted.

She needed to move, but her desk slid toward her. Blocked in a triangle formed by the L-shaped workstation, she decided get back in control by climbing over.

An avalanche of books began.

Janet raised her arms to ward off.

From the corner of her eye, she saw six shelves worth of solid oak come loose from the wall, fully loaded with the office's collection of park history, lore, and goddamned science.

As the shelves swept down behind a hail of sharp-edged hard covers, Janet dove into the kneehole of her desk.

● ● ●

"See you next time, Kelley," Alicia told the owner of the Pic and Sav while she pushed her cart away from the checkout. In addition to some staples, she'd bought more than she'd intended for her and Wyatt, fresh oranges, premium bacon, and $6.99-a-pound baby spinach. Now all she needed was to stop at the Firehole Inn and talk Edith out of a couple of well-marbled rib-eyes.

Suddenly, it felt like the store jumped up and then crashed down. The lights flickered.

Though she tried to clutch the handle, her cart rolled free. A bag she'd balanced in the child's seat tumbled to the floor.

With the next shock, Alicia fell to her hands and knees. Above a grinding rumble, she heard the thud of falling canned goods and the sharper shattering of glass.

God, not again. Even with the thought, she knew this was not a repeat of the tremors they'd been having. More and *stronger* earthquakes.

Her kneecaps went numb from repeated impact with the worn linoleum floor. She cut her palm on a broken jar of Major Grey's Chutney, the sticky brown concoction of mango and ginger mixing with her blood.

It sounded like a train was passing close. Above the din, people yelled.

"Kelley, you okay?" called the owner's husband from where he hung on to the checkout stand.

"Everybody out!" Kelley bellowed in a voice that didn't match her small stature.

Harry the hoarder stood braced in his coveralls, struggling to hold onto his plastic water jugs. He lost one, the tap smashing to spread liquid with rhythmic *glug*s.

The power went. Daylight grayed the area near the automatic doors, and auxiliary lighting came on toward the rear.

The store looked like one of those video clips of a California earthquake taken from the supermarket security camera. Pickle jars fell from the shelves and smashed, cans of corn landed on edge and dented, toilet-paper towers toppled. An unappealing mix of sour odors rose.

Harry watched his water jug drain as though he wished he hadn't paid for it.

Kelley made a staggering run for the exit.

The pregnant woman Harry had jumped line on sat

with her arms protecting her stomach.

Alicia had never felt so helpless.

● ● ●

Kyle clutched Strawberry's reins as the horse continued to surge. Ground waves rolled down the canyon. The trees shuddered, then began to whip. She heard the snapping of their trunks over the ghastly grinding of the earth.

"Get off the horse, Kyle." A faint shout. She caught a glimpse of Wyatt on hands and knees. He held Thunder's reins, but hooves sheathed in steel pawed the air.

A brimmed hat went flying. Thunder reared and plunged and she could no longer see Wyatt.

Kyle dismounted on the uphill side and the ground came up to meet her. Without the steadying pressure of her knees, Strawberry went berserk.

The reins tore from Kyle's hand. Despite the treacherous footing and the hysterical animal, she tried to grab onto the saddle, anything to try and get the animal under control so she would not go into the canyon. Her hand snagged the loop of her climbing rope beneath the saddle-bag and it came free.

With a shrill neigh, Strawberry went over the edge.

Thunder either fell or leaped, but in a heartbeat, he too tumbled into the canyon.

The ground began to slide. From up the hill came an ominous rumble that didn't belong to the earthquake.

Clutching her rope, Kyle scrabbled sideways and got onto an outcrop of volcanic scoria.

Making a last stand on the crumbling shelf, Wyatt stood with his hand stretched toward her. Then the trail collapsed and in dreadful slow motion, he went into the canyon.

Perched on her island of rock, Kyle's vision darkened from the edges. Sound assaulted her, rumbling and clacking over a low vacuuming roar. All she could see was a jumbled mass of rock and earth before her face, with tree roots protruding.

The ball looked identical to one she had once grabbed hold of in Rock Creek Campground. Using the slick muddy roots for a handhold, she'd pulled herself from the filthy flood. There she had crouched and gripped the rough rock while aftershocks rumbled through.

That wasn't right, though, was it? Hadn't she always remembered dragging herself from the water and crawling up onto the slope?

On Nez Perce Peak, Kyle knew there was something about that long-ago morning that she wasn't seeing. With a sob, she knew it was right there, just beyond her wall of darkness.

She didn't want to know what it was.

CHAPTER THIRTY
SEPTEMBER 28

As it finally had when Kyle was six, the ground on Nez Perce stopped moving. It brought the same sense of shock . . . that such chaos could turn to normalcy in a heartbeat. And along with it came the disbelief that she'd survived once again.

Quiet descended, along with a faint rushing of water. Dust choked her throat and gritted against her teeth and tongue.

Her tunnel vision began to clear; swimming bright sparks floating above the jumbled slope. Although she knew all was still, things kept tilting to her left. With a shaking hand, she pushed against the rock. Her shoulder protested and threatened to collapse, but she struggled up and stared out over the slide.

Clouds of rock flour obscured her view of the stream at the canyon bottom, down over a hundred feet. Though boulders still clacked against each other, she cupped her hands and cleared her throat. "Wyatt! Nick!"

It came out a croak.

The only answer was the clatter of collapse as more of

the hillside tumbled into the abyss. God, where were the guys . . . the horses?

She cried out again. What had she gotten them all into, asking Colin to send help and getting Nick here, forcing herself to overcome her nightmares and take Wyatt along into the backcountry?

"Strawberry! Thunder! Gray!" She couldn't see them at all, and that had to mean . . .

Her chest heaved, and a sob tore through her throat. If the horses were buried, then Wyatt and Nick . . .

Alone, she was alone with no radio or anyone who knew where she was. No, it couldn't be . . . somebody had to be down there.

When she'd cried as a child for her parents she'd been destined to failure. This time, she determined to find the others if she had to tear aside every boulder and grain of sand.

Looking down, she saw at her feet the climbing rope she'd pulled off Strawberry. Though she didn't believe in divine intervention, for that matter, in divine anything, this piece of good fortune made her scalp tingle.

Quickly, she picked her way off the outcrop onto the slope where trees were still firmly rooted. Selecting a stout pine, she looped the rope around the trunk and secured it with a bowline knot. Without any climbing equipment to slow her descent, and no gloves, Kyle wrapped the rope around her body and placed her already scarred hands around it.

She planted her feet on the hillside with the rope between her legs, held on tight and started to edge backward down the slope. A few feet down, she crossed onto the uncertain footing of the slide.

Every few feet she stopped and looked around. Each time, she shouted and heard no reply, saw nothing but the ruined canyon wall.

● ● ●

Wyatt lay in the shelter of a pine trunk. Skiing on top of the slide, he had almost managed to stay upright. Then his feet had sunk in and he'd sprawled headlong. For what felt like forever, boulders the size of his head had bounded past or leaped the pine trunk over him. He saw them vaguely, for in his plunge down the hill he'd lost his glasses.

As the rain of rock subsided and things got quiet, all his body parts seemed intact and he felt no pain to suggest internal injury. For a long moment, he lay disbelieving his good fortune. Then the bubble of detachment burst.

He'd seen Thunder and Strawberry tumble end over end in the landslide, screaming in a way that tore at his gut until the raw earth covered them. He prayed they had died cleanly rather than suffocating slowly.

Wyatt tried to stop panting and breathe evenly, but it took another minute before he could croak, "Kyle."

The last he'd seen Nick and Gray, they'd been holding their own. "Nick!" he tried, his throat still too dry to raise his voice.

There was no answer save the whisper of wind through the trees and the shushing of the creek. He tried not to think of being the only survivor out here. Though Nick was a volcano junkie who'd been gung-ho to get to Nez Perce, Kyle hadn't really wanted to go to the mountain. She'd gone along to be game, and if Wyatt's decision to pack in with horses rather than work harder at getting a chopper had gotten her killed . . .

Desperation surged in him. "Kyle!"

All was quiet, except that up the slope somewhere he heard the skitter of gravel. Recalling that the quake had been preceded by the same precursor, he went still and prayed it was too soon for a decent aftershock.

When no rocks came careening down, he tried to push up and found his right ankle strangely without sensation.

"Wyatt?" The vice that had seized his chest backed off a half-turn.

"Kyle? Thank God!" He thrust a hand up, the same muddy color as the rest of the slide. "Here. I've lost my glasses."

There she was above, roping down like a fuzzy mountaineer in his nearsighted view. As she clambered closer, his heart swelled at the welcome sight of her jeans-clad fanny smeared with earth. From the cleaner look of the rest of her, her hair still half-braided, she had not been caught in the slide.

She arrived at his side in a small avalanche of stones.

"Are you hurt?"

"I'm not sure . . . Nick?"

"I saw him go off the shelf, like you."

"God," he said. They stared at each other for a moment. Then she shouted, "Nick!" with an edge of hysteria.

A faint snort came from the lower left hand side of the slope. Kyle turned to him with a questioning look.

"Gray! That you, boy?" Wyatt called. Another snort was followed by a long horsy sigh. "I don't like the sound of that."

"Do you have your radio?" Kyle asked.

"With Thunder." He gestured toward the pile of rubble.

"My radio is with Strawberry."

"Oh." Wyatt thought from her expression that she understood the slide had taken the animals.

Above them, there was a sudden clacking of rocks. His stomach twisted.

"Can you get up?" Kyle asked. "Hang onto this rope?"

Another little shudder. The sound of pebbles sifting threatened to loose his bowels.

"I've got to." He moved his feet, pulling them free of the loose debris.

She freed one hand to help him rise and he got a look at her palm, scraped and slick with blood. She wiped it on her pants before clasping his hand and pulling him up.

The instant he put weight on his right ankle, a stab of pain shot all the way to his brain.

He inhaled sharply. "Shit. I've done something here."

Kyle grasped his arm. "Lean on me."

"You're not hurt?"

"I was up on the rocks above the action," she said in a shaky voice.

Even without his glasses, Wyatt saw the grim look on Kyle's face. "I mean are you doing all right with all this?"

For an instant, he caught a glimpse of something primal in her eyes. "Hell, no, but I have to."

Though he wanted to run off the treacherous ground, the best he could manage was to grab the rope above Kyle. Together, they began a lopsided sideways hobble over stones that looked blurred and turned underfoot. It was amazing how he took for granted his usual sure way of walking in the field.

Kyle steadied them both from behind him and he wondered how she managed with her rope-burned hands. "One step at a time."

"Yes, ma'am." He found a hollow between two larger rocks and his ankle complained again.

"Don't ma'am me. Move your right foot left about six inches."

With Kyle's help and slow painful steps, Wyatt made it onto the forested slope. There, they both let go the rope, and he was able to see well enough to limp along. He cupped his hands once more and shouted, "Darden!"

Nick did not answer, but there was another tortured sigh.

It was difficult to keep up with Kyle as she hurried

toward the sound, but he managed. He didn't want her to face what they might find alone.

● ● ●

Kyle saw Gray first. The big horse lay with his head facing downhill at the base of a trail of broken earth. His front leg lay crumpled beneath his chest and both his rear legs canted at crazy angles. His saddle was empty.

Wall-eyed, Gray struggled to lift his head.

"Broken neck," said Wyatt. "Poor devil."

Kyle's heart surged when she saw Nick sprawled beyond Gray's shoulder. It looked as through he'd stayed on the horse until the last, for his limp hand still held the reins. She reached him and knelt, thinking that the next seconds could change so much.

Wyatt slipped in beside her and reached for a pulse. With one hand on Nick's neck and the other on his chest, he said, "He's breathing."

She exhaled the one she'd been holding.

Wyatt bent closer and squinted. "Describe any injuries you see."

Nick's face was pale, but that might be from the beige dust that coated everything. Although he appeared largely unscathed, if he'd damaged his spinal cord he might never walk upon a volcano again.

"What we need is a chopper," Kyle concluded.

She grabbed Nick's radio, hanging from one of Gray's

saddlebags. Wyatt took it, squinted, and clicked buttons. "Mayday, Mayday. This is Ranger Ellison. We need a medevac stat."

Bent beside Nick, Kyle smoothed back his matted hair and felt the stickiness of blood. On the side of his head where he'd hit the ground, she found a swelling knot. "He's hit his head on something."

Gently, she tapped her fingernail on his collarbone. When he did not respond, she became more aggressive, pinching his earlobe and calling him in a sharp voice. His eyelids did not even flutter. Desperation welled and she screamed, "Nick!" reaching for his shoulders.

Wyatt put a restraining hand on her arm. "Don't move him."

She slumped down. "Sorry." She knew better than that.

"He's breathing, but unresponsive," Wyatt said into the radio. "We're on the south side of Nez Perce Peak. On the trail where the shelf goes along the canyon, the pilot will see the slide."

Tears ran down Kyle's cheeks as she brushed her fingers along Nick's beard. If they had just risen ten minutes earlier this morning, they'd have been well clear of this stretch of canyon. Right now, she'd be calming Strawberry with a soothing hand on her graceful neck. Wyatt would be subdued, Nick ebullient. All of them would have been impressed by the distant sound of avalanche in the canyon.

His report complete, Wyatt moved away and squatted behind Gray's head. Very gently, he stroked the horse's limp withers. The only response was another roll of eyes.

Wyatt unsnapped the flap on his pistol holster. "I hope the dust hasn't clogged this."

Kyle gasped.

He met her eyes. "Look away."

The shot echoed through the canyon.

CHAPTER THIRTY-ONE
SEPTEMBER 28

In the waiting room at the Mammoth clinic, Kyle checked her watch against the wall clock. It had been nearly an hour since the chopper brought them in.

She and an equally filthy Wyatt waited in the crowded anteroom outside the treatment area, drawing stares from others.

"We should have taken Nick to a bigger hospital," she said.

"No second guessing." Wyatt shifted in the plastic chair. "After the way David died, I thought we should bring Nick to the nearest facility."

Kyle cradled a cup of machine coffee in her raw red hands. Nick's words about dying in the field kept playing in her mind.

Wyatt squinted at the wall clock.

"Almost eleven," she read it for him. "Do you have a spare set of glasses?"

"At my house."

Much as she wanted him to stay with her, she suggested, "Why not go and get them?"

"Then I can check on the seismic." He echoed her anxiety over whether the quake had relieved any of the pressure at Nez Perce.

Their eyes met.

Wyatt started to rise and stopped. "Before I go, you sure you're okay?"

Kyle met his gaze. "Truth to tell, I'm numb. I just keep telling myself the quake is over." She put her palm onto the flat arm of her chair.

He looked down at her hand. "You notice there are no significant aftershocks."

She'd been trying not to think about it.

"Could be a sign we're in for more."

"I hope not."

Wyatt got up and winced when he put his weight on his right foot.

"You should get that looked at."

"Since it hasn't swollen, I think it's just a stone bruise." He tested it gingerly. "I've got an elastic bandage at home."

He put his hand on her shoulder and left it a moment. "I hope Nick's all right."

"He should be." Kyle gave a faint smile. "His head has always been hard enough."

She watched Wyatt walk away.

If Nick made it through, how would he feel about how close he'd come to the edge? Surely, this brush with death was going to have an impact on him.

"Please, please," she repeated, as close to a prayer a

she'd come since she was six.

Two men came in wearing neon vests. The larger man cradled his wrist and the other had a seeping cut over his left eye. From their conversation, Kyle gathered all their efforts at clearing the road in Gardner Canyon had been negated as another section of the cliff had collapsed onto the road. The man with the bad wrist told his buddy he was evacuating the area as soon as he was treated and could gather up his family.

A chill ran down Kyle's spine. If it were true that the area of instability underlying the park was as large as the GPS data indicated, even Mammoth might not be safe. Certainly, the people who had been through this morning's quake weren't ready for another one.

A mother came in carrying a crying girl of about six years. Tangled brown curls framed a small scarlet face. The child didn't look hurt, but her sobs kept working up into screaming fits.

It reminded Kyle of herself as a six-year-old, being air-lifted out of Madison Canyon to a Billings Hospital. She lay in a strange bed with high rails like a crib, though she was too big a girl for one. Light came in from an open transom over the door, giving a dim view of beds filled with sleeping children.

Before nightfall, Kyle had been watching the other kids, but though they talked to her, she hadn't answered. In the bed on her left was a girl about five with her arm in a cast. Her mother and father had brought her a new doll dressed in blue to match her pajamas. On the other side was a girl in a green nightgown; she had burned her hands grabbing a stove burner. White gauze made her hands look like paws. She had kissed her parents and promised to never do that again. In the corner of the room was pretty flushed Sally, her mommy had called her that when she came in and asked Miss Darla if Sally's temperature had gone down yet.

Nobody had come for Kyle.

But Mommy and Daddy must get here soon. That was the only thing she had to hold onto. In the morning, they'd come and bring her something, too. Then she'd talk to the other girls.

Footsteps sounded in the hall outside the ward. There was a click and the light over the transom went out. As though someone had clapped their hand over Kyle's mouth and nose, she tried to breath but could only manage a choking wheeze.

Sally stirred. "You okay?"

Kyle could not speak.

"Miss Darla!" Sally called. "Something's the matter with her."

Swift steps approached. The door opened, a switch snapped. Bright light stabbed Kyle's eyes. Miss Darla approached like an angel in white, her cap a sail. "What's this, little one?"

Kyle found her breath and screamed. Once she started, she couldn't stop.

Sitting in the clinic waiting for news of Nick, she bit her lip to keep from sobbing. Tears stood in her eyes.

"You all right, ma'am?" The road worker with the cut on his head asked.

Kyle pushed to her feet and slammed though the door of the nearby ladies room. She barely made it to a stall before the tears came. Great heaving sobs that shook her so hard she had to sit down on the closed toilet seat and hug herself.

She'd been a fool to think studying Yellowstone was something that could be controlled; an idiot to believe it was anything less than playing with fire.

● ● ●

At two in the afternoon, nearly three hours after Nick had been brought in, one of the doctors came from behind a pair of swinging doors. In her thirties, she wore a white coat spattered with blood Kyle tried not to notice.

"I'm sorry I've taken so long to get back to you." She pushed back a stray tendril of her blond hair. "But as you can see, we're swamped." Though her voice sounded serious, she wasn't using the hushed tones with which bad news was usually imparted. "Nick is conscious and oriented."

Kyle nodded, aware that her eagerness set her up for a fall. "He's okay, then?"

"His pupils are equal and reactive. He's doing as well as can be, given that he was unconscious for a while. It would be best for him to get a CT scan, but since we don't have one, I've ordered X-rays." The doctor gestured around at the other patients. "It may take awhile. Since this is an urgent care clinic and not a hospital, if all goes well, I'm thinking of releasing him later . . . but only if someone can stay with him overnight."

"I won't leave him alone," Kyle vowed.

The doctor sobered. "If he gets worse or loses consciousness again I'd recommend the air ambulance to Eastern Idaho Medical Center."

Properly warned, Kyle entered the exam room to find Nick sitting on the edge of a wheeled bed wearing a gray hospital gown. His hair and scruffy beard had turned uniform beige from the gritty landslide. Dirt streaked his arms and blood was drying to a crust where it had dripped down his neck.

"You all right?" She struggled to sound upbeat, but his pallor frightened her.

His trademark grin looked forced as he wiggled his bare toes and waggled his fingers. "All present and accounted for." He looked past her shoulder. "The cowboy?"

"Wyatt turned an ankle, but he's fine. He's gone over to his office to check on the stations."

"With no more aftershocks than I'm feeling, she's probably priming for more."

"I was afraid you'd say that."

"You okay?"

"A few scrapes." She turned up her palms to show the

newly raw skin that had disrupted the healing cuts on her palms. "I was lucky."

"That was a hell of a ride," Nick said. "Old Gray saved my life."

"Um, Nick . . ." Kyle swallowed. "I'm afraid Gray didn't make it." She did not elaborate on Wyatt having to shoot the injured animal. "None of the horses did."

"Ah, shit. The cowboy set a store by Thunder."

"He did."

Nick's eyes went from her dirty clothing to his own stack dumped on a chair. "We look like ragamuffins."

"My gear was . . . buried," Kyle said. "Your bag was on Gray where he fell, but I'm afraid in the excitement of getting you onto the chopper, we left it behind."

"That's okay." He looked fragile with his bandaged head and a lost expression on his face. When she took his hand, his fingers were trembling.

"How do you really feel?" she asked.

"Like somebody snuck up behind me and hit me over the head." With a glance at their clasped hands, he seemed to realize she could feel the quaking in him. "I guess I'm a little rocky, but hey," he brightened, "pretty soon I'll be out of here."

She smiled. "The doctor said if your tests are okay, she'll release you to my custody. She doesn't want you left alone tonight, so I'll get us a room at the hotel."

His grin broadened. "That'll be nice." Putting up a hand, he touched his bandaged head with care. "Course

I'll bet I look like a terrorist in this turban."

She forced a smile. "Can you see all right? Remember things?"

He looked at her steadily. "I remember everything."

"Nick . . ."

For a moment, it was all there between them, a golden summer, a new moon night, and the promise that the past might not be the key to the future.

❖ ❖ ❖

Kyle booked a room at the hotel with two double beds and took a hot shower. Her scraped hands stung when the soap contacted them, but the sensation of being clean was rejuvenating. That, and believing Nick would be all right.

It was a shame to have to put her filthy clothing back on. Without a brush, she webbed her hair together into a rough braid. Scrubbing her teeth with a washcloth, she vowed to buy toothbrushes and something for her and Nick to wear . . . after she went over to Wyatt's office to check the seismic stations.

On the way to the Resource Center, there were constant reminders of the quake. Next door to the clinic at the Mammoth Post Office, one of two white marble lions had been knocked from its pedestal beside the front stairs. As she passed Park Headquarters, she saw that some of the basement windows were broken. The next big house where Chief Ranger Kuni lived had a fallen chimney.

Farther on, the stone chapel had suffered a collapse near the altar. Kyle hoped it wasn't a bad omen.

The Resource Center's front door was stuck in its frame. The large window next to it was open with a floor mat beneath the sill inside.

Wyatt's office door was closed.

"Nobody can go in there," said a young voice from behind her.

She turned to find receptionist Iniki Kuni, dressed in black with matching fingernails.

"Dr. Stone? I didn't recognize you."

"Maybe you will after I get some clean clothes on."

Kyle opened Wyatt's door. His hair looked damp, and he wore a fresh uniform. Now that he was clean, she could see where scratches marked his face and hands.

He turned from the computer. "I told Iniki if she let anybody but you in, I'd rip out all her earrings." His dark eyes searched her face from behind a pair of glasses with an out of date frame style. "Shut that." He pointed to the door.

She did.

"Iniki says she's leaving before the workday is over," Wyatt said. "Says her father can stay and play Chief Ranger if he wants, but she can't take any more earthquakes."

"I've been wondering how much more I can take," Kyle confessed.

Wyatt removed his glasses and set them on the desk, exposing the dark bruise of his black eye. "How's Nick?"

"Awake. They're waiting on tests, but he acts like he's

going to be his old self."

"That's good." It sounded sincere, but solemn as though he meant Kyle was the one who should be happy.

He pushed up from the desk and moved around it toward her. When he was halfway there, a wave of pain crossed his features.

"Your ankle?" she gasped.

He shook his head. "I keep thinking about leaving the horses up there for the buzzards."

She closed the distance to him. "Oh, Wyatt, I'm sorry."

After last night on the cabin sofa, it seemed the most natural thing to go into his arms. Her cheek pressed the side of his clean-shaven face and she smelled soap along with the pleasant scent of his skin.

He held her tighter; apparently heedless that she was getting his uniform dirty. "Thunder would have walked through fire for me."

"Strawberry was so sweet; she'd have done anything for me, too."

A muffled sob escaped. As Wyatt's hands spread over her back, she let tears flow. It felt infinitely wonderful to be comforted by someone who knew her secrets.

Her jacket parted so that they fit together. Chest to chest, they were nearly the same height. Her breasts, spare though they were, pressed against him. His hand slid up to her neck, his fingers stroking her hair. "Kyle," he said in a thick voice.

Awareness washed through her like a warm tide. Not

the frenetic hot passion she'd felt in youth, nor the simple embrace of friendship, this complex mix of comfort and disturbing sensuality suddenly frightened her.

It couldn't have been more than a few seconds from the time her coat fell open until they both drew back and looked at each other. She realized her hands were shaking and put them in her coat pockets.

"It was a 7.1," he said awkwardly.

"It felt bigger." She reached for a tissue from a box on his credenza and blew her nose.

"Less than a 6.0 here in civilization. That's why there isn't more damage."

He gestured toward the computer. The quake's signature began with a wide excursion and gradually dampened over the several minutes of shaking. "That's from Nez Perce Seven, the closest station to the epicenter."

Wyatt zoomed out from his detail of the earthquake to show the hours since. The response showed a chatter of tremors too small for human detection.

"I suppose we can call those aftershocks," she said. Their one hope to avert more activity was if the large earthquake had dissipated the energy and the rising magma had stabilized at depth.

Hours later, when Kyle and Wyatt came out of the Resource Center, the sun had moved west over Sepulcher Mountain. Heavy gray-white clouds streamed over the broad cone of Bunsen Peak north into Mammoth Valley. Standing on the yellowing grass beneath the cottonwoods,

Kyle concluded, "All we can do is monitor and wait. We've got all the equipment in the field that I intend to place."

Across the parking lot, Iniki Kuni hurried toward her compact car.

Wyatt's eyes followed Kyle's gaze. "Are you planning to go back to Salt Lake?"

It was tempting, watching Iniki patch out on the gravel and head toward the park entrance. But she glanced toward the clinic. "I suppose I'll go. I'm not sure when."

A muscle in his jaw bunched. "Let me know when you figure it out."

As he started to limp away, something in the set of his shoulders made her say, "Wyatt."

He turned back, his expression shuttered.

"Look," she said, "I know you're trying to protect me from getting hurt by Nick again."

"As of right now, I officially give up." His hands went into his jacket pockets. "You're buried so deep in your past you wouldn't know your future if it was standing in front of you."

When he walked away again, she stood silently and watched him go. Then she went up the street beside the old Fort Yellowstone parade ground.

Elk grazed in the gray afternoon. Snow was on the wind. And there was no longer any doubt that Wyatt was jealous, not just of Dr. Darden's world-class credentials, but of her feelings for the man.

God, this was too complicated. The memory of

Wyatt's touch sent an electric sensation through her, even as he was going home to Alicia. And she needed to buy some clothes and toilet articles for her and Nick.

The general store was a shambles. She nodded to the lone clerk picking up fallen merchandise. Racks offered sweat pants, T-shirts, and fleece pullovers. Kyle selected clothes, shampoo, disposable razors, toothbrushes, and combs, along with liquid detergent so they could do laundry without the cheap powdered vending-machine soap. "Flashlights?" Since hers were at the bottom of the canyon, she bought three.

The display of cigarettes was behind the checkout counter with the liquor. With an effort, she turned away from both.

As Kyle took the glass-walled circular stair up to the hotel's second floor, blue twilight was falling outside along with flakes of snow. When she put her key in the room lock, the door opened beneath her hand.

Nick looked as tired as she felt. Clean-shaven but dressed like her, in his dirty clothes. Over his wound, a spot of blood had soaked through the gauze.

A draft from the open window swirled around her ankles. The bathroom soap dish sat on the wide wooden sill with an eddy of smoke rising from a Marlboro. "Non-smoking room," he said.

She'd done that on purpose.

Before she could get past Nick into the room, he fixed her with an intent look. "What's going on with the signals?"

Part of her wanted to pour out every detail of what each station had been reading, to pick his brain for what she and Wyatt might have missed, but somehow she couldn't give in to impulse. With his head injury, she dared only dissimulate. "After the big one this morning, things are just chattering along."

Nick raised a doubtful brow, but moved aside to let her in. "Things have felt pretty quiet."

"And they are," she declared, setting her bags on the antique dresser next to an open bottle of Crown Royal and a full ice bucket.

"Drink?" Nick picked up a half-empty glass and took a swig. "I talked them out of a bottle over at the bar."

"Should you be drinking?"

"I'd rather this than the pain meds they gave me." He went to the bathroom for another glass, dropped in ice cubes and poured.

She took it from him. Her first sip burned, the second made her realize she needed to take it slow.

Nick ambled to the window and took a drag from his cigarette. Exhaling a cloud, he extended the pack. She looked at the filters, lined up like bullets. "No, thanks."

"Giving it up again?"

"Someone told me I needed to break the habits of my past." The image of Wyatt walking away produced a hollow feeling in her chest.

Nick ground out his smoke in the soap dish and came toward her with his catlike walk. "Don't give up all your old sins."

"Nick . . ."

"The night of the new moon, it all came back, your smell, the feel of you. Remember the first time we were together at field camp, driving down the canyon? That rock nearly smashed the car."

He picked up his drink and knocked it against hers. "Tonight we celebrate cheating death again."

As if she'd been doused with cold water, she stared at him. "I sat in that waiting room for hours thinking you might die, and you joke about it?"

His face changed, and he leaned against the dresser. "Come on, you know how it works. If I let myself get too serious about the danger, I'd end up stuck in a desk job."

"Would that be so terrible?"

He frowned. "Kyle . . ."

Her cheeks flamed. "I should have known better than to think you'd finally start taking things seriously."

She went into the bathroom and shut the door.

CHAPTER THIRTY-TWO
SEPTEMBER 28

Before he went home, Wyatt drove to the upper parking lot at Mammoth Hot Springs and sat in his Bronco for a while. He stared at the pale travertine terraces deposited by spring flow without really seeing them.

He was still reeling from his reaction to Kyle this afternoon. Sure, he'd suspected how it would be between them, but when he'd finally felt her body against his, it had opened a window he'd merely peeked through before. If they hadn't pulled apart when they had, he felt certain he'd have made an idiot of himself by letting her know how he felt.

Hell, he had let her know. On the mountain when he'd let testosterone and jealousy lead him into a fistfight, when he'd challenged her to figure out why he didn't care for Nick, and again today. But she was so caught up in Nick, she was oblivious.

Twilight snow began to fall as he parked the Bronco and limped across his yard. When he'd been there earlier to shower, he'd checked the front of his house for quake damage. Except for a pot of earth lying on its side, a left-over from summer geraniums, all had looked intact. But had he really left a light on in the kitchen?

Wyatt pushed through into his hall and smelled the comforting aroma of baked potatoes. Before he could reach the light switch, he heard, "Surprise!"

He stopped. "Alicia."

Stunned, he took a second to remember he'd given her a house key. And another to realize that in the day's events he'd forgotten to call and tell her he was back.

She launched at him, her face a pale oval against the darkened hall. On impact, her soft weight was all womanly curves. Kisses rained on his cheeks and tickled his moustache while she murmured, "I called around three and checked with Iniki that you were back, but I made her promise not to tell. I hid my Navigator around back."

"This is a surprise." The scent of roses wafted from her.

She pressed close. "I was afraid something might have happened on the mountain."

"It did," Wyatt said over her shoulder as he gave her a hard hug.

He flipped the light switch. Her black hair made a smooth fall over her shoulders. The cushy material under his hands was some kind of dark velvet that suggested silkier skin beneath.

He stepped back.

Her dark eyes widened when she saw his wrapped ankle.

"The quake set off a slide in the canyon. I turned my foot on a stone, but nothing serious." He wasn't ready to tell her about Thunder. "Let me get out of uniform."

LINDA JACOBS

"I can draw a hot bath . . . for two?"

"I had a shower earlier." He moved toward his bedroom. She didn't follow.

The changes were subtle. A pair of candleholders he remembered from her place graced his nightstand. Thick wax columns smelled of spice. A foot-thick swath of feminine items peeked from his open closet door. A leopard print cosmetic bag lay open on the bathroom counter, with little jars and bottles spilling out.

What in hell was he going to do?

● ● ●

Alone in Wyatt's kitchen, Alicia used the corkscrew on one of the good bottles of wine she'd bought. Her hand trembled, and she spilled red drops that stained the white counter.

She ought to be in the bedroom with Wyatt right now, but this wasn't turning out the way she'd hoped. She'd left the front hall dark so their opening kiss would be more romantic. He'd turned on the overhead light. And she'd never known him to pass on one of her candlelit bubble baths. What had he meant about something happening on the mountain?

She told herself he must be exhausted from a long day in the saddle, especially with an injured ankle. It would probably be a good idea to back off and let him unwind.

Ten minutes passed. The potatoes were in, and they

would keep. The salad waited to be dressed. The steaks were seasoned.

Wyatt spoke from the doorway. "Dinner looks wonderful." He sounded distant.

"I was shopping for goodies this morning at the Pic and Sav when the big one hit. That's a story." She knew she was babbling.

"Are you okay?" His gray eyes flicked over her without the interest she'd expected after their time apart.

"Cut my hand on some glass." She displayed a strip of bandage on her palm.

"I'm glad that was all."

Alicia waited for him to pull her into his arms, but he turned his attention to the wine label, a California Cabernet. She poured for him.

"Nice," he nodded after sampling. "You know, a guy could do a whole lot worse than to come home to all this."

"You want to start the steaks?"

"In a bit." He pulled out a chair, sat at the table and studied his hands. "We lost all three of the horses in the quake and came out by chopper. A big landslide . . . almost killed Nick Darden of USGS."

Alicia sank into the chair next to Wyatt. "No wonder you seem upset." She took a gulp of wine. "Is he all right?"

"Should be. We were damned lucky."

Seeing the haggard look of Wyatt, she recalled his affection for Thunder. "I'm sorry about the horses."

"They were good friends. Old Gray broke his neck . . .

I had to shoot him."

Her stomach turned. "Oh, dear."

They sat for a moment in silence. Then it occurred to her that there was a piece missing from his explanation, and though it probably wasn't the time or place . . . "What about Kyle Stone?"

"She was there. Up the hill on some rocks." His shoulders tensed and he evaded her eyes.

Creeping dread came over Alicia as Wyatt drank off his wine in a single draught. In his room, her clothes, her candles, her cosmetics. With all her heart, she wished she hadn't been so bold.

"So what were the sleeping arrangements up there?" It was like walking out onto a frozen lake, but she couldn't stop.

"Alicia, don't do this." He wouldn't meet her accusing stare. "We had a common bunkroom for the three of us."

"No side deals?"

"For God's sake," he snapped. "Unless you count Darden sniffing out his old girlfriend."

"You can lie to me, Wyatt, but don't lie to yourself." Blood beat in her temples. "I saw the way you kept making mooneyes at her in the Lake Hotel sunroom."

"Get off my back. I just can't stand to watch her make the same mistake she made years ago with Nick. She can do better than that."

With an almost audible click, everything came into focus. The countertop with wine stains. The hum of the refrigerator and the furnace fan stirring warm air, frost forming patterns on the window above the kitchen sink.

"You poor son of a bitch," she said. "You're in love with her."

● ● ●

Wyatt shoved back his chair, dragged Alicia up, and kissed her. It had always been good between them, and he could make it happen again. The last thing he wanted was to lie alone tonight and think about Kyle and Nick.

He should be glad he'd come home to find Alicia part of his welcome. How much darker would his hall have been without her embrace? How empty his bachelor housing?

She was out of his arms. The space she left felt cold. With her back to the refrigerator, she challenged, "If you can honestly tell me you're not in love with Kyle Stone, I'll stay."

"Don't play games."

With a sigh, Alicia said, "I love you, Wyatt."

A test. He reached his hand palm forward and she matched hers to it. He twined their fingers and squeezed but did not answer.

Her tears spilled over, mascara running. "I thought maybe you and I were each other's answer. You could have been mine."

Closing his eyes, Wyatt said, "I'm sorry."

Two hours later, he sat alone in the living room recliner with an ice pack on his ankle. The TV was off and the only light rose from the candles Alicia had left behind. He'd brought them out from his bedroom and eaten steak, salad, and a piping hot baked potato by candlelight. Just because he was by himself didn't mean he had to be a slob.

The spicy scent rising from the melting wax reminded him of Alicia's bedroom. Torn between the desire to call her and the wisdom of leaving it alone, he mentally toasted her and drank off the last of the red wine.

He set his empty glass down so hard it fell over with a clink. Kyle was up at the hotel with Nick, and here he sat trying to pretend it wasn't eating his heart out.

CHAPTER THIRTY-THREE
SEPTEMBER 28

Snow was still falling when Kyle returned with Nick from the restaurant in Mammoth. He held her arm to help her across a patch of glazed ice in the parking lot, although she was probably more in command of her faculties than he. A drink of Crown in the room, a couple glasses of wine, and the medication he'd taken after all clearly had him feeling no pain.

Dressed in the sweats she'd bought, they stopped by the coin-operated washer to transfer their field clothes into the dryer. Nick kept up the banter he'd been throwing at her silence all evening. "At 21,000 feet in Tibet it was colder than a banker's heart. The food was what we all looked forward to, something hot and filling like that steak tonight."

She produced quarters, and he fed the metal slots.

"The Chinese couldn't run the truck mounted seismic unit and get decent data. When we rejected it for poor quality, they killed a couple of the camp dogs and served them to us for dinner."

Kyle grimaced. "What did it . . . ?"

"Like chicken."

She pressed a hand to her mouth.

"You see, some of us had sort of bonded with the dogs, so our punishment did double duty. Finally, I got in the seismic unit and taught the locals how to run it. After that, we got back to eating stewed yak."

"Which also tastes like . . . ?"

"Sorry, no. Like beef. Really, really well-aged."

She laughed in spite of herself.

In their room, he went to the window and opened it to smoke a cigarette. She stood beside him and watched the snow whirl past a streetlight and coat the lawn. It felt like old times, listening to Nick spin stories.

Perhaps she'd been too quick to shut him down earlier when he'd trivialized death. Maybe it was just his way of coping. After all, though he'd figured out she didn't like the dark, he had no idea why.

"How about a nightcap?" He poured himself one as he spoke.

She shook her head. "How are you feeling?"

"Head gives a throb now and then." The patch of blood on the gauze had turned a rusty brown.

Kyle pulled off her boots. In the bathroom, she unbraided her hair and shook it loose over her shoulders. Despite a few streaks of gray, its burnished mahogany was intact. She looked into her eyes and remembered her youthful, sun-reddened face in the bathhouse mirror at field camp.

When she came back into the room, Nick had closed the window. "You wanted to know how I feel. Actually, I'm a little melancholy."

"You?" In her sweat suit, she crawled onto the bed nearest the door and sat against the headboard. "You've been making me laugh for hours."

With a dismissive hand, he waved away his clowning. "You should know I go on like that when I'm afraid to act serious."

She pulled her knees up toward her chest and wrapped her arms around them. "I don't think you've ever admitted that before."

"I thought everyone knew."

"So why are you sad?"

"Guess I've been thinking too much. Close calls will do that to you." Nick came to her and sat on the bed's edge. "That summer, the weekend we stayed here in the cabins, was a time like nothing that has ever happened to me."

"That's flattering, but you must have felt something more when you got married."

"All I can tell you is that was different. I was older, more jaded."

She reached and took a swallow of his drink.

He met her eyes. "You scared me to death, Kyle. You made me want to settle down and raise babies and dogs. That fall I was scheduled to do field work in Antarctica."

She wrapped her arms around her knees and drew into a tighter ball. "Don't you see that you weren't ready when we met, and not when you married." Her voice sounded surprisingly calm. "One of the things that struck me about you when we met again was how little you had changed. I even worried that I wasn't the girl you once knew."

"You haven't changed, babe." He smoothed her hair.

Kyle sat up straighter, a move that pulled her out of his reach. It would be too easy to have a few more drinks and fall under the spell of being on a bed with him. "I've changed inside," she persisted. "Are you willing to?"

"I have. I know better than to run from you a second time." His eyes were as serious as she had ever seen them.

"But are you willing to make hard decisions? To settle down?"

Nick left his drink in her hand and walked to the window. "It always comes down to this, doesn't it?"

"I may be a scientist, but earthquakes and volcanoes scare me witless, especially up close and personal. I don't think I could stand waiting and worrying about you."

"I can't promise to stay out of the field. It's my life." He came back to Kyle and took her hand. "Ask me anything but that."

"I'll bet that's exactly the way you proposed marriage," Kyle said. "Twice."

Nick pushed off the bed. "I'll go check on the dryer."

● ● ●

An hour later Nick lay with his back to the bed Kyle had

chosen. More than once he opened his eyes and stared at the cold sky spawning another swirl of snowflakes. He'd left the drapes open to let some cool in, balancing the steam radiator's relentless enthusiasm.

He wouldn't have thought he'd be sleeping alone. Even when he'd walked out to get their laundry, he'd believed in his ability to talk Kyle into changing her stance.

Wondering if she was asleep, he considered just slipping into bed beside her . . . but his respect for her was too great. He had to play it straight, for no other women had ever brought him close to really settling down.

He lay back and tried not to think. He could count sheep, but the riddle of Nez Perce Peak was more interesting. He'd agreed to come out of the field because he knew Kyle would insist on it no matter how much he wanted to stay. Now, this hotel with all the amenities felt like the sidelines with a big game in progress.

Nick closed his eyes and imagined Nez Perce, pristine and unspoiled, except where wildfires had left their mark. Like any treacherous dormant volcano, it wore a veil of green and masqueraded as a cool and airy peak.

Then, in his mind's eye, it erupted. First, a steam explosion formed a crater, beckoning him to stand on the rim and peer into the inner workings. Already, he could smell acid fumes and feel heat pouring from the chasm.

Nick began to drift; images of rough hot rock, his footsteps crunching over clinker, and the taste of sulfur spun in his head.

In his dream, he was first on the scene and loving it at Hawaii Volcanoes National Park. He watched the high fountains of fire, burbling endlessly into the black of night. Bits of bright liquid were tossed hundreds of feet, sparkling like fireworks.

It was beautiful but treacherous to be out here in darkness. The fresh crust of pahoehoe, the smooth, billowy variety of lava, hid many voids. One might walk across the same spot safely several times, but then luck could run out.

There was a constant low rumble from the earth, a trembling roar pounding through tubes beneath the crust. Great thumps and whumps of liquid lava sloshed against the walls of a vacant chamber, alternating with panting respirations that might have been a monster inside its lair.

Where the river of molten rock met the ocean, it hissed like a dragon. Waves hurled onto the shore and flashed to vapor. The glow lit the underside of the steam clouds, turning them an eerie grayish-orange.

Nick stood near a dark flow that moved slowly like congealing cake batter. Heat radiated toward him as though he stood before an open oven. Upstream, a crack appeared in the top of a rounded lava dome. The fissure burned bright.

Another appeared about ten feet closer.

While Nick watched, the piece of black rock between the cracks began to float, then was submerged in a fresh flood of red. Another section broke free and the stream became a raging torrent. It washed toward the low ridge, not three feet high, which separated Nick from the lava channel.

He turned and ran. The wall of heat that pushed him was so strong he thought his hair might catch fire. For a moment, he wished he was wearing one of those moon suits with the hoods and masks, but they weren't used much because the visors had a tendency to fog, and in a headlong rush they were too bulky and slow.

Nick's foot crashed through the crust, and he went down. The sharp glassy surface sliced his hands. He struggled to pull out of the hole as heat seared through the sole of his boot. Only the insulating effect of the solidified rock kept him from bursting into flame.

He dragged his leg onto the crust and managed to get up. The wind shifted, bringing the stinging stench of sulfur dioxide. Trying to contour uphill, he broke through the crust again. He was on fire, screaming in searing agony, but it was cold, so cold. His whole body was turning to ice. All the light and the life were going out of him, for his luck had finally run out.

Nick woke with a shock, chilled to the bone and sobbing like a child. He'd thrown off his covers and lay naked. Outside the window, snow still fell.

Strong fingers gripped his bare shoulder. "Nick," Kyle said. "You're having a nightmare." She lifted the crumpled covers and smoothed them over his bare body. Her weight depressed the bed as she sat. "They must have turned off the heat after midnight."

He felt groggy trying to focus on the cold hotel room

while the afterimage of lava made the bathroom light Kyle had left on look green. Uncoiling from his fetal position, he swiped at his tears. "Sorry. Damned silly of me."

"I have nightmares, too." Kyle's strong chin divided her face into a Harlequin mask, part dark where the shadows fell.

"Not like this one."

● ● ●

Kyle had never seen Nick this vulnerable. With his tear-stained face and bloody bandage, it was all she could do not to clasp him to her heart.

He drew his knees up and cocooned beneath the covers. Feeling the cold herself, she rose and dragged the spread off her bed, sat back down and wrapped herself. "So tell me your nightmare."

His face began to compose itself back into controlled lines.

She grabbed his hand to keep him from withdrawing. "No bullshit, Nick. Let's have the dream that just woke you crying like a baby."

He grinned. "Did anyone ever tell you you're a relentless woman?"

"Every one of my students."

Even as she held on to him, she felt him slipping away, back to the man who walked the edge. There was only one thing she could think of that might pull him closer, something she'd never thought she was capable of . . . until Wyatt broke down her defenses. If she told Nick about her sixth birthday, let him see inside her and understand the fears she had for both herself and him . . .

"Shall I tell you a nightmare first?" she asked with a calm she did not feel.

"Okay."

With her free hand, she snuggled the bedspread tighter around her shoulders. She still felt cold. "When I was six . . ."

"No bullshit," Nick warned.

"Stay with me. The night I turned six, my family and I were camping in Rock Creek Campground over in Montana. That was on August 17, 1959."

"Oh, Jesus." His expression went stark. "This is no dream."

"I lost my mother and father and our dog Max during the earthquake and flood." Nick reached out his hand. She took it. "In my dreams I found them. Over and over I'd uncover Mom or Dad. Sometimes they'd be perfectly preserved, but their staring clouded eyes said life was gone. The next time I'd find a mass of bloody rags, but I'd know it was one of them."

"Your dreams win," Nick conceded. "No contest."

Kyle hugged her knees and for a moment, the only sound was their quickened breathing.

He nodded toward the bathroom. "No wonder you sleep with a light."

He frowned. "Why didn't you ever tell me?"

"I couldn't talk about it."

Nick gestured for her to come into his arms.

She remained where she was. "Just this week, I told the first person."

"Wyatt." Nick's hands lowered.

"Now your dream," she suggested.

"Mine?" He shrugged. "It's not about anything that ever happened to me."

She felt the house of cards she'd built collapsing. "Then what were you afraid of?"

"I fell into a lava flow. Thought I was dying until I woke up."

Though the old bravado was now firmly in place, she tried once more to reach him. "You don't suppose this dream was your subconscious trying to tell you something?"

He considered. "Maybe it's a sign I'm not to run from the mountain."

Kyle felt as though the tumblers of a lock clicked into place.

Earlier this evening he'd come as close to a commitment as she could ever expect from him. Take up where they'd once left off. No promises of love and undying devotion, of course. There had never been.

Tears welled, and her throat ached. When she told Wyatt about her past terrors, he'd held her, taken on his sorrows as his own.

"There'll always be another mountain for you, Nick."

Kyle stared at him, dry-eyed.

As much as she might wish things were different, it felt satisfying to have an answer, even if it was the one she had been living with for years.

CHAPTER THIRTY-FOUR

SEPTEMBER 29

Kyle didn't think Wyatt had gotten any more sleep than she. Dark circles marked the skin beneath his eyes as he poured some of Iniki Kuni's Safari Blend for her.

"That's the last of it," he grieved. The young girl's desk was unattended this morning.

The Resource Center coffee room bore signs of yesterday's earthquake. Plywood covered the window, and the only unbroken coffeepot was in use.

"Where's Nick?" Wyatt asked.

"Sleeping. When I left him, he looked terrible."

Wyatt paused with his mug halfway to his lips. "I guess you'll be taking care of him a lot from now on."

"No one takes care of Nick Darden."

As she followed a limping Wyatt across the hall toward his office, someone hailed him from the reception area. Janet Bolido wore a tailored suit and pumps that looked out of place in the park.

Her dark eyes were direct, her handshake just shy of a bone-crusher. "Dr. Stone, I'm glad you're here. What I've got this morning includes you."

They went into Wyatt's office. Janet walked behind the desk, took a seat in his chair and placed her palms on his blotter. "What do your signals tell you is going to happen next?"

"It doesn't work that way," Wyatt protested. "We can't predict . . ."

"You did yesterday. Iniki Kuni leaked your email to *Billings Live Eye*, warning of more activity. They went with an exclusive . . . ten minutes later the big one struck."

"Coincidence," Kyle argued. "Our warning was generic, not specific."

"Nevertheless, *America Today* just called me. They asked for whoever predicted yesterday's quake to go on national television tomorrow morning."

"Good God." Wyatt leaned forward. "As in Gene North, live from New York?"

"The same," said Janet, while Kyle tried to register that she was serious.

"What would we tell them?" she asked. "That we know when the next one will be?"

"We don't," said Wyatt, "any more than we knew when that one was going to go. If we were able to do that we wouldn't have been in an avalanche chute and gotten our horses killed."

Janet's expression softened. "I didn't hear about that. Are you all right?"

"Kyle and I are." He pulled out a guest chair and sat, propping his hurt foot in an elevated position. "Dr. Darden from USGS took a blow on the head."

Though Janet did not ask, Kyle added, "The doctors think he'll be all right."

"That's good. Of course, he'll go on the show with you two."

Kyle's vision of Brock Hobart on Monty Muckleroy's couch transformed into her, Wyatt, and Nick on the *America Today* sofa across from Gene North in his wing chair. Yet, Stanton's derision at seeing Brock making predictions on the air held her back. Serious scientists published their findings in peer-reviewed journals, spoke at sanctioned conventions, or at best appeared on productions of *National Geographic* or *Discovery*. Television was the place for folks raising money for treasure hunting or searching for Noah's Ark.

"We won't be going on TV," Kyle said.

Janet's gaze shifted to Wyatt. "I think you will." The implication that he worked for her was clear. "You folks keep telling me your warnings are not precise. Now all you have to do is tell everybody in America."

"Wonderland," said Wyatt flatly. "You want us to calm peoples' fears." Kyle had the distinct impression he was about to tell the Superintendent to shove it.

She put a light hand on his arm and turned to Janet. "When do we have to let them know?"

"By noon."

"We'd like a chance to talk with Nick before we commit."

Janet's smile conveyed victory. "I'll wait for your call."

As soon as she left, Wyatt crossed his arms over his chest. "No way in hell."

"Refusing could cost your job."

"So what? She wants us to tell people everything's all right. It's not." He pushed back his guest chair and took his rightful place behind the desk. "I'm going to take a look at the stations."

While he started his computer, Kyle sipped the coffee she'd allowed to get cold.

"I'm in," Wyatt said after a few minutes of navigating to the Institute website.

"Brock Hobart is probably in, too," she replied. "I wish we could do something to keep him out."

Wyatt looked thoughtful. "The site is already set up so the public can access only certain areas. Why not set up a public access delay on the Nez Perce records?"

"I'm not sure I like that idea." Yet, after hearing Brock Hobart make predictions using their data, she felt the need to do something to slow him down.

Wyatt was already tapping keys. In a few minutes, he had remotely set up the Nez Perce Network so the real time data was secure. It could only be accessed by someone onsite in Salt Lake, by Kyle from anywhere so she could use a replacement laptop for the one lost in the canyon, or from Wyatt's network connection at Yellowstone. All others had to wait forty-eight hours to see the data.

Kyle moved to stand behind Wyatt. "Let's take another look at the focus of yesterday's quake, now that the stations all over the world have measured it. I'm guessing it will give us another point on the Saddle Valley fault plane."

Wyatt asked the computer to plot the point within the earth where the motion had originated. "Guess again. Three miles beneath the cinder cone at Nez Perce."

"Good Lord."

He frowned. "Could that mean the magma has found a conduit and is massing beneath the old eruption site?"

"Bingo," said Nick from the doorway.

He took only a moment with the records. "These small tremors below magnitude 1.0 aren't aftershocks. We're looking at continued harmonic tremors associated with moving magma." Though he still looked pale, what they were seeing seemed to invigorate him. "This is fantastic. We could see a crater form at Nez Perce."

"You mean an eruption?" Wyatt asked.

"Think of it as the volcano clearing its throat. The heat builds until the ground water flashes to steam, and BAM!" Nick brought his fist up beneath the palm of his other hand and knocked the upper one aside.

Sweat broke out down Kyle's back. "When?"

He thought. "If we have more quakes beneath the peak and can track their focus, we might establish a rate of rise for the magma. Otherwise, with this constant background chatter, we wouldn't have any warning."

"No warning?" Despite her perspiration, Kyle felt cold inside. "Wouldn't the background events get stronger as magma nears the surface?"

"That might be a clue," Nick said, "but frankly, with as many steamers as we saw near the summit, the crater explosion could happen any time."

"After that there would be nothing plugging the conduit to stop a larger eruption." Kyle looked at her watch. There was plenty of time before they'd agreed to get back with the Superintendent, but she didn't need any more.

"Nick, Janet Bolido was just here to say we've been asked to appear on *America Today*. I say we take them up on their offer."

He shook his head. "Those interviews can't be controlled. There's no telling how things can get twisted. You go on there thinking you'll say one thing . . ."

Wyatt cut in. "Janet expects us to say nothing's going to happen."

Kyle waved an impatient hand. "We don't know what's going to happen, but people need to know what is possible. Even if we can't be precise."

"Don't say I didn't warn you later," said Nick.

Wyatt gave him a hard look. "Since you've dealt with the press before, we'll keep quiet and let you do the talking."

Nick went out into the hall and disappeared into the men's room.

Wyatt called Janet.

In fifteen minutes, with several callbacks, it was set. New York considered and rejected that *Billings Live Eye* do the interview in the field. Instead, they requested the team of scientists do a live feed from their Salt Lake affiliate studio.

"Tomorrow morning," Wyatt reported. "They'll pay mileage, meals, a hotel, all the trimmings. Even air if we want to fly down from Bozeman."

Kyle looked out the office window. Morning light glared on a few inches of snow, but the roads were clear and shiny wet. Wyatt brought up an Internet weather service and confirmed the region was clear of winter storm activity.

Nick came back into the office.

She turned to him. "Let's drive down."

He did not reply.

She checked her watch. "If we grab our stuff, we can be on the road before noon. We'll stop for fast food and be at my place in time to catch some sleep." After the helpless feelings of yesterday, both during the quake and after, it felt good to be back in control.

"They want us at the studio by 4 AM." Wyatt started shutting down the computer.

Nick leaned against the wall, apparently deep in thought.

While Wyatt's machine powered off, he pushed past Nick and went to fetch his uniform jacket from behind the door. He turned his wide-brimmed hat and looked at it. "Should I wear the full getup for TV?"

"Of course," Kyle said. "I'll need something a bit more formal from my place." She jabbed an elbow into Nick's side. "Earth to Darden."

He turned with a look as solitary as when he'd talked of dying alone. There was something else as well, a determined set. "I'm not going with you."

"Not going?" Kyle echoed. "This is your fifteen minutes of fame, too."

Wyatt put down his hat. "Look, buddy, we may not always see eye to eye, but we need you there, too." He touched his bruised cheek where Nick had hit him. "You owe me."

Nick faced him. "If you're worried about credibility, tell them I'm in agreement that something is going to happen at Nez Perce Peak. I'm going to call USGS and get more equipment, charter a helicopter. There's no way Colin can say no, hell, he's in Asia. I'll get forgiveness rather than permission after we, that is . . . you've, been on national television."

Kyle grabbed his arm.

Wyatt said, "Come on, we need USGS to make this cluster thing complete."

Gently, Nick loosened her grip. "Sorry. By this time tomorrow, I plan to be back on the mountain."

● ● ●

Half an hour after he refused to go to Salt Lake, Kyle stood by the driver's door of the Institute van while Nick saw them off. On the lawns of Mammoth, last night's snow was melting.

"I wish I could change your mind on this," Kyle said.

Wyatt stood at a little distance on the Resource Center porch, not far enough from her and Nick for a stranger to notice. A muscle twitched in his clean-shaven jaw.

"I've got to go back," Nick insisted. The bloodstained bandage still circling his head had the effect of making him look very young.

"Nick, no. You were in the clinic only yesterday."

Wyatt stepped into the yard and walked farther away.

Nick's eyes were clear green, the same as she remembered smiling at her the evening he'd urged her to his tent in the woods.

"Wait for us to come back from doing the show," she insisted. "Monitor this thing from a distance . . . Think of the dream you had last night."

He shook his head. "I can't let a nightmare from the past keep me from living."

Kyle looked at him with dawning awareness. Wasn't that exactly what she had been doing all these years? Waiting for Nick to come back and tell her it had all been a mistake? Examining perfectly good men and comparing them to a shining impossible image of incarnate summer? Behind Nick's shoulder, Wyatt walked alone beneath yellowing cottonwoods. Wind rattled the branches and blew clots of snow off the browned grass.

"You need to start living too, Kyle," Nick urged softly.

"What?" she asked, but she saw him take in that she was watching Wyatt.

"You need somebody, in a way I never have. I don't pretend to like the cowboy, but he's a decent sort. That torch he's carrying is damn near blinding."

Kyle hugged herself against the chill. "He's got a woman."

Nick shrugged. "Back home I've got someone, this year's saint who believes she can weather the time I spend in the field." He smoothed her hair behind her ear. "For you, I could forget she exists."

She gestured toward Wyatt. "Then why push me toward him? Why can't we . . ." she broke off. This had all been settled last night, or thirty years ago.

"If there were just one woman for me, Kyle, it would be you." Nick rubbed his temples beneath the gauze. "But Wyatt told it true. I light where the volcano blows."

"And now it's in Yellowstone." Her words were like chips of stone. "If not, we'd never have seen each other again."

She heard the crunch of Wyatt's boots behind her before he spoke. "We need to get on the road."

She looked at Nick, and her anger drained away. "Take care on the mountain," she whispered.

Wyatt went around to the passenger door of the van and opened it.

Nick looked at him over the roof and glanced at Kyle. "If the press is as bloodthirsty as I've seen them, you're going to need each other."

Before she or Wyatt could reply, Nick walked away.

On the way through the park to the west entrance, Kyle felt as though each mile took her farther from the past. If she hadn't been driving, she would have closed her eyes against the memory of twenty-year-old Nick in a

Wyoming summer meadow; blue cotton shirt tied around his bronzed waist, khaki shorts above muscled calves, green eyes squinting in the high-altitude sun.

How many others had he offered the same line? Sincerity personified, "If there were only one woman . . ."

Yet, she believed him. In his own mind, Nick hadn't thrown her away lightly, then or now. His struggle to choose between her and the mysterious world of live volcanoes had wounded him, and at some level, Kyle believed she was the one who came closest to competing with his siren's song.

She glanced over at Wyatt. So dear and familiar, yet she was aware of him in a way that disturbed as well as enervated. Stanton had told her how he and Leila had gotten together. No fireworks at first sight, just a simple progression from friendship to a kiss that had surprised them as much as it brought relief.

As they left the park and the van passed over the edge of the last caldera, the tightness in Kyle began to ease. Being in the park, especially in the backcountry was at once a breathtakingly beautiful and terrifying experience. She hadn't realized how good it would feel to be out of the line of fire.

CHAPTER THIRTY-FIVE
SEPTEMBER 29

Kyle wasn't sure which was worse, seeing Stanton lying helpless, or watching Wyatt's reaction. The nursing home . . . they'd stopped at University Hospital and found out he'd been moved yesterday . . . smelled of urine and faint rancid cooking odors. Outside the window, dusk was falling. On the sill, a single tired floral arrangement reposed amid fallen petals and stamens.

"You should have seen his room right after it happened," Kyle murmured. "Flowers, cards . . ."

Stanton slept with his mouth open, one side more slack than the other. "I've brought Wyatt," Kyle spoke up.

Stanton opened his eyes. Their bright blue seemed dulled, but he put out his hand. "Yes!"

Taking the emaciated claw, Wyatt engaged in the kind of lie she was prepared to offer. "You do your physical therapy and you'll be back on your feet in no time."

"Yes," Stanton agreed.

Kyle glanced at the dark and silent TV; thankful she wasn't the one lying here without even a game show to break the monotony. "You're looking better," she lied as well. "I don't know if you've heard about the activity we've been having up at Yellowstone."

"Yes," said Stanton.

She wondered how he could have known. "Leila must have told you, maybe Hollis?" Her smile felt forced. "Well, guess what? Tomorrow morning Wyatt and I are going to be on *America Today*."

Before Stanton opened his mouth, horror fingered her spine. She saw it hit Wyatt as well when yet another repetition of, "Yes," was not a rational answer.

She gave a brilliant smile and turned away before either man could catch the sheen of tears in her eyes. Behind her, Wyatt muttered, "Christ."

Kyle stared out the window through a blur. She heard Wyatt recover and render an upbeat story of the New Moon earthquake, along with the Nez Perce Peak landslide. He made no mention of the horses' fate or Nick's head injury.

At intervals, Stanton punctuated the delivery with the single word he was able to speak. Until he couldn't help her, she had not realized how much she'd been counting on his advice.

As Wyatt began to run out of steam, Kyle blinked and the autumn leaves came into focus. She turned from the window. "Stanton, do you remember all those times we talked about predicting earthquakes?"

He nodded. This time she thought he looked at her through eyes of understanding.

"Wyatt and I are in a bind about the TV show. Should

we cry Chicken Little like the global warming crowd?" She put out her left hand. "Or follow our gut instinct and lay things out with logic?" Her right hand lifted.

Stanton's eyes tracked to her right.

She went on, "We saw so many bad signs at Nez Perce Peak that we sent out a warning."

"It got to Park Headquarters right before the latest big quake," Wyatt said.

Stanton shook his head with sudden vigor.

Kyle moved closer to the bedside. "We were wrong to warn them?"

Another headshake.

"Wrong to go on TV?"

Stanton nodded.

She bent closer. "Because you think it's unprofessional, like everybody says about Brock Hobart?"

Stanton indicated that wasn't it.

Wyatt frowned. "My bosses in Yellowstone are okay with us going on TV. Are you worried what the USGS folks will think?"

Not that, either.

Stanton closed his eyes and made a fist of his good hand. His forehead furrowed and he got out, "Hell."

"Hell?" Kyle put a hand on his pajama-clad arm.

He opened his eyes and tried, "Hall . . ."

She looked toward the doorway. No, said another headshake. "Holl?" she asked. "Hollis Delbert?"

"Yes!"

"Has he been here?" led into "This morning?" and "Did he say something about us being on TV?"

"How could he know?" Wyatt interjected.

"I don't know how he found out, and that's only half of it," she fumed. "I'm not letting Hollis dictate us off the show."

● ● ●

An hour later, Kyle stood in the Institute's basement hall outside the seismic lab and stared into the blackness. Drawing a breath, she got ready to run for the light.

Wyatt touched her arm. "I'll get it."

He went into the room and threw the switch. The fluorescents blinked until they settled, shedding a sterile light. The faded map of the world, spotted with historic earthquake epicenters showed the Pacific's ring of fire with Japan and Sakhalin Island as hotspots. The seismograph drums turned slowly as she approached the bank from Yellowstone.

She stopped. "Oh, no."

Wyatt gave a soft whistle.

All of the strip charts were busy with the chattering of almost constant tremors. They were mostly in the 1.0 magnitude range, but occasionally spiked to 2.0s or 3.0s.

Kyle moved to the nearest computer terminal and began entering rapid commands. She brought up the signals from the newest stations they had placed around Nez Perce that were not represented by charts.

Wyatt rolled a chair over and sat at her elbow. "Good Lord."

If she were a believer, Kyle would pray. Such constant tremors surely proved that the magma chamber had found an outlet and was working its way toward the surface. "I wish Hollis were here to see this."

"From what I know of the man, he wouldn't care," Wyatt said. "His vendetta against you is too personal."

A flashing message insisted Kyle check email. She ignored everything on the list except the one from Nick, sent from Wyatt's account at the Resource Center.

Looks like I'll be waiting a day or so to head up. My equipment has been delayed by the winter storm on the coast. I've been in Wyatt's office all day monitoring the seismic. Superintendent Bolido came over and asked me if she should consider an evacuation. When she heard I was mounting a helicopter expedition to Nez Perce, she decided to hold off.

"She probably figured if Nick was going into the park interior it was safe," Kyle mourned.

She glanced at another of the workstation's three monitors. The signal from Nez Perce showed that a new excursion of up to 3.5 had happened only moments before. In Kyle's imagination, it rattled the rodeo trophy in Wyatt's office, along with the nerves of people like Iniki Kuni, but then the little receptionist had already evacuated. "I'd feel a lot better if everybody got out of the park," she told Wyatt.

He didn't reply as he stared at Nick's message. The next sentence said, *Tell Wyatt that Alicia Alvarez came by.*

Wanted to tell him goodbye before she left for Texas. She said he would understand.

● ● ●

Kyle and Wyatt left the Institute van in the parking lot and took her Mercedes. It felt good to put her foot to the floor on the I-80 grade east of Salt Lake. She wondered what had happened between Wyatt and Alicia to send her away, but it was none of her business.

Wyatt sat in silence beside her. By the dash clock, it was past ten. They'd stopped for fast food after leaving the Institute.

As the lights of her subdivision came into view, it felt like she'd been gone a long time. She parked in the drive beside her townhouse and got her duffel bag out of the trunk.

"My couch makes into a nice bed," she said.

Wyatt left his kit and dress uniform in the car.

Inside her foyer, it was dark, but she didn't want to look foolish. Without using her key ring flashlight, she went into the hall and turned on a single light.

Wyatt followed her into the living room and turned on all the lamps.

She set the laptop she'd brought from the Institute on the dining table beside her keys. "Down here's a half bath, but you can shower in mine upstairs."

He glanced over his shoulder toward the door. "I'd

better take your car and go to the hotel by the highway."

She tried to lighten the mood and keep him from going. "You been on TV before?" Even as she spoke, a frisson of stage fright sobered her.

He grinned. "Mr. Rodeo, Live at Five in Bozeman. All the kids screaming and begging to ride the mechanical bronco on camera."

With an effort, she answered his smile. "I'll bet you were right up front."

"Actually, I was hiding on the back row wishing I were home riding a real horse. Kind of the way I'll feel in the morning."

"Too bad Nick didn't come with us." As soon as the words were out, she regretted them.

Wyatt drew himself up, and she felt he was about to head for the door.

"Don't." She put a hand on his arm. "It's over with Nick . . . You must have heard him shoving me at you . . ."

"I heard him. The volcano jock suggesting the stay-at-home guy would make a nice patsy. He made me feel like a damned fool." Wyatt pulled away. "It was bad enough when Alicia called me a poor son of a bitch for . . ."

A fluttering started in her stomach. "For what?"

"For"—his voice dropped, but his dark eyes glowed— "wanting you."

"Is that why Alicia left?"

"When I came back from the mountain, she sensed things weren't the same."

"Nothing's the same." *Her carefully planned existence blown to hell ... Last night's debacle with Nick ...* "Or everything's the same."

Wyatt's hand came up and her heart pounded. He touched her cheek and slid his fingers around to the back of her neck. "You were right the first time. The way we were together, friends, that's all up in the air and it scares me to death."

"It scares me, too," she whispered, feeling goose bumps from his light caress.

"If this were simpler, I'd just grab you and let the chips fall where they may."

A feeling of shyness, as though they were kids getting together for the first time, made her hesitate.

Wyatt sighed and held out his hand, palm up. "Give me your car keys and I'll get that room."

Even as she reached to her pocket for her keys, part of her wanted to throw her arms around him, to embrace the change that had already taken place. "Wyatt ..."

He glanced at her wall clock. "We're going to need what sleep we can get."

It was an excuse, as clear as rain, but he was right. As never before in their lives, they both needed to be their best for the show.

She placed the keys in his hand. "Pick me up at three-thirty so we can make it to the studio on time."

CHAPTER THIRTY-SIX
SEPTEMBER 30

Kyle couldn't sleep. Her light was on, but the brightest bulb could not hold back the darkness. With a muttered oath, she threw back the covers and grabbed her robe. The bedside clock showed two-forty. A draft swept her bare ankles as she went downstairs.

Curling up on the couch, she thought of Wyatt, who in the old days of their comfortable friendship would have been sleeping here now under her spare comforter. Recalling her own breathless reaction to his recent embraces, she asked herself why she had always thought it out of the question. There was the issue of her being several years older, the fact that she'd been his major professor and dissertation advisor, but those were mere convenient excuses for the main reason. She had not been in the market for a man . . . unless he was Nick Darden.

No wonder Wyatt had disliked Nick on instinct, grasping immediately that he had been the obstacle to both their happiness. And while she'd been mooning after Nick, Wyatt had been the one who built the fire that made her forget the mountain night around them.

Kyle remembered asking Franny how she had chosen between the brothers who both wanted to marry her. She imagined the youthful Francesca, tall and slim like her daughter Rachel and her grandchild Kyle. With flashing eyes and a merry wit, Francesca must have had her choice of suitors, whether in her Tuscan home, New York, or Wyoming where she settled to start a family.

"How did I choose?" Franny had mused with a soft expression. "I thought about living without each of them in turn. And the idea of losing one of them made my chest hurt . . . so bad I had trouble catching my breath. He was the man for me."

For all these years, Kyle had thought Nick was the man for her, yet, how could she ask what her life would be like without him? He had never been there to begin with.

As for Wyatt, she recalled how safe and warm she'd felt after telling him her greatest secret. How he'd understood her fears in a way Nick could not begin to comprehend. A vision of the yearning in his eyes as he'd left her tonight started an ache beneath her breastbone.

The hands of her wall clock moved toward three. She went into the dining room to the laptop. With feeling of dread, she turned on the machine and logged into the database.

The activity in Yellowstone was even more volatile than before. Kyle wished she had more experience with what the charts had looked like at Mount St. Helens or Mt. Pinatubo. She could call up some of the signatures from the Earthquake Center, but what she needed to know was how things had looked in the weeks and months before an eruption. Nick would know but, of course, there were no phones in the rooms at the Mammoth Hotel and his cell was in the bottom of a canyon.

Recalling the people in Yellowstone, the road workers and the mother with the crying daughter, the doctor who'd treated Nick, Joseph Kuni staying while his daughter fled . . . thinking of their fitful rest this night, while the background of constant quakes ramped up enough to frighten even the bravest . . . Kyle felt colder than she should wrapped in fleece.

It finally started to sink in that she was going to be on television. With the realization, came the weight of responsibility. People were going to watch, believing that she had a track record of success at warning of disaster.

She went back upstairs and showered, a quick hot blast that failed to warm. Dressed, with her hair caught up in a smooth knot at the back of her head, she peeked out the window at scattered snow flurries. Thankfully, the roads were clear.

While waiting for Wyatt, she scribbled a few introductory remarks about the Institute and the partnership of the National Park Service and USGS in Yellowstone. Her pen scratched as she slashed out most of it.

When she heard her car horn out front, she wasn't ready.

Wyatt made no move to let her drive, so she headed for the passenger door. Though it was warmer here in than in Yellowstone, her dressy black coat, low-heeled pumps and pantyhose were inadequate for the misty autumn weather.

The instant Kyle slammed the door, Wyatt prodded the gas pedal. Something in the set of his profile said he wasn't happy about the choice he'd made to leave her for the hotel.

She reached to touch his wrist. He kept his eyes on the road.

"About last night . . ." she tried.

"Nothing happened last night." He kept his eyes on a stoplight, waiting even though the streets were deserted. On green, the Mercedes accelerated down the mountain, but Kyle sensed the control Wyatt exerted over both the car and his emotions.

She had the same problem, torn between wanting him and trying to focus on *America Today*. "Nothing physical happened . . ."

On the I-80 on ramp, Wyatt glanced at her. "We've got too much else on our plate to do anything but drop this subject."

She resisted the urge to reach toward him again. "We'll let it go . . . for now."

They drove awhile in silence. Finally, as they pulled into the TV station parking lot, he turned his head. His expression filled her chest once more with longing.

"I've been throwing myself at you, ready or not." He stopped the car and turned off the engine. "I'm afraid you're not."

Of course, he'd think that. The last concrete thing

she'd said last night was to agree that she was scared to death. He seemed to have forgotten saying it, too.

Well, maybe she had been frightened before, but there was no arguing with the wisdom of Franny and this ache beneath her breastbone.

The station's front door opened and a young man waved them in.

❋   ❋   ❋

The TV studio made the seismograph lab look low-tech, with cameras on trolleys, wheeled ladders, banks of sound mixing equipment, and TV monitors everywhere.

As Kyle and Wyatt waited for the looming airtime, she gave her hair a self-conscious smoothing. "I told the guy I don't wear foundation, but he put on extra pancake and shadow."

"Got to have some color for the camera." Looking a little orange himself, and with his black eye effectively masked, Wyatt repeated the litany he'd been told. His scrutiny, from her mascara-laden eyelashes to lips slicked with a slash of color, made her feel less a child playing dress-up and more a woman. She smoothed the skirt of her black dress and checked the set of Franny's small diamonds at her earlobes.

"You look nice," he offered, his voice pitched low.

They may have tabled the subject of each other, but her cheeks grew warm. She thought he'd never looked better, standing tall among the studio workers scurrying around to meet the on-air deadline. He wore his ranger's dress uniform with ease, his badge bright on the formal dark jacket bearing the National Park Service crest. At the last minute, he'd decided to forego the hat. "No need looking like Dudley Do-Right."

He shifted his weight from one foot to the other. "Did you check the stations again?"

"I logged on around three. The activity was stronger than ever."

"Uh-oh," he said. It took a second for her to realize his focus was on something past her shoulder.

"I see you made it," said a snide voice at her elbow.

With a sinking feeling, she turned on Hollis Delbert. "What are you doing here?" The makeup on his face above his best navy suit gave her the answer.

"Making sure you don't get the Institute in trouble." Hair lacquer made Hollis's blond comb-over look darker than usual. "When the network called looking for you, I made sure they understood who was in charge."

Before she could come up with a retort, Wyatt shook his head. "Brother, you are a piece of work."

"Dr. Stone? Dr. Delbert?" said the studio aide. "We're ready for you and Ranger Ellison now."

"That's Dr. Ellison," she informed the slender young man who didn't look old enough to shave.

They picked their way over snaking cables to a bare table with three waiting chairs. Kyle's image of her and

Wyatt being interviewed by a friendly anchorperson, maybe sitting around in armchairs or a couch, evaporated.

The aide directed them to sit with Kyle in the middle, helped everyone put on microphones and showed them the earpieces. "Keep your eyes on me at all times. I'll be sitting across from you, pretending to be your audience."

Her mouth went dry. Though she tried to call on her years of lecturing to induce calm, whatever opening remarks she might have come up with flew out of her head. Moreover, if Hollis were going ahead of her, in his capacity as the Institute's Acting Director he'd probably steal whatever intro she came up with.

The studio aide turned on a TV about five feet away and she heard the opening bars of the *America Today* theme. Sometimes, she watched snippets of the show in the morning, standing around half-dressed or brushing her teeth. She had never imagined entering the nation's collective bathroom or joining millions in breakfast.

Kyle pressed her lips to keep in an obscenity. Nick had promised a media circus. She shot Wyatt a glance. "Let's just get through this without losing our cool."

Gene North appeared on the set decorated as Everyman's living room. His black hair contrasted with crow's feet that Botox and a facelift hadn't quite eliminated. Kyle wasn't speculating; he'd had his plastic surgeon on the show.

"Welcome to America," Gene greeted. "Today is Monday, September 30."

His very blond and thin co-anchor, Mitzi McMahon,

introduced terrorism, baseball playoffs, and the weather. A winter storm was moving onshore into Washington and Oregon, likely to become a major blizzard. Unfortunately, Kyle didn't think weather would deter Nick in his return to the field.

Gene North was back. "Let's get to our feature of the day. In less than a month following the September 10th earthquake disaster at Sakhalin Island, there have been two strong shakes in Yellowstone Park."

"Yes, Gene," Mitzi agreed. "What brings these events together is the question of whether earthquakes can be predicted before they do the kind of damage the world saw at Sakhalin."

Gene took over. "This is especially important for the many earthquake prone areas of this country. Everyone thinks of L.A. and San Francisco, but did you know that in 1811 and 1812 the central Mississippi Valley was rocked by three massive quakes on what's known as the New Madrid Fault Zone? That Charleston, South Carolina was nearly leveled by shaking in 1886? Even Manhattan Island is underlain by ancient faults which could be reactivated."

Kyle pressed her hands together in her lap. Whoever had briefed Gene had done a reasonable job.

He went on, "We go live now to our affiliate studio in L.A., and Dr. Brock Hobart, a scientist who has taken credit for predicting all three major quakes."

"Taking credit is right," Hollis muttered. "I don't know anybody who'd give it to him."

Wyatt made a shushing sound.

A split-screen came up with Gene on one side and Brock on the other. Brock didn't look nearly as confident as he had on *Mornings with Monty*.

"Good morning, Dr. Hobart." Gene was warmth personified. "I understand you're developing quite a record for predicting earthquakes."

Brock smiled. "When I put together my theories back in the eighties at the United States Geological Survey, I got little support, so I moved on."

Hollis snorted. "The director suggested Brock not let the doorknob hit him in the ass on his way out."

"So how has earthquake predicting managed to pay your bills?" Gene asked.

"Family money," Hollis continued his commentary.

"Fortunately," Brock braved, "there are people interested in the potential of prediction. Think of the billions of dollars that could be saved worldwide with an accurate early-warning system."

"Indeed." Gene raised a brow. "You claim to have foretold Sakhalin, but I understand you didn't say where in the world it was going to happen."

Brock's smile faded. "Monty had to go to a commercial break before I could discuss the location."

Gene did not look happy. "A commercial is coming here soon. Before we go, could you very quickly tell me about your work in Yellowstone?"

"What work?" Wyatt asked.

"Yes, Gene," said Brock. "After Sakhalin I was looking over the seismograph signatures from the park and predicted both the September 26th and September 28th quakes."

Gene cut in. "Ten seconds."

Brock blurted, "With the full moon coming up on October 10th, if I were in Yellowstone I'd watch out."

Kyle felt as though she'd been running a race. She tried to focus on how her message was different from Brock's, but it was difficult. He seemed sincere in his conviction.

"Wow, Mitzi," said Gene. The *America Today* set faded into a car commercial with fast-driving and loud rock music.

Before Kyle was ready, the show was back.

"Now, before we go to our other scientists, we have a recorded message from Janet Bolido, Park Superintendent for Yellowstone."

Kyle should have known a woman with the ambitions Janet had would not have passed up the opportunity to be on national television, but she was still shocked to see her face on the monitor. The video must have been made yesterday, for she wore the black suit that had looked out of place on a workday in the park.

Standing before a backdrop of Mammoth Hot Springs, Janet extended an arm to encompass her surroundings. "Ladies and gentlemen, I'd like to welcome you to Wonderland. Yellowstone, the world's first and best National Park, has been around for over one hundred thirty years With the stewardship of our fine staff, the support o

Congress, and the Department of the Interior, we should be around for many more."

She took a few steps toward the camera and the operator went to a close-up. "Now my scientists, whom you are about to meet, are some of the world's experts on a volcanic land, as they tell me the park is. And despite some fringe person's warnings about Yellowstone being unsafe, our people freely admit that specific predictions as to the time and place of earthquakes and volcanoes are not yet possible with current technology . . ." She paused and smiled. "But I'll let them tell you that. In the meantime, I want everybody to know that the fall season in the park is one of the most beautiful, and I encourage a visit . . ." The image drew back to show the white terraces of the hot springs and Janet raised her arms. "Everyone come to Wonderland!"

Abruptly, the monitor went dark. "Thirty seconds," said the studio aide.

Caught watching Janet with her mouth half open, Kyle shut it. How clever of her to set it up so she would look good but not have to field questions and risk being put on the spot.

The aide went on, "Remember to look at me when you talk."

Kyle forced her clenched hands to relax. The only other time she'd felt such stage fright was when she defended her master's thesis. But that did not compare, for then she had only faced three kindly professors, who later said the best thing she'd done was admitting when she didn't know something.

As Janet had said, nobody knew what was going to happen in Yellowstone. But since her video had been made yesterday the bad omens were a lot stronger.

The studio lights glared. Perspiration broke out under Kyle's arms. "Three, two, one," counted the aide. A red light appeared on the camera behind his shoulder. She stared at the lens.

Gene's baritone was in her ear, introducing Hollis as the Institute Director, omitting the interim nature of the title. Kyle continued to stare at the lens.

"Dr. Stone?" Mitzi said. "That's cute, you know . . . rocks."

The studio aide waggled his fingers. Kyle dragged her gaze from the mesmerizing headlight of the camera, looked at his narrow face with startling dark brows and a pencil moustache, and tried to imagine him as her only audience.

Mitzi went on, "I understand you and your colleagues also made a prediction that came true."

This was it, Kyle reasoned, the only chance in this charade to get her message across. "Unlike Dr. Hobart I've spent many years studying Yellowstone." She talked to the aide. "Dr. Ellison and I were in the field during the New Moon Earthquake, along with Dr. Nicholas Darden, a noted volcanologist from the USGS. After we saw the mountain's summit smoking and other signs, we felt things pointed to more large quakes and thought it prudent to warn park officials." She felt pleased with the calm in her voice. "Now the possibility of an eruption . . ."

"A volcano?" Mitzi shrilled. "I thought Dr. Hobart was talking about earthquakes."

In Kyle's earpiece, Gene North broke in. "I'm going to ask the Institute Director, Dr. Delbert, about that. What is the history of volcanic activity in the area?"

Hollis sucked in his breath. Kyle didn't know if she was on TV or whether the camera had just homed in on Hollis's nose hairs. While he continued to sit frozen, she heard Wyatt whisper, "The caldera."

Kyle broke in, "There have been large eruptions in the past, at around two million years ago and 1.3 million. And the great explosion that created the basin holding Yellowstone Lake took place around 630,000 years ago."

"Whoa." Gene whistled. "Sounds like we're about due."

She hadn't meant it that way. There was a fair amount of slack in all geologic methods of age dating and she wasn't about to set her watch by them. But she'd come on the show with the idea of getting people to take this latest round of activity seriously. Her nostrils flared as she took the only stand she could. "You've done the math, Gene. Today Yellowstone is under siege by constant tremors, an almost certain sign of magma on its way to the surface."

"Ranger Ellison?" Mitzi asked. "Has there been any discussion of evacuation?"

Kyle felt Wyatt hesitate. Then, taking a deep breath, he bent forward, "I understand some Park Headquarters residents have already left."

A hubbub broke out in the studio audience in New York.

Gene's joviality was extinguished. Rather than pursue the obvious inconsistencies in Janet Bolido's performance, he changed the subject. "What about Dr. Hobart's prediction for the full moon?"

"There's no question in my mind," Kyle said, "or in the opinion of Dr. Darden of USGS, that something is going to happen, be it Dr. Hobart's full-moon earthquake, a steam or lava eruption, or something much worse." She expected Gene to cut her off, but he was quiet. "If we saw a repeat of what happened 630,000 years ago there would be no dining rooms with college students serving prime rib. No mountains, lakes, or waterfalls. No buffalo, bear, or bison. No Yellowstone Lake with cutthroat trout and nesting osprey. All the geysers and hot springs blown sky-high." She saw the wide eyes of the young studio aide. Her cheeks felt hot; sweat trickled down her sides. "There would be no Yellowstone . . . no one in the surrounding towns would survive."

● ● ●

The red light on the camera winked out. Bright light ceased to drill Kyle's eyes.

The aide stood in front of the desk doing a deer-in headlights impression. "No Yellowstone?"

The look of panic on his face made Kyle wonder if she' gone too far . . . but just like Brock Hobart, she believe every word she had said.

Hollis shoved back his chair. "Jesus Christ!"

As she stripped off her mike and earpiece, the aide put the TV monitor back on. A cruise line commercial ended and Gene told Mitzi, "Powerful warnings from Yellowstone." He looked thoughtful. "My brother-in-law lives in Cody . . ."

Hollis soldiered on, "Are you out of your mind?"

Still sweating, but feeling cold, Kyle gathered her black coat and started for the exit.

Hollis called after her, "Don't even think of touching the van and equipment."

She turned back, hot words ready, but Wyatt was there. His steady eyes warned her not to rise to the bait. With careful control, she said, "Those items belong to the Institute."

"Fine," Hollis gasped. "Then you don't belong. You're fired."

After all that she'd been through this morning, Kyle shouldn't have any adrenaline left. Yet, its sharp sting ran down her arms. "You don't have the balls."

"Watch me. Stanton and Colin aren't around and Radford will be on my side when he hears what you've done to frighten people."

Wyatt tugged her arm. "Come on."

The studio help began to gather. She fought the urge to tell Hollis off.

Wyatt's grip tightened. "Kyle."

A local TV reporter from the morning drive time show walked toward them.

Kyle bit her tongue and allowed Wyatt to draw her away.

Hollis's stridency carried. "Don't try going to the Institute. Security won't let you in."

On the way out of the building, Wyatt offered her the keys to her Mercedes.

"I'm too mad to drive." Her voice shook. "He fired me. He fucking fired me."

Wyatt's gaunt face looked infuriated, but his features softened as he met her eyes.

"So help me, Wyatt, if you say you're sorry . . ."

The corners of his mouth twitched. "I won't. You're tough enough to take on ten SOBs his size."

"Can he fire me?"

Wyatt sobered. "Colin and Radford put him in charge, so I suppose he can. At least until all this sorts itself out."

"I'm afraid we haven't got that kind of time."

CHAPTER THIRTY-SEVEN
SEPTEMBER 30

Morning sun shone full when Kyle and Wyatt entered her townhouse. She stood in the hall, ran her hands up and destroyed the knot her hair was in. "I feel awful." She threw her coat onto the sofa.

Wyatt raised his arms and stretched his long back. He shrugged out of his uniform jacket and tossed it beside hers. "I was sweating like a pig during the broadcast."

"Ditto."

He glanced toward the stairs. "I checked out of the hotel, but I could use a run through the rain locker."

"Gentlemen first," she offered briskly. "There's soap and shampoo. Clean towels under the sink." He got his bag from the car and took the stairs two at a time.

Kyle moved to the dining room table where the replacement laptop beckoned. God only knew what was happening in the park by now. She booted up and went online. It seemed to take forever for the Institute site to come up. After clicking through the public areas to the entry for the Yellowstone Network, she keyed in, "Max." Kyle had never had another pet.

A little hourglass appeared. It stayed too long for the usual login.

Kyle's fingers curled. "Come on, come on."

Upstairs, her shower went on.

A dialog box declared, "Your password is either invalid or has expired."

"Son of a bitch." It had to be Hollis. He'd had time to get from the TV studio back to the Institute and cut off her access.

On instinct, she reached for her cell phone.

It was in the bottom of the canyon on Nez Perce.

She looked toward the wall instrument in the kitchen and pushed halfway to her feet. With gritted teeth, she imagined railing at Hollis, "Stanton and I built the Institute while you were in elementary school. Now put my goddamned password back."

Even as she raged, experience told her it would do no good. He'd probably go into a full-blown asthma attack. And until he calmed down, probably in a matter of days rather than hours, she stood no chance of reasoning with him.

Subsiding back into her chair, she tried logging on a few more times in case there had been a mistake. Then, with rapid keyboard and mouse adjustments, she exited the site she'd helped develop. Closing the laptop lid, she listened as the hard drive wound down along with her pulse rate.

The silence brought a sting to her eyes. She remembered the dismal storage basement of thirty years ago, that

Stanton had transformed into one of the premiere seismic research facilities in the world. She heard the laughter of so many students, of her and Wyatt bent together over a monitor while they planned a seminar that was both educational and entertaining. For Stanton's sake, for Wyatt, for Xi and all the others, she could not let Hollis get away with this.

It might take a little while, until Colin was back in the country, but she vowed she would have her job back . . . and see Hollis in Siberia.

The shower noise ceased. With a glance at the ceiling, she considered her nearly bare larder. Frozen concentrated orange juice, maple flavored bacon she could microwave; maybe stir up some eggs with them in the same dish. At least she had some espresso grind Jamaican Blue Mountain that would brew up with fortitude.

As she was spooning the aromatic coffee into the filter basket, Wyatt's footsteps sounded on the stairs.

"Make mine strong enough to walk."

She turned and felt a little shock at seeing him in gray sweats and a T-shirt rather than his uniform. Comb trails marked his damp hair and he smelled clean. A flash of image in her brain . . . of simply stepping forward into his arms, but she thought she'd better get her own shower.

"Hollis cut off my password," she said.

Instead of swearing as she expected, Wyatt's smile remained in place.

"This is serious." She pointed a spatula at him. "What

are you grinning about?"

He leaned against the counter and crossed one bare ankle over the other. "Just wondering if Hollis is suicidal enough to turn off website access from Yellowstone National Park."

Her spirits lifted. "Your office! Of course Hollis won't dare shut you down. He knows Janet Bolido would have his head."

Wyatt took the spatula from her and brandished it toward the refrigerator. "I'm ready for bacon and eggs . . . and," he looked at the black outfit she'd worn on the show, "you are overdressed."

With the now familiar flutter in her stomach at the timbre in his voice, Kyle hurried up the stairs. She turned the taps and thought that he'd been considerate, showering quickly and leaving plenty of hot water.

With a smile, she rummaged beneath the sink for a bottle of shower gel that had been a gift from Leila a few years ago. When she released the cap, the aroma of forest evergreen rose on the steam. The soap smelled so luxurious that she washed her hair with it as well as her body. Scrubbing with the slippery suds, she recalled the night she'd compared her lean frame to Alicia's bounty. Now, as surely as she knew her own name, she knew Wyatt wanted her and not Alicia.

Stepping out of her steamy bathroom, she smelled bacon. A smile curled her lips at the image of Wyatt overseeing her frying pan. But why not? Nick was the useless one in the kitchen.

Her closet offered an array of khakis, jeans, her few good dresses 'ke she'd worn to the studio, and her thick, ankle length fleece robe. There were also the black long john style pants and pullovers she'd worn at the Nez Perce patrol cabin.

She reached for her usual jeans and hesitated. Though she knew she looked damned fine in denim, she decided that this morning was a time for breaking out of the mold. As rapidly as things were changing in Yellowstone, her life was also driving forward at breakneck speed.

Might as well enjoy the ride.

Going to a drawer, she chose a pair of dance pants with a little flair. A cropped top that left a few inches of bare skin showing at the waist went on without a bra. Smoothing her hair with a brush while warm air flowed from her dryer, Kyle noted that those few threads of gray hardly showed.

Though she'd washed off the studio makeup, she opened the medicine chest and came up with a cake of blush her neighbor Christine had given her for her birthday. As she smoothed some onto her cheeks, she watched her face in the mirror soften.

That little ache inside her, the one she'd felt when she saw Alicia and Wyatt together at the Lake Hotel, had been for him after all. Knowing he was downstairs cooking their breakfast made her reflection smile.

* * *

Wyatt heard the whisper of Kyle's bare feet on the tile. When he turned, he couldn't believe what he saw. Her hair, falling softly over her shoulders, invited him to touch. A cropped top outlined her breasts, with a hint of smooth skin at its base. So slender, she looked younger than she was, younger than he was. Her eyes were blue-green tourmaline as deep as the sea.

"I feel better." She raised her hands, stretched, and lifted her hair. The bottom edge of her top rose, exposing a few more inches of waist.

He wasn't feeling bad himself, as he imagined bending over and teasing her belly button with his tongue. The image instantly had him wondering what he'd been thinking to put on his soft sweat pants without any underwear.

Trying not to make a prize idiot of himself, he turned and faced the counter as she edged past.

Though there was plenty of room in the small kitchen for Kyle to move around him without touching, her hip grazed his on the way by. From the corner of his eye, he caught a smile on her lips.

Before he could make a grab for her, the smile turned to a frown, her nose wrinkling as she lifted the skillet from the stove. Only then did Wyatt smell that he was burning the last strips of bacon.

"Think we can salvage this?" She glanced over her shoulder and he wondered if she meant to sound seductive.

Through his glasses, the blackened strips looked hopeless.

She studied the already heaping platter of bacon he was proud of and added the burnt pieces at the side. "You never know, we might get hungry."

"I'm already starving." Wrestling his libido, he reached for the carton of eggs instead of Kyle.

"I'm starving, too." Yet, she reached to turn off the stove burner.

He looked into her shining eyes. Deeply embedded was a flash of something he'd seen before . . . over a beer in a cozy booth, outside her townhouse the night he'd nearly taken her in his arms, when they had broken apart after embracing in his office.

If she had been any other woman, he'd swear she was coming on to him.

Well, two could play. "I'm trying to prepare a culinary delight, here." His tone was teasing. "If you don't let me cook . . ."

Her hand touched his; her thumb made a slow circle on the back.

Wyatt swallowed.

Self-control had its merits, but when her fingers moved to trace the lines of his palm, his physical reaction was immediate. This time he could not bring himself to turn away.

Kyle raised her eyes from his hand to his face and the unmistakable passion in her gaze was no longer intermittent. "You said last night that you were afraid of this."

Yeah, and how stupid had he been to say that? Here was the woman he'd been in love with for years, yeah, Alicia had said 'love,' not 'want' as he'd misquoted last night.

Wishing for Nick's gift of gab, Wyatt raised Kyle's hand and placed it on his chest. "My heart's pounding like a hammer, but it's not because I'm scared."

"I'm not either." She moved her fingers in a slow circle over his T-shirt, making him want to strip it off.

"Last chance, lady." He pressed her palm against him. "To stop me doing something you don't want."

"I want," she said. Her other hand took off his glasses and set them beside the sink.

"Kyle." He sank to his knees, his hands on her hips, turning her into him.

She gasped, spread her arms, and gripped the edge of the counter. But she did not push him away.

He pressed his mouth to her stomach, not teasing the way he'd imagined, but fervently.

She didn't move, either to welcome or reject him. He turned his head and pressed his cheek against her smooth skin, praying she wouldn't change her mind.

Then he felt her hand in his hair. She cradled his head, pulling him closer.

Wyatt managed to get to his feet and look down into her eyes. Without his glasses, her features appeared soft.

He slid his hands up her arms, under the loose sleeves. Skimming his lips over the hollow of her throat, he murmured, "God, don't let me louse this up."

They bumped noses. It made him feel seventeen. When their lips came together, he felt the curve of her smile. It stilled as they explored each other, gently at first. Her firm spare flesh matched his, as though they'd been poured from the same mold.

She broke the kiss and pulled back. Her lips were parted and deeply pink.

Lost in the best feeling he'd ever known, he said, "Don't say no, Kyle, for God's sake."

"I won't."

❋ ❋ ❋

As Kyle led Wyatt by the hand up the stairs, his sweats accentuated the long lines of his body. She felt the ache inside her chest again, knowing that what they were about to do would change the landscape forever. Yet, as they entered her bedroom, she made no move to turn aside. Their relationship had changed and there was no going back.

Though their embrace downstairs had sealed their fate, the walk up had broken the mood enough to make her feel awkward at the prospect of disrobing.

Standing beside her bed, she said, "I'm no good at this. I've been alone too many years."

Wyatt moved closer. "Right now, I don't feel any good at it, either." Ever so slowly, he bent to her. It seemed to take a long time while the care with which he moved underlined that she was both delicate and treasured. Finally, his parted lips brushed hers. He drew her bottom lip into his mouth, a gentle tug that pleaded for response.

Kyle didn't move, poised on the verge. Wyatt's tongue traced the seam where her lip met the inner flesh of her mouth. Their hands were still clasped.

"What's going to happen to us . . . after this?" she murmured.

"You said you wouldn't say no." He cradled her cheek with his palm.

"I'm not saying no, I'm just . . ."

"Talking too much." His kiss smothered her words. This time he was no longer gentle; but dragged her against him.

She pulled back once more. "I want to be clear that I'm just wondering . . ."

Wyatt gave her a rogue's smile. "Who knows what will happen anytime? Will the volcano blow? Will this make things better or worse?"

He was right. Though there were no guarantees to the future, she could not imagine turning away.

Her hands caressed his back, tugged his T-shirt free of the waistband of his sweats and found bare skin. He drew in his breath. "I need to tell you, though. Alicia didn't accuse me of wanting you."

Kyle frowned. "She didn't?"

"No."

Wyatt deftly tucked his leg behind Kyle's and she felt him take her down on the bed. They landed together, nose to nose, laughing softly. Propping himself up on an elbow, he focused on her with nearsighted eyes.

"Nope. It seems Alicia knew some things better than I did myself." He smoothed Kyle's bare stomach and she felt again the sense of rightness between them.

"So what did she say?"

"She said I was in love with you."

 ● ● ●

Kyle awakened more slowly than usual, with a languid feeling of well-being. Twilight filtered through her bedroom window. She had a vague recollection of Wyatt tucking the blankets around them after they'd gone downstairs to eat, come back up, and made love again. How sweet it had been to drift into much-needed slumber.

This was foreign, the way lying with him made her bed seem smaller, yet not crowded. Even the room looked less large, but now the dimly lit bower imparted a sense of intimacy rather then one of darkness closing in.

Wyatt shifted her closer with a gentle tug until her bare back was warm against his chest. She pressed his hand to her breast and could no more imagine taking back what had happened than she could deny her own name. The first time had been fraught with the urgent haste of feeling too long denied. The second had been slow and sweet. The beauty was in the details, for though the act of love was always the same, each time was different.

Wyatt whispered, "You awake?"

She answered by placing her hand over his.

With his other arm, he reached to snap on her bedside lamp. "Little dark in here." She flinched at the brightness.

The bedside clock said almost 7 PM. "I can't believe we slept so long."

"We both needed to rest . . . after everything." It all came rushing back, Hollis firing her, the crescendo of seismic activity, Nick heading back into the park interior.

Wyatt pointed to a coil of rope on the floor. "Is that what you used to climb out the window?"

The memory of hanging outside in the middle of a thunderstorm embarrassed her. "I should have known better."

"On the contrary," he said, "Most people never think about an earthquake, but when I hear glasses rattling in my cabinet, there's nearly always a reason."

"I really missed the mark that night."

"I don't think you did. After you told me you'd panicked for no reason, I checked the records at the earthquake center. There was a disturbance in Alaska at about 2:30 AM Mountain Time that you may have detected."

"So you don't think I'm crazy."

"Not even a little bit. Come here."

He settled back and drew her against his side, her head cradled on his shoulder. His warmth seeped into her. Here, she'd been impatient with him for being negative toward Nick, when he'd been so right.

How could she have thought three sun-gilded weeks with an inconstant young man were the ultimate idyll? She should long ago have focused on the fact that Nick had left her without a backward glance. The only explanation was that she'd used him as a shield against becoming intimate with anyone else . . . an effective means of keeping her secrets.

The telephone rang.

She jumped and sat up on the edge of the bed to grab it. Before she could say hello, Nick's voice was urgent in her ear. "Kyle? All hell has broken loose up here."

"What's happening?"

"Who's that?" Wyatt mouthed.

"Nick," she murmured, then said into the phone, "Wyatt's here with me."

"He needs to hear this, too," Nick said crisply. "Haven't you been watching people running for the hills on TV? Haven't you seen the seismic data today?"

"Bad news," she said. "After the show, Hollis fired me. Cut off my network access."

"Ducky. Well, tell Wyatt I've been using his account all day. Kyle." He paused. "I think she's gonna blow."

She went still inside. The fact that Nick had been the one to resist such a prediction made it doubly terrifying. She looked at Wyatt, saw that he had heard, and felt his hand on her arm.

"I thought you might be in the field by now," she told Nick.

"The winter storm's already pounding the West Coast, but my supplies got here an hour ago. I've got a chopper coming to fly me up in the morning."

"But you can't go if you think . . ."

"I have to."

"Don't leave until we get there." It was foolish, she knew, to want a last chance to talk him out of it in person.

"Be here by first light and you can see me off at the helipad. Otherwise, I'll need you to monitor from Wyatt's office."

She didn't hesitate. "That's the only place we can get real time data. But, Nick"—she pleaded one more time—"you know how many volcanologists have died on the job."

"Hey, as you said on TV, do the math. The moon won't be full until October 10th."

The back of Kyle's neck felt stiff, all the boneless comfort she and Wyatt had generated replaced by urgency. "With all those people on the run, has Janet Bolido called an evacuation of the park?"

"No," said Nick.

CHAPTER THIRTY-EIGHT
SEPTEMBER 30

Yellowstone Superintendent Janet Bolido was barricaded in her office with her TV on. The twenty-four-hour news network had picked up the Yellowstone story like a terrier with a new squeak toy.

In a live-action shot from Gardiner, a fat guy in a dirty T-shirt packed his car beneath a streetlight's illumination. "I'm getting all my stuff, case I don't get back."

In the next scene, an elderly woman with a drawn face stood in front of a tidy bungalow. "Our house is all mine and Dave got no insurance." She laughed nervously. "Course I guess insurance doesn't cover a volcano."

Janet twisted her hands together. All day she'd been watching similar scenes from Montana, Idaho, and Wyoming. Cities and towns up to a hundred miles from the park were emptying, as people stated their intention to get out, "at least until after the full moon."

Outside, horns blew from the traffic jam in the hotel parking lot. The bottleneck was the only route onto the narrow dirt track to Gardiner since the canyon road was closed. She looked out the window and saw the line of cars and campers moving at a crawl.

The list of messages Janet was ignoring was impressive: TV and radio stations from as far away as Vermont, somebody from Monty Muckleroy's show.

How was it possible she had such rotten timing? Twenty-seven years at Interior, sucking up to all the right politicos, to end up by blind dumb luck in the middle of this?

She channel surfed and found *Billings Live Eye* in Gardiner. Carol Leeds held her jeans jacket closed against a brisk wind as she reported on the exodus north.

Another earthquake, larger than the others today, knocked a coffee cup full of pens off Janet's desk. A glance up at where the massive bookshelf had been before going to the scrapheap sent a clutch through her.

Get out, she thought. Catch the next plane back to Washington and let somebody else handle this.

The hell of it was that she'd never been good at making decisions. And she had never been in charge of a situation where peoples' lives were threatened.

Her office door opened without a knock. Joseph Kuni's impressive figure in his pressed uniform filled the doorframe. His stormy gaze from beneath salt and pepper brows took her in, along with the TV.

Stepping in, he watched silently as Carol Leeds reported, "There has been no word from park officials, but many employees are taking matters into their own hands and leaving."

"I just flew in from a meeting in Denver," Kuni said in

a controlled voice. "Am I to understand you have not ordered an evacuation?"

Janet cleared her throat unnecessarily and pushed to her feet. "Yesterday, I talked to Dr. Darden, the volcanologist, and he said . . ."

"That was yesterday." He dripped disdain. "Did you see *America Today* this morning?"

She nodded without meeting his eyes.

"So what are you going to do about it?"

Her mouth opened. No sound emerged.

Kuni advanced on her. "I think, Ms. Bolido, that you are going to issue a statement calling for the evacuation of Yellowstone, and that you are going to do it right now."

Feeling as though her legs went weak, she sat back down.

Interpreting her silence as resistance, Kuni loosed his famous temper. "Or I will do it for you!"

● ● ●

"I'm not going back to Yellowstone," cameraman Larry Norris told reporter Carol Leeds and *Billings Live Eye* manager Sonny Fiero. It was after 11 PM at the end of a workday that had begun before daybreak.

Sonny's moon face expressed displeasure from behind his elevated desk. Carol slid a hip onto the polished wood and looked down at Larry. "Don't you know what's happening right now? Every major network in the country is mounting an expedition to Yellowstone. We've got to salvage our exclusive."

Larry wasn't much for talk; that was Carol's job. And though she'd overridden him plenty in the past, he'd never been quite this upset.

Carol went on, "We'll charter a helicopter and be the first reporters to show the smoking peak from the air."

Sonny smiled and flicked ash from his cigar. "I like it."

"Are you both crazy?"

"Come on, Larry," Carol said. "How am I going to do this without you?"

"Take Sonny. He knows how to operate a camera."

The newly minted station manager seethed. "I've got to run things from here." He waved a stubby arm. "Look, it's your job to cover Yellowstone, has been for twenty years."

"Twenty years ago I didn't have Donna and Joey." He felt a wave of pride, for his hardworking gamin wife and for Joey, a bookworm who excelled in school as compensation for not being able to play sports.

Carol tried again. "I've got Louisa in high school, but I'm not going to miss the story of a lifetime."

"We've all got to pick our priorities," Larry said.

Sonny stood up to his full five-foot-one. "So pick this. If you don't have a job, how will you take care of your family?"

Larry pushed up and towered over both Carol and Sonny. "Are you threatening me?"

Carol stepped between the two men. Her hand felt light on Larry's arm, but it restrained him. "We were in dangerous places during the '88 fires and got out just fine. Don't go off half-cocked over this and lose your health insurance."

CHAPTER THIRTY-NINE
OCTOBER 1

Long past daybreak, Wyatt drove Kyle's Mercedes into Gardiner, Montana. He'd taken the long route around the northwest corner of the park, watching for patches of accumulated snow and black ice while Kyle slept.

He tried to get back the euphoric feeling he'd had when she took him into her bed, a sensation of losing the boundaries between himself and her. But Nick's call had catapulted him back to reality and made him question the wisdom of laying his feelings all out. What chance did he really have against a flashy globetrotter?

Crossing the deserted Yellowstone River Bridge, he caught a glimpse of Alicia's townhouse. Her Navigator was gone and so, he assumed, was she. An image of her big liquid eyes and generous mouth failed to move him; she'd been right to leave him.

He glanced at Kyle who was rubbing her eyes. A crease on her cheek marked where she'd lain on her jacket.

She looked at him and smiled.

Confidence renewed, he reached to smooth the fold in her skin.

With a broader grin, Kyle shoved her coat into the floorboards and raised the seatback. "Did the Pied Piper come through?"

"Must have." Only one moving car was in sight and the buildings appeared dark inside despite the dreary morning.

Wyatt pulled the Mercedes up in front of a surprisingly open service station. "I could use some coffee."

Inside the old-fashioned place with a mechanic's bay alongside, he greeted a big red-faced man in work coveralls. "Hey, Landers. Still here?"

"Could say the same about you."

"Got things to do in Mammoth," Wyatt said, "but you ought to clear out."

Landers shook his blond head. "Everybody ran like rabbits yesterday. Now this morning those earthquakes have plumb stopped."

"Stopped?" The last time they'd seen the park records, the rumbling in the earth had been almost constant and on the increase.

Landers put a hand flat on his linoleum counter. "Steady as a rock."

Wyatt couldn't believe that. Tremors must still be going on at a level lower than a person could detect.

Thankfully, it was fifty miles to Nez Perce Peak.

● ● ●

Kyle went to the ladies room and washed up, feeling as though her eyes were full of sand. Yet, as she smoothed her tangled hair and twisted it into a thick braid, she couldn't help but be heartened by the memory of Wyatt's fingers combing through it.

He hadn't said he loved her; just that Alicia had come up with it. But with a smile, she realized he would never have uttered the word without meaning it.

If someone had asked her a week ago to name the people she loved, she would have begun with Stanton and Leila and then . . . she would have had to name Wyatt. All those days and nights of working together had bred the trust that allowed her to confide in him about Hebgen Lake, before she ever realized they'd be lovers.

In the seconds that followed, she felt a quiet adjustment inside her. Of course, she loved him, had loved him for years as her most cherished friend. It had just expanded like the fullness in her chest, the polar opposite of the emptiness she would feel at his loss. Franny had been wise to teach her that litmus test.

When she came out to the car, Wyatt had bought her coffee and doctored it with cream. Taking the wheel, she drove them past the park maintenance barns and up to the kiosk at the north entrance. A striped boom blocked the highway and she stopped.

"Let me handle this." Wyatt got out and walked up to the small building.

"Hey, Teri," Kyle heard him say say to the small ebony-haired woman who alone manned the border into the park. She didn't look large enough to enforce anything, but the look on her face said she'd throw a drunk and disorderly onto the hood of a car and cuff him in a heartbeat.

"We must get to Mammoth," Wyatt said.

"Off limits." Teri wore a .45 on her hip.

Kyle couldn't believe this. She'd been certain no one would question Wyatt's right to break the evacuation order. Thinking to help, she shut off the engine and got out.

"Come on, Teri," Wyatt said. "If it's safe for you to be here . . ."

"We drew straws for the duty, everybody who didn't have family." Her jaw squared. "Maybe the National Guard will take over later if they have to call them out, but right now it's just me." She looked thoughtful. "You know they only left one person because they didn't think anybody would want back into the park."

"Teri, you have to let us in," Wyatt insisted. "This is important."

The young ranger's expression softened, but she stood her ground. "I'm sorry, Wyatt."

Kyle stepped forward. "I'm Dr. Kyle Stone of the Utah Institute. You might have seen me with Wyatt on TV?"

Teri's eyes widened. "I didn't see the show, but they've been playing parts of it over and over on *Billings Live Eye*."

"Then you know how serious the situation is. Now Wyatt and I have to access some very important data from his computer in Mammoth."

Teri spoke to Wyatt. "They said on TV she got fired. She was wrong about scaring everybody. They all ran and this morning everything's fine." Her slight quaver conveyed how badly she wanted to believe that.

"It's not fine," Wyatt said. "All of us are sitting on top of the teakettle's whistle."

Kyle tried again. "Right now, you're stuck here not knowing what might happen. How about you let us get to Wyatt's computer and we promise to call you . . . if it looks like you need to clear out?"

Teri looked at the empty town. A moment more of weighing duty versus common sense and she offered Wyatt her hand. "Deal."

Kyle guided the low-slung Mercedes carefully up the dirt track into the park. Unspoken between her and Wyatt was the worry that Nick had carried out his plan and left at dawn for the backcountry. Although the arctic front was still on its way, the intermittent snow showers had subsided, leaving a weather window for a helicopter.

The closer they drew to Mammoth, the more she dreaded finding out.

They came down the hill into a ghost town. The hotel parking lot lay deserted. No lights brightened the dull morning in the Headquarters or Admin buildings. Not even the local elk were on the lawns.

When she pulled up in front of the Resource Center, she was surprised to see smoke issuing from its chimney. "Maybe that's Nick."

"I hope so," Wyatt agreed. "He'll know what's been happening since last night."

Inside, Radford Bullis greeted them from his corner office. "Thought I'd stay until you got here."

"Who said we were coming?" Wyatt asked.

"Darden."

Kyle looked down the hall toward Wyatt's dark office. "Where is he?"

"Eagle Air from Gardiner flew him up this morning. Guy's got brass balls. He had a moon suit flown in from USGS and winter gear in case he had to hike out. He said he'd call from his satellite phone to Wyatt's office at noon."

"I wish he had waited for us," she said.

"You got a death wish, too?" Radford misunderstood, thinking she had wanted to go. He stared at the burning logs in the fireplace, his bushy brows knitted. "I've got Polly and our boys down in Gardiner. I was going to head up to Bozeman with them, but since the quakes have tapered off, maybe I should stay."

"No, Radford," Kyle said. "Twice now we've had major events preceded by a period of seismic quiet. If anything, I'd say it's ominous."

"Take care of your family," Wyatt urged.

Kyle felt numb, as they talked about the impossible in calm tones.

Radford started to go and turned back. "Colin Gruy is flying back to USGS from Sakhalin today. When things settle down, we'll have to sort out things with you and

Hollis." He shook his head. "Stanton was always right about you two needing a referee."

Radford clapped Wyatt on the back and his broad bulk disappeared through the doors of the arctic entry.

She watched him go. "I'm not sure that was a vote of confidence."

Wyatt led the way to his office, started his computer, and brought up the Institute website. Kyle watched over his shoulder as he typed in his username and password, and hit the return key.

A dialog box declared, "Your password is either invalid or has expired."

"Shit!" Kyle kicked the desk leg with her hiking boot.

"That can't be right." Wyatt peered intently through his glasses. "Nick was using this account last night."

"Hollis knew you'd bring me here to get into the system."

"You're probably right." Three failed attempts to log on caused the site to lock Wyatt out.

She jumped up and paced a narrow oval between the desk and the credenza. If only Radford hadn't left, maybe he could call Hollis and talk sense into him.

Wyatt was already on his feet. "Radford's cell number was on my phone I lost in the canyon. I'll get it from his office."

Kyle followed him into the lobby. Radford's door was locked.

Wyatt turned to Iniki's desk. "She should have all the numbers."

He tugged, but the desk drawers didn't budge.

"What about somebody who can pull rank on Hollis?" Kyle suggested. "Janet Bolido?"

"The brass keep their cell numbers under wraps."

She continued to cast about. "We'll call Colin, no, he's on the plane."

Her hands made into fists. She felt like going back into Wyatt's office and kicking his computer, or better yet kicking Hollis's ass all the way to Sakhalin. She'd never forgive him if anything happened to Nick.

CHAPTER FORTY
OCTOBER 1

Nick studied Nez Perce Peak from the Saddle Valley. His view was unobstructed through bare trees left standing from the fires of '88. He'd had the helicopter land in the divide downslope from the cabin along the Saddle Valley Fault and stowed his equipment and camping gear at seismograph station four.

Using binoculars and a topographic map, Nick plotted out areas he wanted to stay clear of. Any of the reentrants that led down from the peak could be potential paths for a *nuée ardente*, a pyroclastic avalanche of gas and particles that would seek the path of least resistance. You got caught by one of those and ash would plug your mouth and nose until you suffocated, unless the air was superheated, in which case a single searing gasp would destroy your lungs.

He had observed one of the deadly and fascinating events at the Soufrière Hills volcano on Montserrat in the West Indies back in 1977. High on the slope when the nuée rolled out of the crater, he'd had no place to run. With a pounding heart, he had raised his Nikon and watched the roiling cloud come at him through the lens. As flashe of St. Elmo's fire illuminated the clouds above the crater, the electrical charge in the air from particle friction stood Nick's hair on end.

The nuée came on, slowing on the broader areas and leaping down the narrower gullies. Expecting to be burned, buffeted off his feet, Nick snapped photos as fast as his auto-wind would cycle. If the camera made it, he hoped the community of volcano lovers would see the images as a fitting memorial.

Through the lens, he watched the cloud approach. The mass billowed over him and cut his visibility to zero, the stench of sulfur everywhere. Hunkering down, he waited for death. No time for regrets or what ifs.

To his amazement, he realized the cloud was composed of fine dust and surprisingly cool. Within moments, it lifted.

Hardly able to credit his fortune, he blinked grit from his eyes and realized the main body of the flow had passed around a hundred yards from him.

His pictures were spectacular.

The quake in the canyon had been another close call, but not a signal to run from the mountain as Kyle had imagined. In his mind's eye, he saw her, slim and lovely, and tasted regret that he couldn't lead two lives, one with her and the other in the field.

With his traverse planned to the top, Nick set out walking. Using a portable gravimeter, a million times more sensitive than the average bathroom scale, he measured gravity variations as the mountain lifted from magma's upward press. The instrument could detect an inch of elevation difference by measuring the gravitational field to the center of the earth, nearly 4,000 miles below. Along with the gravimeter box, the size and weight of a car battery, he also carried silica tubes in his pack to collect gases on the crest.

Two hours later, he felt on top of the world. He stood on the mountaintop, frigid wind tearing at his parka and waterproof pants.

The weather ceiling did not obscure his view of the ranges surrounding Nez Perce. Over the shoulder of Mt. Chittenden to the southwest, he caught a glimpse of the Tetons nearly a hundred miles away. Thick clouds streamed into Jackson Hole, the winter front on its way.

Nick slid off his pack, brought out his water bottle, and took a pain pill for his throbbing head. He capped the bottle, sat, and rested on the ground littered with lightweight reddish cinders. When he'd run into the marble-sized material a few hundred yards down from the crest, he'd found it tougher walking than usual.

As he had done each time he climbed to the summit, he studied the shape of the mountain for clues as to what a new eruption might look like. There were several possibilities.

With magma beneath the peak, he thought the relatively soft material of the cinder cone might be ejected to form a small crater, as he'd told Kyle and Wyatt. Alternatively, if the molten rock located the zone of weaknes along the Saddle Valley Fault, it could come rocketing to the surface along a long fissure, something he had not mentioned.

Or the whole mountain could blow. Nick was betting his life that didn't happen.

He'd taken gravity readings all the way up, marking the positions with stone cairns. Data taken later in the same spot would reveal whether the cone was shrinking or swelling.

He drew out one of the silica tubes for a gas sample. The largest fumarole vented about thirty yards down from the mountain summit. Three days ago, when Nick had approached the three-inch opening it hissed like a kettle. Today a foot-wide aperture to hell roared like a furnace. Yellow crystals of sulfur rimmed the opening.

Nick donned leather gloves, knelt on the upwind side and turned his face away from the hydrogen chloride fumes. Feeling the heat, he wished for the moon suit he'd left at his camp. Next time he came up, he'd have to wear it.

After taking samples at two smaller fumaroles, he checked his watch. Already eleven, no way he could get back to call Kyle by noon. He'd considered lugging the four pound telephone up with him, but had wanted to collect samples.

Being up here alone was a two-sided proposition. He relished having a front row seat to watch a dormant volcano come to life, yet he wished Kyle were here to see it with him. It would even be nice to have Wyatt to joust with.

Nick started back down the mountain, stopping to take gravity readings in the same places as before. He searched for evidence the mountain continued to bulge.

● ● ●

"Come on, Nick," Kyle said to the silent telephone in Wyatt's office. The clock on the computer said it was almost one.

"Our boy is probably just caught up in the excitement," Wyatt said.

"I wish we could call him, but Radford didn't give us a number."

"If he's walking around, he's not set up to take calls. The antenna must be aimed just right to pick up the satellite signal."

"I can't stand this." Kyle fidgeted with a piece of glassy obsidian on the desk.

Wyatt studied her restless hands. "I suppose I should be pleased his being an adrenaline junkie came between you."

"That isn't really the problem." She tossed the stone from hand to hand. "I would hate this waiting and wondering what danger he's gotten into, but the bottom line is that he chooses his love affair with volcanoes over everything. It's the only commitment he's ever made."

Wyatt sipped coffee he'd made from powdered instant. "I guess after Marie and the others you could say I've never made a lasting commitment."

Kyle reached for his hand. "This thing with Nick has taught me that I don't believe in miracles either. But, whether we knew it or not, Wyatt, you and I have been committed to each other for a long time."

The telephone rang. She and Wyatt both started.

He passed the receiver across the desk to her.

"Nick?" Her mouth was dry.

"I'm on the mountain." He sounded far away, as though more than miles separated them. "Set up a temporary camp at station four."

"We saw Radford before he left with his family. He told us you'd gone."

"Thanks for doing this."

"Anything for you," she said, with lightness she did not feel. "How's your head?" An image of him, pale in a bloodstained bandage made her close her eyes.

"Only bothers me when the pills wear off."

Anger broke through. "Nick, you shouldn't be . . ."

"Save your breath, Kyle," Wyatt stage-whispered

"What are you seeing from the seismic stations?" Nick evaded.

The focus of her pique shifted to Hollis. "Not a thing." Across the desk, Wyatt was bringing up some of the older data, as it was all they had. Ruefully, she realized they had only themselves to blame for setting up the roadblock. "That weasel Delbert cut Wyatt's security access. We can only get to the public data that's forty-eight hours old."

"That's no good," Nick grumbled. "This morning I

made a gravity traverse to the peak and back. In the hour between readings, the mountain swelled rapidly."

"How rapidly? We've already seen unprecedented rates of rise."

"Up over a foot," he related dispassionately.

"A foot an hour?" She clenched the receiver. "Nick, get out of there."

"Call the chopper," Wyatt said loudly. "Start walking down now."

Kyle cast a worried look out the office window. Still no sign of the front, just cloudy bright. "If you don't leave before the weather socks in, you may not be able to."

As though she and Wyatt had said nothing, Nick went on, "It's too bad you can't look at the GPS data from all the stations. That would give us a picture of what's bulging where."

"If I can get that information, will you come down?" Kyle bargained. "We don't need your gravity data if we can get to the changing elevations another way."

"Any type of data will help us. What we learn here may save lives in some more populated volcanic area." When she did not reply, he said in a lower tone, "Kyle . . . I don't really have a death wish."

She didn't have an answer for that. "Stay by the phone, Nick. I'll call you back as soon as I have something."

"I want to go back up and take some more readings on the east side," he said, "so I won't be able to take incoming calls."

"Nick."

"I'll keep the phone with me and call you every ten minutes," he promised.

As soon as the line was disconnected, Kyle told Wyatt. "Start establishing a baseline from the GPS records in the public area. I'm going to get us back in."

"How? Colin's probably still on the plane from Tokyo."

She began punching buttons on the phone. "I'm calling Hollis."

Listening to the ringing, she considered how to play it. Butting chests wasn't likely to be the best approach with him drunk on his imagined authority.

On the third ring, he answered. She envisioned him behind the desk he'd set up facing the door for intimidation.

"Hollis, this is Kyle. I'm in Wyatt Ellison's office at Yellowstone."

"What are you doing there? I thought the park was evacuated."

She controlled her tone with an effort. "We're trying to get some vital real time data for Nick Darden at USGS. He flew into the park this morning to measure gravity and discovered Nez Perce Peak is swelling at a foot an hour."

"Good God." Hollis's imperial tone was replaced by uncertainty.

"The thing is," she said evenly, "Wyatt is having some trouble logging in to the site. We need to give Nick the safest place to wait until he can be picked up by helicopter."

Hollis was silent. She wondered whether he was

suspicious of her story or realizing the magnitude of his mistake.

Wyatt reached his long arm across the desk and took the receiver out of her hand. "Get with the program, Hollis. You might try firing Kyle, but you can't cut off the National Park Service without getting your ass into a serious sling."

She heard Hollis sputtering as Wyatt kept talking. "Right now, no one knows except her and me that you cut off my security access. But if they find out what a childish stunt you pulled with Darden's life at stake, you're going to be looking for a job." He handed the receiver back.

"If they find out?" she heard Hollis say faintly.

"Nobody has to know," she told him. "Unless something happens to Nick."

Five minutes later, they were in. Kyle pulled up the GPS elevation data and compared it to the information that was several days old. The mountain had come up three feet the day the quake killed the horses, twice that yesterday, and they confirmed that the rate was now a foot an hour and rising.

"Maybe Nick is still set up at station four." Kyle spoke around a lump in her throat. "Let's call and warn him."

CHAPTER FORTY-ONE

OCTOBER 1

The first jolt of the quake knocked the satellite phone off the chest containing the seismic station equipment. The second sent Nick sprawling.

Lying on his side, he had a view down the Saddle Valley and up the north flank of Nez Perce Peak. He told himself there had been plenty of tremors, so many that he should be inured to them by now.

This was different.

There was a noise like an approaching plane, but he didn't believe a military fighter would be in the vicinity. Rather, he suspected the frenzied rush of heated rocks and gases, hurtling up the final vent toward the surface. The din continued to grow.

He glanced at his watch. 1:12 PM. Locating his camera, he figured there was no sense being the only one to see what happened next.

With hands that shook, he raised the Nikon and tried to focus. The quaking of the ground grew more violent and he lay on his stomach and planted his elbows.

He saw it first, of course, because of the great difference between the speed of light and sound. The peak in front of him seemed to shimmer as though seen through heat waves. Reddish cinders danced.

Then there was lift, almost in slow motion as the top quarter of the mountain peeled free. Seen through the telephoto, it looked as though Nick sat directly in the path of millions of tons of flying rock. He steeled himself not to flinch or stop taking pictures.

The concussion shoved his chest and he collapsed with his face in the dirt. Now, nothing was in slow motion. The explosion of sound first surrounded and then penetrated him. His bones vibrated. A sharp stab of nausea unsettled his internal organs and he feared losing control of his bowels. Pinned by the pressure wave, he lifted his hand and touched wetness on his cheek. His eardrums must be bleeding.

Here it was. What he'd desired, angled, and prayed for. In awe of Nature's display, he felt completely insignificant. What happened in the next few seconds would decide his fate . . . or at least whether he was to survive this initial eruption. There was no telling how many or how large subsequent blasts might be. Whatever he might wish now, he was stuck with his decision.

And what he'd told Kyle about being killed by a volcano.

If the side of the crater had broken down, resulting in a lateral outburst, he'd be done for already. The fact that he was still alive meant this force was directed upward. Shoving his camera inside his parka, Nick managed to make it to his feet.

As the shock wave subsided, rocks thrown out of the volcano, known as bombs for obvious reasons, peppered the sky.

He'd heard about rock falls. The secret was to dodge the bombs, a dicey experience, while trying not to panic. Especially not to turn your back and flee, when every instinct screamed, "Run for your life."

Nick's feeling of being inconsequential rose. Even as he braced like a tennis player about to receive service, he knew one false move could mean a broken limb or being smashed in the chest or head.

Above the mountain, a dark column rose into the sky. Tongues of what looked like flame leaped from the mouth of a new crater where the relatively soft cinder cone had been. Fumes stung his nose and made his eyes water. Blinking, Nick struggled to focus on the incoming missiles.

There came a mean-looking one, an irregular, twisted bomb shaped like a piece of driftwood. He started to feint left, then watched its spiraling path and stood his ground. It landed a few feet away, finishing the job on the satellite phone.

"Son of a bitch." Definitely no life flight now.

Here was another pitch, headed straight for the plate. He jumped right and watched it crash to earth. Adrenaline surged as another projectile landed in the middle of the solar panel for the station. Bits of silica and plastic flew.

More rocks fell, glowing crimson and ochre, and giving

off steam as they landed. Nick darted this way and that with the sinking sensation that his opponent was running him all over the court. Several plum-sized pellets hit, one on his shoulder and the other on his foot. Both stung and he felt the heat through his clothing and boot.

He decided it would be better to seek cover than continue the deadly game of dodge ball. Gasping for breath, he snatched up his backpack and dove behind the storage chest.

With his pack as protection for his head and shoulders, he hunched down behind the barrier and looked toward the eruption's source. Rocks the size of cars ejected from the crater to bounce and tumble down the flanks he'd surveyed not two hours ago.

The violence did not diminish. Protected from rocks coming in laterally, Nick peeked up from under his pack for those falling out of the column of ejecta. As fast as they were coming, he heard one auger in nearby before he saw it. Then another landed uphill, giving him just enough warning to jump aside before it jounced and rolled to lie hissing on the tarp. Smelling hot sulfur, he kicked the missile aside and watched it continue downhill.

It began to happen with chilling regularity. With horror, he knew it was no use watching out. He would either be hit or not.

All the while, he prayed there would not be a pyroclastic flow. His position low on the flank of the mountain would be a death trap should a mix of hot rock and gases come rushing down the volcano.

With a crash, a red-hot bomb hit the chest three feet from Nick. Small bits flew, embedding themselves in his forehead and cheeks, and burning like branding irons. With a cry, he clawed at his face, tearing at both rock and flesh. His hands came away slick with blood.

God, it hurt. Even with the slivers removed, he felt the raw searing and smelled scorched flesh along with smoke and rotten eggs.

A moment later, a new and noxious odor filled his nostrils. Heat flared . . . the tarp over the chest was on fire.

Wind whipped up the flames and forced him from his shelter.

More bombs hissed and sizzled through the air, some streaking in on his left with a sound like a passing bullet. He could hear nothing out of his right ear. It ached deeply, yet felt as though it were plugged with cotton.

A baseball-sized rock struck his right hand, smashing his little finger as neatly as a hammer blow. Pain exploded in his head.

He wasn't going to get out of this. The thought sounded crystal pure against the cacophonous backdrop of noise assaulting his remaining ear.

Fighting back from the edge of giving up, he scanned the slope for a better hiding place. It was barren, but for dry grasses he believed would soon be a raging brushfire. Around fifty yards upslope was a copse of aspen, but that would burn as well.

Nick gauged the wind and decided. Instead of just holding his pack, he shrugged it on. His moon suit lay nearby. Grabbing the heavy material, he slung it over his head and shoulders and began scrambling upwind of the fire.

A bomb landed on a nearby boulder and shattered both. Shards flew in all directions, and more small fires started in the nearby grass.

It could only have been a few minutes since the eruption began, but he was already reduced to staggering uphill on trembling legs. Thinking of how worried Kyle would be when she realized what was happening, he managed to keep moving.

With an eye on the sky for falling bombs, he put his foot down on a loose rock. It turned, his ankle followed, and the next thing he knew he was on all fours. Trying to steady himself, Nick managed to set his hand down on a glowing fragment and burn his palm through his glove. His breath hissed in through his teeth and he swore. With his head hanging like a whipped dog's, he waited for a fresh assault of pain.

For like the solid earth, his pain was layered. Topmost was the sharp agony of his seared face and neck, like a never-ending scream. Next, his smashed finger refused to go numb even in this cold. He pulled off his bloody glove and saw white bone where the meat had been stripped away. And beneath those pains were the deep aches of numerous and distinctive bruises where rocks had struck until he was like a punch-drunk boxer.

Nick rocked his weight back and forth between his hands and knees in preparation for getting to his feet. One and two and . . . nothing. His arms and legs shook with the futility of the task.

Another wave of tremors propagated through muscle and bone. He turned and looked up at the rim of the crater.

He'd been lucky so far today, as he had been all during his career. To keep his good fortune coming, he now ignored a sharp jolt of quake and lifted his good hand. His injured finger sent an arrow of pain that seemed to pierce his skull, but he managed to transfer his weight and move a knee forward.

Sweat ran down his cheek and dripped from his chin onto the rocky ground as he crawled. Twenty feet, fifty, and the slope steepened. Dark sparks began at the periphery of vision and closed down into a tunnel before his face.

He had to keep moving, but despite determination, he felt himself going down. His cheek landed hard, more insult to his burned flesh. In fact, pain was the only thing keeping him conscious.

In just a minute, he'd go on, but for now, he lay still. The cold wind found his sweat and started him shivering.

With an effort, Nick raised his head and looked toward the summit again. This time, he had to swipe blood out of his eyes and blink until his sight cleared.

Kyle would be so pissed at him for dying up here.

CHAPTER FORTY-TWO
OCTOBER 1

N ick doesn't answer," Kyle told Wyatt as she replaced the receiver and wiped her damp palm on her trousers.

He concentrated on the computer screen. "Look at this."

The signal from seismic station four was like nothing she'd ever seen. Similar to the harmonic tremors Nick had pointed out, but this pattern had symmetrical excursions that went on for three or so cycles, subsided, and then renewed with greater amplitude. The effect was to draw something that looked like threads on a screw.

As they watched, the signal from the station flat-lined.

"Think things just got quiet up there?" Wyatt asked.

"Not a chance." Kyle tried to breathe. "Station four is off the air, just like Nick's phone."

A shimmer from the surface of Wyatt's coffee attracted her eye. It was on the move, a sure sign that tremors were passing beneath Mammoth.

Wyatt brought up station five, near the crest of Nez Perce Peak. It too had gone off line.

"What about the others?" Kyle gripped Wyatt's shoulder.

"I'm clicking as fast as I can." It took mere seconds to discover that the core stations surrounding Nez Perce had all gone down at precisely 1:12 PM.

Kyle pressed her fist to her mouth. "Keeping fanning out."

He did. The first station they found that had recorded past the time was in the Lamar Valley. It showed that the screw-shaped signal continued.

A sudden rumbling shivered the office windowpanes and shook the ancient walls of the Resource Center. A distinct resonance Kyle remembered from once hearing a grain elevator explosion forty miles away. Long and rolling, it grew louder by the second.

Wyatt swiveled his chair and looked out the window.

Kyle was already on her way to the door. She heard Wyatt's boot heels clacking behind her as they went through the lobby and out onto the lawn. Hugging herself against the biting wind that presaged the cold front, she walked away from the Resource Center so it wouldn't obstruct her view of the southwestern sky.

As the initial roar began to subside, Kyle saw a dark plume rising miles away in the direction of Nez Perce Peak. Much taller than it was wide, like every textbook picture of a classic Plinian eruption column, described by Pliny the Elder at Vesuvius where hundreds of thousands died.

"God," she said. "Oh, God. Nick." The chill air did not seem to contain enough oxygen.

Wyatt put his arm around her. "I'm sorry, Kyle."

Numbly, she stared at the roiling smoke pushing toward the stratosphere and tried to maintain hope. She continued to be awed by the column's massive height.

"It doesn't look big enough to have blown up the whole mountain," she hoped. "More like a sustained release from a crater."

"Perhaps." Wyatt sounded doubtful.

"Maybe he's alive." Yet, his satellite phone was dead, and there was no signal from seismic station four.

There was no reply from Wyatt.

"He was over a mile from the peak," she argued. "Just because the equipment was damaged doesn't mean Nick didn't take cover somehow." This was foolish, but once the seed was planted, she couldn't stop it growing.

"Kyle." Wyatt's face was sober.

"Yes," she insisted. "The eruption has stabilized."

Wyatt squinted through his old pair of glasses.

Though she had trouble imagining going near the mountain . . . "After St. Helen's exploded, there were helicopters and planes in the air right away. Some of the best news footage came from 15,000 feet."

"But another blast, a bigger one could happen at any moment," Wyatt said.

Something shifted inside her. "Wasn't that true then? Isn't it true every time a scientist steps onto an active volcano?"

Though Nick and the others who walked the edge were unarguably daredevils, she was the one who'd tried to have it both ways. To study Yellowstone from a distance, while rationing the time she dared spend there. Yet, she went through life trusting oncoming cars to stay on their side of the highway line, believing in the ability of a many-ton aircraft to fly, in short, fearing earthquakes and the dark because she had never shed the baggage of her past.

Kyle watched the eruption cloud billow skyward, realizing she and Wyatt were the only people who knew Nick's position. If he could be found, given needed medical care, God forbid if it were only to retrieve his remains, they had to act fast.

"Wyatt, what was the name of the helicopter charter Nick used?" A raven, wings spread to catch a lift, cruised from the roof of the Resource Center to a nearby tree. "Some bird name."

"Eagle Air."

"Let's go."

They rushed back to his office. She dialed the number Wyatt found in the Internet White Pages. As the ringing went on and on, she felt like screaming.

After nine tones, a man answered brusquely, "Arvela."

"Is this Eagle Air?"

"Yeah. Johnny Arvela. I own it."

Across the desk, Wyatt sat in his guest chair, legs crowded by the scarred Park Service desk. She felt the tightness in him as he listened third-hand to the conversation.

"This is Kyle Stone calling from up in Mammoth," she told the pilot. "You flew Nick Darden to Nez Perce Peak this morning?"

A snort, then, "I flew the crazy SOB."

"I'm calling because Nick needs to be picked up and brought back down."

The man laughed, but he didn't sound as though he found anything funny. "He said the mountain might blow. Well, sister, have you taken a look out your window in the last few minutes?"

"Look, I'm with the Utah Institute of Seismology. Did you happen to see me on *America Today*?"

"I surely fucking did," Arvela answered. "Based on your own prediction, your buddy is one crispy critter. And if you think I'm going to fly back up there, you've got another thing coming. My family and I are getting out of here."

Kyle sensed his readiness to hang up. "If you won't help, do you know any other pilot who might? Being on the scene to film an erupting volcano could mean a lot. Whoever gets the first footage will certainly be on the news."

Awaiting the verdict, she met Wyatt's concerned dark eyes. Then she followed his gaze out the window and saw that snow had begun falling in earnest. If they didn't move soon, they might be socked in. "Please," she appealed.

"I know one guy with the cast iron balls you're looking for. Chris Deering."

"Thank you," Kyle said.

Wyatt grinned and put his feet to the floor, ready to go. She shook her head, grabbing a piece of paper to write down the number Arvela gave her.

"Not there yet," she told Wyatt, dialing the cell phone of the other pilot.

The call was answered on the first ring. "Deering." Though clipped, the deep, certain voice inspired her confidence.

"There's a volcano erupting in Yellowstone," she said. "How'd you like to be first on the scene?"

Deering chuckled. "I'm already going to be."

Her mouth dropped open. "You what? Where are you?"

"You caught me in West Yellowstone. We can see that sucker blowing from here. Another five minutes and I'll be in the air with a photographer."

"How many passengers can you carry?"

"Six, but I'm not waiting around here on anybody."

Her heart sank. "What if I told you a volcanologist from the United States Geological Survey is on the mountain? I'm Dr. Kyle Stone, and Ranger Wyatt Ellison and I have lost communication with Nick Darden from Park Service Headquarters here in Mammoth." She threw a desperate look at Wyatt, wishing he could come up with the magic words she needed.

To her surprise, the mention of Nick being on the mountain was the key. Deering said, "I'll land in front of Headquarters in half an hour." He paused. "Weather permitting."

As Kyle hung up, she cast a worried glance out the window at the swirling flakes. "We're on," she told Wyatt, who had subsided back into his seat. "Chris Deering will fly us."

"No kidding?" He pushed up. "Deering was the one who picked up David . . ."

"Weather permitting," she advised.

Wyatt frowned. "This is one bitch of an arctic front. Wind chill on the mountain's going to be well below zero."

Kyle looked at her lightweight, hoodless down jacket lying crushed on the seat. "The pilot said he'd be here in thirty minutes."

"Then let's get some winter gear from my place."

She slung on her coat while he put on his heaviest uniform jacket.

"Wait," he said. "We forgot to call Teri."

But when he called the guardhouse at the north entrance, there was no answer.

"She probably took off when she heard the eruption." Kyle gathered her coat and headed into the hall.

Pausing to turn off the coffeepot in the employee lounge and scatter the ashes on the lobby hearth, Wyatt led the way through the arctic entry. As he opened the door, a gust caught it and slammed the portal back against the clapboard outer wall. The front had most definitely arrived.

Kyle followed him out, struggling to see as the driven snowflakes battered her eyelashes. Sure enough, this wind cut through her clothing as though she wore nothing. By the time they reached Wyatt's Bronco, her cheeks and nose hurt from the frigid gusts.

When he turned onto the road to his house, the snow

let up a bit, allowing Kyle a hazy view of the long shoulder of Mount Everts across the Gardner River. She could only imagine the distant eruption cloud.

Three minutes later, Wyatt parked in front of his duplex. Once more, Kyle followed his slightly longer-legged stride through the blowing chill. When she was halfway across the lawn, an earth tremor rolled through.

Wyatt put his key to the lock as another, sharper shock triggered. "I swear I didn't do it," he joked.

She tried to smile.

Inside, he flicked the hall light switch. Nothing happened. He moved swiftly to the kitchen. Kyle heard snapping and saw no illumination.

"I'm surprised the power stayed on as long as it did," she said.

Wyatt came back into the dimness of the hall. She expected him to head with alacrity toward wherever he stored his winter gear, but instead he came to her. "Ten deep breaths." He held out his arms and smiled beneath his dark moustache that she now knew was silky and soft.

"Got time for three." She stepped forward until they were chest to chest; layers of down compressed against his wool coat. Though one of his buttons dug into her breastbone, she pressed closer.

Wyatt slipped his hands up under her jacket and spread them over her back. She felt him inhale deeply and did the same, finding out how quick and shallow her respirations had been.

"We'll find Nick," Wyatt said. "He'll be all right."

She wished that were possible.

They held each other in silence, while gray light slanted through the small glass pane in the front door and filtered in from the kitchen. In the midst of chaos, the feel of Wyatt and the even rise and fall of his chest reassured her.

Though their embrace probably lasted less than a minute, when they broke apart she believed she could face the mountain.

CHAPTER FORTY-THREE
OCTOBER 1

W yatt waited with Kyle on the porch of the locked Headquarters Building. He shoved at his bulky coat sleeve and checked his watch's LED readout. "Two fifty-seven." Cold from the stone rail seeped through long underwear, fleece pants, and an outer "windproof" layer, so he eased back to his feet.

"Coming up on two hours since we last heard from Nick," Kyle observed. Looking a little like a tire company ad, she was swathed from neck to thighs in his thickest roly-poly parka. A pair of his ski pants bunched above her boots.

"The chopper will be here soon," he said.

She rewarded his effort with a faint lip movement that might be a smile. "I hope the pilot can make it."

Though the snow had let up, the wind weaved it into sinuous snakes, undulating across the road. Wyatt had seen it like that a hundred times, an inauspicious omen of deeper accumulation.

Feeling the wind chill on his hands, he reached into his pack. First, he encountered the topographic map he'd put in, thinking of sketching the changes to the land's contour. Then he rummaged beneath the map for insulated gloves.

A faint *whump-whump* came from above.

Wyatt saw Kyle strain her neck to see, but there was nothing except clouds heavy with snow.

The rotors' chop grew louder, along with the engine's whine. A dark speck emerged from the low ceiling over Cannon Hill's rounded slope. Wyatt shielded his eyes against the white glare.

Gradually, he made out the same royal blue helicopter he'd flown in the day David had died. Through the reflection on the windshield, he could see the helmeted pilot, concentration obvious in the set of his shoulders. In the left front seat sat a pale-faced woman who stared at Wyatt and Kyle then turned to speak to someone sitting behind her.

The chopper lowered. Wyatt scooped up his pack and shouldered it. When Kyle was slow to follow, he paused. "You're not afraid to fly?"

"Hell, no." Her jaw squared, and she grabbed her own pack off the rail. "I'm just a little leery of getting blown out of the air."

"Tell me about it." He raised his voice to be heard over the rotors, watching the chopper's propellers blow snow off grass and sagebrush. He had no fear of flying, but he suspected with this cold front they were going to get bounced all over the sky.

The skids were down, the aircraft out of place in the road. He and Kyle ducked their heads against the frigid windstorm and ran toward their ride.

The person in the rear seat opened the door and Wyatt recognized the ponytailed cameraman from *Billings Live Eye*. Seeing the video unit at the ready, Wyatt instinctively held up an arm to avoid being filmed. To his surprise, the man set it aside and extended an arm to help Kyle get in.

As she clambered over the guy, who made it clear he was keeping the window seat on the pilot's side, Wyatt glanced forward at Carol Leeds, in jeans and a light jacket, a few red curls escaping from a Peruvian style hat.

Wyatt climbed into the helicopter, shoved past the guy with squatter's rights to the window, and settled in the middle seat with Kyle on his left. Just the place you didn't want to sit in case of trouble.

He no sooner got seated than Carol turned with a predatory smile and shouted over the din, "Dr. Stone. And Ranger Ellison."

"That's doctor," Wyatt yelled automatically, then wished he hadn't let her count the first coup. He was still angry over her editing of their interview, and didn't intend to show up on *Billings Live Eye* again.

Ignoring Carol Leeds's mention of their names, he introduced himself and Kyle to the cameraman, who said he was Larry.

The pilot, a leathery man in his fifties, whipcord thin, turned with a smile of recognition for Wyatt and spoke to

Kyle. "Chris Deering. Tough about your buddy."

"We hope not," Wyatt said.

"Is the missing guy Nick Darden the volcanologist?" Carol asked.

"The same."

Deering's veined hands darted over the intricate instrument panel, flipping switches and adjusting dials. Wyatt recognized the altimeter reading around 7,000 feet, fuel tank comfortably near full, and artificial horizon showing the helicopter sitting flat.

The pilot twisted the throttle on the end of the collective control between the seats and lifted the inclined bar slightly. As the engine ran up, the chopper began to shudder. His other hand feathered the stick between his knees, his feet poised on the foot pedals.

With the noise level rising, Wyatt picked up the headset stuck in the seat pocket and put it on.

A moment later, the helicopter left the ground, bumped back down, and bounced up again. It skittered sideways in the buffeting wind. Finally, as though Deering's hand held his craft to earth, he lifted the collective and let the Bell surge into the sky.

❀　❀　❀

Kyle settled against the left rear bulkhead. Though her bare neck was at least six inches from the window, she felt chill air sheeting off the glass. Intense vibration and noise from the engine and rotors made her glad for the noise-dampening headphones.

Having the press along was a bad omen. She'd envisioned some photographer who wanted to make it into *National Geographic*, but she should have known. This Carol Leeds who'd distorted their words on the day of David Mowry's memorial service was more interested in sensationalism than in being respectful. After Kyle and Wyatt's appearance on *America Today*, a local TV personality like Leeds was probably salivating at the chance to view the volcano with the scientists who'd supposedly predicted it. Nick's potential misfortune gave added spice to an already titillating story.

Kyle looked out the side window. It seemed eerie to see Mammoth so empty. Where the skids and the rotors' buffeting had not disturbed the snow, it formed an unbroken blanket over the highways. If she didn't know better, it might seem a scene from a tranquil Sunday morning.

"Ms. Stone . . . uh, Doctor." Carol Leeds's avaricious tone dispelled the peace. "I understand you were fired from the Utah Institute."

Wyatt nudged Kyle. She tried to ignore the bait.

The ground turned indistinct then disappeared from view. As she'd expected with the gusty weather, the flight was like driving a rutted back road with frequent dips.

"Ms. Stone?" Carol said again.

Kyle's teeth set.

Wyatt put a hand on her arm. She suspected he meant

461

to warn her off, but she was fortified by determination not to let Hollis win. "As Acting Director, Delbert's position at the Institute is somewhat ambiguous. It remains to be seen whether he has the authority to let someone go over a professional difference of opinion."

Carol looked back at Kyle with sharp green eyes. "This seems more than a difference of opinion. Was there something personal between you and Dr. Delbert?"

Wyatt chuckled. "Kyle and Mr. Comb-over?"

She gave the reporter a hard glare. "Worrying about my job politics is ludicrous when we've got a live volcano in Yellowstone for the first time in thousands of years. Everybody within a hundred miles has fled while Wyatt and I have a friend out there . . ."

Her words breaking, she faced the blank white window. Was Nick huddled down in a safe place, lying hurt, or worse?

As they flew farther south, the air grew rougher. The helicopter lifted like a penthouse elevator, then headed abruptly for the basement. What redeemed the ride was that the ceiling began to lift behind the arctic front.

As they flew out from under the low clouds, Kyle caught a glimpse of the long line of Specimen Ridge out the right side. Out her window, she saw the snowy bottom of Lamar Valley, the rocky riverbed marked by a line of cottonwoods.

She pressed her nose to the glass to look straight down at a herd of several hundred animals. Though small specks, she could tell the difference between the round dark humps of buffalo and the paler brown elk. Thinking of their ancestors who had roamed the land during other times when ejecta columns billowed into the sky, she wondered how many had been too close and perished. How many died of starvation when they found their sturdy necks unequal to brushing aside ash the way they muscled through snow to graze?

She tried not to think of Nick in the same context as other victims of Yellowstone's violence . . . or of men and women in a Madison Canyon campground.

With five aboard, it began to grow warm. Sweat flushed Kyle's chest and sides, and she eased the zipper of Wyatt's parka and put her forehead to the cold window. Rivulets of moisture rolled down the inside of the glass.

In the front seat, Carol turned to Deering. "How much longer?"

"Ten minutes at most."

Bending forward, Kyle looked out the windshield. As the cloud cover continued to break, an electrifying vista opened. Snowcapped peaks rose on the left, the fifty-million-year-old Absaroka Range where Stanton and his students had discovered an imposter in youthful, violent Nez Perce Peak.

Deering banked to follow the valley south, the shrouded sun brightening over the right side of the aircraft. As they passed beyond the Thunderer's jagged cliffs, the head of the long valley lay revealed, an impossible image of impenetrable smoke and churning ash.

Kyle gasped.

"Here we go," said Wyatt. He scrabbled in the top of his pack and yanked out a topo of the terrain that used to be.

Larry said, "We should never have taken off once we knew the thing was erupting." But despite his words, he was already raising his camera.

Carol grabbed Deering's arm.

He shook her off and put a finger out to touch a photo clipped to the dash in front of him. Pictured was a plump redhead with her arm around a young woman with even brighter hair, both standing in front of his blue helicopter. "Keep the faith," he told the women Kyle assumed to be his family. Or perhaps he spoke into his microphone to encourage her and Wyatt in their quest to find Nick.

Wiping the pane once more, she peered toward the cloud of superheated gases, rock and ash. Blue-black like the lowering sky before a thunderstorm, it billowed and retreated unpredictably, unfurling in an endless stream. As she watched, an explosion of white surged into the sky.

"Steam eruption," said Wyatt.

Seeing such awesome power unleashed, transforming green ridge and golden valley to shades of gray, was difficult to comprehend. She dared not dwell on what might happen if this first eruption merely cleared the vent's throat.

Kyle wanted to tell Deering to hurry, to find Nick and get them all out of here. Yet, at the same time, there was a sense of reluctance to rush toward an inevitable and terrible revelation.

As they flew toward the peak on a direct line, the stench of sulfur penetrated the cabin. Already uncomfortable wearing too many clothes in the overheated space, the taste of rotten eggs sent a wave of nausea through Kyle. Taking deep breaths through her opened mouth, she noted the white paper top of an airsickness bag sticking out the top of the seat pocket.

The already unsettled sky developed deeper potholes. At a teeth-jarring plunge with a sharp bottom, Kyle clutched the armrest and noted the bunched muscle at Wyatt's jaw.

"Jesus," said Carol.

Deering said, "That's enough," putting the craft into a turn away from the dark column. Gradually, the turbulence eased. With a glance over his shoulder at Kyle, smile lines crinkling at the corner of his eye, he spoke to Carol. "Thought you wanted to get up close and personal."

"Start filming, Larry," she said, though he was already at work. "I'll set up the satellite phone." She ordered Deering, "I need you to fly a two-twenty degree heading to line up the signal."

Ignoring her, he turned back to Kyle. "Where do we start looking for Dr. Darden?"

She studied the altered landscape. The top of the peak where the cinder cone had protruded was gone, but the three great spines of basalt still angled away from the crater. Snow on the peak had melted more than halfway down. Fresh landslide scars marked where frozen ground water had flash-melted to form mud slurry.

"When we last spoke, Nick was at our seismic station four," Kyle said. Starting at the ruined crest for reference, she swept her eyes down the decapitated mountain. Jagged volcanic bombs littered the upper slopes. Seen at a distance of about a mile, those ejected boulders must be as big as Volkswagens. Above the tree line, where scrub brush and grasses had grown, the ground now lay as bare as the cinder cone had been. All but the tallest brush was buried in gray ash; the rest had either burned to bare sticks or was still aflame.

"But Nick also said he was thinking of heading back up," she managed.

Wyatt looked startled and she realized he hadn't heard Nick's side of their last conversation. "If he started walking when you two hung up, he could have made it pretty far."

Kyle grimaced. If Nick had been that rash, there'd be little hope of even finding his body. "He said something about wanting gravity readings on the east side."

Wyatt nodded. "First let's keep it simple and assume he stayed where we last talked to him. We'll branch out from there."

"But where is station four?" She looked down at the terrain that looked unfamiliar both because she was in the air and due to the landscape's colorless hue making everything look alike.

Wyatt put a finger to his map. "You see the spine that

heads north from the peak and ends above Saddle Valley?"

"Got it." The rugged dike separated a huge slope of boulder talus on the west and thick forest on the east. Unlike at Mount St. Helens, where a lateral blast had blown down miles of timber, Nez Perce's eastern forest remaining standing, limbs bowed beneath a drab cover of ash.

"Follow the ridge down to Saddle Valley," Wyatt instructed, "then west down to station four." He bent forward and showed the map to Deering.

The pilot banked and put the chopper into a dive that made Kyle's stomach lurch. Wyatt's shoulder pressed her against the bulkhead as the G forces increased.

"Hey," Carol said. "I never did get a satellite signal."

"We're doing search and rescue now," Deering clipped.

He leveled out over Saddle Valley, flying at around two hundred feet.

Kyle scanned the slope for the seismic station. There had been a brushfire, no doubt ignited by a glowing bomb. The charred area covered several hundred yards and had burned out upon reaching a line of trees. A hundred feet or so up a steep hill, blackened vegetation surrounded a copse of boulders, a landmark Kyle had used before to help locate the station while on horseback. With the normally pink rhyolite rock covered in soot, she almost didn't recognize it.

A five-foot mast stood out from the blackened slope, its solar panels canted and smashed. The burned tarp lay on the ground. What had been the plastic storage chest formed a black and bubbly drape over the lump of batteries and recording gear.

Deering brought them into a hover over the ruined gear. Beside Kyle, Wyatt reached for her hand. In the same instant, she recognized the smashed casing of Nick's satellite phone.

Carol spoke into her headset. "How could anybody have made it through this hell?"

CHAPTER FORTY-FOUR
OCTOBER 1

Could he have taken shelter in those rocks?" Wyatt pointed to the copse.

"Maybe," Kyle hoped.

Nevertheless, after several minutes of slow reconnaissance, Nick did not appear to hail them.

"What now?" Deering asked.

"I suppose we should see if Nick climbed back up the mountain," Kyle said.

The pilot began to apply more throttle.

"Wait," Carol said. "Let me and Larry out here."

"What?" asked her cameraman. His medium weight rain gear was no more suitable for the weather than Carol's denim jacket.

"Look at this view," she advised. "A clear shot all the way to the summit. I'll be able to get a signal and phone in the first eyewitness account before anybody else gets here." She scanned the sky as though looking for other aircraft.

Having been hired for dual purposes, Deering diplomatically hovered.

Carol twisted in her seat toward Kyle and Wyatt.

"Larry and I will look around for Dr. Darden here."

"I can imagine the story if *Billings Live Eye* finds Nick," Kyle challenged.

To her surprise, Carol shot her a direct look. "You have every right to dislike me, but, like you, I have a job to do." Her voice softened and Kyle had to strain to hear it above the helicopter's racket. "If we find Dr. Darden, and he consents to be interviewed, we'll talk on camera. Otherwise . . . I promise no pictures."

Carol acted sincere, but Kyle sent an inquiring glance at Wyatt.

"We can use all the eyes we can get," he said.

The reporter's alert gaze flicked down to their clasped hands, then she turned to Larry. "You in?"

He gave the eruption cloud a baleful glare. "Let's do the story and get out of here before this whole place blows."

Once Larry went out the rear door in a blast of cutting wind and Carol vacated the front seat, Kyle moved to take her place. Deering once more lifted off and flew up along the valley.

Wiping condensation from the windshield with her fist, she noted a promontory where the footing would be easier than in the valley. "Nick probably would have walked up that way."

Deering guided the Bell above tree line. Wyatt spoke into his microphone. "Surely he wouldn't have had time to get all the way up here."

Kyle hoped he was right. Below, volcanic bombs dotted

the barren surface. There was no sign of Nick's bright parka or the moon suit. But if he'd been struck down, he might already have been buried by the rain of particles.

Turbulence hit once more and Kyle's stomach lurched. As Deering banked, they bumped and tilted. Squinting out at the lowering visibility, he fought the controls. "This ash fall may put an end to our search window."

Kyle rubbed her chest to ease the tightness and tried to believe Nick hadn't been in the line of fire.

"What if he had some warning?" she hoped. "Something that caused him to get out of the exposed valley?"

Wyatt bent forward. "I'd have headed up to the spine. Hidden out in some rocks where I was safe from bombs and had enough elevation to avoid a *nuée ardente*."

Deering nodded and flew toward the great dike. On the way, they flew over the Nez Perce patrol cabin, nestled below the ridge. Several holes in the roof attested to falling missiles.

"Surprised it didn't burn," Kyle said.

They headed farther up the irregular backbone of dark rock. A past fire had burned the hillside, making way for young pines that bristled over the slope.

"If your friend hears us, he'll come into the open and signal," Deering suggested.

The ridge top was narrow, in places only a few feet wide. "Can we fly lower for a better look?" Kyle asked.

"The winds along the knife-edge are treacherous," he replied. "I crash-landed up here during the '88 fires."

Kyle sucked in her breath and stared at the rugged terrain.

"The visibility is going fast," Deering said. "We need to pick up the others and get out of here."

Ash continued to drift like gray snow. Yet, seen through filtered light, the column erupting from the cone seemed to be diminishing.

"See," Wyatt observed. "It's quieting."

Deering shook his head. "Can't take a chance on that lasting."

Despite wanting nothing more than to be a thousand miles from this mountain, Kyle turned to the pilot. "Set me down. I'll look for Nick on the ground."

Wyatt's hand gripped her shoulder through the thick parka he'd loaned her. "Set us down, she means."

"You can't cover any distance with that ankle."

"I'll have to." But as he bent to touch the bandage, a twinge of pain passed over his face.

Deering looked at them both. "Anybody who gets out may have to stay behind while I fly away."

"If it were someone dear to you down there . . . ?" Kyle proposed.

Deering glanced at the photo taped to his dash. "Kendra . . . my girl's learning to fly . . ." He gestured to the young woman with bright hair. "If she went down, I'd run through a forest fire to find her." But with the next turbulent rut, he shook his head. "Be that as it may, I can't land on the ridge."

"Go higher, then." She pointed. "Up where the slope eases. Just let me out and I'll start down, looking for Nick as I go."

Deering studied the clearing visibility. "I guess I could do that."

"I'm coming with you," Wyatt said again.

"And I told you no. Somebody has to find Nick and you'll just slow me down."

He hesitated a moment more, fiddling with his boot. "All right, but we won't go far."

"And if you have to leave . . ." Kyle said.

Wyatt's hand slid from her shoulder down to stroke her fingers. "If we leave, you'll freeze to death in this wind chill."

"I'll get down to the cabin. Build a fire and eat the emergency rations. You need to go pick up those reporters before they get hypothermia."

"You've got a goddamn answer for everything, don't you?" He shook his head. "Nobody could say you were scared now."

As Deering began to climb once more through bumpy air, she realized Wyatt was right.

Unfortunately, that ended as soon as her boots touched earth. The ground shuddered like a shivering dog. Wind knifed at her face, ears, and torso while she struggled to zip Wyatt's parka and get on her gloves. The chill factor must be minus twenty, the risk of hypothermia real.

Kyle watched the helicopter take off and head down into

the valley. Moments later, it lost elevation, hovered, and landed on a flat spot low on the ridge. Wyatt climbed out, waved Deering off, and began to limp up the summit trail.

She wanted to shout for him to go back down and meet her near the cabin. But despite her raised arms and wild gestures, he was a tiny figure far below who probably couldn't see her signal.

Worse, there was no evidence of Nick amidst the strewn boulder field. Seething at the knowledge that if he lived he was no doubt thrilled with the mountain's display, she was surprised to realize it was affecting her, too.

Perhaps it was the scientist in her, but there was something exhilarating about the charged air. Nez Perce's change from peaceful, snowcapped mountain to angry, heated monster was both shocking and awe-inspiring. She'd only experienced such transformation once in her life, and as a terrified child, been unable to process it.

A gust of wind struck Kyle in the back and sent her sprawling uphill. As the gale drove back the plume and cleared the worst of the sulfurous fumes, she saw for the first time the jagged edge of the vent.

It was closer than she'd thought, less than a hundred yards. No more rocks ejected from the crater, and the ash column had faded from deep charcoal to a steamy gray.

That pale hue gave hope. If the eruption at 1:12 PM had released the built-up pressure it might be weeks, months, or even years before any further activity. In the meantime, steam from the melted snow meeting hot rock would tend to form smaller phreatic explosions, like flinging water onto heated stones in a sauna.

Kyle stared up the hill, while the steady wind continued to hold the cloud back. From all over the world, volcanologists were no doubt en route to Nez Perce Peak in order to stand where she did.

She began to climb.

Her boots dug into the soft mix of cinders and ash. Two steps forward and one back, trudging around the twisted bombs that ranged in size from softballs to Suburbans. Foot by foot, she advanced toward the unknown, urged on by the ancient drive of a student of the earth, to be the one who made it to the top of every mountain.

Moments later, Kyle stood on the rim and stared into the fresh raw wound. The top of the mountain had been replaced by a bowl at least three hundred feet deep. Freshly broken rock littered the cindery surface as it did on the outside of the crater. At the bottom was a black hole around four feet across with yellow sulfur coating its lip. Inside the crater where the wind did not reach, steam billowed and ascended sinuously from the vent.

Gazing into hell's gateway, Kyle realized that if Nick had crossed the line where she stood, he'd never be found.

❋ ❋ ❋

Wyatt saw no sign of Nick as he toiled up the summit trail along the rocky spine. Sweating beneath his parka, he scanned the scree on the west side, checking to be sure Nick hadn't fallen into a crevice between the large boulders. He also looked into each of the dense thickets on the eastern slope. His ankle, which had been better this morning than yesterday, was hurting again.

A few minutes ago he'd seen Kyle up on the crater rim, something he could not imagine her doing for mere curiosity. After redoubling his effort in case she'd found Nick, he lost sight of her as the wind brought a cloud of steam into his line of sight.

The tremors ramped up from a shudder to several sharp jolts that nearly threw him off the path. Gaining his balance, he tried to hang on while a ground roll of at least magnitude 5.0 went by. He hoped it wasn't worse for Kyle up higher, but suspected it was. Wanting to rush to her side, he knew that if this level of quaking kept up, he'd be stuck in place no matter what happened.

Crouched in the center of the trail, it was amazing how quickly he went from overheated to trying to turn his face away from the frigid air blasting at his cheeks and nose. With the ground this unstable, there was no way he could climb. Much as he hated to admit it, Nick must be dead . . . probably had been since the first eruption at 1:12.

Above the rocky spine, up in the trees, wisps of smoke rose from a wildfire set by the lightning thrown off by the eruption or a falling volcanic bomb.

Hearing a faint whopping, he looked up to see a helicopter circling. He waved and hoped to attract Deering's attention, but this was a different aircraft. Painted olive drab, it looked like surplus from the Vietnam War. Even at a distance, he could see it was packed with passengers, their cameras trained on the reborn volcano. If this group, and there, a fixed-wing appeared from behind the peak . . . with them in the air, then Deering should still be able to fly.

Wyatt craned his neck, but saw no sign of the Bell.

As the arctic front's assault grew more feral, he considered the merits of warming before a crackling fire. Hot beef stew, Kyle's recipe. Hell, he'd settle for canned, even welcome blankets of coarse, scratchy wool.

Down the slope sat the Nez Perce patrol cabin.

Wyatt snugged the hood of his parka closer around his face until he peeked out through a narrow tunnel. Though he wanted nothing more than to sprout wings and get off this powder keg, he had no choice but to try and survive until help arrived.

He prepared for the effort of getting to his feet, but before he could move, a low frequency rumble began to be audible. Accompanied by renewed tremors, it sounded as though the Devil rolled barrels in the bowels of the earth.

❂　❂　❂

Larry filmed Carol as she spoke into the satellite phone. Then he panned around and up the long slope toward the fuming peak. Fine ash created a hazy effect, but she was right about this being a wonderful vantage point. With the wind holding the steam back, he could see the crater rim through his viewfinder.

He could even zoom in and make out a tiny figure, practically skiing down the loose surface of the upper cone.

Behind him, Carol said into the phone, "We're watching the rescue effort from the last known position of USGS scientist Dr. Nicholas Darden. There is no sign of him here, so it is assumed he headed up the peak. Right now, we can see Dr. Kyle Stone near the mountaintop searching for her colleague. Formerly of the Utah Institute, Dr. Stone appeared yesterday morning on *America Today* to predict just such a debacle as has occurred."

Larry watched Kyle run, hoping she didn't fall for the ground was shaking constantly. The dull resonance he'd sensed beneath the howl of the wind rose.

"Standing here is like riding in the back of a truck on a rutted road," Carol reported. "There have been several larger shocks in the last few minutes . . ."

All at once, the sound surged upward into a shriek that made Larry imagine the flight deck of an aircraft carrier. A sharp shock of earthquake struck, the sensation of an elevator dropping a few feet and jerking to a halt. He braced his feet and kept the camera running.

Through the LED screen he watched the crater rim dissolve. Then an explosion tore the peak apart in eerie silence.

"My, God," Carol screamed. "It's going up."

Out, thought Larry, as a boiling mass that looked and

behaved like an avalanche of gray snow poured down the mountain. Glowing, incandescent, shot with electricity. As the jet-like sound subsided, Larry heard the flow. Hugging the lows on the mountain's face, it gave forth an animalistic growl, mixed with an ominous clacking.

Beside him, Carol's mouth was open; she appeared to scream. He staggered up and shouted, "Run!" but she stood frozen.

He grabbed her arm and gestured to a man-high stack of boulders up the slope. They needed to get behind it or they would have no chance.

Still, she did not move. Unable to manage holding the camera and dragging Carol, Larry let the video unit drop. It bounced off a twisted chunk of lava rock, landing soundlessly amid the clamor.

The flow came on, billowing, surging; enveloping everything in its path.

CHAPTER FORTY-FIVE
OCTOBER 1

From the upper end of the mountain's eastern spine, Kyle watched the crater's side collapse. Impossible to think she'd stood there only moments before with the faith of a child in Santa.

As the nuée poured over the rim, her throat constricted. She knew she could never outrun this fiery gathering of broken rock and ash, tumbling particles that threw off lightning spears and charged the air with ozone. It thrust forth from the mouth of the declivity and spread over the slope with a horrible energy. Constantly shifting, forming new shapes, it sprang down the mountain like a leopard dropping from a branch onto prey.

Knocked to her hands and knees by a quake, Kyle watched annihilation wing toward her, furious, alight with a reddish glare.

She struggled to her feet; half running, half sliding down the gravel slope on the east side of the spine and into the forest. With no time to escape, she sat with her back against the nearest large pine and pulled her pack up to protect her head. Knees drawn to her chest, she unzipped

Wyatt's parka and ducked her face inside, creating an air pocket in case part of the nuée crested the ridge and dropped down over her.

Her ears already ringing from the piercing note preceding the eruption, she flinched at the cacophony of the surging current. It managed at once to whoosh, roar, and clank, like a flash flood she'd once heard in a desert wash.

She took a big breath, wondering if it would be her last, and wished she had let Wyatt get out of the helicopter with her so he'd be here to hold her . . . but no, if she were going to die she'd want him to live.

Listening with horror to the uproar, she suddenly realized it had reached the peak of its crescendo and began to lessen. When no roiling cloud overtook her, she inhaled with care.

On a puff of foul air, she tasted the taint of burned matches. Hugging her knees, she tried to tell her knotted muscles to relax.

When the sound and the sulfur fumes diminished, she decided to climb back onto the spine and see if she could see Wyatt. Leaving her pack at the base of the tree, she dragged herself back up the slope to the ridge top. Though the wind shoved her shoulders and tore at her hood, she planted her feet against the earth tremors and looked down the west valley.

Ash coiled like smoke in the air above the dying avalanche. The path of newly deposited gravel and sand size material formed a meandering path down the lowest downhill route. It had passed close to the ridge where Kyle had hidden out and even closer down near where she'd last seen Wyatt. But what chilled her even more was that the place they'd left the journalists beside seismic station four had been overrun and buried.

It was time to get off this mountain. Her watch read 5:55; with the lowering ash cloud, a premature darkness began to fall. The thought of night sent an arrow of alarm through her. After the violence of the last surging flow, she had to accept that she might be the only person left alive down here.

As she faced the mountain's ruined summit, another glowing avalanche poured over the edge like fumes from an acid-filled beaker. After a moment, the eerie combination of rumbling, hissing and clacking once more assaulted Kyle's ears. Flying rocks burst from the expanding cloud. Beneath her feet, the ridge heaved and shuddered.

Then, deep in her chest came a vibration so low and ominous it was felt rather than heard. Her bones trembled.

The mountaintop exploded.

She had no more than an instant before a shock wave hit, a great thunderclap that lifted her like a huge hand and thrust her back off the ridge. Tumbling end over end down the scree, she felt her shoulder, hip, and one knee impact the ground. Her momentum halted by a thick tree, her vision narrowed to what was before her face. Her escape options must be as thin, for if the helicopters and the plane she'd seen had escaped the blast, they'd be winging on prayer for clear air.

Kyle shoved to her feet and ran, headlong down slippery evergreen needles, and over exposed roots. Her heart raced and her breath came in hitches. More than once she tripped over deadfalls and went sprawling.

Somewhere nearby must be the lava cave Nick had told her about. If she could make it there . . . wisdom had it that one of the few survivors of Mount Pelée's 1902 eruption on the island of Martinique had been in a stone jail, while the rest of 27,000 citizens died.

On their way to the cave, before she and Nick were distracted by the fumaroles on the cinder cone, they were near a cairn of boulders on the ridge. He'd pointed it out as a landmark. He had also said they would need a climbing rope so as not to get trapped.

She didn't have a rope now or a choice.

The approaching flow crested the ridge, puffing like a locomotive. If she were overtaken, she could be surrounded by material as hot as 1,500 degrees.

There must be some clue to the cave, rather than this monotonous high-angle slope studded with pines. As she dared a glance over her shoulder, a bolt of St. Elmo's fire radiated off the front of the flow, causing her to duck and swerve.

With heat assaulting the back of her head, she saw a ring of rock to her left that might surround the cave's opening. Sliding toward sanctuary with stones peppering her skull, she didn't think she could make it. Then she saw the sinkhole in the mountainside, where jumbled rocks had collapsed beneath an arch of smooth, dark rock.

Kyle dove like a base runner. If she landed hard enough to break bones, so be it.

The filthy cone of last season's snow came up to meet her, capped in places by the sugary white of this winter's beginning. The impact caught her on the chest and she slid down, shushing over cold crystals. She felt as though she rode a roller coaster into the dark.

She tangled in something that felt like tree branches and came to a jolting halt. Her head just missed smashing into the rock floor.

Flush with adrenaline, she staggered up, fought her way free of the dead pine lying against the snow cone, and plunged into blackness. The light from the entrance shone farther than she had imagined, a silvery glow that suffused the rocky walls. Every few steps, she looked over her shoulder toward that beacon, gradually watching the illumination recede.

She hadn't realized how much she was counting on that dwindling spark until she turned to find total blackness and knew the ash cloud was upon her. The hot blanket seared her exposed face and neck until she burrowed deeply into the parka's hood. Holding her breath against the fumes, arms out before her, she continued her blind flight.

Fifty feet, perhaps a hundred, she ran. Her gloved hands hit first, a warning, but not in time to prevent her crashing chest-first into a solid rock wall. She twisted wildly, feeling the urge to suck in a lungful of air, sweet or foul.

God, what did it matter? She was surely surrounded by poison gas, she couldn't see, and her hair and clothes were probably about to burst into flame.

Still, she fought the rising impulse to inhale. Shoving off the rock, she tried to recall which direction was away from the cavern opening, and moved in that direction. God, let this not be a dead end.

Light, she had a flashlight in the inside pocket of Wyatt's parka. How stupid of her to have panicked and not remembered. The snaps ripped and she fumbled inside, then removed her gloves so her fingers could find the metal cylinder and drag it out.

She pressed the switch.

Nothing happened.

For a moment, she thought she was blind. Then she shook the light and heard the sifting of the broken bulb inside.

Kyle gasped. She dropped the useless flashlight and heard it roll away over rock. Hot air rushed into her throat, sulfurous and heavy with dust, so thick that she choked.

Yet, the furious sound of the beast that pursued her had abated, for she had not only heard the tinkle of glass in the flashlight, but now she registered her own rough breathing.

She continued to inhale and exhale rapidly. Time to get out of here, but as the air quality continued to improve, she realized the tunnel she had run through must have curved round a corner and she'd lost the light. Her eyes strained into utter darkness, while the earth began to heave and shudder once more.

Kyle's legs folded and she went down. Her chest rose and fell in an ever-increasing tempo that merely sipped when what she needed was a long drink of pure sweet air. Curling into herself, she hugged her knees against her chest.

As the heat from the expended flow dissipated, cold seeped into her from her wet pants and the natural refrigeration that had kept a cone of snow unmelted through a summer's heat.

Dark . . . dark, and so cold, wet . . .

Her fingernails dug into her palms. She squeezed her eyes shut as tears stung her lids.

She would not go back there. No matter how black it was or how violent the earthquakes, she would stay in the present. Blood slicked her hands where her nails broke the skin, the pain connecting her with reality. With her head pressed to her knees, she pretended it was dark because her eyes were closed.

Terror swelled in her chest, not for her present danger, but because she didn't want to see . . . didn't want to recall what had been walled so many years on the other side of a delicate partition within herself.

A tear broke and rolled, warm against her cold cheek. And another.

"Daddy."

When she had dragged herself out of the freezing flood of the Madison River onto the pile of rock and grit, shivering so violently that her teeth knocked together, dawn had grayed the canyon. And in that wash of pale light, Kyle had seen her father.

He lay with his chest barely covered by the rags of dark plaid shirt. One arm reached toward her, an invitation to safety, love, and all she'd believed shattered. Sobbing, she crawled through the mud, ignoring the cuts and scrapes from sharp edges of stone.

When she touched his cold hand with her own freezing fingers, it didn't move. She grabbed his wrist and tried to shake his arm, but it was stiff and unyielding, as though he had turned into a pillar of salt like Lot's wife in the Bible.

"Daddy?" Her voice rose.

There was something the matter with his eyes; they stared yet he did not act as though he saw her.

"Wake up!" she shrieked, prodding his chest with a fingertip and then pummeling with her fists. "Daaaadddy!"

Another of the tremors that had come without warning all night shook the Madison Valley. And in the next instant, she heard a swooshing and looked up to see the beginnings of an avalanche about a hundred feet above her and her father.

She dragged at his arm. He didn't budge, and she saw he was buried up to his thighs. Though she felt the growing gut sense that Daddy was dead like Grandma and Grandpa Stone, gone away to Jesus, she clung to his hand.

The approaching mudslide gathered speed. And as surely as if she heard her father speak, she knew he wanted her to leave him.

Kyle scrabbled across the slope away from the hissing river of mud and rock. Slipping on the liquefied surface, she plopped back into the rising cold flood, opaque and brown like coffee with cream. It was all she could do to fight being washed away, but she flailed with her arms and legs the way Daddy had taught her. Toward a ball of tree roots and uprooted earth that protruded from the slide, something she could grasp to pull herself out.

When the ooze stopped sliding, she couldn't see Daddy anywhere.

Perhaps an hour later, as she huddled on the shore in the mud-stiffened rags of her clothing, she heard voices and the splash of oars.

Sitting in the same fetal position in the black lava cave, Kyle realized she'd been about to give up. To let the constant earthquakes that seemed to be increasing in intensity and the darkness immobilize her.

With her back to the rock, she realized it was no longer sucking the heat from her body. Rather, it was the other way round, as the floor and walls began to radiate warmth.

In a single motion she was on her feet, touching the stone with her palms for confirmation. Such sudden and rapid heat flow this near the ground surface this far from the peak could only mean one thing, that another, even larger eruption was imminent.

With a hand on the wall and the other extended before her, she began to walk. Counting her steps, she figured she'd come less than twenty feet when the tunnel curved sharply at the place she'd run into the wall. Beyond, she saw a blessed faint glow.

Dry-mouthed, she hurried toward the entry. And stood looking up at least fifteen feet to the rounded opening in the ceiling. Not even a gecko could make its way up there; the rock around the entrance appeared too rough for even suction-cup feet, supposing one could hang upside down.

Kyle turned to the dead pine, imagining she might use it as a ladder, but try as she might, each effort to raise it was like wrestling an octopus.

She began to sweat and stripped off the parka. The cone of snow was softening and darkening as the heat flow melted it down.

"Help," she shouted, and, her voice rising, "Wyatt!"

There could be no answer, she knew. If anyone had been out on that slope, they'd be dead. Yet, she shrieked on and on. Each time she tried to stop, the grip of hysteria was too great.

Finally, sobbing, hoarse, and feeling stupid for losing it so badly, she slumped back to the floor. Air from above chilled her sweating brow. And though she grew cold again near the entrance, she could not imagine once more walking away from the light.

How gray it already looked outside with all the particulate matter in the air. Her aching throat closed further at the thought of night falling on the mountain.

She began rooting through the pockets of Wyatt's coat, wishing she hadn't lost her pack. No food, no water, except the ash-sprinkled snow cone that was rapidly melting.

The air in the cave continued to warm. From outside, she began to hear a crackling that defied identification until she smelled something burning. Of course, the hot gases or the lightning thrown off by static electricity had ignited wildfires.

With the recent snows, it was probably too wet for the trees to catch, but the stench of burning under-story grew stronger. Within minutes, Kyle saw the first wisps curl into the cavern like smoke down a chimney.

Her heart rate accelerated. As the smoke continued to come in, forming eddies, she watched a stray tendril waft down the lava tube. The smoke moved in the direction she'd just come from.

Was it possible the cave had another entrance?

She shook her head. In places, lava rock was so porous that one could lift boulders measuring three feet on a side over their head. She had faded photographs of her and Nick doing that at Craters of the Moon National Monument in Idaho when they'd gone there during field camp. The drawing effect of the cave must be because there were small vents to open air.

On the other hand, the lava had run out of the tube, leaving the void behind. There could be a large enough exit for her to escape.

Kyle stared into the maw of the tunnel. If she stayed where she was, she was dead. One way or another . . . poisonous gas, another eruption, or dehydration in this pit with no way out. Could she face the darkness with no guarantee?

She had to. If she didn't make it through, she'd never see Wyatt or Nick again.

Facing down the blackness, she asked herself for the first time . . . how bad could just being in the dark be? In the past hour, she'd faced far worse.

She forced her chest to rise and fall more evenly while determination strengthened her spine.

During the next lull in the earth tremors, Kyle managed to shove to her feet. She slung Wyatt's coat around her waist and secured it with a knot.

Bending, she pawed into the snow to a slightly less filthy layer and scooped up a double handful. No matter that her raw hands dyed the edges with blood, she crunched ice until her thirst was reasonably quenched.

As though force of will could make it so, she envisioned the other opening of the cave, a place where the lava flow had spread out over the shield of mountain. She would push past horror and anything else in her way to reach that exit . . .

And after she did, she might never again be able to muster adrenaline for imagined peril. She would live in a world where she could decide whether or not to use a goddamned nightlight.

With a last look behind her, Kyle took the path she'd traveled, back into darkness.

CHAPTER FORTY-SIX

OCTOBER 1

It wasn't the dank, musty smell, or the ever-narrowing walls of the tunnel that seemed to lead into the bowels of the mountain. Not even the spider web that caught Kyle across the mouth and made her flail wildly. It was the constant sense that something was about to strike her in the face that kept her heart galloping.

That, and she couldn't seem to breathe.

Slow, she admonished herself, the litany she'd recited through the years whenever she had the misfortune to end up in darkness. But, though she managed to get her respiration rate down a little, there still didn't seem to be enough oxygen in the rapidly warming air.

Nonetheless, she carried on, feeling as though her head were wrapped in some kind of suffocating cloth. With her once-more gloved hands waving before her nose, she brushed the ceiling and found it lowering almost directly in front of her. She stopped and bent, feeling for open space and finding a passage no more than three feet high. If she got down and crawled, she might . . .

Get out of here, her inner voice shrieked. Time to turn

around and run back to where she could gulp even smoke-tainted air.

Gritting her teeth, she moved forward and found a duck walk sufficient to negotiate the low point. In this crouched position, the heat radiating from the rock was more noticeable. Trying to ignore the constant quakes rumbling like distant thunder, she made a sweep before her with her hands to make sure she would not hit her head upon arising. Then she shoved up from the floor.

She shuffled a foot forward but . . . which way to go now?

Although the general slope was downhill, here the floor seemed a perfect plane.

She chose a direction and moved. In three steps, she felt the rock above begin to slope down. Quickly, she executed an exact U turn and began to move forward as quickly as she dared. In four steps, the ceiling began to come down again.

She stopped, her hands curling into fists. A sound of frustration escaped her dry throat. Her eyes straining as they had been for long minutes, Kyle looked back over her shoulder and tried to decide whether she was coming or going. With time running out, she tried to feel lucky. She turned and looked forward again. All her senses strained to perceive some texture in the utter blackness. "Please, God," she murmured.

There was nothing . . . but then there was . . . some indefinable nuance in the darkness that simply felt right.

She moved and this time the rock above stayed the same height so she was able to walk without stooping. In a moment, she could feel from the floor's downhill slope that she followed the way of gravity, where the lava would have drained. And, though it might be her imagination, the blackness ahead did not seem so absolute.

❀ ❀ ❀

Kyle began to move more recklessly. Her hands encountered no obstacle as long as she steered toward the faint suggestion of light.

Gray brightened to silver and she began to believe her prayer might have been answered this time.

Yet, she prepared herself for the worst. The opening would be no larger than her head. The ceiling was about to collapse between her and freedom. The heat radiating from the walls presaged a fresh outpouring of lava.

Nonetheless, she followed the sloping floor. With each step, the illumination grew stronger.

When she lacked about a hundred feet to the entry, she could see the patch of light, at least three feet tall and about as wide. Panting, she put on a burst of speed.

Kyle emerged into monochrome twilight and was immediately struck by the cold. Her chest muscles rebelled and it took a gasp to draw in air that stabbed at her lungs.

As fast as she could, she fumbled the jacket from around her waist and put it on. With wind-driven flakes of ash falling almost sideways, she blinked and tried to duck away from their assault.

The contrast between the light outside and total darkness was great, but as her eyes adjusted, she realized she'd thought there was a lot more day left. Her watch revealed it lacked a few minutes till seven. Not quite sunset, but she guessed that under these conditions there would be no more than fifteen minutes before it would be too dark to tell white from black.

She scanned the lowering sky and saw steam billowing from the crater. What were the chances any of the aircraft were still in the area?

Hearing no engine noise, she turned her attention to the pine-studded slope. Here the incline was at least fifty degrees and she thought that in the cave she'd lost quite a bit of elevation. Thankfully, she'd left the wildfire above where it would burn toward the mountaintop. Off to her left about thirty yards, she made out the dark shape of the rocky spine and realized she couldn't be too far from where she'd seen Wyatt alight from the helicopter.

Sidestepping on the steep slope, Kyle began to make her way down. It was rough going in the semidarkness, as the contrast between rocks, roots, and solid footing ebbed. Ash coated the trees, making them look flocked as if for Christmas in the last of the dying light.

Despite having braved the blackness of the lava cave, she felt a stab of alarm as night fell. The familiar sensation made her long to reach for her pocket flashlight, thoug she knew it lay broken where she'd dropped it.

But she wasn't going to think about the dark now. She had to find Wyatt and the others. They couldn't all be dead.

Yes, argued logic, they could. There were dozens of ways Nick might have died.

Asphyxiated, bull-dozed by a boulder, blown to bits in the crater . . .

As for Wyatt, he might have been caught by the glowing ash cloud and turned into a mummy like the bodies found in Pompeii and Herculaneum.

Bitter liquid rushed up the back of her throat.

Kyle swallowed the burning bile.

Wyatt, at least, had to be all right. She would not think otherwise. Near the ridge, there was no sign that the flow had crested it. He could even be nearby, as she didn't think he'd have gotten far on his bad ankle.

Cupping her hands, she shouted, "Halloo!" God, but her throat was raw.

The pines soughed and the earth continued to rumble.

"Wyatt!" she tried. "Nick? Anybody?"

Looking around the slope, she noted wisps of steam drafting from the ground not twenty feet to her right. Another field of fumaroles, this one much farther down the mountain.

The seeping gas, along with the heat she'd felt coming from the rocks in the cave, made her speed her steps. It shouldn't be much farther to the clearing around the cabin and it would be a bit lighter out from under the forest canopy. But, she cautioned herself, the gas along the Saddle Valley fault could be so thick by now that she'd walk into a poisonous death trap.

All at once, the wind brought a faint rhythmic chop from the west side of the ridge. Kyle stopped and listened for several seconds, as the engine noise first grew louder and then receded.

Heedless of the uncertain footing, she began to run. Though it must be impossible for the chopper pilot or passengers to see or hear her, she cried, "Help! Down here!"

❊   ❊   ❊

Larry couldn't believe his ears, but that was definitely a helicopter, and it was getting closer. And unless he climbed out of the rock pile he and Carol had taken shelter in, out into the freezing twilight wind that was sure to give him frostbite, there was no way in hell the pilot was going to see them.

For the past hour or so, listening to numerous extrusions blast from the crater, he'd huddled against Carol. Dressed as they were, to leave the rocks meant certain death. Just a remaining there might.

As the whopping continued to grow louder, he said, "Hear that?"

Carol sat slumped with her head on her chest. Even though he'd saved her life by dragging her upslope and behind the boulders, she'd been despondent ever since.

Now, she raised her face to him, and he saw a spark dawn. "Deering's come back for us?"

"Maybe. Let's go!" Larry shoved up and kept his head tucked to avoid bumping it on the low ceiling of the dugout they'd burrowed into.

The chopper noise was static and he couldn't tell which direction it came from. As Carol started slowly to move, he staggered out on legs stiff from sitting on cold stones. When the arctic blast hit him, he gasped.

Once in the open, the sound of rotors was a lot louder. An even stiffer wind began to beat at him as he turned and saw Deering's Bell hovering over the rock pile. Inside the cockpit, the pilot lifted one hand in salute.

"Carol!" Larry shouted. He looked back to their shelter and saw her coming out with her arms folded, shivering.

Deering brought the chopper down and landed in a vortex of blowing cinders and soot from the wildfire that had passed through earlier. Larry ducked his head, squinted his eyes against the projectile storm, and grabbed Carol's arm. Together, they ran for it.

Once inside, with Carol in the front seat and he behind, shedding dirt onto Deering's leather seats, Larry put on headphones and asked, "How'd you know where we were?"

Deering concentrated on lifting off. When they were airborne and about fifty feet up, he pointed toward the seismic station, largely buried in ash. From this vantage point, was obvious that the hot debris flow had contoured the hillside and managed to miss the boulders by mere yards.

"Saw where you dropped that," Deering went on.

Larry looked and saw where he'd lost the camera. Even draped in several inches of ash, the shape was recognizable.

Through the headphones, he heard Carol regain her spirit along with her bitchiness. "The story of a lifetime and no pictures."

Deering looked over his shoulder and gave a Larry a look of sympathy. Unable to hold his temper, Larry burst out, "You're upset because I dropped the camera to drag you away from that flow? Pissed because I saved your life?"

"Here's the deal," she came back. "I'll owe you for my life. You owe me a Pulitzer."

Thinking of his family and how close he'd come to dying, Larry decided he could damned well find some other job that had health insurance for Joey's asthma.

Bending forward, Larry tapped Carol's shoulder. "No, this is the deal," he said. "You'll have to collect in another lifetime, because I just quit."

❂   ❂   ❂

In her headlong rush, Kyle tripped over more deadfall, each time staggering up and renewing her speed.

Ahead, the forest began to thin. Aiming for open space, she heard a sudden loud crack like a shotgun, followed by streaking hiss.

The sky lit with a red glow that nearly blinded her. Ahead, she made out someone standing with an arm raised to launch the flare. The unnatural light also showed what might be a body on the ground.

As the signal began to fade, Kyle lost all sight in the bright afterimage. She stumbled forward, yelling, "Who's there?"

Wyatt and Nick . . . one of them was down. And it must be them, for who else would know about the signal gun in the cabin? Blindly, she tripped over uneven ground and fell onto her hands and knees with a sob.

Boots crunched at a run over the rocky ground and stopped before her bowed head.

She couldn't see detail. Were those Wyatt's lace-up winter boots or Nick's two-tone hikers?

Hands touched her shoulders through the parka. "Kyle."

Arms enfolded her and pulled her up. Her cold cheek found the material of a jacket covered in gritty ash.

"Wyatt . . ."

His embrace tightened until her bruised ribs protested. She ignored it, pressing closer. "I was so afraid for you."

Wyatt's lips brushed her temple and she didn't care that both his mouth and her skin felt like sandpaper.

"You're safe." That was all that mattered right now. The rest of the world could wait while she savored this gift.

"Ten deep breaths," Wyatt murmured at her ear. His thumb traced the track of one of her tears.

The helicopter crested the ridge. A spotlight cast them

and the swirling ash in dazzling white and black shadows.

Wyatt let her go. Kyle looked at Nick who lay with his eyes closed. Though his face was covered in a sticky-looking mess of blood and dirt, she could see the angry patches of blisters peeking through.

The chopper noise rose to a scream. The black shape behind the blinding light came down into a hover less than fifty feet away. Dust rose in a cloud and dirt pelted Kyle's face as the skids touched down.

"Nick?" she screamed.

Wyatt tapped her shoulder and shouted, "He's pretty weak, but I hope he'll be okay." His glasses were so streaked she couldn't imagine how he saw through them. "Time to go."

The ground gave a jerk. "God, not now," Kyle exclaimed, knocked sprawling to the earth along with Wyatt.

From where she landed hard on her back, she could see the dark interior of the helicopter, an instrument glow on Deering's face as he maneuvered the controls with a set jaw. To her amazement, a filthy Carol Leeds rode shotgun with Larry in back. Kyle tried to get to her feet, but the quake continued.

Wyatt crouched nearby. For a moment, she thought he was looking at her, but then she saw he was transfixed by something behind her. Just as her father had watched death march up Madison Canyon, now Wyatt's gaze revealed the same stark terror.

Mere yards uphill, parallel to the linear trace of the

Saddle Valley fault, the ground was splitting open to reveal a line of brilliant red. It was like looking at the interior of a steel furnace.

Kyle froze. She tried to swallow, but her throat was too dry.

"Let's go!" Wyatt's shout galvanized her. They made it to their feet together and Wyatt dragged Nick up over his shoulder into a fireman's carry.

They reeled across the heaving ground toward the chopper. Deering was upping the power, the rotors' scream deafening to her ears that were still abuzz from when the peak exploded. A glance over her shoulder revealed thick crimson lava oozing from the fissure.

She saw that Nick's eyes were open and that he was staring at the phenomenon. He might act flippant sometimes, but now his nightmare of burning to death in molten rock was reflected on his face.

The helicopter shuddered, both from the ground roll and Deering's run-up. Then it lifted off. Kyle started to cry out to him not to leave, but that was worse than useless amidst the cacophony . . . and she knew he had to get the machine out of the way or no one would survive.

Another look behind showed a scarlet flash, as the lava broke free and sped in a liquid flood toward them. She and Wyatt made it the last few feet to where the Bell maintained a low hover.

She leaped for the chest-high skid and the thick metal caught her in the diaphragm. With her breath driven out in a whoosh, she turned to see Wyatt sling Nick over the support where he dangled by his armpits. Now, as Wyatt jumped and grabbed on, their combined weight shifted the Bell into a sharp starboard list. She felt the heat on her back from the molten river and drew her legs up, getting her breath and shouting at Nick and Wyatt to do the same.

The helicopter slipped sideways and down. In a second, Nick would start to scream and then it would be her turn. She squeezed her eyes shut, every muscle cringing as she strained to pull herself up.

Ever so slowly, she felt the craft begin to lift. With a surge of hope, Kyle opened her eyes and saw it was enough to keep Nick's boots out of the lava. Yet, even as it rose, the chopper was still crippled by the uneven load. She looked up at the slanting rotors and prayed.

The rear door opened and Larry, looking like an ash-covered scarecrow, lay on the floor and stretched his arm toward them.

It was no use. She couldn't reach up without falling off the skid.

The next few seconds seemed to last forever.

Then Deering managed to bring the Bell upslope of the fissure and start to bring it down again.

Kyle's feet touched the ground.

Nick let go of the strut and crumpled.

Wyatt bent to him.

Larry scrambled up and got out. He grabbed Kyle's arm and gave her a push into the helicopter. With a shove from Wyatt on his backside, Nick was in, too, gasping and puffing at Kyle's side.

Despite his hurt ankle, Wyatt fairly vaulted into the rear seat, landing hard on Kyle's thigh. Larry followed and slammed the door.

"Let's get out of here!" he shouted to Deering.

With four of them crowded in the rear seat like sardines, they held on as the helicopter took off in a nose-down attitude to catch the lift. Out the windshield, they had a front row view of the widening fissure along the Saddle Valley Fault. To both the west and east, great fountains of lava spewed into the now-dark sky.

When the engine's scream muted to a drone in her headphones, Kyle heard Nick say, "Yee haw."

She turned to him. "I take it that means you're all right?"

"Thanks to the cowboy. He found me crawling and got me out of harm's way." Nick grinned, but it was mostly grimace as he gestured to his bloody face and neck. "These burns hurt like hell." He pointed to his gloved hand and she saw that the fleece was also blood-soaked. "Broken finger, busted eardrum . . ." His smile grew stronger. "But did you see the eruption? The most glorious thing I've ever seen."

As the Bell flew higher, everyone turned to watch the glow from the crater. The eerie light tinged the underside of a renewed cloud of ejecta into the night sky.

Nick leaned forward. "I can't wait to get back up here

. . . map out the flows . . ."

Wyatt gave him an incredulous look.

Kyle reached across Nick's shoulders to get Wyatt's attention. He turned, their eyes met, and she shook her head.

"You walk the edge," Wyatt told Nick. "I'll watch."

"You mean we will," said Kyle, as she and Wyatt shared a grin.

CHAPTER FORTY-SEVEN
OCTOBER 2

Just after midnight, Deering's helicopter touched down at University Hospital in Salt Lake City. After Nick's unquenchable enthusiasm had convinced everyone he was not in critical condition, Deering had flown Carol Leeds and Larry Norris to Billings. There, ash had been falling very gently, putting a pale gray blanket onto the half-emptied town.

Now, seeing a chopper on their pad where life flight usually landed, the University's hospital staff came out at a run. Upon seeing the blood on Nick's face and hands, and the ash covering him, Kyle, and Wyatt from head to toe, they had to be assured there had been no car bombing. Though Nick insisted he was good to walk, Wyatt practically shoved him into a wheelchair just inside the hospital door. Then, limping himself, he insisted on pushing Nick down the hall to the ER.

Kyle stayed behind to see Deering off. "I can't tell you how grateful I am that you were willing to do all that you did."

He stood with his helmet under one arm, "They say

I'm a wild man." His gaunt features creased into a smile. "You'll get my bill."

She laughed and brushed ash from her shoulders in a little cloud. "Were you serious about contracting with Nick to make additional over-flights as this thing unfolds?"

Deering's face sobered. "Tell you what. I saw you on *America Today*, and if you check things out before we fly, we've probably got as good an opinion as any."

But she couldn't check things out for him as things stood now. Power-mad Hollis had cut her out of her world, and damned if she wasn't going to get back onto the network before this new day was over.

To Deering, she said, "What if I told you we really don't know what's going to happen? We make educated guesses, better ones every year as our technology advances, but the fact remains that something huge could happen in Yellowstone virtually without warning."

"It sounds like waiting for terrorists to attack, to get hit by lightning, or for a meteor to fall out of the sky . . . you've just got to live with it." He stuck out his hand.

"Amen," she said, accepting his firm handshake.

He put on his helmet and went to the cockpit. She remained on the roof for his run-up and watched him take off into the city-washed night sky.

Inside the hospital, the wait in the ER was several hours while a major car accident was sorted out. Finally, Nick was seen, his burns bandaged, finger splinted, and the doctors insisted he stay overnight for observation and a

CT scan in the morning.

With no means of transportation and no inclination to leave Nick alone, both Kyle and Wyatt decided to take turns cleaning up in his hospital room's bath. As the gift shop was closed at this hour, there was no chance of buying even a clean shirt.

"You can wear hospital gowns," quipped Nick from his bed, looking like an ancient mummy with his head, neck and cheeks swathed in gauze. He plucked at the gray material. "Don't you envy me in this?"

Feeling the scratchy ash that had penetrated Wyatt's outer parka and winter pants, and through fleece to her skin, Kyle started opening cabinets looking for extra gowns.

"Over here," said Wyatt after a moment of rummaging through drawers.

Kyle opened the bathroom door. "I think the last time we were in this position, I said 'gentlemen first'." She gave him an unquestionably intimate smile, fraught with memory of yesterday morning at her townhouse. Then she laughed. "This time, I say to hell with that."

❁ ❁ ❁

Wyatt watched the door close behind Kyle, aware of Nick peering at him from between the bandages. Standing by the bed, Wyatt ruffled a hand through his hair, sending a rain of sandy particles onto his shoulders and the floor. "Oops."

He glanced around to find a place to sit without making too big a mess and he decided to wait until he could get cleaned up.

"Wyatt."

He met Nick's gaze.

"I think you were upset the other day when I was telling Kyle about the torch I'd seen you carrying."

A flash of irritation penetrated even his haze of exhaustion. "You did make me sound like a patsy."

Nick shot a significant look at the bathroom door. "It seems to me your patsy days are behind you."

Wyatt thought for a moment. "If that were true, how would you feel about it?"

Nick's grin crinkled the edge of his cheek bandage. "I'd say congratulations."

Wyatt smiled in return.

The laugh lines around Nick's eyes settled. "Kyle's the best, always has been, and I treated her badly. She and I both considered whether we could have a second chance but that was all nostalgia."

"It looked a little more intense than just old home week," Wyatt countered.

Nick spread his hands. "Okay . . . but there were two reasons it could never have worked." He ticked his index finger. "One. I'm married to the mountains."

Wyatt nodded without surprise.

"Two. If Kyle hadn't been so careful keeping the world at arm's length so she wouldn't have to face her past, sh and you would have come together long ago." His eyes twinkled. "It just took some shaking up to get there."

* * *

Kyle stood in the shower, letting hot water run over her aching neck and back muscles. If there had been a tub, she'd have drawn a bath and lay down in it. After the extremes of cold and heat of this day, the beating she'd taken from repeated falls on the mountain, and the sleep deprivation . . . Jesus, that had begun with the early rising for *America Today*, and it had been over thirty hours since Nick's call had wakened her and Wyatt from their post-lovemaking nap. After all that, she should be thinking of nothing but a soft pillow.

Rather, she kept wondering what was happening at Nez Perce. Outside the door, she imagined Nick doing the same. As she had on the crater rim, she appreciated the lure of studying dynamic change in the earth. Now, she understood she'd been doing that all along, watching five earthquake records. She had simply been too shell-shocked from her childhood experience to risk going through it again.

Kyle turned off the water and dried herself on a thin towel. She caught a glimpse of her face in the mirror, her cheeks and neck laden with patches of pink, the remnants of burns from the *nuée ardente*. What startled her was the serenity she saw in her eyes, something that had been absent since her sixth birthday, in a peaceful campground beneath a silver moon.

Vowing to put that part of her past where it belonged, she focused on smoothing some of the hospital lotion onto a few of her more livid bruises.

With Kyle leaving the bath in her gown and Wyatt coming in wearing his briefs, they brushed past each other in the doorway. Though there was adequate room to get by without touching, Wyatt paused, cradled her cheek and pressed a light but lingering kiss onto her lips.

Nick was asleep in the bed, the room lights dimmed but not extinguished. Kyle smiled at his consideration, and without disturbing him, lay down on the room-wide window seat. The last thing she recalled was Wyatt curling up next to her.

❀ ❀ ❀

At 2:41 in the afternoon, rested and ready for battle, Kyle stepped off the University shuttle bus in front of the Institute. Wyatt, with his ankle wrapped in an elastic bandage, came down the step behind her. Nick emerged through the door gauze-wrapped to the eyes, and brandished a fist. "The mummy versus Hollis Delbert."

Kyle figured Nick's cocky attitude stemmed in part from a clean bill of health on his head scan. Yet, she said to him, "You take it easy. You're supposed to be hurt, remember?"

"Wish I had my dress uniform for this," Wyatt said

He wore his dirty fleece that he'd talked the ER staff into not cutting off him, as did Kyle and Nick, along with their parkas that she'd sponged off so they were merely dirty rather than disgusting.

With no campus security in sight, they marched three abreast up the sidewalk and entered the building basement, where it opened in the rear at ground level. Though she and Wyatt had been there only three days ago, she inhaled the earthy smell of rocks, the ink of the seismographs, and an academic chalk-like odor with a sense of wistfulness.

Hollis wasn't in his office. His Tectonophysics class on the fourth floor would end at 2:50.

Kyle went behind Hollis's desk, settled into his chair and nudged his computer mouse to see if his machine had the security on. Immediately, his screen came alive with the seismic signal from the Pelican Cone station, only a few miles west of Nez Perce.

"We're in," she said.

Nick pulled the guest chair away from the wall and brought it around behind the desk to straddle. Wyatt sat on the desk, his back to the door.

In the hall, the bell clanged, signaling the end of classes. A moment later, there came the sound of many feet and voices from upstairs as the classrooms emptied.

Kyle focused on the Pelican Cone record. The display was the one for yesterday's eruption. It showed the twenty-four-hour record for October 1, starting with the oscillating sine wave of rising magma. At 1:10 PM the tornillo, or screw-shaped signal, appeared, signaling the final turbulent rise to eruption.

Later in the record of the afternoon, Kyle noted the continued quakes, background rumbling punctuated by the sharp excursions that had knocked her on her ass multiple times. There was the big one that had ripped open the Saddle Valley fault to form a fissure that fountained lava as they scrambled for safety.

Kyle clicked forward to today's record.

Nick whistled. "Thar she blows again." He pointed to another tornillo just after noon, followed by a large reverberation and more lower case grumbling.

"What in hell do you think you're doing?" Hollis shrilled from the doorway.

Kyle kept watching the computer. From the corner of her eye, she saw Wyatt turn his head with slow deliberation as though Hollis were the intruder. In the chair beside Kyle, she felt Nick's body make a subtle transformation from alertness to a slack posture.

"I said, what are you doing with my computer?" Hollis advanced into the room.

Wyatt shoved off the desk and towered over him. "As Park Service, I have a perfect right to be here and look at the records."

"Who's that?" Hollis pointed at Nick, who lifted a hand to his bandaged forehead and grimaced as if he were in pain.

"That?" Wyatt echoed dryly. "Don't tell me you don

recognize Dr. Nicholas Darden of USGS Volcano Hazards?"

"Nick Darden?"

Nick turned. "The same. Haven't seen you since the Geophysical Society meeting in San Diego, Delbert? Say what, ten years?"

Kyle pushed a button on the mouse and toggled to look at yesterday's eruption from the Pitchstone Plateau station.

Hollis looked at her again and inhaled a big breath. "Kyle," he said with tight control, "you've been fired. You have no right to be in this building, much less at my desk."

She ignored him.

Wyatt moved a step closer to Hollis, who took an equal pace back. "That's what we've come to talk to you about."

He stepped. Hollis retreated.

"You remember when Kyle and I called you from my office, and I said nobody needed to know you'd cut off the park's access to the website . . ."

"Right," Hollis said warily.

"Well, we said that if nothing happened to Nick, nobody need know about your slimy little trick."

Kyle turned and faced Hollis. "We'd be happy to keep our end of the bargain, but there's just one little problem." She gestured toward Nick, who appeared so infirm it was hard to see how he managed to stay in the chair.

Wyatt advanced again. "Yes, a problem."

"What's that?" Hollis blustered, fetching up against the wall.

"It looks to me as if something happened to Nick," Kyle said.

Wyatt put a hand on Hollis's shoulder. The smaller man looked scared.

"Now, here's what you're going to," Wyatt instructed. "You're going to turn in a letter of resignation addressed to Stanton, with copies to Colin Gruy and Radford Bullis. In this letter, you will indicate that you intend to pursue other interests and that you appoint Kyle Stone as your interim successor."

Hollis started shaking his head.

"You can probably get on again at UCLA," Nick suggested quietly, "as long as I don't call my friend the Chairman and tell him you were responsible for nearly getting me killed. If Kyle had seen the tornillo before the eruption and warned me, those minutes could have made the difference between this," he gestured toward his head, "and me walking away without a scratch."

Kyle met Hollis's eyes and shrugged. "Your choice." She went back to dinking around from seismic station to station.

Hollis opened his mouth and closed it. He looked at Nick, who held out his hands and lifted his shoulders in a 'what can you do?' gesture.

"All right." Hollis sent Kyle a glare of hatred, and without another word, left his office.

Wyatt was already heading for the door as Nick and Kyle scrambled to their feet. Hollis's footsteps were rapi on the tile floor, so they had to rush to the hall to watch him reach the exit.

"Yee haw," said Nick.

In the lab across the hall, the portable seismograph made a dutiful record of Hollis slamming the door.

EPILOGUE
JULY 2

By midsummer, Nez Perce Peak had erupted twice more, building a lava dome inside the crater and spreading ash on the cities and towns to the northeast.

The Friday afternoon before the Fourth of July weekend found Kyle in the Institute lab studying the pattern of bumps and thumps that marked the new era in Yellowstone seismology. She brought up a map from the website that compiled the historic earthquakes in the area. The largest number and the most intense magnitudes had been in the western part of the park and outside it near the Hebgen Lake Fault System, as well as within the outline of the 630,000-year-old caldera. Next, she plotted the quakes since last September 10th when the swarm that led to eruption began. Contrary to the past, there had been a marked diminishment of activity in all the western areas.

She turned from the computer monitor to Stanton, who sat beside her in his wheel chair.

"One should never assume they've got things figured out," she tempered, "but I think the opening of the Nez Perce vent released some of the pressure we saw building for years beneath the caldera."

"I wouldn't argue with that," Stanton replied with the slow and deliberate speech he'd developed through long months of therapy. Fortunately, he was right handed so his still-drooping left side did not prevent him from light duty as a Professor Emeritus, filling in some for the void left when Hollis returned to UCLA.

"Knock, knock," said Leila from the door. She looked as lovely as ever in silk and pearls, her silver hair in soft waves. In contrast, Stanton was tieless and wore khaki trousers; having declared that life was too short to go around overdressed when he had trouble keeping his fork steady at the dinner table.

"What are your plans for the weekend?" Leila asked Kyle.

"Thought I'd drive up to Yellowstone this evening."

Leila checked her watch and advised, "You should get on the road so you'll get there before dark."

Kyle looked at the wall clock and found there was probably just enough time to make it to Mammoth before summer night fell. "I'll go soon."

But once Stanton and Leila had gone, she turned back to the computer and brought up her email.

Nick's latest message was from the Andes, where he and a group of South American geophysicists were conducting gravity studies on a newly smoking crater that had been dormant for over sixty years.

As soon as this project is wrapped up, I want to come back to Nez Perce. Some folks may think the small eruptions released the energy, but you and I both know Yellowstone is the world's largest supervolcano.

"Thanks, Nick," she thought. "*Here I was feeling pretty good about things, and you have to bring me back to earth.*"

In the meantime, you keep watch over Nez Perce and the Wasatch, and I'll see you in the fall. P.S. I miss your smile.

Kyle's lips curved into a full-blown grin. If she and Nick had been friends first, instead of lovers, they might not have lost all those years.

She pushed back her chair, locked up the lab and went out to her Mercedes. Her overnight bag was already stowed in the trunk.

Anticipating a lot of traffic if she drove through the park from the south, she took the longer but faster route around the west side. It was high summer, the potato and wheat crops of eastern Idaho emerald green where elaborate aluminum irrigation machines rolled through the fields. The air was so clear that she could look to the east and see the tips of the Grand Tetons. About fifty miles south of West Yellowstone, she entered the Targhee National Forest.

The 'Land of Many Uses' had been intermittently logged with vacant fields of stump stubble alternating with deep forest. The afternoon sun set off a strobe effect of light and shadow on the highway.

Kyle knew that beneath the mantle of vegetation lay the Island Park Caldera, the relatively small fifteen-mile-wide crater from the eruption of 1.3 million years ago. It also happened to mark the edge of the gargantuan two-million-year-old eruption, which had left a hole fifty by forty miles and rained ash over the western half of North America.

Once in the park, she drove through the open meadows along the Madison River. Here she crossed into the youngest 630,000-year caldera. Spying grazing elk and buffalo alongside wading fly-fishermen, she lowered her window and drew a breath of clean mountain air.

North of Madison Junction, she passed back out of the caldera and headed for Norris Geyser Basin, occasionally closed due to soil temperatures in the boiling range along the nature trails.

Dusk was falling when she caught sight of the small Headquarters community. Inhaling the familiar scent of sage, pine and earth, she felt she was coming home.

When she turned in at his duplex, Wyatt was waiting in the shadow of the porch.

As she got out of the car, the moon began to rise over the eastern horizon.

Wyatt came to her through the blue twilight, wearing faded jeans and a pullover, carrying a bottle of Lite and a Guinness. "Little late tonight?"

She took the proffered beer, knocked it against his and drank. "Made it by dark."

"Only just."

She looked again at the lemon orb of moon.

"Full tomorrow." Wyatt took her drink, placed it with

his on the trunk of her car, and put his arms around her from behind.

She leaned back, enjoying the feel of his muscle and warmth. "I'm learning to see the full moon as something other than a symbol of a single disastrous event in my life."

Wyatt's embrace tightened.

"I'm even trying to enjoy this time of evening. It's as though everything is more sharply defined before darkness falls."

He bent and his lips and moustache brushed her neck. "I wish you could spend more time here."

She smiled. "I may be able to soon. I just hired Cass Grain out of Menlo Park, and she loves the kind of administrative nit-picking I plan to hand off to her."

"Cass is a true supporter of romance," Wyatt said dryly. "Hungry?" he went on. "I've got rib-eyes from the Firehole Inn."

Picking up their beers, they got her bag out of the trunk and went inside.

Over dinner, she told him her theory about Nez Perce easing the pressure on the magma chamber beneath Yellowstone.

Wyatt forked up some baked potato. "Don't let Superintendent Kuni hear you say that."

"How so?" Kyle sipped some of the red wine Wyatt had poured for them.

"Now that the park has reopened, Joseph plans to use the proceeds from the Wonderland Campaign to augment the scientific program. He doesn't ever want to be caught asleep at the wheel like Janet Bolido."

Thinking how much better suited the former Chief Ranger was to manage the park, Kyle said, "I wonder how Janet's doing since she fled back across the Potomac."

"Do you really want to know?" Wyatt asked.

She took another bite of the succulent steak Wyatt had cooked medium rare the way she liked it. "That's great about Kuni's commitment to research, since my theory about things being quieter since Nez Perce blew could be totally wrong. In fact, I got an email from Nick today, warning us not to get complacent."

Wyatt grinned. "You know it's against Nick's nature to want anything calm."

She toyed with her wineglass. "It's funny. Carol Leeds's latest series was about how we were 'wrong' to warn of a major eruption at Yellowstone."

He rose and picked up both their plates. "I guess she didn't think Nez Perce put on a big enough show."

Kyle joined Wyatt at the sink and started rinsing the dishes.

He turned off the water. "Leave those."

In his room, Wyatt snapped on a lamp. "We were wrong . . . this time."

Kyle faced him across the bed, her fingers on the buttons of her blue cotton shirt. "It may not happen in our lifetime . . ."

He shrugged off his pullover.

"Or for thousands of years . . ." She stripped her shirt down her arms and dropped it, stepped out of her jeans and left them in a heap on the floor.

Wyatt slid beneath the covers and held them back in welcome.

She climbed in and his long limbs twined around her. Their mingled exhalation warmed the pillow.

"But it will happen," Kyle said.

Closing her eyes, she took a second to perform what had become her ritual since last fall. She sent up a prayer for frightened little girls and everyone else who relied on fate to get them through the night.

"Wyatt," she murmured against his chest.

He spread his hand warmly over her back. "Hmmm?"

She drew a deep breath. "Turn out the light."

PROLOGUE
Houston, Texas
July 1, 1988

Black smoke billowed from the roof vents. At any second, the flames would burst through, adding their heat to the already shimmering summer sky. Wood shingle, Clare Chance thought in disgust, a four-story Houston firetrap. She drew a breath of thick humidity and prepared for that walk on the edge . . . where fire enticed with unearthly beauty, even as it destroyed.

Fellow firefighter Frank Wallace, over forty, but fighting him, gripped her shoulder. "Back me up on the hose." Although he squinted against the midday glare, his mustachioed grin showed his irrepressible enthusiasm.

"Right behind you," Clare agreed. In full turnouts and an air pack, she ignored the sultry heat and the wail of sirens as more alarms were called. Helping Frank drag the hose between gawking by-standers and shocked apartment residents, she reflected that the toughest part of the job was watching lives inexorably changed.

1

A commotion broke out as a young Asian woman, reed thin in torn jeans, made a break from the two civilians holding her. She dashed toward the nearest building entry crying, "My baby!"

Frank dropped the hose, surged forward and grabbed the woman. "Javier," he grunted. "Take over."

Javier Fuentes, lanky, mid-twenties, took the handoff and restrained the woman from rushing into the burning building. Her dark eyes went wide as she screamed and struggled. Her short legs kicked at Javier's shins.

Adrenaline surging, Clare demanded. "What floor?"

"4-G . . ." the woman managed. "He's only two. "

"Let's go," Clare told Frank without bothering to ask why the child had been left alone. As she bent for the hose, her sense of purpose seemed to lighten the weight of her equipment.

They headed in.

The building's peeling doorframe had been defaced by purple graffiti and the interior stairwell smelled faintly of mold and urine. New and sparkling in the seventies when oil jobs had enticed northern immigrants to Houston, the housing had fallen into disrepair.

At the second floor landing, Clare and Frank met smoke. She tipped up her helmet, covered her face with the mask and cranked the tank valve. Beside her, Frank wordlessly did the same.

As they moved up, Clare made sure the hose didn't snag around corners while Javier and others fed slack. Business as usual, so far, and they would find that young mother's child.

At the third floor and starting blindly toward four, Clare

elt the smoke grow hotter. She crouched below the deadly
eat and told herself that she could breathe. Positive pressure
revented fumes from leaking into her mask, and the dehy-
rated air cooled as it decompressed.

In, out, slow . . .

Isolation pressed in with the superheated atmosphere. She
ouldn't shake the feeling that Frank had left her, belied by
is tugging on the hose. At times like these, she had to keep
er head on straight. No giving in to claustrophobia and no
ought of turning back.

If you misguessed the dragon in the darkness, you would
ay with your life.

Fourth floor hall, and Clare went onto hands and knees.
arkness and disorientation complete, she concentrated on
eping the hose in line and her breathing steady. The worst
miliation was if she sucked her tank dry and had to make
ignominious exit.

Ahead, Frank cracked the nozzle for a bare second. Heat
mmed down as the spray upset the thermocline. He hit the
ve again. A glimpse of not quite midnight winked from
e shadows, now there and then gone. Clare ground her
th and her chest tightened as they approached 4-G.

he door stood ajar. A good omen, she hoped, as she and
nk accepted its invitation and crawled inside.

rapes and couches blazed, giving off toxic gases that
de her glad for filtered air. The ceiling sheetrock was
ned away, revealing the space beneath the roof where stor-
boxes blazed. Did they contain old clothes and junk, or
cious family heirlooms from Southeast Asia, belonging to

the young woman who waited below?

A thousand degrees from above drove Clare and Frank onto their stomachs. While hot water rained onto shag carpet, she inched along, one gloved hand feeling the way and the other on the hose. If you let go of your lifeline, you could lose orientation, the sure first step to a mayday situation.

Through the drop-spattered mask, there was no sign of life in the living room and nothing that looked like a crib or play pen. Clare looked toward a door that must lead to a bedroom but flames licked at the frame and walls. No haven there. Sick with the possibility of failure, she dragged herself toward Frank. She had not yet told a mother that her child had died in a fire.

If hell existed, this must be its antechamber. Frank lay ahead of her, directing the hose. By the tugs, she felt him move forward, risking the dragon backing around and coming down with searing breath. Clare found herself staring at the constantly changing colors of combustion, unable to resist the inferno's splendor. Her love-hate relationship with fire hurt most at times like these.

An ominous rumble began, the vibration resonating in her chest as though the dragon cleared its throat. Cold horror of the heat.

Through the steam cloud from the power cone, she caught a shifting in the rafters, a barely perceptible sideways slide. She couldn't grab Frank's collar to warn him, couldn't do anything except scream his name into the maelstrom.

One moment, Clare was crawling toward him. The next, she disappeared in a shower of light.

SUMMER OF FIRE
LINDA JACOBS

It is 1988, and Yellowstone Park is on fire.

Among the thousands of summer warriors battling to save
America's crown jewel, is single mother Clare Chance.
Having just watched her best friend, a fellow Texas
firefighter, die in a roof collapse, she has fled to Montana
to try and put the memory behind her. She's not the only
one fighting personal demons as well as the fiery dragon
threatening to consume the park.

There's Chris Deering, a Vietnam veteran helicopter pilot,
seeking his next adrenaline high and a good time that
doesn't include his wife, and Ranger Steve Haywood, a man
scarred by the loss of his wife and baby in a plane crash.
They rally 'round Clare when tragedy strikes yet again, and
she loses a young soldier to a firestorm.

Three flawed, wounded people; one horrific blaze. Its
tentacles are encircling the park, coming ever closer,
threatening to cut them off. The landmark Old Faithful Inn
and Park Headquarters at Mammoth are under siege, and
now there's a helicopter down, missing, somewhere in the
path of the conflagration. And Clare's daughter is on it ...

ISBN#1932815295
Gold Imprint
Available Now
US $6.99 / CDN $9.99
www.readlindajacobs.com

RICHARD D'AGOSTINO
RITE OF PASSAGE

"There! Shine your light over there."

"Frank, it's just some sand trickling."

"SHUT UP, damn it! Do you hear that?"

"Yeah, I hear it. It's the dirt under your boots."

"I'm not moving, Jack."

"Frank? What is it?"

Stone ground against stone. The earth shook. Walls trembled In a gush, sand poured from slots in the wall. Dust swallowed the ai

A secret sanctuary has been breached.

And so begins the tale of a prehistoric crystal cylinder seal, d covered in a passage beneath the base of Cheops' Pyramid. Becau of its ultimate secrets, Egyptologist Dr. Karl Cassim's only daugh is taken hostage; Cairo's Minister of Police betrays his office; a the chosen must prove their worthiness by passing through the Sev Gates of Osiris. With the assistance of American astronomer Jul Rutledge, renowned British Egyptologist Sir E. Osborne Hunsd museum curator Nancy Gottlieb, and the very things he debunk — gods, curses, and magic — Dr. Cassim discovers a prophecy warning for the New Age of Man. Everyone's life will be change

Maybe even yours.

ISBN#1932815546
ISBN#9781932815542
Gold Imprint
US $6.99 / CDN $9.99
Available Now
www.rdagostinobooks.com

DAVIE HENDERSON

WATERFALL GLEN

When Kate Brodie inherits Waterfall Glen it seems like the start of an exciting new life. Full of romantic notions, she swaps her dull routine in San Francisco for life as a Highland lady.

But the stunning beauty of the glen belies a troubled history and uncertain future, and Kate's imposing new home, Greystane House, is full of disturbing revelations about her family's past. Each portrait on the ancient walls tells an unnerving story, while the empty rooms echo with rumors of a centuries-old curse that takes on new significance when unsettling events threaten the small community whose fate lies in her hands.

The only person Kate can turn to is a man haunted by equally troubling events, a man she has every reason not to trust. Only with his help can she find a way to defend old values against the materialism of the modern world. Only together can they lay their ghosts to rest.

ISBN#193281583X
ISBN#9781932815832
Gold Imprint
US $6.99 / CDN $9.99
Available Now
http://daviehenderson.bravehost.com/

For more information

about other great titles from

Medallion Press, visit

www.medallionpress.com